Critical Praise for Steve Thayer

Saint Mudd

"Fascinating . . . A raucous tale of gangsters, newspapermen, corrupt police, and the FBI."

—*Minnesota Monthly*

The Weatherman

"I read *The Weatherman* with mounting excitement and a sense of involvement which few novels can elicit in me these days. It has one of the highest take-off points of any novel in recent memory . . . and from there it just keeps on shooting the thrills and suspense . . ."

—*Stephen King*

"Masterful ... even the savviest readers will change their minds about who the killer is several times before the heart-stopping conclusion."

—*Chicago Tribune*

Silent Snow

"Thayer uses his mastery of historical detail to build his own spellbinding version of the Lindbergh kidnapping. He also balances the icy clarity of his investigative thinking with the welcome warmth of his characterizations. And in the end, he leaves us with the chilling thought that the snow might never melt on some buried secrets."

—*New York Times Book Review*

The Wheat Field

"Steve Thayer's *The Wheat Field* is an extremely intelligent, well-written but decidedly adult foray into murder ... a deeply satisfying and complex tale that examines how human beings react in different ways to the seductive lures of power, money, and lust."

—*Washington Post*

"I am an old man in love with a ghost."

"That's the kind of line that can really grab a reader. Steve Thayer uses it at the beginning of *The Wheat Field,* a novel as haunting as its opening suggests ..."

—*New York Times Book Review*

The Leper

"Who wants to read a novel about a leper? Anyone who wants to be enlightened, educated and entertained by bestseller Thayer's unusual but awe-inspiring hero . . . a relentless crusader for Hansen's disease sufferers, whose rights as US citizens were too long compromised by fear. This book deserves a wide readership."

—*Publishers Weekly*

"One of the characters in this novel asks who'd want to read a book about a leper? If it's this book, the answer is almost anyone. This is quite simply a wonderful novel, one that delivers on the promise Thayer displayed in previous novels such as *The Weatherman* and *Silent Snow.*"

—*Booklist*

Ithaca Falls

Steve Thayer

Conquill Press
St. Paul, MN

ITHACA FALLS

Cover Design: Linda Boulanger

Library of Congress Control Number: 2014958782

Thayer, Steven Leonard

Ithaca Falls: a novel / by Steven Leonard Thayer – 1st edition

ISBN: 978-0-9908461-1-6

Conquill Press/April 2015

Printed in the United States of America

10 9 8 7 6 5 4 3 2 1

For

Larry Thayer

1950 — 2010

"What a guy."

A Song of Sing Sing

It was raining the night of the execution. No thunder. No lightning. Nothing that dramatic, just a slow, dispiriting drizzle falling on the thousands of people who had gathered outside the gray precincts of the notorious prison on the east bank of the Hudson River. Inside the death house guards were listening to a new Philco that crackled with static as it warned of a deadly Nor'easter working its way up the Eastern seaboard. But the lethal winds being generated by that storm had yet to arrive.

Eighteen cells had been expressly built for Death Row, designed and constructed by a man who was himself a prisoner. A trained stonemason. Down a dank corridor was a little green door. Through that door was the death chamber. And the chair. And that was all. A prison within a prison, constructed and dedicated to one electrifying end. Execution. In fact, when Death Row was completed in 1904, the stonemason prisoner was executed there. Put to death in his own design. The last walk from the cells to the chair was forty feet. On this night, only one man was scheduled for that short, long walk.

"Is there anything I can do for you?" said the priest, speaking through the leper-squint.

"I'd like to see a movie," said the prisoner to the iron door.

"I'll ask the warden. Is there anything I can get you to read?"

The condemned man closed his Bible. He wasn't really reading it. Just studying the words. "There is one book," the prisoner told him. "When I was a teenage boy it was a favorite of mine. Slaughterhouse Five. *The author's name is Kurt Vonnegut."*

"I've never heard of the book, or the author. A Harvard man?"

The prisoner, once a large, able-bodied, and handsome man, mustered a wide grin. "Cornell," he told him.

"Yes, that makes sense."

Then the condemned man listened to the fading footsteps of the prison chaplain as he hurried off in search of the mysterious request.

Cell 17 was nine feet by twelve feet. Slightly smaller than a room. Slightly larger than a grave. The contents were a bunk, two blankets, and a bucket of cold water—this for drinking, washing, and flushing the toilet. As a cup could be fashioned into a weapon, the prisoner had to slurp the water to his mouth with his hands. One light bulb burned overhead. It was embedded in the ceiling so the prisoner could not access its sharp glass. This light was controlled by the guards outside the cell. And there was that Bible. The Catholic Bible. An iron door with a leper-squint closed and locked with an emphatic clang, followed by a loud bolt shot. Guards peeked in on the prisoner every fifteen minutes, all day and all night. The keyhole was protected so that the prisoner could not stuff it with gum or paper, delaying guards while he attempted suicide. On the western wall of the death house was a row of eighteen windows, each ten inches wide and twenty-four inches long, mere slits in the thick walls. Iron bars drilled into the limestone framed the narrow view. The windows overlooked the river.

It was nearly an hour before the priest returned. The prisoner was lying on his bunk with his Bible over his heart when he heard the familiar voice at the door.

"I'm afraid our modest prison library doesn't have that particular book, so I made a phone call to the New York Public Library. Got hold of an ornery young man just as they were closing, who nonetheless conducted a search for your book and your author. He told me neither one of them exists . . . at least not in the New York Public Library."

"That's because the author is only nine years old," he told the priest, with the ghost of an Irish smile on his face, "and the book has yet to be written."

"Why that particular book?" he asked the prisoner.

"Because I am unstuck in time."

The priest laughed. Then paused. "I saw him play once . . ."

"Saw who play?"

"The great Bobby Bill. The man they called the Ghost Runner."

The prisoner, still lying on his bunk, sighed. A heavy sigh. "I'm not him."

"He came up to Holy Cross with the Big Red in those years before the war. My God, that man could play football."

"I heard he fell in the bloody fields of France."

"No. He disappeared in the bloody fields of France . . . or so the story goes."

THE GHOST RUNNER

The story, as it goes, began in those years before the war. Before the world changed. Football was a block and run game back then. And the great Bobby Bill was a football legend—the all-American quarterback of the Big Red of Cornell. He was like a Greek god. So athletic, so sculpted and handsome, he fell just short of pretty.

Bobby Bill was playing quarterback when the new stadium opened in 1915, and that was before they built the giant crescent. Before it became Crescent Field. The stands back then ran only about halfway up the hill. Up at the top of the hill was a parking lot. Fans could park up front and watch the game from their cars. That year, 1915, the Cornell Big Red were the national champions. First time ever. Bobby Bill might have played another year after that. Might have been the year he disappeared.

Football stadiums were going up all over America. When they built the new stadium in Ithaca, they were careful not to touch a large grove of trees that stood tall down at the south end of the field. Stately pines ended up serving as an evergreen backdrop in the south end zone. These trees were known as the Woods. An acre of beautiful pine as an extension of the playing field. There had never been a stadium quite like it.

Bobby Bill, the all-American quarterback, would often break away for a long touchdown run. The man could outrun them all, that's how fast he was. And thousands of fans along with the players and coaches on the sideline would be screaming their hearts out as he sprinted by them. "Run, Bobby, run!" The glory of Saturday afternoons.

Now, if he was running for a touchdown into the south end zone, the great Bobby Bill would just keep on running. Disappear into the trees. Into the Woods. The Ghost Runner. The fans loved it. Nobody knew the exact route he'd take, but he would usually sneak back to the bench through the north end of the stadium. It was like a magic act.

Then one Saturday afternoon—no one seems to remember what year it was, but it was near the end of his time at Cornell, and the football game he was playing in was all but over. It was a muddy game, everybody remembers that. Might have been Harvard. The leaves were off the trees. The sky was gun-metal gray. The rain was November cold. Couldn't see any numbers. No faces. Just twenty-two spirits in constant collision out there on the field. Still, everybody knew Bobby Bill. Remember, the man moved like a Greek god. Near the end of the fourth quarter he broke away on one of his long patented touchdown runs. Through the mud he ran. Through the rain. And then he disappeared into those woods.

Six points. The fans in the stands, those sodden fans, those faithful fans, went crazy. Seasonal madness. But the great Bobby Bill never came back that day. Cornell went on to lose. Most guessed he just kept on running.

There was talk of a girl. Of a broken heart. Rumors swirled of drugs, and gangsters, and illicit bets. But there was little investigation. In America, a man has a right to disappear.

It was said a classmate spotted him in France during the war. In the Army. Up on the front where the fighting was heavy. But just as he never returned to the football game that muddy day in Ithaca, the great Bobby Bill never returned home from the war.

Or so the story goes.

THAT SONG OF SING SING

"And you say you were a detective?"

"In my day," the prisoner told him, "I was one of the best."

"But you tried to kill the governor . . . a man who two days ago was elected President of the United States."

"No, I tell you, I was shooting at another man altogether."

"Still, you are a convicted assassin." The priest got no reply. "The warden has again denied your request to attend movie night . . . there being a Death Row policy against it. And that one-armed police captain came to see me. He was asking about you."

Now there was a long silence on both sides of the door. The prisoner had hoped against hope that he might be allowed to see a movie. Any movie. Indulge a former passion. He thought of the one-armed cop who had helped put him away. The silence continued and the prisoner at first believed the priest had at last given up on him and left him alone. But then he heard the one-word question through the squint.

"Mendicants?" *he was asked.*

"Beggars," the prisoner told him, sitting up on his bunk. "The practice of begging. I believe it's also an order of friars."

"That is correct. The Mendicants are an order that depend directly on the charity of people."

"Coelacanth?" *the prisoner asked the chaplain, wanting the definition.*

Again the hush, as if he had finally stumped the faceless man in the collar. But then the priest answered through the squint. "It's a fish found only in fossil form. The term is sometimes used to describe something that is totally out of date."

"Very good, Father." This was a game they played. Vocabulary.

"I shall miss you, my friend."

"And I, you, Father."

After the priest had gone, the prisoner stood before the narrow window on what was scheduled to be the last night of his life—the end of a life written in italics, somehow separate from the life he had really lived. The cool and wet November air filtering through the bars felt good against his face. Mitigated his need to cry. The murky outlines of a thousand souls stirred on the river bank beneath him. Some had come to cheer his demise. Others had come to pray for his pardon. Still others had just come to watch. But all of them wanted a show. So the son of an Irish mother grabbed hold of the iron bars and through the rusty screening he sang his mother's favorite song. It was a song he had heard sung over and over again at the memorials honoring his fallen comrades, those brave spirits who had perished that blue September morning when the towers fell. Though he often confused the lyrics, he raised his voice anyway, and he sang his living heart out. The crowd, standing below in the rain, fell into an unearthly silence at the sweet, melodious strains of a voice they knew to be his.

"Oh Danny boy, when all the flowers are dying
And I am dead, as dead I well may be
You'll come and find the place where I am lying
And kneel and say an 'Ave' there for me ..."

When he had finished the requiem, the quiet outside was so intense only the drizzle could be heard. The need to shed tears returned, but he swallowed that need and stared with moist eyes through the inclement weather that surrounded the infamous prison known around the world as Sing Sing. Three miles across ever-darkening water, on the west bank of the river, the prisoner spied the faint lights of Rockland on the Palisades, while a mile above the village he was witness to a gathering of storm clouds. Storms had always been his undoing. His downfall. The crazy winds of time. It was those crazy winds that were blowing the Halloween night he washed over the falls in pursuit of the assassin who had come to Ithaca to kill Franklin Delano Roosevelt.

"I dwell in shining Ithaca. There is a mountain there, covered in forests . . . It is rough, but it raises good men."

—*Homer's* Odyssey

The Halloween Storm

All day long a Canadian cold front had been sweeping south along the Great Lakes, bringing with it winds gusting up to forty miles per hour. By the time these pre-winter blasts began blowing across the state of New York, they were colliding with hot air that had bubbled up from the Gulf of Mexico. At noon it was 72 degrees in sun-shining Ithaca and students in their shirtsleeves were on the Arts Quad tossing footballs. By 6:00 p.m. the temperature had nose-dived thirty degrees. The barometric pressure was falling even faster. Then the sun went down. Darkness fell. And all hell broke loose.

For years Cornell University had turned a blind eye to the drunken revelry of Halloween, so much so that in each succeeding year the costumed debauchery grew even more base than in the year before. On that storm-ravaged evening the drinking had begun early. Even before the last rays of daylight slipped from the sky and blackened clouds swept over the campus, there were devils and witches down on their knees vomiting into the grass. By 7:00 p.m. hordes of students dressed as ghosts and ghouls were parading up and down the steep slopes between the hallowed halls, most of them clutching glasses of beer and screaming as if possessed. Near 8:00 p.m., in the deep shadows of the towering elms on Libe Slope, one could hear the guttural groans of drunken sex, and by 9:00 p.m. cars were being overturned and set ablaze. The only thing preventing the entire evening from turning into a full-blown riot-cum-orgy was the oncoming weather.

To add even more drama to the mayhem, the Ithaca Motion Picture Company was filming a movie on campus. It was a costumed piece in the horror genre, most probably one of those bloody *slasher* films the kids could never get enough of.

He was an ex-cop in possession of a PhD, and he set his trap by the moon and the stars. The professor did not believe in astrology. He was a man of science. He believed in astronomy. He was in pursuit of a killer. A serial killer, he suspected. The professor believed this killer was also a man of science who would strike again on this night on this campus, not because it was Halloween, but because the moon in the eastern sky was barely half-full, and the stars would most likely be hidden by the cloudiest month of the year. The murdering bastard was all but guaranteed the darkness he craved. What this murderer could not have anticipated, any more than the university professor, was the intensity of the storm that was brewing.

The professor of criminal justice stood beneath Eddy Gate fingering a letter his late wife had once written to him from faraway Oregon. The inscription above the arched entrance to the ivy-coated campus was in Latin: "*So enter that thou may become more learned and thoughtful.*" Above the exit: "*So depart that thou may become more useful to mankind.*"

The good professor was departing on foot down College Avenue, absentmindedly reading the old letter beneath the streetlamps, when from behind he heard a blaring horn and found himself in the beams of a low-slung, high-powered roadster. A bright yellow beacon on wide tires speeding through the night. The car nearly ran him down. He jumped from its path, the letter flying from his hand. He retrieved the handwritten memories from the street and then watched, a bit bemused, as the sporty yellow car curved away from him and raced up the hill. A rich kid with his girl hurrying to beat the rain.

The speeding car was followed a minute later by the heavy clip-clop of a horse pulling a hay wagon, the bales topped off by a dozen students, their faces hidden behind Halloween masks. They were laughing hysterically.

The professor stepped from the street to the curb as one of students held up a lantern. The boy was dressed as a wolf. "Hey, Professor, find your killer yet?"

"Sh*uuu*t *uuu*p! That's not nice," came the voice of Little Red Riding Hood.

"They say it's driven him mad."

"Well, that's what he gets for teaching that stuff."

"Shit, I think *he* killed her."

"His own wife?"

"You guys are *sooo* drunk."

"I thought he was leaving."

"Yeah, go on back to Harvard Yard, Professor Flatfoot."

All of this was said in passing, in masked anonymity, and the widowed professor listened as the horse-drawn wagon filled with students clip-clopped up the curved avenue, their taunts dissipating in the night.

He had waited a lifetime to marry his high school sweetheart. His beautiful Katelyn. Then she got pregnant and he cheated on her. Now both women were dead. Murdered. The professor folded the letter along its worn creases and returned it to the breast pocket inside his coat. Over his heart. Then he turned his collar to the cold winds off Cayuga Lake, that fantastic oddity of water that often created its own weather and then sent it racing up the hill. The smell of oncoming rain was sharp. Come morning it would be November. The ugly month. The month of fallen leaves and naked trees.

The professor of criminal justice was now walking the edge of Collegetown, where the shops and the sidewalk cafes were darkened and closed in an effort to protect them from vandalism. Thunder rumbled over the hills to the west, inching closer by the minute. Street lamps flickered off and on as the coal plant out Pine Tree Road was already losing electricity. The bright klieg lights of the motion picture company illuminated the nearby gorge, but even those generators were shutting down in anticipation of the storm. After weeks of forensic research and days of preparation, the professor's plan for the killer's capture was on the verge of being washed out. He picked up the pace until he arrived at the corner where College Avenue overlooked the Cascadilla gorge.

SUSPECT IN A STORM

There was just enough wind to flutter a vampire's costume cape, allowing the professor to spot his suspect from the Collegetown Bridge. A bolt of lightning lit up the sky and there he was, in silhouette, climbing the stairs that led up the steep cliffs from the creek. The ex-New York City police detective stood perfectly still, but his heart was racing with anticipation. He watched as the apparition moved slowly through the faltering light of the street lamp that topped the gorge. The cop in him took note of the way the dark figure inched its way up the crooked stairs with a noticeable limp, a walking cane supporting a bum leg. Thunder followed the lightning strike. It rumbled through the gorge. Finally at the top of the steps, the ghostly silhouette tipped his head to the threatening skies, his cape flapping behind him.

The professor had blanketed the campus with students he had come to trust, though like the students aboard the hay wagon, how many of them still trusted him was hard to say. The students had whistles. When the murderer of Ithaca women was spotted, the students were to whistle for help.

The winds picked up. Sang songs in his head. Echoes of his past. Choir music. Political speeches. The pretty voices of the women he had loved. These women haunted him to no end. He used his fingers to clear his ears. Clear his mind. Besides the weather, there was one other problem, and it was a big one. It was Halloween night. And screaming women were everywhere.

OF CRIME SCENES PAST

Three weeks before that Halloween night, back when the autumn foliage was nearing peak color and the air in Ithaca was still redolent of summer flowers, the body of a beautiful and keenly intelligent woman was found in the early morning hours, splayed atop a boulder. This woman, a popular news darling, had just been appointed to a vacant seat in the United States Senate. Now she was known to Ithaca police as victim number two, and she had been mutilated to an extraordinary degree. The body had been discovered in the Cascadilla gorge, halfway between Collegetown and downtown. Her throat had been so deeply cut that her head had fallen off. It lay face up a few yards away, beside the rushing water.

The professor of criminal justice had stood stone still at the crime scene and taken in every gory detail, and with just as much internalized emotion as he had felt when he had come across the killer's first victim.

"Did you know the senator?" the lead detective asked him.

"Yes," he answered. "I knew her." He did not tell police that in secret, she had been his lover. The man had come home to Ithaca in pursuit of old dreams. Now he was living a nightmare.

The boulder before him was saturated with blood, and the ground around it was soaked in a two-foot circle. Murder as a presentation. There are several reasons to *stage* a murder scene. One is to mislead the police and redirect the investigation away from the main suspect. Another is to make the victim's death look like a suicide or an accident in order to cover up the murder. The third reason is *shock* value in order to create fear. These murders were shocking, more shocking than anything the ex-cop had seen in his days on the streets of New York City.

Before the Ithaca murders, the professor had believed unnatural death was merely another science. He thought if all cops were on the same page they could, working together, outsmart and apprehend even the most diabolical killers. His goal was to revolutionize police work. Bring it in line with the new century. So he wrote a more practical textbook on homicide investigations, with detailed case studies and crime scene photographs so explicit the book was not sold to the public. This revolutionary textbook ended up in police training academies from the East Coast to the West Coast. Then he followed it up with an even more controversial textbook on sex crime investigations, with even more horror laden details and more explicit photographs. These books were not only based on his experiences, but they were the results of hundreds of interviews with death investigators across the country. In police circles the professor of criminal justice was a shining star, because when it came to homicide, he literally wrote the book.

But these Ithaca murders not only shattered his world, they were out of his world, as if committed by a madman from some other time.

THE LECTURE

Bailey Hall sat in the heart of the Cornell campus. It was really an auditorium, with a steep main floor and a horseshoe balcony. The hall could seat two thousand people. Concerts were held there. Week in and week out, every one of those main floor seats was filled for the professor's lectures on the psychology of crime. Not only was the subject fascinating, but the man giving the lectures had a voice like velvet. A voice ringing with rectitude.

Working now with two gruesome murders, the professor of criminal justice created a criminal profile of the still unidentified suspect. He then presented the profile as a lecture at Bailey Hall, focusing his efforts on victim number two, the senate beauty found murdered in Cascadilla gorge.

As was the case with the first victim, the senator's throat had been cut right through to the bone. The chest was open below the lungs, and the heart was missing. The uterus was nowhere to be found. With the exception of a bloody white blouse found beside the fast-running water, her clothes had also vanished.

Despite advances made in criminal detection, the time of death was still the hardest thing to nail down. Partially digested food was found in the remains of the victim's stomach. The partly digested food, along with increasing rigor mortis, indicated the senator's death had taken place about three or four hours after the food was eaten, so the county coroner's best guess was that her murder had taken place somewhere between midnight and one o'clock in the morning. This fact left reporters muttering the oldest cliché in journalism. *"The autopsy raises more questions than answers."* Why was a United States senator strolling the gorge alone in the middle of the night?

The victim's white blouse, the professor told the packed auditorium from the stage, was knifed repeatedly and saturated with blood, indicating that her face may have been covered with the blouse at the time of the attack. Here, to the astonishment of all, he held up an enlarged photograph like a movie poster of the bloody blouse found at the crime scene. The blouse was so violently shredded and blood-soaked that little of its original white color was left showing. The audience gasped. Some of the students, most of them girls, got up and walked out. They said he was sick, that he was turning the murder of two intelligent women into an academic exercise. Or even worse, he was exorcising his own demons at their expense. But to the students who remained, and quite a few of them remained, the ex-detective explained how murderers were caught.

"The murderer covered his victim's face to avoid eye contact," the professor went on, as if it were just another lecture.

"This is called *depersonalization*. She was, I believe, a targeted stranger."

"Or was she targeted because of you?" The loud taunt was the voice of an angry female student, and it came from the back of the hall as she was exiting.

The professor pretended to ignore her. But then another young woman seated up front respectfully raised her hand and with considerably less hostility asked, "Isn't it more likely, Professor, that she was killed because she was a United States senator?"

This girl had a point. In recent years a number of powerful women in the Northeast had been murdered, their unsolved cases spread over five states. But victim number one was not a politician. She was an Ithaca housewife. "If that were the case," he said, answering her question from the stage, "then we would have a serial killer with a political agenda. Extremely rare. A misogynist bent on altering the future for women by murdering their leaders. Serial killers and political assassins are historically two different animals."

The remarks from the audience had thrown him off his game. Frustrated him. The audience seemed fully aware of his personal involvement in these murders. "Leaving the victim nude is the best way to leave the least amount of evidence," he went on, his velvet voice rising, his face reddening. "Her killer took her clothes to deprive the police of clues. The victim's head, wrapped in the bloody white blouse, was dropped by accident. He may have heard somebody coming and hurried off." Here he paused. The stillness in the hall was spooky. "Technically, the victim's death resulted from the severance of the left carotid artery, the murderer having cut her throat from left to right. The wounds were inflicted with a strong-bladed dagger, extremely sharp, and it was used with a great deal of force. It appears the dagger was held in the left hand of her attacker. It also appears the murderer had some anatomical knowledge, for he attacked all of the vital organs, though it was not necessarily the work of a doctor or a medical student. The harvesting of these organs was more like *ripping out* rather than *surgically removing*."

For the sake of research, the professor explained to his audience, police divided murderers into two distinct categories—the ordered and the disordered. "The disordered killer is an uneducated person who kills and then runs," he told them. "The rage is impulsive. The disordered killer could be suffering from any number of disorders, including schizophrenia and paranoia. The ordered killer, on the other hand, is an educated person who plans an attack and then carefully follows the ensuing investigation. The rage is actually a controlled rage. The ordered killer is a psychopath. In Ithaca, we are dealing with a psychopath. The theft of the heart and the uterus was a direct assault on love, procreation, and commitment, the three things women hold most dear. The severed head was to be his trophy. For victims he seeks out attractive, intelligent women with good backgrounds, which is why he searches for his prey near the university."

Up to this point the remaining students sat spellbound. Breathless. It was what the professor told them next that invited their skepticism. For despite his vaunted reputation as a lecturer at the university, his young audience did not yet understand the science of crime. "This killer, this collector of women's body parts," he told them, leaning over the lectern, "is between forty and sixty years old. He is not an only child, but he is the firstborn. He has a superior intellect, with a college education. He has no children. He is left-handed. He prides himself on his appearance, almost athletic in spirit, and he moves well in society. He is also a drug user . . . perhaps opium, but more likely cocaine. He dabbles in movies. Film studies. He is gregarious and outgoing, even charming. A good talker. He uses these skills to manipulate people. He has the ability to separate his life as a murderer from his life as a respected member of the community . . . Dr. Jekyll and Mr. Hyde without the potion. These women are not his first murders. He killed as a young man. He misses those days."

The professor put a hand to his forehead to shield his eyes from the bright lights. As he looked out across the auditorium floor, he could read grave doubt in the faces of his students, now supremely skeptical of the things he was telling them. In some of their faces he could even read pity. About the only thing he did not tell his audience that day was when this collector of women's body parts would strike next.

THE MURDER CLUB

The lecture on the Ithaca murders by the professor of criminal justice and ex-New York City police detective was the talk of the town. His detractors said he had gone too far. His defenders said he had simply done what he had been hired to do —teach the science of crime. From the controversy and the publicity that ensued, the killer had to know the professor was on to him. The best way to lure a psychopath out into the open is with disinformation, so the university announced that the professor would be taking a leave of absence in order to pursue his research. But word soon spread on campus that he was emotionally unstable and a suspect in his wife's murder. The administration wanted him out of town. In all likelihood, the faculty was told, he would not be coming back. He bought his train ticket and he said his goodbyes.

It was at this point the professor gathered together his most trusted students. They met in secret, and the students dubbed it the Murder Club. Their meetings took place in the clock tower, where one of the girls played the chimes. From the tower high atop East Hill they could look out over fair and shining Ithaca and map their strategy.

"He will strike on Halloween," the professor assured his Murder Club, "on the eve of my departure from the university, making me look even more like a suspect. A disgruntled employee. The killer will be costumed in formal wear, with a long black cape reminiscent of Victorian England. He will be wearing a hat of the type that is no longer in fashion, and beneath the hat will be a small black mask to hide his face. He will be carrying a walking cane and feigning an injured leg, limping to evoke sympathy. The cane is actually a weapon. Beneath his coat he will be carrying his murder kit . . . knives, ropes, handcuffs, and poisons. He will strike between nine p.m. and midnight, with the full cover of darkness, but not be out so late that he will arouse suspicion. In order to prevent another murder, it is imperative he be apprehended before he chooses his victim. He does not return home without killing."

And so the stage was set. Halloween came. The university professor packed his bags. His murder club blanketed the campus. The police covered Ithaca. The sun slipped from the sky and the drunken revelry began. But then came the storm.

THE SUSPENSION BRIDGE

The mysterious silhouette wearing a hat of the black slouch type limped north on College Avenue, walking cane in hand, into the heart of the campus, his long, flowing cape flapping in the gusts. The professor fell in behind him, moving through the night with the stealth of a ghost. A magician. Now cloud-to-cloud electricity was added to the storm, and the most harrowing of winds came howling up out of the gorge. Dead leaves swirled by him in cyclone patterns and the first raindrops slapped his face, but the ex-cop kept his suspect in sight. When the shadowy cape moved, the professor moved. When the specter stopped, the professor stopped. This disappearing game went on for a quarter mile, until the man in the cape stood directly beneath the flickering street lamp at Campus Road. There he stopped, a malignant shadow steeped in coruscating light. Then the black slouch hat began to swivel ever so slowly as the suspect turned his head to look behind him. The professor stopped beside a tree, using it for cover, and in doing so he caught a glimpse of a pair of small black eyes, indistinct in the night. Then a blinding crack of electricity illuminated the copper-colored clouds. A barrage of thunder shook the earth. The power failed, the lights went out, and all of Ithaca went black.

The professor felt his way along the avenue like a blind man, hurriedly shuffling his way from tree to tree, while his suspect disappeared into the darkness. Rain started to fall. It was then he heard an appalling scream—not the scream of a drunken coed, but instead a mortal scream of terror that is instantly recognized by all. The professor feared the worst, that he had failed, that all of his calculations and preparations had not stopped another murder. Suddenly a whistle was blowing up the hill near the old chapel, and then another whistle. Across the Arts Quad, the girl in the clock tower, a member of the Murder Club, struck up the chimes. It was a requiem that had never before been heard on campus. The requiem was to be played only if the whistles sounded. Somebody was yelling, "Murder! Murder!"

The professor was off and running blindly, into a crazy north wind, a burning feeling in the pit of his stomach. All he had to go by was the sound of the whistles and the echoes of those horrible screams. Out of the corner of his eye he saw witches, ghosts and drunken ghouls scattering for cover, but he could not tell if they were running from a murderer or just trying to get in out of the rain. Rockets of lightning lit up the sky like the Fourth of July, and he saw the man in the long cape dart past the chapel and race away beneath the clock tower. He was no longer limping. The professor pursued him with the passion and the speed of the great athlete he once was, momentarily forgetting that his youth was far behind him. His suspect's black cape flapped in the wind like the wings of a bat. The professor could hear voices trailing behind.

"He's chasing the killer."

"Another girl has been attacked."

"She's alive! Get a doctor!"

The voices and the whistles were being drowned out by the thunder and the rain, furious and torrential. The professor ran by President's House only to again lose his suspect in the storm. A horrible wheezing sound filled the air. He feared it was coming from his own lungs. It was there, catching his breath before the Gothic mansion, that he was first consumed with the haunting feeling that he had made this ghostly run once before, that he had chased this man in another life, in another time. But he had neither the time nor the inclination to parse his emotions. It was just a feeling, and he filed it away and moved on.

As bad as the weather was, it seemed to be allied with the law. Lightning again illuminated the campus, and the malignant shadow of a caped man could be seen skirting the grounds as if in a spotlight, fleeing down the steep slope before the library in the direction of the Fall Creek gorge. The professor chased him down Libe Slope, fighting to keep his balance on the slippery hill. The driving wind and the drenching rain were in his face, an energy so potent it could force back the hands of time—and whenever it seemed his suspect had at last eluded him, a bolt of lightning would once again illuminate the campus hills and he would spot the caped specter racing away from him. The killer was panicked. The professor could sense it in his flight. This psychopath had not been expecting a trap. He had thought of his pursuer as a mere college professor. The professor, on the other hand, with his military training, his police training, and his superior knowledge of the criminal mind, had clearly been expecting him. In his heart he was still a cop—the one entity a psychopath fears.

It was near the foot of the deep-sloped hill where the chase began to go awry, and for reasons the university professor could not explain. Perhaps it was the weather, or maybe it was his exhaustion, both physical and emotional, but he became suddenly disoriented, and he stumbled and fell. Hit his head, hard. His mind was now spinning in circles. The night was suddenly strange and disconcerting, running backwards, as if removed by one degree from reality. Everything seemed out of its proper place and time. Exhausted-looking jalopies were parked along the curb, every one of them black. In the brief flashes of the storm they looked as if they might be Model Ts. He put his hand to his head, where he could feel a welt swelling above his eye. He had bruised his knee and twisted his ankle. Bolts of lightning lit up the sky. The sound of thunder was incessant. The rain was coming at him like machine gun fire. He struggled to his feet and then doubled over to catch his breath. He grabbed his aching leg and tried to wring out the pain.

His suspect was moving toward the bluffs that led down to the suspension bridge over Fall Creek, where the fierce waters sluice through a narrow corridor. He was probably hoping to lose his pursuer in the woods on the far side. The professor fought to keep his balance as he staggered across the street. His clothes were soaked, his chest heaving, his feet drenched in muck. Still he marched face-first into the storm and lurched over the bluff. The gusts of wind and rain were blinding. He was chasing the shadow of a man who was stumbling down through the trees, but with a burst of adrenaline he was fast upon his suspect. He tackled him from behind and they both tumbled down the hill, just short of the bridge. They wrestled off the beaten path to a cliff jutting out of the rock. Far beneath their tangled feet lay Fall Creek, roaring down from the hills like a flash flood, a wild river of water destined for Ithaca Falls.

The woods above the gorge were as stark and dark as the professor had ever seen them, so dark that he could not make out the face of the man with whom he was wrestling. He knew only that he was the murderer he had long been searching for, the knife-wielding serial killer. Still, he had the sense he was struggling with an older man, and even in the wind and the rain, this man smelled of wintergreen. The killer was yelling at him, taunting him, but the actual words could not be heard over the roar of the storm and the rushing of the water. Each was struggling to hold his own against the other, against the crumbling stones beneath their feet, and against the weather—a life and death struggle on a rocky ledge above a gorge overflowing with raging water. They were both tiring, the killer more so, and just when the professor thought he was getting the best of him, that he could wrestle this knife-wielding maniac under arrest, there was a brilliant flash of white light and a great cracking sound. It was a force so ferocious that it shook the earth. Tree branches came crashing down around him. He could feel the rocks shifting beneath his feet. He released his suspect and held on to a rocky ledge, fearing for his life, his legs now dangling from the cliff. Ironically, he could still hear the chimes from the clock tower, only now it was Lord Tennyson's *In Memoriam. "Ring out the old, ring in the new; Ring out the false, ring in the true."*

The caped suspect, now freed from the professor's grip, scrambled back up the cliff to the path and stumbled toward the suspension bridge, his formal wear hanging on him like a scarecrow's, filthy, sodden and torn. The professor gathered every ounce of strength he could muster. He pulled himself to the cliff and rested there on all fours, faint and nauseated. He gagged and choked. He spit up blood. His hands were cracked and bloody. Still, he got to his feet and faltered through the trees toward the suspension bridge over the water.

The bridge was not for the faint of heart. Some students spent four years at the university and never set foot on the rickety thing. It spanned the gorge one hundred and fifty feet above the water and even on a mild day it swayed in the breeze, while far below the violent torrent crashed down through the jagged notch. The professor stared across the bridge in astonishment. It seemed he would not have to race across the bridge after all, for there the man was, ghost in a storm, standing dead still at the center span, showing the resilience of a horror-movie villain. The killer covered his waxen face with his cape. The professor started across the bridge, clutching his leg. But much to his surprise, this killer, this collector of body parts, did not run. He did not move an inch, even in the howling winds. He held his place on the bridge and shouted words the professor could barely comprehend, a high-pitched and bewitching voice crying Cassandra warnings into the storm. "Now only two men must die and all will be changed. Go back. You can't stop it. Not in this time." They were words to that effect, though the professor was no more sure of their content than he was of their meaning. Whatever their meaning, it was not in the ex-cop to break from the chase.

THE FALL FROM THE RICKETY BRIDGE

And so it was on Halloween night that these two opposing spirits found themselves locked in mortal combat in the midst of a tempest on the rickety bridge that spanned the chasm. The killer fought like the madman that he was, using his cape and his cane as weapons. As for the professor of criminal justice, what should have been a case-ending apprehension seemed instead a prologue to the next chapter in his life. He was wet and cold, and more exhausted than he had ever been in his life. The welt across his brow from his tumble down the hill had opened wide, and the blood was running into his eyes. The electrical storm, the rumbling thunder, and a wind that rolled over Ithaca's hills like Satan's breath were now conspiring against him, and all the time a killer was swinging wildly at his head with a gold-headed cane. The professor was fighting both a madman's fury and nature's fury, but he was also wrestling with the demons of his own past.

What happened next happened in flickering shadows, in wind and rain, and in the first icy flakes of pre-winter snow. Suddenly and without warning, a wind like an avenging spirit spun both of the combatants in circles and then sent them flying over the cables, somersaulting through the air and into the gorge. A deathly plunge into a chasm of raging black water.

The professor clung to the killer's cape as he fell through the wind and rain and then hit the rushing water below. They were in the rain-swollen creek now, a devil of a stream lacking in both soul and compassion, and it was tearing apart both good and evil. The university professor could hear much more than he could see, and what he heard most was the angry roar of fast-moving water. He reached out and again grabbed on to the killer's cape, both of their heads barely above the torrent. He made an attempt to swim, but his efforts proved futile when matched against the current. So he hung on for the ride, fighting to keep his head above the rushing water as he raced beneath the shadow of a road bridge. And then, before he could do anything to stop it, they were both tumbling over Ithaca Falls.

It all had to have happened in a matter of seconds, but in his mind his descent into the abyss was one long, excruciating minute after another, and every second of it played out in slow motion. He was plummeting, a tremendous free fall few persons ever experience. The sudden exhilaration of life before death. The force and sheer volume of the water was throwing him at the rocks beneath the falls, and death should have been instantaneous. But suddenly he was instead spinning in circles, upside down and inside out. A liquid vortex was drawing into its center his entire life and all that surrounded it. Water from this vortex was shooting into his mouth and up his nose. He could not breathe in, nor could he spit out. And there was something else going on. Something incalculable. Timeless. Not death, but a suspension of life. A dream from which he could not wake. Then he felt his left leg snap just above the knee. That pain was all too real. He was now separated from the caped killer and was on his own against the raging water. And just when he thought he could hold out no more, that his brain was going to burst and his lungs were going to explode, the current loosened its death grip and his head was spat free. He gasped for air. Gasped for another chance at life.

It was almost as if he had been spat into another time. The falls were behind him now, but the entire vista seemed different, incongruous, somehow out of context. Then another wall of water was bearing down on him with a deafening roar, and the professor was once again driven under. Again he was consumed with the feeling that he was being dragged through time. His broken leg felt as if it was being torn from his body. He was struggling to swim, struggling to surface, but the sheer force of the raging water was overwhelming, and this timeless force kept pulling him down, until the inevitable happened and he smashed his already wounded head into a submerged rock.

He was drowning. Even beneath the water, the professor could see his blood swirling away from him. Leaving his body. His highly-educated mind was going round and round in watery circles. A pinwheel. A kaleidoscope. A phantasmagorical life flashing before his eyes. His only solace was that if he was meant to die in this lawless water, it was almost certain that his suspect, that diabolical collector of body parts, would die along with him. The professor had stopped tumbling. Stopped struggling. He was suspended timeless in a watery grave. Then all went black and he at last gave up the fight and surrendered to his fate. The professor of criminal justice floated ghostlike in the cold water, eagerly anticipating the bright light that was said to await the dead.

He was not a religious man. His experiences in the war and his secular education had driven the Catholic God from his bones. But if there was an afterlife, a real and meaningful life after death, perhaps his beautiful Katelyn would be there, holding out her hand to him, forgiving his sins and guiding his spirit into the heavens. Either way, the last earthly feeling he could remember was of his battered and broken body as it settled face down into the rocks and sand, but he could not tell if the rock and sand were a part of the shoreline, or whether he had settled into the sandstone at the bottom of Fall Creek, just south of Ithaca Falls.

"The past is never dead. It's not even past."

—William Faulkner
Requiem for a Nun

BOOK ONE

ITHACA, NEW YORK

1929

The Dinner Party

It was a candlelight dinner. Timeless in its beauty.

Viewed from the luxury of distance, the High Victorian Gothic mansion on East Hill appeared warm and inviting that springtime evening, its towering bay windows ageless in the firelight. However, on a stormy night in the dead days of an ugly month, the craggy bluestone house might appear forlorn, or even haunted, a place one would not dare visit, much less reside. But on this starlit night, inside President's House, those gathered around the long oaken table in the mahogany dining room were enjoying a perfectly fine and friendly feast, while piano music waltzed out of the parlor.

The 1920s were still roaring. Thriving. Bubbling with enthusiasm. A new American president had just been inaugurated. Herbert Hoover was his name. A Stanford man. He had been elected by a landslide. And why not? Times were good. Those gathered for dinner were not only the proud and the privileged, but they were characters of every means and mind. Among the two dozen were men of science and men of letters seated alongside crazed poets, radical philosophers, and some horny-handed boys from the state's farming districts. Cornell University, growing in both stature and wealth, was singled out not only for the eminence of its faculty, but for the extraordinary range of its course offerings and the exceptional diversity of its student body—so much so that the women gathered at the table were not just the wives and relatives of the professors, but were themselves students, graduate students, and tenure-tracked professors. It was this forward thinking, this romantic ideal, that attracted intelligent young women to the storied hills of Ithaca and to the halls of the university. These women and men were already seated and about to enjoy a dinner of quiet and elegant timelessness when the last guest arrived, dressed in an ill-fitting brown suit that looked as if it might not even belong to him. He walked with a pronounced limp.

Seated at the head of the elongated table was President Emeritus H. W. Hightower, PhD. It was his dinner party. He gave a warm and welcoming smile to his late arrival, a smile interpreted by everybody in the room who knew the old university president as a beam of academic approval.

There was no hush and no drama as John Alden limped his way to the dinner table, for not only was Alden the last to arrive, but he was virtually unknown to the others at the table. If he was forty-some years old, he was in his youthful-looking forties. He was even younger in appearance when considering the fact that he himself was a university professor with a lifetime of experience that few academics possess. He was by the standards of the day a curious-looking man. A thick head of sandy brown hair was showing strands of gray, but it was dry hair and somewhat unkempt, and he wore it much too long considering the times. His face showed few signs of aging when compared to the other men in the room, and he still possessed the body of the athlete he once had been. But he had a boxer's face, as if somehow it had been rearranged. Made to look different. He was taller than most of his peers, and in his youth it was said his potent nose and wide Irish grin could not be ignored. The prominent nose coupled with his solid height had made for an awkward student who had grown into an imposing man.

Still, it was not his nose but rather the intensity of his blue-gray eyes that people in the room first noticed, and not in a wholly comfortable way. The intellect behind those eyes was obvious, but there was also the troubled stare of a man who had known much pain and misery. President Hightower had considered passing Alden off as the soldier he once had been. Perhaps as a veteran of the Great War. But that would begin a web of deceit hard to untangle. Might it not be better, he suggested, that they stick with the plan?

The ebony walking cane that supported his recovering left leg was topped with a fine head of gold, the type of cane a rich man would carry simply for appearance's sake. Anybody watching him hobble across the room to the dinner table that night—and quite a few people were watching him—could see that the pretentious cane fit him no better than the suit. John Alden looked out of place, as if this were the first chapter in a new life. Yes, all of the men at the dinner table that night were dressed in suits and ties; it was just that their suits and ties were much better than his. Theirs fit. Alden took his seat, and with an awkward gesture he smoothed his polka dot tie beneath his bulky vest and then pulled the chair tight. The gold-headed cane dropped to the parquet floor with an embarrassing whack, and he let it be.

He had been a guest in few New York mansions, though John Alden had on occasion slipped through the doors of some of the renowned homes on Park Avenue—sometimes with a warrant, and sometimes without. Even so, the fireplace that dominated the east wall of the dining room in President's House was the largest and most ornate fireplace he had ever seen. He was seated directly across from it. This great fireplace rising up and above the mahogany wainscoting was an eye-pleasing blend of gray-green marble, and on this candlelit evening there were just enough logs ablaze in the hearth to ward off the chills until the summer weather arrived. Behind the president's chair was an enormous clock, a grandfather clock built by the Ithaca Calendar Clock Company to exacting specifications—a uniquely intricate design, its modern day mechanisms openly displayed in an antique cabinet. The past encasing the future. John Alden and President Hightower shared an interest in *horology*, the science of measuring time and the art of creating timepieces. The house was filled with clocks.

"Are you the mystery man my uncle has squirreled away in the attic?"

John Alden turned to his left when she said that. She was a gorgeous girl, blonde and slender and brimming with the joy of youth. He was quite taken with her. Like a lot of men, he was painfully shy around beautiful women, so he was appreciative when one of them talked to him first, especially a woman as pretty as she was. "I like to think of it as the third floor," he told her with as much wit as he could gather.

"Are you the one who broke his leg and hurt his head?"

It was the same lovely voice, only now it was coming from his other side. He turned his head to his right, momentarily confused. She, too, was a gorgeous girl, with the same short blonde hair he had just encountered on his left, and she, too, possessed that remarkably slender figure brimming with the joy of youth. Her smile was electric, as was the smile of her sister. He had been seated between identical twins whose beauty in the candlelight was as bewitching as it was radiant. They were even dressed the same in the most stylish and costly dress of the day, a beige and lace flapper number that emphasized sleekness and was meant to show off long, lovely legs beneath the flounce.

"You must be the president's nieces I was told about, though nobody mentioned you were exactly the same." He caught a glimpse of the retired university president at the head of the table, and he took note of how much the old man was enjoying his surprise.

"I'm Amanda Parrish," said the twin to his right.

"And I'm Belle Parrish," said the twin to his left.

"A and B," he acknowledged. "How will I tell you apart?"

"Oh, it really doesn't matter," they said, almost in unison. And then they both giggled the same exact giggle.

The wine being served the guests that evening was a Baco Noir from the Finger Lakes region, a full-bodied, deep red cabernet with hints of dark cherries and ripened raspberries. It was a local favorite. But at John Alden's plate there stood instead of wine a tall glass of ice beside a conspicuous bottle of Coca-Cola. He had requested it. Alden reached for the Coke. "I understand you both spent the winter in Spain?"

"Yes," Amanda told him with excitement in her voice. "The country is tearing apart. There's going to be a war."

"Yes, I know," he said, pouring the Coke over the ice.

"You know Spain?"

"I know of the war to come." Alden caught his tongue before he had said too much. Then he quickly apologized, it having dawned on him that he had yet to introduce himself. He had spent the winter recuperating, not socializing. "I'm sorry . . . my name is John Alden. I'm going to begin teaching at the university in the fall."

"John Alden," repeated Amanda. "Like the Pilgrim on the Mayflower?"

"Yes. I'm actually a descendant."

"What subject will you be teaching?" asked Belle.

"Crime," he answered.

"Crime? How fascinating," replied the other twin, as if by force of habit they took turns speaking.

He stole a sip of the Coke. "Are you students at the university?"

"No," Amanda told him. "We're actresses. We're in the movie that's being made here."

"Yes," confirmed Belle. "One of us gets killed."

"Which one of you gets killed?" Alden asked the girls, sincerely interested.

"We don't know yet," Amanda told him. "We've never before had to worry about that. You see, John, we do *everything* together."

He nearly choked on his Coke. "Everything?"

Amanda—or maybe it was Belle; he could not tell them apart—whispered into his ear, and she whispered for good reason. "Everything," she seductively repeated.

He tried to wash away his embarrassment with another swig of Coke. He had to be careful not to drink or eat too much. There was still a lot of the evening left for him, and the headaches were frequent. John Alden rubbed his injured leg. The laudanum prescribed by President Hightower had worked its magic. Four months of constant pain had given way to merely an irritating soreness.

It was then that he first noticed her. She was staring at him across the table, a dark-haired girl with a lively gleam in a pair of big brown eyes, eyes that made her seem almost pixie in appearance, more cute than pretty, and strikingly familiar. The girl was, without doubt, a student, for behind the gleam in those beautiful eyes there manifested a keen intellect. But he also detected a trace of jealousy, not the malicious kind of jealousy, but the envious kind, as if she wished she were the one with whom he was exchanging pleasantries. She seemed to be paying no attention to the well-to-do student seated beside her, or perhaps he was paying no attention to her. It was plain that she had been watching him as he talked with the twins. She smiled his way with a perfect row of snow white teeth. His wife had had that same snowy smile. He returned her smile with one of his own, or the best that he could come up with.

The enormous clock at the end of the room echoed the hour. John Alden flinched at the sounds. Westminster chimes. *"I summon the living, I mourn the dead."* The unexpected loudness and the dark beauty of the chimes brought the room to a hush. Then as if on cue, President Emeritus H. W. Hightower, PhD, rose from his chair to speak.

Long after President Hightower had passed from the scene, one of his beloved students, a prominent alumnus, wrote a tribute to him in *The Cornell Book: Essays from the Past.* He described the former university president as round, pleasingly plump, and exceedingly cordial, like a wise and elderly snowman with fundamental warmth of spirit. "The glow of goodwill shines in his face," he wrote. "Everything about him—his advanced age, his moustache, the spectacles precariously balanced on his rotund nose like Teddy Roosevelt, his clothes, his speech, and in particular his manners—said that he was a man of the nineteenth century and not wholly comfortable living in the twentieth. And even though everybody he befriended in those last years knew the old president had passed his prime and that his influence on education was on the wane, they still held him in high regard and with a touch of nostalgia, a renaissance man left over from the Gilded Age. In other words, when President Hightower spoke in that mellifluous voice of his, his radio voice, people still listened, the way they listened when he had ruled the university with an iron fist and influenced higher education across the nation."

Much too flattering, Hightower would have said of the article, but with an element of truth as to his standing at the university on the night of the candlelight dinner.

"Thank you for being here tonight," he told his invited guests. "We don't do this enough . . . not like in the old days . . . but then, tonight, I refuse to wax sentimental. Tonight is about the *future.*" At the mere mention of that magical word there was a surprising round of applause, because by 1929 the word *future* had become synonymous with the word *utopia,* an unyielding conviction that somehow ordinary people were destined to be successful. And rich. When the enthusiastic applause abated, President Hightower went on with his speech. "This dinner is very special for me personally, because tonight I officially welcome home my nieces Amanda and Belle Parrish from their long, and I'm guessing, glorious winter in warm and faraway Spain." Now there was a polite and respectful round of applause for the two girls seated beside John Alden. "They are," he continued, "my identical nieces, as you can plainly see, and I might add . . . identical trouble." This brought a round of affectionate laughter, followed by more applause. The girls blew kisses his way. "This is a special evening for another reason, for after our sumptuous dinner here," he told them, "we shall retire to the parlor of this most magnificent house, where others will join us, and where I promise you a guest speaker the likes of which you have never before seen or heard." Now a hush fell over the dining room, the very kind of silence the old university president had been hoping for. Out of the corner of his eye he saw John Alden hiding behind his glass of Coke. He went on with his speech with the skill of the showman some thought he was. "In point of fact," he said, lowering his voice to nearly a whisper, "I promise you more than a mere speaker. I promise you a man who will leave you thinking hauntingly about this evening long after you have left this house, and long, long after you have left the university."

"Is it the Great Houdini back from the dead?" shouted a physics professor at the far end of the table.

Amid the roiling laughter, President Hightower laughed a hearty laugh himself and shot right back. "His story is better than that of the late Harry Houdini, my fine physics friend. In point of fact, the physics of his story alone will addle your mind."

THE PARLOR GAME

By the time dinner had concluded, another forty persons had gathered in the parlor. These after-dinner guests had been invited to hear the guest speaker and then partake of dessert. They were all a part of the university crowd except for those from the Ithaca Motion Picture Company, who were there on a break from shooting their latest feature. When the dinner guests had filed into the ornate sitting room, the parlor was packed to its French doors. Every chair was occupied and men were standing along the walls, several of them sharing a match to light cigarettes. Even the servants could be seen standing on tiptoes at the back of the room. An orchestra stage stood before a large bay window, the night providing a black backdrop.

A raised podium stood off to the left of the audience, and a Steinway baby grand piano sat off to the right, its middle keys having been played down to the wood. A timeworn sea captain's chair was placed at center stage, like the witness stand in a courtroom hearing. In keeping with the mood of the evening, only candlelight and the flickering flames of another glorious fireplace illuminated the room. Anticipation was high—that collective giddy kind of high. The wily old university president had been building suspense all week by dropping puzzling hints about a dark and mysterious guest.

The house as a whole retained the aura of frayed grandeur, but the word *parlor* did not do justice to the space in which they were gathered. Often called the Gold Room, it could hold a hundred people, and often did—an elaborate venue for poetry, literary readings, music, and guest lecturers. The walls were decorated with gold leaf, and they climbed to a twelve-foot ceiling with gold filigree panels. Candelabras that held fifteen candlesticks each were fastened to the left and to the right of a blue marble fireplace. The maple flooring was polished to a golden shine.

Before the night's entertainment could begin, there was some business, or at least the pretense of business, that had to be attended to. Since some of the university's most important patrons were in the room, it was imperative they be assured, once again, that the university was on sound financial footing.

The school's finance administrator, a man named Livingston Hughes, stood behind the podium with the mien of the prominent banker he once had been. His nose seemed perpetually in the air, as if a stick had been wedged up his backside and no force on earth could get it out. Nobody particularly cared for the man, but he was good at what he did. He was in charge of the university's finances, a responsibility he took great pride in, boasting daily about the size and growth of the school's endowment, which owed its success to a booming stock market in which the university was heavily invested. By the spring of 1929, the New York Stock Exchange had become a form of entertainment—its seemingly never-ending rise followed religiously. Everybody was getting rich, including the university. In the past year alone, shares of Du Pont had gone from 310 to 525; Montgomery Ward from 117 to 440; and General Motors was selling at 199. Historians of the day would record that their fellow Americans were feeling lucky, grateful, uninhibited, healthy, and happy. They certainly were that night in Ithaca.

The ex-banker turned finance administrator gave what sounded like a financial pep talk. He told the assembled audience, "The fundamentals of our economy are strong, and the university has strategically positioned itself so as to accumulate wealth at an astounding pace. Perhaps our much beloved President Coolidge said it best in his outgoing State of the Union message. Let me quote . . ." Livingston Hughes then read the message from the former American president as if he were reading a pronouncement off of parchment paper. "'No Congress ever assembled, on surveying the state of the Union, has met with a more pleasing prospect than that which appears at the present time. In the domestic field there is tranquility and contentment . . . and the highest record of years of prosperity. In the foreign field there is peace, the goodwill that comes from mutual understanding. We should regard the present with satisfaction and anticipate the future with optimism.'" Here the man paused and produced a tobacco-stained smile. "Ladies and gentlemen," he said, "I could not agree more. If I may paraphrase our students, let the good times continue to roll." Then the school's finance administrator left the stage to an enthusiastic round of applause.

With everyone in the room assured Cornell University was on sound financial footing, President Emeritus H. W. Hightower took his place at the raised podium. He was a Yale man by birth who had come to Ithaca as a young professor filled with all of the vigor and idealism that youth has to offer to teach the sciences. His plan as a young man had been to one day return to the college in New Haven, with its secret societies so holy that no one dared speak their names. But he fell in love with the gorges and the waterfalls and all of the legends that flowed from them, and he fell in love with the university on East Hill. So he stayed in hopes of one day making Cornell the equal of Harvard and Yale, Princeton and Dartmouth. His interests, too, changed over the years. He moved from teaching into administration and more and more he left the science of nature behind, gravitating instead to the science of the mind. This was perhaps the reason he so took to John Alden. The man piqued his curiosity and challenged his intellect in ways no other man had done before.

"And now," he announced with an almost childlike delight, "the moment you have all been waiting for …"

"It's about time!" came an impatient cry from the audience.

This brought a smile to his face. "Yes," he responded, "tonight is about time. You were not invited here on an old man's whim, I assure you. I took great care in putting together tonight's invitation list." He really was a showman, with near a carnival barker's flair for the dramatic. "I needed tonight's guests to be the most forward-thinking academics of our day, and I intentionally left off the list those who refuse to open their minds to the possibilities, both good and bad, that the future holds for us. And so . . . let me begin at the beginning . . ."

John Alden watched the presentation from a chair alongside the wall, fairly close to the podium but still a part of the audience. His enthusiasm did not match President Hightower's. The heat from the candles and the fireplace was causing him to perspire. He rubbed his sore leg and wrestled with the butterflies in his stomach. He longed for something to drink, but feared he had already had too much Coke. He felt a caffeine buzz. The opium that had lately spared him so much pain was beginning to wear off.

"One morning last autumn," President Hightower said, beginning his story, "the morning after the Halloween storm, to be precise . . . and that would make it All Saints Day, wouldn't it? Of course it would, but I digress. It was quite early, and I was out for my morning hike. The streets through campus were still wet from the hellish deluge the night before. Tree branches were down everywhere and puddles were the size of ponds, but the maelstrom had passed in the night and a glorious autumnal sun rose behind the woods to the east. My hike that morning took me down into Fall Creek gorge, where, to my surprise, I came across a man lying at the edge of the creek, which was still heavily swollen from the rains. It was as if he had washed up on the shores of Ithaca like some shipwrecked sailor. Indeed, by all appearances this man seemed to me to be quite dead. Yet upon further inspection I discovered he was merely unconscious, although severely battered. I managed to bring him around, and there being nobody up and about at that early hour, I practically carried him back up the hill and then here into President's House, where I immediately sent for a doctor. He had a broken leg and a fractured skull along with numerous cuts and abrasions. After a week of the most excellent care, he recovered enough to tell me a story so incredible that I have kept his four-month presence in this house a secret . . . until tonight." Here the old university president paused and took a deep breath, as if he himself were still having a hard time believing the story. "It seems . . . and having seen his physical condition that All Saints morning, I have no reason to doubt it . . . that our gentleman visitor had fallen from the Rickety Bridge into the Fall Creek gorge and then washed over Ithaca Falls." There was an audible gasp from the audience because everyone in the room was familiar with the infamous bridge and the deadly stretch of water that ran beneath it. "Yes," he assured his guests, "the man had fallen one hundred and fifty feet into the water, and then tumbled another one hundred and fifty feet over the falls to the torrent below. Now, I'm sure all of you remember the Halloween storm . . . a devil of a night if ever there was one, and one of the worst storms we've had in years . . . so you can imagine the violence of the water pouring over the waterfalls on that ungodly evening. That he survived to tell me anything at all is a miracle, for we know all too well how many unfortunate souls have lost their lives in Ithaca's famous gorges. Well, our mystery man has had all winter long to recover from his brush with death, and, with the melting of the snows, I can keep him on ice no longer. Ladies and gentlemen, without further ado, here tonight to share his incredible story with you is Mr. John Alden, eminent professor of criminal justice here at our very own Cornell University."

There was a light and very curious round of applause as John Alden struggled from his seat in the audience and limped up to the captain's chair at center stage. He dropped into the stiff wooden chair and placed the walking cane on the floor. He could see President Hightower's beautiful twin nieces whispering to one another. He could see the big brown eyes of the pixie-faced girl staring at him with bewilderment. He looked and felt like a caged animal in a zoo. The audience seemed mildly disappointed with him, and he felt openly hostile toward them. It was plain to see that they had been expecting more of the evening than the sob story of a man who had fallen into the drink and then lived to tell about it.

At the very back of the room an assistant football coach leaned into an aging colored man, also an assistant coach, both of them standing against the wall. "He kind of reminds me of Bobby Bill. He's got that look . . ."

"Yeah, he does. Whatever happened to Ole Bobby Bill?"

"The war . . . they say."

"Yes, you heard me correctly," President Hightower went on from up at the podium. "Mr. Alden claims to be one of our own, though I'm sure none of you has ever before seen him in the halls, or even heard mention of his name on campus. Nor have you likely ever heard of the discipline he claims to teach. Criminology. The scientific study of crime." Here he paused again to build their curiosity. "You see, my friends, Mr. Alden is a very special guest. He comes to us from the twenty-first century. Mr. Alden won't even be born until the year 1968."

What happened next could be measured in heartbeats. With the first beat of the human heart following the announcement of John Alden's birth year, there came the momentary shock of silence within silence. Another beat later came disbelieving grumbles. By the time the human heart had pounded three times, the room was filled with laughter and murmurs, as if the audience was at last being let in on a joke they did not particularly care for.

John Alden did not like being laughed at. The collection of candles reflecting off of the gold-coated walls made everything look aflame, like he was a guest in hell. He loosened his polka dot necktie, which now made him look even more disheveled in the ill-fitting suit. His socks kept falling down and he kept pulling them back up. He was mad at himself for having allowed the old bird of a university president to talk him into this nonsense. He avoided all their eyes and put on his most serious face. This evening was going to be a lot harder on him than he and President Hightower had imagined.

"If I may continue," President Hightower pleaded with his fat, stubby hands high in the air. "If I may continue," he repeated as the room quieted down. "Please hear us out. We've been planning tonight's entertainment for over eighty years." This brought about a round of polite laughter, and the distinguished H.W. Hightower, PhD, was allowed to continue with his presentation. "The man you see before you," he told them, "was born John W. Alden in Ithaca, New York, on the thirteenth day of January in the year of our Lord . . . 1968." Again he was forced to raise his hands for silence as the groans began. "He attended West Hill Elementary School, Ithaca Middle School, and finally a new Ithaca High School, which, if I understand him correctly, is to be situated on our old Percy Field, where he not only led the football team to a conference championship, but he graduated at the top of his class in the year 1986. The consummate student-athlete. With a bit of wanderlust in his young heart, Mr. Alden left Ithaca and joined the Army, specifically the military police, where he ended up serving in a war on the Arabian Peninsula. After his Army stint he found his way to Harvard Yard on a piece of federal legislation called the GI Bill and graduated magna cum laude in the year 1995, having earned a bachelor of arts degree in psychology with a minor in English literature. Then in the year 1996, Mr. Alden did a very curious thing with his Harvard education. He joined the New York City police department, which I understand is to grow enormously in both size and prestige."

"Who ever heard of an educated flatfoot?" The question was raised in the back of the room and brought yet another round of laughter.

"Gentlemen, please," President Hightower implored, "hold your editorials until I am through." He shuffled the notes in his hand. "Mr. Alden rose through the ranks, as they say, until he reached the coveted rank of Detective: First Grade, and was awarded a highly sought position in the department's famous homicide division. Not only did Detective Alden solve murders in New York City by day, but by night he continued his education, eventually earning a doctoral degree in forensic psychology at NYU in conjunction with the John Jay College of Criminal Justice in Manhattan."

"No such college exists." This comment came from up front.

"Crime is not a science," shouted another.

"It was only a few years ago," President Hightower reminded them, "that psychology was not considered a science. This university helped change that." Again he returned to his notes. "Now where in the future were we? Oh yes, after ten years of solving some of the worst and most puzzling crimes imaginable, Mr. Alden wrote a textbook on the science of murder. He left the New York City police department in the year . . . 2008. Yes, in the twenty-first century. Mr. Alden returned home to Ithaca, where he married . . . his high school sweetheart . . . and accepted a position teaching criminal justice here at the university." He looked up to see if he still had everybody's attention, and to make sure John Alden had not fled the room. "But how did he get here, you ask? This is where the story gets interesting . . ." Now he ignored his notes altogether. He leaned over the podium and spoke in a voice so whisper-like that the whole room leaned forward to hear him. This was better than radio. "It seems in the year 2010 a killer is afoot in Ithaca, a devilish assassin with a penchant for knife play. Yes, a master criminal that even the great, but sadly fictional, Sherlock Holmes would be hard pressed to apprehend. But on a stormy Halloween night in the year 2010, much similar to the stormy

Halloween night we suffered through last autumn, the renowned John Alden, professor of criminal justice, laid a clever trap for the fiend, and on that night of drunken revelry . . . and isn't it nice to know some things will never change . . ." Here the room exploded with tense laughter at his little joke, as they were clearly enjoying the show. ". . . And on that night of drunken revelry, in the midst of that terrible storm, Mr. Alden came upon the fiend in the act of murder, and not only did he save a young woman from succumbing to the dagger of a madman, but he pursued that madman through the campus, down the steep grade of Libe Slope, over the cliffs of the Fall Creek gorge and on to the Rickety Bridge. It was there he finally overtook this most diabolical of killers, this collector of body parts . . . and it was there, suspended one hundred and fifty feet above a raging torrent of water, on planks of wood rotting beneath their feet, that a life and death struggle between the forces of good and the forces of evil ensued. During this struggle, in the midst of thunder and lightning, the two combatants were torn from the bridge, thrown into the raging waters, and then washed over Ithaca Falls."

John Alden sat in silence, listening to all of this, staring intently at the flickering candle flames and the melting wax. There were times it seemed when he, too, got caught up in the story, but most of the time he just sat there stewing, perturbed his story was being turned into a cheap melodrama. A silent movie.

The president emeritus waited for his guests to digest everything he had told them. He took a deep breath and caught his second wind. He returned to his normal speaking voice, his let's-get-down-to-business voice. "What happened next," President Hightower said to his captive audience, "is what we are here tonight to figure out. Mr. Alden, himself, is not sure of what exactly happened, but putting our two highly-educated minds together, we have come up with a theory . . .

that theory being that Mr. Alden, through a rare and extreme combination of forces, both natural and supernatural, a *perfect storm,* as he calls it, was washed through some kind of time portal, a liquid vortex, and ended up back here with us, where I found his near-lifeless body alongside the creek."

President Hightower paused at this point. No one was laughing. No one stirred. The audience seemed more baffled than anything, the lot of them staring at John Alden like a laboratory specimen. As college pranks go, this one appeared particularly dark and bizarre. The murder story had clearly shaken the women. It was not the type of hoax usually staged by an eminent and erudite university president.

"Ladies and gentlemen," President Hightower announced, "your job in this room tonight, through what I hope will be sharp questioning and deductive reasoning, is to prove that the man you see seated before you is a charlatan. A fraud. A con man. A sly, but convincing, actor. I've been trying to trip him up for the past four months, and though I find that some of his answers challenge the intellect, I've yet to catch him in what I call a *true gaffe.*" Here he steadied himself for the task ahead. He pulled a gold watch from his vest pocket and checked the hour. "Now, for the sake of the future, Mr. Alden and I have laid down a few rules." He snapped the watch closed and returned it to the vest pocket over his ample belly. "This is not a debate. Mr. Alden claims his answers are historically accurate. Some questions he simply will not answer. And always remember, Mr. Alden suffered serious injuries to his leg and to his head. Those facts are indisputable. Until he fully recovers, he is a guest in this house and on our campus. Tonight, I want you to ascertain whether or not he is a guest in our time."

The first man out of his chair was Nolan Dunn, a career academic. He would not even look Alden's way, instead addressing the question to the president emeritus. "If this be not a cosmic joke, President Hightower, and our guest truly holds a PhD, then why is it you constantly refer to him as Mr. Alden instead of the much honored Dr. Alden?"

President Hightower removed the spectacles from the bridge of his nose and put on his sly and totally disarming smile. "Ye gods, Professor Dunn, the man does not earn his doctorate for another seventy years. So I honor him with Mister. Now please, direct your questions to Mr. Alden."

The next question was asked by an ungainly and poorly-dressed student who was standing alongside the wall to Alden's left, a local kid by all appearances. A townie hiding behind thick glasses and an undernourished shell. His name was Jim Dorn, a lab assistant at White Hall. He avoided Alden's eyes, and his question seemed intentionally frivolous. "In your mind, when will the good times end?"

At last it was John Alden's turn to speak. The man had been confined to his bed over the long, snowy winter. It was only in the past two weeks that he had been able to get outside for some slow, painful walks and some badly needed fresh air. He did not yet know these people, and they did not know him. The audience waited impatiently to hear the sound of his voice, to take note of his attitude, and to judge his response to their inquiries. They were expecting a joke, so he fixed them with the truth. "October of this year," he told them with no uncertainty, "1929. The stock market crashes. Entire fortunes are wiped out in a matter of days, and the ten years that follow become known as the Great Depression. At its worst, one in every four Americans will be out of a job. The university you are all so proud of will barely survive."

"Nonsense!" came the angry voice of the finance administrator, Livingston Hughes, the very man who had just assured the audience the good times would continue. "Sheer and utter nonsense," he bellowed, "and dangerous talk, President Hightower."

In an instant the air had gone out of the room. John Alden had popped their party balloon. "Little men like you will be throwing yourselves out open windows," he said, dismissing Hughes. Suddenly they were no longer having fun. With just that one answer he had pulled the economic rug from beneath their feet. Threatened their good times. And there was something else they noticed. His voice. It was a smooth, commanding voice, the likes of which they had never before heard.

It was another student who spoke next, a young man fumbling with a cigarette. He rose from his chair with a question that had more weight to it. During the prosperous 1920s, despite the efforts of academics like H. W. Hightower, the undergraduate population of America's universities was overwhelmingly affluent. College students endorsed conservative Republican presidential candidates by an even larger margin than did the general electorate. "Foregoing the easy prediction that four years hence President Herbert Hoover will be reelected in another landslide," the young man said, "who after that will be our next elected American president?"

"In four years' time," Alden told him, "America will be deep into the depression of which I just spoke. Herbert Hoover will be thrown from office on his ear and will live the rest of his life in infamy, his name synonymous with ineptitude and financial failure."

"And the next president?" The skeptical student asked again, still fingering his cigarette.

"Franklin Delano Roosevelt sweeps into office in 1932, promising America a New Deal. He is reelected three times, making him the longest serving president in American history."

The room was raucous. Outside of New York's large cities, there was not a lot of enthusiasm for the debonair Franklin Roosevelt. Now the comments were coming fast and furious. The most forward-thinking academics of the day were not taking kindly to their host, or his special guest.

"Roosevelt! Good God, another Harvard man."

"He's been governor barely a month."

"An intellectual lightweight trapped inside a cripple's body."

A fairly serious-looking young man rose in the back of the room. President Hightower guessed him to be an adjunct professor, but the university was growing too fast for him to remember every single face. "Since you're predicting economic depressions and presidents and such," the young man said, "can you tell us . . . will the world ever again go to war?" He held up his left arm. There was no hand attached to it, only an unsightly three-pronged prosthetic.

"Yes," Alden told him, unflustered by his wounds.

"When?"

"The war in Europe begins in 1939. America enters the war in 1941."

"What triggers this second world war?" the wounded veteran wanted to know.

"A man of incomparable evil."

"What's his name?"

"I can't say."

"Is it Roosevelt?" someone shouted.

Now laughter returned to the room. They seemed determined to make a fool out of him. The man who had lost his arm below the elbow shouted from the back of the room. "Don't keep us in suspense, Mr. Alden; are we victorious?"

"Historians will call it our finest hour," he answered, raising his impressive voice.

"Well, thank God for that." The one-handed veteran took his seat with a victorious smile.

A rich kid standing to John Alden's left had another question. He raised his hand, more mocking than polite. His name was Royal S. Copeland III, son of the United States senator from New York. He was the boy who had been seated next to the brown-eyed beauty across the dinner table. Now he stood along the wall, smirking, with his college buddies. Copeland was a rather handsome young man, and he had won a small part in the movie being shot. President Hightower pointed to him. The room quieted. The popular student blew a stream of cigarette smoke into the air. Then he pulled his pocket watch from the vest of his expensive suit, with just the right touch of flair, and he checked the time. "As you've stepped out for eighty-some years, Pilgrim, won't your wife be missing you?"

More laughter. They were having fun again. Alden was not. "She's dead," he told him. The room again fell silent. He had them riding a river of emotions.

A gentleman stood near the front of the room, a man gentle in appearance and in demeanor. As a matter of fact, he was the only person in the room that night who bothered to properly introduce himself. "Mr. Alden, I am Professor Robert Short Roth. I head the English department here at the university. I took note of the minor in English literature you claimed to have earned from our friends in Cambridge. Can you tell us . . . which works of our contemporary writers will pass into the realm of literature?"

John Alden did not hesitate with his answer. "F. Scott Fitzgerald and Ernest Hemingway."

Again the room descended into disorder. "Fitzgerald? That Princeton brat hasn't been relevant in years . . . if ever he was."

"Literature is what lasts," Alden reminded them. "Their writings will last for generations."

"Hogwash. They'll both die in drunken obscurity. President Hightower, your guest is preposterous."

The old university president began to think too much of the Finger Lake's fine wine had been served at dinner. "Gentlemen," he implored, stepping forward, "remember the rules."

Now another man, an older gentleman who was a Catholic priest, rose from his chair in an attempt to restore some order and dignity to the evening. The room quieted at the sight of his collar. "It seems to me, President Hightower, that we are ignoring a key element of Mr. Alden's fantastic journey."

"And what would that be, Father Dougal?"

"Mr. Alden," the priest continued, now directly addressing the guest, "this criminal with whom you wrestled on the Rickety Bridge . . . like Sherlock Holmes and Professor Moriarty in a death dance at the Falls of Reichenbach . . . do you claim that he, too, fell from the bridge and was washed over Ithaca Falls?"

"I do."

"Well, then . . . is it possible, even probable, that this murderer of yours also fell through your so-called time portal . . . that you in all probability dragged him along with you?"

John Alden was a lapsed Catholic. In his time he had had little respect for priests. "For your sake, I hope not."

Again President Hightower raised his hands. "Rest assured, my friends, I found nobody else in the water that morning."

"We should thank our Lord," said Father Dougal as he sat down. "One crackpot is quite enough."

The evening was not going well. John Alden felt trapped in a room of burning fire. His hostility was giving way to sickness. Blue cigarette smoke was clouding the gold room. By the time the next questioner rose to his feet, Alden was feeling faint. This inquisitor was a quiet but intensely intelligent-looking man. Thomas Baker-Ward, MD. The diagnostic type. He removed the spectacles from his narrow face and put the end piece to his lips. "Since we're dealing in abstract theories here . . . is it possible, Mr. Alden, that you were, in fact, killed in your tumble from Ithaca Falls . . . and this is your afterlife?"

President Hightower could not help but interject. "Our shining Ithaca as heaven . . . what a fascinating theory."

"More likely hell," said Dr. Baker-Ward, in a humorous exchange.

"I've thought of that possibility," Alden told him. "Or I could be in a coma and this is just one long, crazy dream."

"Are you insane?" the doctor asked.

"I've thought of that, too."

The quiet but intense Dr. Baker-Ward was ready with his diagnosis. He turned to the audience. "Severe depression," he announced. "Despondent over the death of his wife, Mr. Alden threw himself from the bridge. He survived against all odds, and now he concocts this fantastic story to cover his overwhelming shame."

"Oh, my God," exclaimed the rich Copeland boy, standing along the wall, "the ole pilgrim tried to *gorge out*."

Now another Cornell doctor, a Victor Ecarius, was on his feet with a counter diagnosis. He was tall and lean, an almost satanic-looking man, with a sharp beak. And there was something disconcerting about his eyes. The colors were off. "Thank you, Dr. Freud," Dr. Ecarius said, with deep sarcasm in his voice, "but I think that is not the case. Mr. Alden's answers are overflowing with certitude and sincerity. It is obvious to me that he truly believes what he says. A complex case of amnesia would be my guess. He cannot remember the past . . . therefore he cannot deal with the present, so he creates a future."

It was during this psychology discussion that John Alden came to realize that none of the women in the room had yet spoken. He interrupted the argument up front. "Perhaps the ladies in the audience might be curious about what life holds in store for their daughters and their granddaughters in the twenty-first century."

To his surprise the first hand up in the air was that of the brown-eyed beauty who had been staring at him from across the dinner table. He acknowledged her hand and she stood with some trepidation. She had a soft but sincere voice. Again, hauntingly familiar. "How did your wife die?"

The question caught him off guard. He swallowed hard. "I can't say."

Royal S. Copeland III, forever the wise-guy, spoke up again. "Cheer up, Pilgrim. If you're telling the truth . . . your mother-in-law is not even born yet."

There was some nervous laughter. The spoiled rich kid had a point. A stupid point, but a point nonetheless.

Beautiful brown eyes took her seat and an anxious girl seated next to her jumped up in her place. "Does a woman ever get elected President of the United States?"

John Alden smiled at the hopeful look on her face. "No, I'm sorry, not in my time. But before I left, the first African . . ." Here he paused. He chose his words carefully. "Just before I was displaced," he told his audience, "a colored man was elected President of the United States."

LATER IN THE EVENING

The library in President's House was warm and intimate and redolent of good Scotch and pipe tobacco. It was a room that reeked of knowledge and understanding, but John Alden paced the rug like a prisoner with a bad limp. In his hand was a bottle of Coca-Cola, in one of those "wonderful old bottles," as he put it. Too much caffeine and his bizarre performance in the parlor had created an ill-tempered stir in his mind as well as in his stomach. A green-shaded reading lamp sat on a small table, providing the late-evening light. It was the same type of green-shaded lamp that could be seen burning in every window of every dormitory on a study night. Alden was grateful for its incandescent glow. He'd had quite enough of candles. A large log crackling in the hearth provided warmth.

Above the fireplace hung a portrait of the university's founding father, a man who had made a fortune in the telegraph industry and then used the state's land grant laws to create a private-public university out of farmland and woods—a university that would grow into a remarkable institution. Alden wondered if any man could be as noble in life as Ezra Cornell appeared in oil.

To his left hung a black oaken wall clock, a mechanism of intrinsic beauty and perfection. The recently invented clock consisted of two pendulums, one a slave and the other a master. The slave pendulum drove the clock's hands. This allowed the master pendulum to remain free of any mechanical task that might disturb its rhythm. The intricate clock was accurate to within one second a year. Never in the history of the world had time been measured with such precision.

John Alden paused before a shelf of books. On the top shelf an hourglass served as a bookend. He turned it over, sipped his Coke and watched the sand slip slowly through the glass neck. They were all there. The classics. At a glance he spotted Emerson's *Essays,* Dante's *The Divine Comedy, The Odyssey* by Homer, *The Confessions of St. Augustine,* and *The Imitation of Christ, Two Years Before the Mast,* and *The Thousand and One Nights.* Still, the longer he browsed the spines, the more he noticed titles and authors he had never heard of before, gold-stamped titles bound in wonderfully worn leather, as handsome a collection of books as he had ever seen, as if they had been perused many times and then passed on with humility to the next generation. Alden was about to ask about this enticing book collection when the old university president interrupted his thoughts with an observation. "You're unhappy."

He was seated in his favorite chair. The nearby table held whatever material he was studying at the moment. President Hightower struck a match and lit his pipe, tossed the match into the fire, and then puffed repeatedly. Cherry tobacco smoke filled the room. The old man seemed quite pleased with himself.

"You turned my predicament into a parlor game," John Alden complained, still facing the curious collection of books. "A source of entertainment . . . and a cheap act, at that."

"I gave you cover, Mr. Alden."

"How so?"

"Instead of an unemployable lunatic limping through campus spouting nostrums to future events . . . you are now a visiting professor. An eccentric. A living, breathing challenge to logic and reasoning. A mysterious wise man who keeps people guessing. Unlike say, Princeton or Dartmouth, with their evangelical piety, we have cranks of every twist at this university. You will fit right in."

He finally turned to President Hightower. "Am I to thank you?"

"Actually, Mr. Alden, you were quite good tonight. I thought you had some of them . . . until, of course, you mentioned the Negro president. But it was nice to end on a light note."

Alden smiled, probably his first real smile of the night. "You have much to learn, my learned friend."

"Evanescent," Hightower said to him.

"Fleeting," he told the president emeritus, defining the word. "Transitory. Something that is vanishing, or likely to vanish." He fired right back. *"High technology?"*

President Hightower paused for a second, but it was only a second. "Technology on a higher plane would be my guess."

"Good guess. Scientific technology involving advanced or sophisticated devices, especially in electronics or computers. The phrase enters Webster's Dictionary in 1964. In 1969 it's shortened to *high-tech.*"

"High-tech," the old man said, contemplating the phrase. "I like that."

It was a game they played while he recovered. President Hightower would test Alden's knowledge of the English lexicon up to 1929, and John Alden would educate Hightower to words and phrases that were to be added to Webster's Dictionary up to the year 2010. But Alden could never tell if the old man was helping exercise his brain after the head injury, or if he was just trying to snare him in a verbal trap.

"He's coming here, you know."

"Who is coming here?" Alden asked.

"Governor Roosevelt is coming to the university."

"When?"

"Semester's end. He's been invited to speak at commencement. Does that worry you?"

"Why should it worry me?" Alden wanted to know.

"While it's true I do not hold the governor of New York in as high esteem as you apparently do, it would seem from your prognostications earlier this evening that the most straightforward way to alter America's future would be to kill Franklin Roosevelt."

"That's a terrible thing to say. Besides, the man I'm looking for is a misogynist. He preys on women."

"But you claim he said to you on the Rickety Bridge, *'Now two men have to die . . . and you can't stop it this time.'*"

"Yes, something like that."

"Two men?" Hightower raised an eyebrow. "Interesting. If we assume one of them is Governor Roosevelt . . . who would be his other target? Perhaps it is you."

"He could have killed me in my time. Instead, he murdered my wife. Besides, in the big picture, I'm hardly on par with Franklin Roosevelt."

"Then we have to figure out what you are doing here."

John Alden limped in a half circle until he was opposite the old man on the other side of the room. His suit coat was open, his vest was unbuttoned, and his ugly tie hung like a noose. "What do you think I'm doing here? You must have formed an opinion by now."

"I think you're chasing your own death."

Alden downed the last of his Coke and set the clear green bottle aside. "I'm chasing a man. I just don't know that he's here."

"Here in Ithaca, or here in 1929?"

"I don't know."

"There have been no murders in Ithaca. Certainly no violence of the nature that you have described."

"He could have washed up in the year 1925, or 1921, or 1915. He could have been here for years . . . just waiting for me. He's a serial killer. If he's here, he'll kill again. Especially if he knows I'm here now."

"*Serial killer*? I've never heard the term. Police talk?"

"Criminal science. A person who commits a series of similar murders." With that bit of knowledge, John Alden noticed a sudden flash of concern in the old man's face. "What is it?"

"As I recall, there was a series of murders in Upstate New York . . . all of them women . . . back before the war. But I don't know that the cases were related."

"What kind of women?"

"Several of them were suffragists. It's why they made the news."

"A woman's right to vote, and to run for political office."

"Yes. Upstate New York was a hotbed for the women's suffrage movement, as it was for the abolition movement before it. Seneca Falls, Rochester, Auburn, Skaneateles… where the leaders of these women lived and worked."

"And that's where these murders took place?"

"Some of them, I'm sure."

"Do you remember when these murders began?"

"Again, you're taxing my memory, Mr. Alden . . . but I believe the first suffragist killed was in Seneca Falls in 1916. I remember because it was the year after Cornell's Big Red football team was crowned national champions." He paused to dwell on what he had just said. "A strange way to remember things . . . but then I'm old."

"When did these murders stop?"

"I believe the last suffragist killed was around 1920, with the end of the war."

"Or with the passage of the Nineteenth Amendment to the United States Constitution." John Alden stared at the thousand years of history that lined the bookshelves. "He's here. I can feel it."

"Well now, maybe your man was here tonight . . . even asking you questions . . . but isn't it more likely your serial killer, as you call him, would strike in New York City, which you claim as your old stomping grounds?"

"I've checked the New York City newspapers. There have been no killings there of his nature. Besides, that vortex forms here in Ithaca, and it forms here for a reason." It was then that the wall clock struck midnight and proceeded to play its own version of St. Michael chimes. Alden waited impatiently as the clock tolled twelve times. "You can't stop talking about all of the great thinkers gathered here in Ithaca. I'm begging you to put the university to the task. Its full resources. Why am I here? And more importantly, how do I get home?"

The old man smiled. "It took a lightning strike to get you here. I imagine it will take a bolt of electricity to get you home." President Hightower removed the pipe from his lips and glanced up at the wall clock, the focal point of the room. "After the Great War," he told Alden, "the times changed. The colleges and the universities changed. I got them through the transition, but my day had come and gone. Even I could see that. So we passed the torch. They gave me the title *president emeritus* and they let me stay here in President's House. I'm allowed an occasional lecture, and I preside over a few selected ceremonies, but I no longer run the university. In current academic circles, my power is minuscule."

"You have the power of persuasion."

At this the old man chuckled. "It's been nearly thirty years, Mr. Alden, and I'm still adjusting to life in the twentieth century. I'm a horse and buggy man in an age of automobiles. You can hardly expect me to convince my colleagues that I have unique insights into the twenty-first century."

John Alden thought back to the parlor game and to the sheer antagonism it had wrought. It was then he remembered one of the few bright spots. "Who was the dark-haired girl . . . big brown eyes, pretty face . . . asked about my wife?"

President Hightower allowed his mind to wander over the questioners. "Caitlin something," he answered, not really sure of her last name. "She plays the chimes in the clock tower. I believe there's a concert tonight."

"Did you say Katelyn?"

"Yes."

"Spell it."

"C-a-i-t-l-i-n. She's a member of the senior class. Psychology, I believe. Curious, don't you think . . . that of all the possible questions pertaining to the future . . . she chose to ask the personal." He shrugged his shoulders. "Women," he said, and he went back to puffing on his pipe.

"On the subject of lovely and mysterious women . . . you failed to mention your nieces were identical twins."

"They are my sister's grandchildren, actually."

"I don't believe I saw their parents at dinner."

"Their father is dead. Their mother is in Manhattan."

"Where in Manhattan?"

"Bellevue. I'm guessing you're familiar with the institution."

John Alden plopped into a chair and rubbed his aching leg. "I am."

"There is a fine line between genius and madness," President Hightower told him. "I ended up on one side of the line.

My unfortunate sister and her offspring have all ended up on the other. We don't talk about it. In this day and age the stigma of mental illness is worse than tuberculosis . . . tantamount to leprosy." The president emeritus blew a stream of smoke at the ceiling. "So tell me, Mr. Alden, does the future hold much hope for those going mad?"

John Alden did not like the way he was being stared at. "No, there is still no cure, but there will be new drugs to manage mental illness by correcting the chemical imbalance in the brain."

"Name one."

Here he sensed one of Hightower's traps, as if he was expected to make up a stupid name for some futuristic drug. He stared at the empty bottle of Coca-Cola. "Lithium," Alden said, "will be discovered to have miraculous effects on manic depression."

"Lithium, you say? An element of the periodic table, where it sits just below sodium. Lithium bromide is currently being used as a sedative."

"Yes."

"Interesting. And were you ever prescribed any of these new drugs?"

John Alden hesitated before answering. "I was."

They both sat in unpleasant silence, the warm air having gone out of the evening, the fire in the hearth reduced to embers. President Hightower was a respected psychologist, a retired university president, and the only friend John Alden had in the world in which he now found himself living. Still, he could not shake a feeling of unease.

"Eminence grise," Hightower finally said.

"It's French," Alden told him, defining the phrase. "It means the power behind the throne. An advisor or decision-maker who operates secretly or unofficially. *E-mail,*" he shot back. "The word enters Webster's Dictionary in 1982."

President Hightower put his aged mind to work. "A verb, or maybe a noun . . . and my guess would be that *e-mail* is mail that is to be delivered electronically, as if by telegraph. Hardly revolutionary, I would think."

John Alden smiled for only the second time in the evening. "You're better with the new words than I am with the old words. How do you do it?"

"Simple extrapolation," Hightower answered. "The same as you."

"Explain."

The old university president leaned forward in his chair and offered his first real diagnosis of John Alden's situation, while all of the time his eyes continued evaluating his visitor through a cloud of cherry-infused tobacco smoke. "You have suffered through a traumatic experience, Mr. Alden. In going over Ithaca Falls, you also took a blow to the head, not to mention the cumulative effects of the emotional blows I suspect you've suffered over the past few years. As a result of the injuries to your body and mind, and to your spirit, you've created an alternate universe, a future world right here in Ithaca. You've taken the edge of science and politics in 1929, and you've applied it to the twenty-first century. You tell of a great storm on Halloween. We had a great storm on Halloween. It was the night before I found you. You talk of a world with pocket telephones, but it takes little imagination to imagine a telephone without a cord. You spoke of a bright yellow sports car that almost ran you down, but we have yellow sports cars right here in town. Young Mr. Copeland owns one. It's a beauty. Yours is some of the most forward thinking I've ever encountered, but it's still based on extrapolation . . . taking the known facts and using them to project unknown facts." Here the old man leaned back in his chair and paused with a long and satisfied puff of his pipe. Then he gave a nod to the black clock on the wall with its master pendulum swinging free. "You're not from the future, John Alden. You're just very good at reading the future."

Rumors of Resurrection

It is hard to say where rumors of the plans for the prisoner's resurrection began, but once they hit the New York City newspapers, these rumors took on a life of their own. After the execution, Cornell University would claim the body. A university lawyer would get a court order forbidding an autopsy, thus preserving the corpse. The dead prisoner would then be packed in ice and returned to Ithaca in a special train car, and then driven up the hill to the laboratories of White Hall, also known as Hell Hall. There the executed man, it was believed, through adrenaline shots and electricity, or some other such means, would be brought back to life—like Frankenstein's monster, only handsome and with an Ivy League education. These rumors of resurrection followed rumors of an escape attempt, which followed rumors of an armed rescue. As ridiculous as they all sounded, the rumors were being made believable by a sensational press, a gullible public, and by the prisoner's extraordinary accuracy when it came to predicting future events. Not only had he seen coming the stock market crash of 1929, but he was now being blamed for it. Electrocute the messenger.

On the other side of the issue were those who worshiped the man. Because of the prisoner's economic forecasting, they had been able to rescue their life savings. He had also predicted the recent election of Franklin Roosevelt to the office of President of the United States, four years ahead of everybody else. To many he was a misunderstood hero —a man framed for an assassination he had tried to prevent, found guilty of a murder he did not commit, and then sentenced to die in the hell hole that was Sing Sing prison. They, too, did not believe he had been sent from the future. They believed he had been sent from heaven.

On Thursday night, execution night at Sing Sing, ten thousand protesters gathered in Times Square in Manhattan for a prayer vigil. Demonstrations in support of the prisoner were also being held in Catholic Ireland, Protestant England, and secular France. State troopers stood guard at wooden barricades that had been hastily erected across roads leading to the prison. Heavily armed guards surrounded the prison walls as people, both for and against the scheduled execution, gathered in the light rain, sandwiched between the enormous stone walls and the great river that ran before those walls. Some people climbed atop the large rocks overlooking the prison grounds. Then another rumor filtered through the crowd. It was said a special executioner had been hired to make damn sure that at the appointed time, 11:00 p.m., the prisoner died—and that the son of a bitch stayed dead.

The minute hand was creeping up on 8:00 p.m. when the prisoner, lying on his bunk, overheard radio warnings of the approaching storm, followed shortly thereafter by the first rumbles of thunder rolling over the Palisades on the western shore. The giant radiators outside the cells on Death Row ran hot and cold. Literally. They were either stone cold or boiling hot, making a comfortable temperature a rarity. On this night they were boiling hot. Near the cell's iron door where the prisoner's white-stocking feet were, the temperature was unusually warm. Near the window, where his head lay on a sweat-stained pillow, the night air was cold and damp. No comfort would be found on this night. Twelve of the eighteen cells in the death house were occupied by men, while three cells were reserved for women. But seldom were there women on Death Row. Three cells nearest the chair were left unoccupied, as the condemned men were moved to them in the hours before the execution. Sing Sing could execute as many as five men on a Thursday night. These last three cells were so near the electric chair that the condemned could not escape the stench of burning flesh or the death rattle of an ineffective overhead vent meant to dissipate the fumes. The place was a fire trap.

"Do you believe in the resurrection?"

The prisoner sat up on his bunk at the sound of the priest's voice and stared at the talking door. "Yes, Father, I've heard the rumor. It's amazing what people will believe, isn't it?" He had once been a proud member of New York's finest, an author and a scholar, but his life was now reduced to cold stone walls and the sorrowful voice of a faceless priest slipping through a slit in an iron door.

"Yet you yourself have asked us to believe you are from the twenty-first century."

"Don't you believe that I am, Father?"

"No," answered the priest. "In fact, I suspect you're a ghost of the past."

"But you believe Christ arose from the dead?"

"I do."

"So, why not me?"

"Because you're not Jesus Christ."

Now the prisoner laughed. "More than a few people have accused me of thinking that I am."

"I do not want you to die alone. You must have family . . .?"

The prisoner lay back down on his bunk, resting his head on the rancid pillow and staring at the water-stained ceiling. "There's no one in this time, Father. Let us say our goodbyes."

"But we all have someone. A girl, perhaps?"

"Yes, there was a girl," the prisoner told him, with a touch of lament in his voice. "But that was in another life."

"That one-armed detective came to me again. He wants to see you."

"I don't want to see him."

Again there was silence at the door. The first stab of lightning penetrated the cell, and more thunder rumbled across the river. The prisoner at first believed the prison chaplain had given up and walked away. Then he heard, "Ad hominem?"

The prisoner smiled. "It's Latin. It means to attack the man instead of his ideas."

"It's an appeal to emotions or prejudices rather than reason," the chaplain told him.

*"Same difference," replied the prisoner. He thought back to his English literature studies at Harvard. "*Bildungsroman*?" he asked the chaplain.*

There was a long pause on the free side of the iron door. At long last the prisoner heard from the chaplain. "I swear to God . . . I'm stumped."

"Finally got you," the prisoner said with a kind chuckle.

"Is it one of your new words?" the voice asked.

"No, Father. A bildungsroman *is a novel about the moral and psychological growth of the main character."*

OVER THERE

I*t was Simms who spotted him. Moving through the mud. Through the rain. It wasn't his face he recognized as much as the way the man moved. He did not slog through the mud the way other soldiers did. He strode through it. Tall and straight. A leader of men. Simms leapt from the truck. Collapsed in the muck. He got to his feet, breathing hard. Put a hand to his chest.*

"Bobby!" Simms cried. "Bobby Bill!"

He was an officer now, a captain, and he turned Simms's way. "Simms, you old cad."

They embraced in the middle of the road. In the middle of France. Simms's column was in retreat. The captain and his column were reinforcing the front. Both men were with the New York 69th. Piercing whistles arced the sky, and the sound of artillery exploded in the distance. The air, even through the rain, smelled of mustard. Sickly sweet.

Simms stepped back and saluted. "So it's Captain, now."

"I bribed a general."

Simms reached out and touched the captain's face, an almost feminine move in a combat zone. It was as if he was reaching for a piece of his past—some romanticized past that had almost died in the war. "Look at you," Simms said. "Not even a world at war could mar that pretty face."

"Is it rough up there?"

Simms spit out a hacking cough. "I took a little gas." He gestured over his shoulder at the walking wounded. "Some of the boys got it bad." Then he found a smile. "It's like slugging it out with the Harvard eleven in the mud. But if anybody can break through . . . it'll be you, ole sport."

"I'll give it my all." The army captain patted his shoulder and then moved on.

Simms called after him, not wanting to let go. "I'll see you back in Ithaca. We'll have a victory beer in Collegetown and talk of the way we were."

But Simms's odyssey did not lead back to Ithaca. He lies buried in France. His brief encounter with Captain Robert A. Bill of the New York 69th was recorded in a single paragraph in a letter to a college friend.

Or so the story goes.

His Beautiful Katelyn

The old university president had messed with his head. In the days that followed the candlelight dinner, John Alden questioned his sanity. He found himself living not in his Ithaca, but some mythical Ithaca—that Ithaca of legend he had heard so many stories about while growing up. There was no radio station in this day and age that would play his kind of music, but still he could hear the lyrics of an anthem rocking through the years—about God having mercy on the man who doubts what he believes in.

He had a headache. John Alden put the barrel of a revolver to his lips and blew his Coca-Cola-infused breath across the bore. It was .38 Super automatic, the latest and most powerful pistol in production. He'd bought it off an ROTC colonel. In practice rounds the Super .38 bullets made holes the size of a fist. He was after a serial killer, and this time he wanted to be more prepared.

Sitting alone now in his third floor room, the gun at the tip of his lips, John Alden felt spasms in his injured leg. He stared at the wad of opium on the nightstand, the magic that would relieve his pain. The half-empty bottle of Coke stood next to it, and next to the Coke lay the letter from the breast pocket of his coat. It was a letter that had traveled with him through time. The paper was crinkled and water-worn now, the ink faded. But her words had survived.

Watching him blowing kisses to a gun barrel from the wall across the room was a framed photograph of a Cornell football player. The young man, a clean-cut, all-American type, was mugging for the camera. No helmet on his head. A football tucked under his arm. A stiff arm to the lens, one foot off the ground. And a pretentious snarl on his face. From the outdated uniform, John Alden guessed the brown-toned photograph to be pre-war. Perhaps that championship season.

Outside it was raining, a fine-sifted drizzle that had grayed this corner of New York for days on end. The resonance of the drops on the roof was incessant. He lowered the .38 from his lips and dropped his head. He thought of the Caitlin girl who had asked about his wife during the parlor game, the pretty girl who played the chimes in the clock tower. Then he looked at the letter and remembered his own beautiful Katelyn in his own beautiful time.

"Cheer up, Pilgrim. If you're telling the truth . . . your mother-in-law is not even born yet."

John Alden sat up and fixed his eyes on the two-dimensional football player in the picture frame across the room. Then he reached for the letter, and the Coke, and he recalled in detail the trip he had made to Oregon in the days after the war.

A TRIP TO OREGON

The man's ability to move through the night like a ghost, to see but remain unseen, had served him well while with the military police, and it had served him even better while fighting crime on the streets of New York City. Seldom did he have to literally break into a home or a business. He usually slipped through an unlocked door or an open window. And then he disappeared. When he reappeared he had usually found what he had come for, a document, a diary, a ledger book, or maybe a gun, and then he was out the door without anyone ever knowing he had been there. Better than a burglar. Sly as a magician. Stealthy as a spirit. Unscrupulous. Immoral. And illegal.

The first time he used this criminal talent of his in peacetime was when he went to see his high school sweetheart after returning home from the war. She had married and had moved across the country to Portland, Oregon. He brought along a gun, a Colt .45 Army automatic. He was angry. He was tired from the travel and wet from the rain. "Katelyn," he said in a soft voice, "wake up." When she did not respond, he spoke a little bit louder. "Katelyn . . . wake up."

She was asleep in the bed alongside her husband, their backs to one another. He watched her stir at the sound of his voice.

"Wake up, Katelyn!"

That one she heard loud and clear. She bolted upright and saw his silhouette in a chair at the foot of the bed, the mere shadow of a man, like one would see in a dream.

"Switch on the light," he told her.

She reached over to the bedside table and turned on a small lamp. A dim forty watts. More shadows crisscrossed the room. She stared at him sitting there, fear and disbelief in her eyes. This was her hometown sweetheart, the man who had taken her to the Homecoming dance in the fall and to the prom in the spring. This was the man to whom she had lost her virginity on a blanket of moss below Ithaca Falls. She had not seen him in five years. He was dressed in a fatigue jacket. Wore it over a wrinkled shirt. His sandy hair was long and unkempt and fell down to his collar. He had not shaved in days. His eyes were red. His face was weathered. Beaten. He no longer looked like a school boy. He looked like a man. A very angry man. In his hand was a black pistol, as lethal an object as she had ever seen. He knew she hated guns. He stared at her. Stared right through her.

She was dressed in a red pajama top, the pullover type, with three buttons running down the front. It accented her breasts. Her hair was still that long and lovely deep brown that he recalled from their high school days, and it fell down across her shoulders with the sweep of an ocean wave. Even roused from a deep sleep and scared for her life, she was as pretty as he had dared to remember. She had once been the forgettable girl in the school choir with the wide, rosy cheeks and the intelligent brown eyes. Other girls, undoubtedly jealous, had bluntly asked him what it was he saw in her. He saw the woman in her. He saw the beautiful young woman in her long before anybody else.

It took a full minute for her husband to wake up. As the former teenage lovers sat staring at one another in deathly silence, the man of the house squinted against the unwelcome light before reaching for his glasses and then spotting the intruder sitting in a chair at the foot of his bed. He might not have seen the gun, or maybe his reaction was instinctive, but he threw off the covers in a rage and swung his legs out of bed. "What the . . ." he exclaimed.

The ex-MP fired one shot across the man's lap, hitting the alarm clock on the nightstand. The gunshot and the exploding clock carried the sound of a bomb. "Get back into that bed," he ordered. The man quickly jumped back into bed, and then he reached for his wife.

"Get your hands off of her," came the next demand. He stared at her husband with a look that could kill. "Put both of your hands under those covers and you keep them there," he ordered. "Katelyn, fold your hands in your lap where I can see them." He was used to giving orders. The young couple did as they were told. "Now, introduce us, Katelyn."

She swallowed hard and the first tear rolled down her cheek. "This is my ex-boyfriend from Ithaca. This is my husband . . . Michael."

It was the first time in years that he had heard the sound of her voice, and she was crying and introducing him to her husband. "It's nice to meet you, Michael," he said, with the gun pointed squarely at the man's chest. "And actually, I was her boyfriend when I left Ithaca. Isn't that right, Katelyn?"

"Yes." Her sweet voice was barely audible. The gunshot and the exploding timepiece had unnerved her.

He stared at her husband, sitting helpless in his own bed. The man appeared lawyerly and studious, almost the opposite of what he had expected. His eyeglasses were of the latest fashion, small and sleek, and he had noticed the man wore an expensive watch on his wrist, even in bed. "Do you think, Michael, had it been me sleeping in that bed that I would have allowed a man to break into my house and get this close to Katelyn?"

"What do you want?" the husband asked.

His gun hand was rock steady. "First of all," he said, "let's get something straight. Katelyn does not get hurt tonight. Nobody points a gun at her. Nobody touches her. I came here tonight to shoot you, you son of a bitch, and unless I get the explanation I believe I'm entitled to …"

"Are you crazy?" the husband wanted to know. The question was not rhetorical, but he got no answer. "Why this way?"

"Apparently, this is the way my Katelyn wanted it to be. I wrote her letters while I was overseas. She didn't answer them. I tried to get home, but there was a stop loss order. Do you know what that is?"

"No."

"That means you don't get out until they say you get out, even though your enlistment is up. I wrote Katelyn letters from a hospital bed. She never answered those, either. When I finally did get home, I went to her mother's house to find out where she was. The woman basically told me to get lost. I found out through friends that she had married and was living out here in Oregon. So I rode a train clear across this country to see her, but I didn't want to just drop in. So I called her up. My beautiful Katelyn hung up on me. I'll bet she didn't tell you that. I've been sitting for three days in a cheap hotel room watching the rain fall and thinking about what I should do next." He stated his case to the husband through heavy breaths, as if he had run all the way to their house. His once smooth voice was now filled with rancor. "All I really want is an explanation," he said. "When I left Ithaca, I had a girlfriend. When I got home, she was married and living a continent away. Don't you think I'm entitled to an explanation, Michael?"

The man glanced over at his wife and then back at the .45 automatic still pointed at his chest. "Yes, I think you're entitled to an explanation."

"Don't you think a quiet lunch would have been preferable to this?"

"Yes, I think she should have had lunch with you."

"Is there any reason I have to keep pointing this gun at you?"

"No, please stop . . . it's not necessary."

He lowered the gun but made sure it was clearly visible, balancing it across his knee. He was sitting at a right angle to his target. Standard military practice. "I've traveled three thousand miles for an explanation, Katelyn . . . and this man's life depends on it."

She shook her head in frightened bewilderment. "I don't know what to say . . ."

He quickly raised the gun and again pointed it directly at her husband's chest. Only now he was squeezing the trigger. "That's too bad for you, Michael."

The man was frantic. "No, wait . . . wait. Katelyn, please, talk to him."

It had been the Homecoming dance, and everybody at Ithaca High was waiting to see who was going with whom. He was the tall, brainy quarterback on an undefeated football team that seemed destined for a championship, so everybody was shocked when it was Katelyn Richter that he asked to the dance—the shapely, smiley girl that played the piano and sang in the school choir. Yes, she was pretty, but she didn't hang around with the cool kids. They ended up dating throughout the school year, and more and more he left his football playing friends behind and spent his time with Katelyn. They went to the movies. They had loved the movies. They went to the prom, had a ball, but their relationship had remained sweetly platonic.

He lowered the gun, only an ounce of pressure away from pulling the trigger. "I'm curious . . . what did she tell you about me, Michael?"

"Not much," the husband said, breathing hard. "That you dated in high school. That you were smart. That you got accepted to Harvard, but you joined the Army instead."

"You must've thought that was really stupid."

"I don't judge."

"I couldn't afford Harvard. Ironically, now that the government is willing to pay for it . . . I no longer give a shit."

One star-sprinkled evening, with graduation staring them in the face, the star quarterback and Katelyn Richter set out on a midnight picnic at Ithaca Falls. The night air was unusually warm for that time of the year. They spread their blanket on a bed of moss a quarter mile below the raging falls. The isolation, along with the roar of the rushing water, was heavenly. It was as if nothing had changed in a thousand years. One could easily imagine a tribal chieftain standing in full regalia atop a cliff contemplating the moon and the stars and the defense of his Cayuga people. Every now and then a plume of icy mist from Ithaca Falls would wash over them and they would hold on to one another tight, afraid they might be swallowed up in time, like the lovers in *Brigadoon*.

"Do you ever feel," she had asked him, "that we've been this way before? Perhaps in another life?"

He was eighteen and had never really been out of Ithaca. He thought the question odd. "Where is that coming from?"

"My grandmother," she told him. "She was quite a character. She believed we skipped a generation, and then we came back. Strangely, she was quite emphatic about it."

Their high school years were coming to an end, and already she had begun to change. He noticed it first in her eyes. Where they were once bright, brown and innocent, he now detected a trace of sadness. She was growing up, becoming less a schoolgirl and more a serious young woman. In a lot of ways it scared him. His ego had allowed that she was eternally grateful for his attentions. She was proud to be the quarterback's girl and to be seen on his arm as they walked the steep streets. Now she was changing in a way that suggested she knew there was more for her out there in the world than just a local yokel football player and a life in Ithaca.

So there had been a sexual desperation to their passion that night below the falls. The thing he remembered most about that wonderfully erotic night was the kiss. There was just that one kiss. The gorge was famous for the sounds it carried, so from the moment he began stripping her, their lips never separated. They swapped tongues, they exchanged breaths, but their mouths were inseparable. They wanted only to feel. Another plume of mist from Ithaca Falls swept over them, freezing them both in that moment in time. He would always remember that evening for the kiss.

But in the weeks that followed that night below Ithaca Falls, the sex did not bring them closer together. It drove them apart. And Katelyn was the one who was pulling away.

The memories of that night beneath Ithaca Falls were causing him to sweat. He stared at Katelyn, in bed with her husband, and he shook his head in amazement. "For a girl who believes in reincarnation . . . you must have known I'd be back." But she revealed nothing. "Why is it you can't talk from your heart, Katelyn? Why is the emotional truth so difficult for you?"

"You ask what happened," she said, sitting up in the bed, her husband helpless by her side. "Life happened. I was living." She was angry now, the anger that accompanies sorrow and fear. "After you left—and you did leave me—I changed. I was growing up. I wanted to go places. I wanted to see things. I wanted to date other men. I wanted out of Ithaca. So I left. My girlfriends from college and I went to Jamaica . . . and that's where I met Michael. We fell in love, and I followed Michael out here to Oregon."

"And my letters?"

"They were waiting for me when I went home to Ithaca to visit my mother. I didn't know what to say."

"How about . . . 'sorry you're in a war, I'm having the time of my life.' That about sums it up . . . doesn't it?" He watched as she cried. Then he fixed his eyes on her husband. "Why do you think she's crying, Michael?"

The man glanced over at his young wife, tears streaming down her face. "I think she's crying because she now realizes how much she has hurt you . . . how much we have hurt you . . . and that we could have handled this a whole lot better."

He tapped the gun on his knee, still agitated. "Now that I'm back and you know the situation . . . would you be willing to divorce her?"

The man was stunned by the question. He regarded his wife, searching for the right answer. He studied the gun and the ex-MP holding it. "No," he declared.

The ex-MP returned his attention to the woman he loved. "I'd join you in shedding a few tears, Katelyn, but I don't have any tears in me."

She wiped her eyes and looked up at him, perhaps remembering the all-American boy he once had been and now seeing the crazed man he had become. "I am sorry. I am sorry for all of the hurt and pain I have caused you . . ."

"I didn't come here tonight in search of an apology," he said, interrupting her. "Certainly not an apology at the point of a gun."

"You asked me to speak from my heart," she admonished him. "In my heart I know that what I did to you was wrong, and that I'll spend the rest of my life regretting it. And I am sorry for that . . . I truly am. But I don't love you. I don't know that I ever did. I love Michael. He's my husband, and you can't change that. Not even at the point of a gun."

The world does not stop and wait for soldiers to come home from war. It never has. More and more the ex-MP was feeling sorrier for her than he was for himself, as she sat on the bed in her pajamas with tears streaming down her face. "Well, I thank you for the explanation," he said. "I wasn't expecting an apology." Now he turned his attention back to her husband. "That leaves us with quite a dilemma here, doesn't it, Michael?"

"What's that?" the husband asked, tiring of the ordeal.

"Let me see," he said, rolling his eyes. "I count breaking and entering, assault with a deadly weapon, possession of an illegal firearm, and threatening your life. By my reckoning, I'll spend the next ten years in an Oregon prison, and you will spend the next ten years crawling into bed with my beautiful Katelyn."

"We won't call the police," the husband assured him.

"We won't call the police. Just go," Katelyn pleaded.

"I trust you, Katelyn, I really do. But I don't know him."

The man promised again. "No police. This is all one big misunderstanding and I'm glad it's all out in the open . . . all cleared up."

The ex-MP sat there tapping the gun against his knee, contemplating years in prison, and trying for the first time since his school days to imagine a life without Katelyn. "Do you own a gun, Michael?"

"No."

"Okay, this is the deal," he said, settling on a plan. "In exchange for you not calling the police, I'll leave the state of Oregon tonight and never come back. Of course, I only see one way to test your trustworthiness." He stood and held out the gun to her husband. "This is a .45 automatic. It holds seven shots. There are six left. Hold out your hand."

The man cautiously held out his hand to him. The angry veteran turned the gun barrel around and handed it to him. "Take it. Point it at me."

The young husband whose home had been broken into, the man who had been humiliated in front of his wife, took hold of the .45 automatic and leveled it at the ex-MP. It was a full metal gun and he had to hold it with both of his hands. "All right," Michael said, in a voice filled with hostility, "you listen to me now. I want you to leave here. This is our house . . . you get out."

A faint smile crossed his war-scarred face. "Did you hear that, Katelyn? Did you hear how his voice has changed? His whole demeanor has changed. That's what a gun does to a man. But did you also notice that I haven't changed? Not a quiver. It's almost as if I'm still holding the gun, isn't it?"

"You get out of here," the husband repeated, the gun shaking in his hand.

"You know, Michael, you'd be doing me a big favor right now by pulling that trigger."

As the two men stared at one another, stared death in the face, Katelyn reached over and gently pushed down on the barrel of the gun, bringing it to rest in her husband's lap.

The war veteran watched this with a lump in his throat, a feeling he had not experienced in years. When he spoke again his tone was softer, a tincture of regret in his voice. "You don't have it in you, Michael. You're lucky that way. Once you kill a man you can never go back to being what you were, no matter how hard you try." He wiped his mouth with the back of his hand. "What time is it?"

The man now in possession of the gun glanced at the watch strapped to his wrist. "It's two o'clock in the morning, for God's sake."

"Time to go. But before I leave, Michael, I think you're owed an explanation. You have to understand the hell of war and the loneliness of the military. For years the only thing that kept me going was the thought that someday I was going home to Ithaca, and I was going to marry Katelyn. And then I got home and Katelyn was gone . . . and there was no way the real Ithaca could live up to the Ithaca I had created in my mind. So I got on a train and I just . . ." He gave this explanation while staring at the floor. When he was sure that his time with Katelyn was up and there was nothing else to be said, he lifted his head and stared down at the man he had come to shoot. "With your permission, I'd like Katelyn to walk me to the door."

She got out of bed, not waiting for anybody's permission. Katelyn slipped her arm through his as if they were going for a stroll in the park, and they left the bedroom, leaving her bewildered husband holding a gun in his lap.

PARTING WAYS

They walked down the stairs to the living room arm-in-arm. He opened the front door wide and they stood side by side, staring into a night that was black and timeless. It was still raining. That Oregon kind of rain. Drizzly and unending. "You should be with your husband," he said to her.

But she did not respond. Instead she asked, "Where will you go?"

"I don't know. I'll just get out there on the road and . . ."

"You should go to college now. I'm sure Harvard still wants you."

He turned to her. "Later tonight, maybe in the morning, your Michael will call the police . . ."

"No, he won't."

"No, it's okay. I'll be out of the state by then." The breeze picked up and the damp Pacific Northwest air washed over them, the way the mist from Ithaca Falls had once washed over two souls filled with passion and youth. "I want to get back," he told her. "I want to get back to where we were . . . and I don't know how."

"You can't live in the past."

The lost veteran took her in his arms and held her tight. He remembered watching the girl in the choir as she sang her heart out. He saw them dancing together in the school gymnasium. They were naked together beneath the raging falls, wrapped in an eternal embrace, their lovemaking spent. "There ought to be a law," he said to her, "that a woman has to marry the man who loves her the most."

"That would be a good law," she whispered, "but I'm afraid we wouldn't obey it." One last tear rolled down her cheek.

"I love you, Katelyn." Then he broke away from her, pushed through the door and disappeared in the rain.

Hell Hall

The president emeritus tried to tell John Alden that his trip to Oregon had probably come after the world war. The first world war. The Great War. That he had served not in some desert on the Arabian Peninsula, but had instead fought on the muddy, bloody battle fields of France. It only made sense. What possible interest could America have in the Middle East worth going to war for? No, the old scholar reasoned, he had listened to the man's stories the whole winter long. And he concluded they had all taken place not in the future, but in the past.

SPRINGTIME AIR

Nowhere in all of New York was the passage of time more welcome than in the storied hills of Ithaca, when another hard winter melted into oblivion. In the springtime air of 1929, the self-described time traveler, the man who had tumbled over Ithaca Falls in pursuit of what he called a serial killer, slowly recovered along with the weather. Each new day the sun rose higher in the sky, and the enigma known as John Alden grew stronger. He now strolled freely over the campus terrain, still using a cane, but with less of a limp. For many at Cornell this was their favorite time of the year. Winter's arctic cold was a ghost of days gone by, the snow had done a vanishing act, the waterfalls and waterways that snaked through the university campus were overflowing with new running waters, and the atmosphere was one of optimism as thousands of students marched towards commencement.

The three men stood in the sunshine before White Hall, watching a protest rally organized by the Moral Way—John

Alden, H. W. Hightower, and Father Wallace Dougal, the Catholic priest who ministered Sage Chapel and the spiritual leader of the Ithaca branch of the Moral Way. He was the same priest who at the dinner party had suggested the serial killer might, too, have been dragged through time.

Situated high atop East Hill between the clock tower and the chapel, White Hall was the first building constructed for the new university shortly after the Civil War. It was a sprawling Second Empire French structure that had once housed the entire school, but by the time John Alden's broken body washed ashore, the building had been displaced by newer and more elegant structures, and the hall had become an eyesore. The scientific experiments conducted inside its walls had also sullied its reputation. It was not long before White Hall became known among the student body as Hell Hall.

"So tell me, Mr. Alden, is this old edifice still standing come your day?"

"It is," he told President Hightower as they faced the entryway, the noisy rally on the lawn of the Arts Quad off to their left. "As a matter of fact, it ends up a National Historic Landmark. Retrofitted, retooled, and readied for another hundred years. One of the wonders of modern architecture will be the preservation movement . . . making old buildings look and work even better in the future than they had in their past."

"And Ye Olde Chapel?" asked Father Dougal, in his quaint but forceful Scottish skirl.

"Still standing in all of its glory, Father. But I'm afraid what you call nonsectarian will be seen by outsiders as non-religious. And the university, even with a chapel, will still be seen by many as a Godless place."

Hightower shrugged his weary shoulders. "Again, Father Dougal, isn't it nice to know some things will never change."

"Search as you may," the priest told them, "with the exception of Hollywood, there is no such thing as a Godless place."

On this day the Ithaca Motion Picture Company was taking advantage of the sunny weather to film a scene from their latest movie on the steps of Hell Hall. It was a simple two-camera set-up. The movie appeared to be a costume piece, perhaps the French Revolution. The decrepit hall served as a backdrop. Besides the camera crew, there were the actors, including Belle and Amanda Parrish, the identical twins from the dinner party.

The rally was small, but loud. They were there to protest the making of the movie. The three men stood and watched intently as the director, clearly annoyed by the protesters, called for action on the well-trodden stone steps of the entryway.

"It's actually a night scene," Father Dougal told them. "They use a blue tint to make it appear dark. Then they'll cut the rally noise and dub in the voices."

"Are you a fan of the movies, Father?" Alden asked.

"Movies," the priest told him, "are the devil's work. But one must know thine enemy."

A Catholic priest ministering secular Cornell had raised eyebrows. What was next, some asked—a Jew? It was President Hightower who had made the controversial hire, and he and Father Dougal were fierce debaters. Intellectual opponents. The two men could never agree on anything, including the role of religion at a strictly nonsectarian university. They were an odd pair. The priest tall and lean, and gray. The president emeritus short and squat, and just plain old. But like President Hightower, Father Dougal had taken a keen interest in John Alden, mostly, he said, because he knew a deeply troubled soul when he saw one, but also because the agile priest perceived a measure of religiosity being played out in John Alden's story, even though he had yet to determine what that story was, or more importantly, what it was not.

Both of these academics had expressed concern about Alden's psychological state as they watched the former detective leaning on his cane, the sun in his face, gazing about the campus where he claimed he would one day teach—in the town where he claimed he was to be born some forty years in the future. He was still wearing his ill-fitting suits, but the necktie was usually stuffed into his coat pocket. There were days when he was the only man on campus without one. He seemed fascinated with the cars chugging up and down the precipitous hills. A few of the newer Model As had made it to town, but the Model Ts were still the most popular means of transportation. Occasionally a roadster would speed by, a conceited preppy behind the wheel. And a wide grin would work its way across Alden's face when he spied a horse-pulled cart slowing up traffic, horns honking in its wake.

"John W. Alden," the priest said, almost to himself. "Why does that name ring a bell?"

"Does it?" Alden asked.

"Might you be any relation to the ghostly Bobby Bill?"

"Do you mean the old Cornell football player? Long before my time. Why do you ask, Father?"

"I do believe his given name was Robert Alden Bill," Hightower said, suddenly interrupting. "Class of '17, if my memory serves. Father Dougal's first year on campus. My God, could that boy play football. Do you remember him, Father Dougal . . . he had that silly magic act? The only really good trick he did was his disappearing act. He'd sit on stage in a chair and our colored football coach, Coach Night Train, would throw a big crimson blanket over him. A minute later the coach would whip off the blanket. And, by God, he'd be gone. The kids loved it. He did the same at games. He would disappear into the woods behind the south end zone. Remember?"

"I remember the boy all too well," said the priest. "I never cared for him, nor did he care for me. Bobby Bill was a loud, lapsed Catholic. A wise guy, and something of a mystery man himself."

"How so?" Alden asked.

Again Hightower interrupted to explain. "Like you, he was a local boy. Big, strapping kid. Might have had some Iroquois in him. He was smart, too. After running wild over our gridiron for three or four years, he suddenly vanished. Didn't even stay for graduation. The next I heard about him was when the Army reported him missing in action during the war. The Ghost Runner."

The priest looked John Alden up and down. "From what I remember about the lad, President Hightower, he did resemble our Mr. Alden here."

Hightower, too, looked Alden up and down. "Yes, I see it now."

"And would this ghostly Bobby Bill be the football player in the picture I found hanging on the wall in my room when I at last came to?"

"It would," Hightower told him. "Go down to Memorial Hall. It's at the north end of the football field . . ."

"I know where it is."

"Of course you do. The Cornell Athletic Hall of Fame is there. Search the walls," Hightower advised him. "I'm sure the boy can be found in the team photographs."

They heard the director shout "cut," and they turned their attention back to the making of the movie. A cop with a billy club extended his arms and kept protesters from rushing the set. Classes were in session, and now students were allowed to run in and out of the hall before the next take. Most students shot past the protesters with barely a nod of recognition.

John Alden spotted her in an instant, his heart inexplicably drawn to her big brown eyes. She breezed up the stairs with a load of books in her arms. It was the Caitlin girl from the dinner party, the student who had asked about his wife. She was as pretty and as healthy as the spring day. The sun gave her hair a copper-tinted hue, framing her face as if for a magazine spread.

There was a boy with her. That rich kid from the parlor. The smart-ass son of a bitch with the stupid questions. *"As you've stepped out for eighty-some years, Pilgrim, won't your wife be missing you?"*

"You seem inordinately interested in that girl."

"She reminds me of somebody," Alden told the old university president.

"As if, perhaps, you knew her in another life?"

"Perhaps. Who is that boy she's with?"

"That would be Mr. Copeland," Hightower told him. "Royal S. Copeland the Third. Son of the honorable senator from New York." On the way up the stairs young Copeland had tossed an empty pack of cigarettes onto the walk. "Please pick that up for me," said Hightower, perturbed. "I will not have my campus trashed."

John Alden kept his bad leg straight as he bent over and retrieved the cigarette pack. He noted the brand. Chesterfields. "Is he a student?"

"Yes."

"And what is he taking up?" Alden asked as he watched the young couple disappear into the hall.

"Space, mostly. He's known about campus as the *royal pain.*"

Father Dougal also eyed the scion of the Copeland family as he disappeared into the hall. "Best lesson for that boy would be a good whipping."

They had come to Hell Hall to view the famous brain collection of Dr. Victor Ecarius, the overbearing head of the department of biology. The brains were currently housed on the second floor. John Alden told President Hightower that he had heard of the bizarre collection, but in his day the human brains that had not yet been destroyed had been locked away in a basement closet, the controversial research on them having been halted for decades. It was also in Hell Hall where John Alden was scheduled to give his first guest lecture of the 1929 school year.

"Will you be joining us, Father?"

"It is the timelessness of a man's soul that interests me, President Hightower, not the size and shape of his brain."

"Besides the making of movies, Father Dougal does not approve of Dr. Ecarius," he explained to Alden, "nor does he condone the work being done here."

"Just don't be fooled by the doctor's highfalutin' talk, Mr. Alden. Ecarius is a simple grave robber. A common butcher. His kind have been with us since Genesis."

And with those edifying words, John Alden and H.W. Hightower left the imperious priest standing in the springtime sun with his small army of protesters as the two men walked through the movie set and then ascended the stone steps of Hell Hall.

A COLLECTION OF BRAINS

For years Dr. Victor Ecarius had been collecting the brains of willing donors, those curious souls who died and left their bodies to science. But when he could, he also collected the brains of criminals and indigents, those poor souls who were unwelcomed in life and whose bodies went unclaimed in death. It was university president H.W. Hightower who had initially granted approval for the collected works. What was the harm, he thought, in studying a few unwanted brains? But along the way Dr. Ecarius had begun collecting human hearts, livers, kidneys, and various other body parts, including, it was rumored, human penises and the testicles that went with them. By the time of John Alden's arrival, the brain sets alone had grown to more than six hundred, each one of them perfectly preserved in a large jar of formaldehyde. One of the advantages to having a university planted in the middle of nowhere was that they avoided the attention such a controversial collection would have garnered in a big city. Cornell was centrally isolated and proud of it. Still, during his years as president, H.W. Hightower had taken a considerable amount of grief over the science being practiced in Hell Hall.

Dr. Ecarius was one of the tallest men on campus, sporting shiny black hair that should have gone to gray years ago, but for some reason never had. This stringy hair was slicked back across his anvil-shaped head. Tarlike. But it was his face people feared—a pale, acne-scarred and hawkish face, with one black eye that had a shrewd glitter to it, and one crimson eye with an odd sideways cast, almost as if the mad scientist could keep an eye on two different things at the same time. Nobody was ever sure if the man was born with this wandering crimson eye, or whether it was the result of some grievous injury.

The doctor was wearing a white lab coat over his shirt and tie. He did not frighten President Hightower, but he scared others to death. The people at the Ithaca Motion Picture Company had been so impressed by his frightfulness, both in reputation and appearance, that they had cast him in their Halloween feature. As the villain. His hands were large and bony, with long spidery fingers. A surgeon's hands. Alden shook that hand and sized up the doctor in an instant, his years of police work at play. Few men intimidated John Alden, but that would not stop Victor Ecarius from giving it his best shot. After the introductions were made, Hightower hung back, pretending to admire the brains encased in formaldehyde.

Dr. Ecarius nodded his head. "I very much enjoyed your parlor game, Mr. Alden. It's the talk of the town. You were very entertaining."

"All in all I was asked an odd lot of questions considering the amount of knowledge that was made available to the people in the audience."

"I'm sure I don't know which my colleagues found more astonishing . . . your claim to be from the future, or your claim to be a Harvard-educated detective."

They moved between two rows of tables, each table crammed with specimen jars. "And how would you react, Dr. Ecarius, if after years of research some head case came along at a dinner party and suggested all of your theories were bunk? Psychology, pathology, economics . . . all of it bunk?"

Ecarius cringed at the language. "*Head case? Bunk?*"

President Hightower shouted the definition from across the room. "It's short for *bunkum,* Dr. Ecarius. It means nonsense. It's a relatively new word. *Head case* should be self-explanatory."

"Remarkable."

"Oh heavens, yes," Hightower went on, "Mr. Alden possesses the most amazing vocabulary. You won't believe some of his phraseology. What was last night's word?"

"*Hazmat,*" Alden reminded him.

"Yes. *Hazmat* . . . short for hazardous materials. It seems those scoundrels at the University of Chicago are going to split the atom, so there is going to be a lot of hazardous material around in the future."

"*Anachronism?*" Ecarius asked John Alden, wanting the definition.

"Something out of its proper place and time," answered John Alden.

"Yes," Ecarius told him. "*Anachronisms* are everywhere in Ithaca. One has only to look. Have you traveled all this way in time to declare my work *bunk,* Mr. Alden?"

Dr. Ecarius had set out to prove that the size and shape of the human brain was directly related to intelligence. Humans had larger brains than animals, and so humans lorded over them. Men had larger brains than women; therefore, men were smarter than women. Whites had larger brains than blacks, and the average educated man had a larger brain than a common criminal, and so on. In vociferous defense of his divisive research, Ecarius would rightly claim that the Europeans were years ahead of the Americans in this particular field of study, and he was determined to catch up.

John Alden leaned his cane against a table and hoisted a jar containing a brain suspended in the clear liquid. "From what little I remember reading of your research," he said, examining the specimen, "I believe you eventually declare your own theories bunk."

"Well, bravo for me. That will require a healthy measure of academic integrity, will it not?"

Watching the two of them talk was the student Jim Dorn, the skinny lab assistant with the thick glasses. The local boy. He stood beside a sink, drying wet beakers with a towel. Dorn was outwardly nervous and appeared just as suspicious of the visitor as their visitor was of him. It was, after all, this scrawny townie who had asked the first snide question in the parlor at President's House. *"In your mind, when will the good times end?"*

John Alden picked up another jar. Viewed from a distance, the contents appeared to be charcoal resting in formaldehyde. "What the hell is this?"

"Hell is a very good word for it. That is the brain of a murderer electrocuted at Sing Sing." Ecarius pointed to an operating table sitting on a platform before a tall window at the far end of the room. The table was smothered in electrical cables, many of them attached to a ghastly-looking head cap, which was attached to lethal-looking electronic equipment. "Jim Dorn and I have been experimenting with the effects of small doses of electricity on the human brain."

"Electroshock therapy," Alden announced.

Ecarius seemed pleasantly surprised. "You've heard of it?"

"It's still in use in extreme cases . . . mania, catatonia, and schizophrenia. Have you tried it on humans yet?" Alden shot an inquisitive look Hightower's way.

"Not yet," Ecarius assured them. Then he added, "But if the right case should come along ..."

"Do you think it's possible that I have brain damage, Doctor?"

"In a spill like the one you allegedly took over Ithaca Falls, temporary lobe damage would be a distinct possibility. However, long term amnesia is more fiction than fact."

"There is nothing wrong with my memory."

"Of course not. You just can't remember what century it is."

On many of the specimen tables there sat potted plants, green and thriving, out of place among the preserved body parts. Alden fingered one of the plants and then put his fingers to his nose. "Wintergreen," he said, identifying the plant. "It's a poison, isn't it?"

"Oil of wintergreen is a very strong poison. It takes very little to kill, but it smells and it tastes quite refreshing. It's actually used in candies and *eau de toilette* . . . in minute amounts, of course."

"Of course. And the marijuana plants?"

"We're also studying the effects of cannabis on the human brain."

"There's an entire generation waiting to help you with that research, Dr. Ecarius."

"I'm pleased. Electroshock therapy, cannabis . . . we must be doing something right."

John Alden picked up another jar. He had been a homicide detective in New York City and thus he was unfazed by blood and guts, but the contents of this jar momentarily froze him. For the first time that day, Ithaca's man of mystery seemed vulnerable.

Ecarius saw it. "The human heart," the doctor explained to him. "That particular heart belonged to a young woman. A suffragist, I believe. If I remember right, her husband murdered her."

"And did you collect his heart?"

"I believe he's still at large. Fascinating, though, isn't it? For all of my studies of the human brain, I still find that so many life-altering decisions are made with the human heart."

Alden placed the jar with the woman's heart back on the table and continued limping past the tables. "I'm looking for a man, Dr. Ecarius."

"So you've said."

"He's drawn up a criminal profile of this man," Hightower said, shuffling across the room to join the conversation.

"A profile?" asked Ecarius.

"Yes," Hightower explained to the doctor. "It is the detailed portrait of an unknown subject's personality and motivators."

"How can you detail his personality if you don't know who he is?"

"We do it based on his crimes," Alden told him.

"So, in effect, you're working backwards. First you discover what he is, and then you use that conjecture to find out who he is and, hopefully, where he is."

"They've actually reduced crime to a science," Hightower told him.

Dr. Ecarius seemed more curious than the rest of the wine-soaked crowd that was at the dinner party. "So tell me about this man you are after, Mr. Alden."

John Alden wound his way around the head of the table and started down another row of body parts. Ecarius trailed after him, and Hightower followed them both. From outside the open windows came the sound of the movie director screaming obscenities at the protesters. "He's an educated man between forty and sixty years old who lives here in Ithaca. He's left-handed. He has some anatomical knowledge, but is not necessarily a physician."

"That's it? That is your so-called profile?"

"For now, that's all I'm comfortable sharing."

Dr. Ecarius shook his head, supremely skeptical. "Are you familiar with the Salem witch hunts of the seventeenth century, Mr. Alden?"

"I am."

"Of course you are. You're a Harvard man. What you're describing sounds to me like a witch hunt. That description you just gave fits a hundred men at this university, including me and several of President Hightower's staff."

"A profile is just another tool for apprehension, Doctor."

"A very dangerous tool, it would seem. And exactly what is it this man has done?"

"He has a penchant for murder."

"And whom did he murder?"

"He sliced up two young women. He stole a body part of one of them . . . tried to steal the head of another."

"When?"

Here John Alden stopped without answering. Before him on the table, floating lifelike in a pool of formaldehyde, was a human fetus. If replanted into its mother's womb, the tiny thing almost looked as if it could continue its quest for birth. Again Alden shot a look Hightower's way, asking with a glance if he had really approved this aspect of the grotesque collection.

"Come, Mr. Alden," President Hightower implored him. "Your class. We'll be late."

With a quizzical look on his face, the Harvard-educated detective hoisted yet another jar of formaldehyde. It was obvious he could not readily identify the body part he was staring at. "And what is this?" he asked, holding the specimen up to the odd-colored eyes of Dr. Ecarius.

Clearly tiring of his visitor's act, an unsmiling Dr. Victor Ecarius stared at John Alden's distorted face through the clear liquid. He stared long and hard before he finally answered. "It's a uterus," he said. "From the Greek word for *hysteria*."

THE CLASS OF '29

For his first guest lecture in their time, President Hightower was to present the ex-detective from New York City to an advanced psychology class. He reasoned these students would be the most intellectually curious about his state of mind. The class was being held directly beneath the laboratories of Dr. Ecarius. In fact, if the seemingly mad doctor put his ear to the floor, he could take in the entire lecture. It was a cave-like and musty hall with no windows. Plus, the walls needed painting, the floors could have used a coat of wax, and there was a perpetual coldness to the room that kept everybody shivering, even on a hot day. It was a short distance but a far cry from palatial Bailey Hall, but it was here that Professor of Criminal Justice John W. Alden was to be introduced to the class of 1929.

Rows of wooden desks climbed tiers to the back of the room. There were less than one hundred seats, and word had spread quickly. Students poured into their seats, as did curious faculty members. Soon people were standing along the walls and sitting on the floor. Up front, behind the lectern, a large blackboard ran the width of the room.

The time-traveling professor and the president emeritus stood up front by the lectern as the audience settled in. Electricity filled the air. "Are you nervous?"

John Alden pulled a necktie from his coat pocket and slipped it over his head and beneath his collar. It was a flattering red tie and it dangled there. "I'm not sure this idea is any better than your parlor game." He picked up an eraser and cleared the blackboard with the grace of a man who had done it a hundred times. "White," he stated. "In the future the blackboards will be white boards. We'll use erasable black ink."

"Fascinating," said Hightower, "though the logic of ink over chalk escapes me."

"Logic didn't get me here."

"Oh, I sometimes think you enjoy playing ignorant, Mr. Alden."

"How so?"

"You find it to your advantage to play the part of the big Irish cop with the out-of-joint nose and the sheepish grin . . . instead of the Harvard-educated detective from a good Ithaca family, with the sharp beak and the keen eye."

John Alden put down the eraser and brushed the chalk from his hands. White dust floated before them. "And do you know what I think, President Hightower?"

"What?"

"I think you sent letters to your friends at the Cornell Club down on East Forty-Fourth Street in Manhattan and you asked them to make some inquiries at the police department about a Detective John Alden who had worked in the homicide division. And when they wrote back to you and said there was no record of a Detective John Alden, you were more curious than you were satisfied. So you sent more letters to your friends at Harvard and asked about a former student named John W. Alden. And when they wrote back and told you there was no record of any such student, you were still more curious than you were satisfied. For charlatan that I may be, I still possess a Harvard education, and I still possess an intimate understanding of detective work in New York City. Try as you may, you cannot erase that."

Now the seedy lecture hall was filled to capacity and people were crowding the doorway. Hightower lowered his voice. "Perhaps you are only a brilliant criminal of our time masquerading as a brilliant detective from the future."

"Perhaps. But do you know what my brilliant skills, detective or criminal, tell me?"

Students were leaning forward in their seats, straining to overhear what was fast becoming an intense discussion. "Please share, but quietly."

John Alden tightened the red noose around his neck and buttoned his coat. "I've detected that it was not mere coincidence that you were in the gorge at first light following the electrical storm on Halloween."

"I hike every morning, you know that."

"Yes, sir, you do, which is why I strongly suspect that I'm not the first person you've pulled from Ithaca Falls. Nor, I suspect, am I the first man you've seen stumble out of the gorge seemingly out of his proper place and time, muttering insane visions about the future. That is the reason you hurried me back to President's House and hid me in the attic for four months. It is why you turned my trauma into a parlor game. You really did want those people to expose me as a fraud. But they couldn't do it. Your so-called brilliant minds could only subject me to their laughter and their ridicule." He motioned to the people now crammed into the lecture hall. "Is that what you've planned for me here today?"

The president emeritus smiled his sly, wicked grin. He stepped to the lectern, quieted the class, and then introduced the guest lecturer. And then he wished John Alden well and left him to his own devices. The old man turned and waddled up the steps through the crowd, his back to the lectern. "I'll audit the class from the back of the hall. Keep your chin up. Make use of that wonderful voice of yours."

"So tell me, President Hightower," Alden asked, loud enough for all to hear, "the others you've pulled from the falls . . . did they ever get back?"

Hightower did not turn around. He simply waved his fat and weathered hand in that dismissive manner of his. "Ithaca, Mr. Alden, is filled with ghosts."

THE LECTURE

On a table to the left of the lectern there sat a large hourglass alongside an unopened bottle of Coca-Cola. John Alden had requested both. Without announcement or explanation he walked to the table, cracked open the bottle of Coca-Cola and downed a healthy swig. Then he flipped over the hourglass. Students watched with unsmiling faces as the sugary white sand began passing through the neck. Refreshed, he approached the lectern with the same academic bravado he had possessed in his previous life at Cornell. "I am here today," Alden told the class, "to teach the science of crime."

No sooner had he spoken those words when a young man's voice called out from the back of the room, near the top rows. "Are we to take you seriously?"

He gripped the lectern and addressed the class as a whole. "As President Hightower told you, I was a New York City homicide detective."

"That's not all we've heard." This from another young man.

John Alden kept his calm. "What else have you heard?"

"That you're a lunatic."

"A *lunatic*?" Alden surveyed the class. "Define the word." Nobody spoke. "Anybody?"

She had a smoky voice, low-pitched and brimming with self-confidence, confidence in both her sex and her intellect. "It's from the Latin word *luna,*" she announced. "Roman goddess of the moon. It is the now discredited belief that lunacy fluctuated with the phases of the moon. The word dates back to the fourteenth century."

"Very good, Miss ...?"

"Dewey," she told him. She was seated just a few rows up and dead center, where she could look him square in the eye. "Caitlin Dewey."

"Very good, Miss Dewey. I can assure all of you that the phases of the moon do not faze me." At his play on words there was a slight ripple of laughter. John Alden breathed a sigh of relief and proceeded with his lecture. "We meet our victims for the first time in death. Police detectives afford themselves an emotional insulation by not projecting a personality onto a murder victim. This is very important. Good detectives have it down to a science. I realized this early on in my career as I listened to my partner talk about the victim during my first murder investigation. By all accounts she was a vibrant and effervescent young woman, newly married, and pursuing a higher education at a college in Manhattan. And yet in listening to him talk of her, the woman, for all intents and purposes, had no name. She was just a vic. A victim. Her goals and ambitions were reduced to the places she had been in the last twelve hours of her life, and to the people she had been with. We were now looking for a suspect. A perp. A perpetrator. An un-sub. An unknown subject. The language of crime is very cold, but it is also very thorough. Murder reduced to a science."

Now John Alden unbuttoned his coat, picked up a piece of chalk and wrote across the blackboard the word *paraphilia*. "This is a fairly new term," he explained to the class. "It was only added to Webster's Dictionary in 1925. *Para* is Latin for deviance. *Philia* is Latin for attraction. *Paraphilia* . . . an attraction to deviance." He went on, composing a list on the board. "There are six sexual deviations. They are voyeurism, sexual sadism, exhibitionism, incest and rape, pedophilia, and masochism. In Ithaca, we are dealing with a sexual sadist."

A young man up front interrupted. "Are you saying there is a murderer loose in Ithaca? A sexual sadist?"

"Before the war you know as the Great War," Alden answered, "there were, I've learned, a series of murders in Upstate New York . . . all of the victims progressive women. As I understand it, nobody was ever arrested for these killings. When a man tortures and murders, it is usually sexual. When one man tortures and murders multiple victims, it is always sexual. The torture is a substitute for the sex act."

Another girl sitting on the steps tentatively raised her hand. "They say you claim to be from the future. Are there going to be murders here in Ithaca?"

"I had an accident," he told her.

Royal S. Copeland III, seated next to Caitlin Dewey, piped up. "The ole pilgrim got drunk and fell into the gorge." Now there was much laughter in the room.

"I suffered a head injury, Mr. Copeland . . . and I was quite sober."

The boy seemed surprised that the guest lecturer knew his name. He did not like it. "How do you know who I am?"

"I only remember what I remember. I only know what I know." John Alden went on with his lecture. "There are four kinds of sexual homicides. Domestic violence . . . a husband rapes and then murders his wife. The rape assault . . . a man rapes a woman unknown to him and then murders her. The lust murders . . . this is a premeditated murder based on a sexual fantasy. And the serial murder." John Alden turned back to the blackboard and spelled out the words *serial killer*. Underlined it. "Serial murder," he explained, "is the killing of three or more separate victims with emotional time breaks between the killings. This cooling-off period ranges anywhere from a few days to a few months."

"Or in your case . . . a few centuries." The tasteless remark again came from young Copeland, but now with even more hostility in his voice. There was nervous laughter in the room, but Caitlin Dewey appeared irritated.

John Alden was unperturbed. "Let's concentrate on the here and now. Serial killers are intelligent, charismatic, and extremely manipulative. They are supremely confident in their verbal skills. They target a certain type of victim. Let us pretend our serial killer likes intelligent women with no children. That is why he hunts near the university. Many serial killers have a fascination with police procedure. They may even interject themselves into the investigation. Despite all of their strengths, they have a glaring weakness. A serial killer is a very insecure individual. They are what we call *control freaks*. Their ultimate high is the moment they have their victim under control. They enjoy the publicity of their crime for the same reason. They are in control. In this case the newspapers of the day will feed his addiction, and he will feed theirs. That is the nature of the two beasts." He went on. "Our serial killer engages in purposeful postmortem mutilation of his victim for shock value. If he has the time, he will decapitate the victim and take her head for a trophy, or help himself to some other body part."

Here he paused. Put down the chalk. The sand was slipping through the hourglass. The musty smell of packed bodies permeated the room. Already John Alden sensed he had them in the sweaty palm of his big hand. He stole another swig of Coke. "Serial killers are the ultimate extension of evil. The sex act is secondary. Instead, the killer is sexually excited by the cruelty of his acts. His pleasure is derived by watching his victim writhe in pain. The serial killer operates in an emotionally detached manner. It's almost as if he's following a script. That script is usually based on his sadistic fantasy. Serial killers tend to increase their killings to the point where they have a complete disregard for the risks. That is most often when they are caught. When finally captured, they display a total lack of remorse."

The students sat in stunned silence. Nobody in their time had ever before talked so openly about sex and murder, and with such exacting detail. John Alden allowed time for everything he had told them to sink in. Then he again picked up the chalk and returned to the blackboard. "If you are a homicide investigator," he said, "you write this on your bathroom mirror so that you see it each and every morning." He wrote the words in bold script: ***Things are not always what they appear to be.***

Everyone in the hall fixed on the words. Then the rich kid slowly raised his hand, a mocking gesture coming from him.

John Alden indulged him. "Yes, Mr. Copeland?"

Royal Copeland nodded to the words on the blackboard. "Wouldn't that there be the story of your life?"

John Alden rested his eyes upon the young man seated next to the prettiest girl on campus and thought of the privileged life the kid must live. The words of F. Scott Fitzgerald came to mind. *"The rich are different from you and me."* Royal S. Copeland III was the son of a powerful United States senator. He had his pick of any college in the world. His every childish whim had been indulged. His every adolescent wish had been fulfilled. He was, Alden believed, destined to graduate from Cornell a worthless shit. To live a meaningless life. "Yes," John Alden told him, underlining the words on the blackboard, "this is the story of my life. Don't ever forget it."

GIRL OF HIS DREAMS

She was waiting for him out on the Arts Quad—Caitlin Dewey, the psychology student from the candlelight dinner, the brown-eyed intellectual beauty who had calmly and succinctly defined the word *lunatic*. The movie people had packed up and moved on. The protesters were gone. The sun was still strong in the sky, and the grass was brilliant shades of green, while white blossoms decorated the magnolia trees. Other students kept John Alden at arm's length and derisively referred to him as the Pilgrim, but this girl approached him coming out of Hell Hall without hesitation. "We've never been formally introduced," she said to him. "I'm Caitlin Dewey."

"Hello, Caitlin. I'm John Alden." He extended his hand. "It was certainly not my intent to avoid you," he told her, taking her hand in his. No electricity coursed through his veins at the touch of her skin, but he did find her hand warm. Inviting. Familiar. His attraction to her had been immediate. She had a thick head of chestnut-colored hair that she wore down to her shoulders. Her face was highlighted by high, round cheekbones that would keep her looking forever young, and her smile was one of those perpetual natural smiles John Alden so admired because he himself could never smile worth a damn.

"How are you recovering, if I may ask?"

He lifted the cane and shrugged his wide shoulders. "My leg is about eighty percent, but my head still isn't on straight. Where are you from, Caitlin?"

"Oregon," she told him. "And you . . . do you still see yourself as having lived in another time?"

That she was from Oregon surprised him. He had thought for sure she was an Ithaca girl. "Yes, Caitlin Dewey from Oregon, I do."

"Some dreams," she told him, "are so vivid that people often mistake them for something they think actually happened."

He nodded his head. "I heard you were a psychology major."

"I'm working on my senior thesis."

"And I'll bet you need a case study."

"You're very perceptive."

"Well, I'm a detective . . . or, at least, I was a detective."

"Still, you shouldn't be predicting murders, especially at a coed university. Half the girls in that lecture were scared to death."

"Well, it's a scary subject."

"I'd like to help you. Help you figure out just where you were a detective . . . and when."

"And how are you going to do that?"

"Through therapy."

The chimes rang out over the hills. It was the top of the hour. The quad was suddenly flooded with people scurrying in all directions. Students stared at the two of them as they passed by. Royal S. Copeland III leapt down the stairs and blew past them. "He's too old for you, Caitlin. *Way* too old." Then he was gone.

"Actually," said Alden, "I'm *way* too young. And your boyfriend there is everything that's wrong with America . . . now and in the future."

"Ignore him," Caitlin said. "And he's not my boyfriend."

John Alden mustered up a skeptical grin. "So, I'm to lie on a couch and you are going to unlock the mysteries of my mind through the *psychobabble* you learned at Cornell."

"I'm sorry . . . *psychobabble*?"

"Psychological jargon," he told her, defining the word, "used inaccurately to talk about personal problems. The word is added to Webster's Dictionary in 1975."

She had a curvy figure, perfectly rounded in all the right places, but not distracting. And she had those pouty lips, the kind of lips a man wants to kiss. "In what direction are you heading?" he asked her.

"Toward the future, Mr. Alden. Or the clock tower, for now."

He liked her sense of humor. Alden turned and stared up at the tower, the tallest landmark on the highest hill in Ithaca. "That's right, you're a chimesmaster." He noted the time on the tower clock. "You know, historically, particularly in Europe, towers have been the bastion of imprisonment and execution. The most famous, of course, being the Tower of London."

"Did you study that at your crime college?"

"We did. The history of capital punishment. The most egregious example," he told her, "was in the state of Schaumburg, Germany." He pointed up to the giant clock hands attached to the face of the tower. "Officials drilled a hole in the clock face. The heavy steel hands were sharpened to a razor's edge. Then from inside the tower the convict's head was thrust through the hole. Spectators could literally watch the last minutes of a man's life tick away."

Caitlin Dewey stared at the clock hands up on the tower and swallowed hard. "Well, here at Cornell," she assured him, "we only practice the perfect execution of the chimes."

"Yes, I know. Music runs in your family."

They started toward the tower. "How would you know that?"

"Caitlin Dewey, as I heard it, was years ahead of her time."

"Was? And who exactly is it that you think I am, Mr. Alden?"

He smiled. A natural smile this time. And John Alden and Caitlin Dewey walked on, seemingly in perfect rhythm, up the hill toward the clock tower.

The Opium Den

It was a large, ivory-colored Victorian, somewhat faded in appearance, and it sat on a hill on yet another steep street just off campus. Curtains in each window of the house were kept drawn day and night except for the bay window at the front of the house. Every night in this downstairs window burned the warm glow of an Oriental lamp.

There was no porch light on this house, and the light from the street lamp did not reach up the hill—so that only the shadowy figure of an inscrutable man could be seen climbing the stairs through a light rain.

John Alden knocked softly at the front door, not really sure if there would be an answer. Or an admittance. He had come alone this night. His leg was bothering him. The Caitlin Dewey girl was on his mind. He felt an inordinate hostility for the senator's son, Royal S. Copeland III. And he still could not wrap his aching head around the day and age in which he found himself stranded.

He turned up his collar to the weather. The door opened slowly, followed by a gracious bow and a humble nod. "Mr. Alden . . . man of dreams to come. Welcome to my house." She spoke the words as if he were an old friend, though he had only been to the house once before, and then only as a guest of another.

John Alden stepped inside. "I'm honored that you welcome me into your house."

"The honor is very much mine." She bowed again. Lady May was her name, and in her youth in her native Shanghai she must have been a knockout. Her long hair was still raven black, and she was attired in a deep red robe, bound closed with a midnight blue sash. Faint and delicate flower patterns ran through both the sash and the robe, all of them connected by nearly invisible vines.

Young, unmarried women were gathered in the parlor of the house, reading or just quietly chatting. They smiled as he passed by in the hallway. But he had not come for them.

They moved through the kitchen, where an elderly Chinese man abruptly stopped fussing with his tea and bowed to the woman of the house. Lady May acknowledged his bow with a simple but elegant nod of her head. Then a skeleton key appeared from beneath her sleeve, and she unlocked the basement door. John Alden followed her down the stairs.

The basement itself was badly lit, a faded incandescent yellow, and it was cluttered with the common rubble of a large house. But the passageway to the rear was clear and clean. Carpeted with rugs. Here another door was unlocked, a small, green door, and the lady from Shanghai led the way down an iron stairwell that had a slight twist to its descent. This was a sub-basement, sometimes found in the large Upstate homes. Most of these sub-basements came with their own legends. They were used to hide runaway slaves as a stop on the Underground Railroad in the days before the Civil War. Or they were once the wine cellars for the Finger Lake vineyards. More likely they had simply been used to store fruits and vegetables. This sub-basement dwelling was candlelight dim, and John Alden was again reminded of the dinner party at President's House. Not a pleasant memory.

Lady May parted a black curtain at the foot of the iron stairs. Two steps later, she parted a copper chain-link curtain. Then she held forth her hand, and John Alden stepped into the den.

A sweet but bitter odor overwhelmed his senses. Fire from a potbelly stove staved off the cellar dampness that follows an

Ithaca winter. The candles in the den were rare spermaceti, the waxy substance from the head of sperm whales, and they burned with an incomparable brilliance, casting a pure and radiant light on everything and everybody they touched. Finely woven rugs carpeted the floor, each overlapping the other, creating a lush kaleidoscope beneath his feet. The room was lined with plush couches and deep cushioned chairs. A half-dozen men were lying about, most of them silver-haired patrons of the university. John Alden removed his shoes and took a seat at the end of a couch, at the slipper-covered feet of H.W. Hightower. The old man smiled, his most welcoming smile. The president emeritus was cocooned in a gold robe and, surprisingly, did not look the least bit ridiculous. His state of relaxation was refreshing.

John Alden removed his suit coat and handed it to Lady May. "I'm not crazy," he said to Hightower.

"I never meant to imply you were, Mr. Alden."

Conversations in the den were spoken just above a whisper, but because of the tranquil atmosphere they were as clear as the sound of college debate. "You're a Yale man, right?"

"Yes, I earned my degrees at the colleges in New Haven."

"Skull and Bones?" Alden asked.

Hightower remained silent.

John Alden enjoyed a quiet chuckle. "Skull and Bones . . . aren't you supposed to get up and walk out of the room at the mere mention of that name, or some crap like that?"

The president emeritus was amused at the slight, clearly enjoying the company. "The secret societies have been with us since the founding of Harvard in the seventeenth century. I doubt they've disappeared in your mythical twenty-first century."

"They have not . . . and it's not a myth."

"The societies do much good . . . they just do it secretly." Here Hightower paused, studying the anguish apparent on the younger man's face. "*Alden,*" he said, "the name is old English, isn't it? It means old friend?"

"Yes, that's its meaning."

"And your mother's heritage was Irish?"

"My grandparents emigrated from Kilkenny. I'm afraid I inherited a lot more of her Irish temperament than I did the stiff upper lip of my father's ancestors."

The others in the den seemed to ignore the conversation, or they listened to it as one would listen to music in the background. Across the room Lady May set a wad of opium on a wire and then heated it above one of the white candles. When the fruit of the poppy was stewing well, when the aroma was biting and inviting, she packed the potion into a bamboo pipe. Then she floated gracefully across the rugs and presented the dream-fried drug to John Alden. He took the pipe from her with a grateful nod. Then he smoked the bitter-tasting magic in a glass bowl over a flame, as if he had been smoking it all his life. He could hear the juices gurgling in the stem. His eyes watered with guilty pleasure. The pain in his leg vanished. The aches in his head melted away. He felt free and uninhibited. "I am not crazy," he said again. Only this time his voice was free of rancor.

"Every place you go," Hightower told him, "everything you see, your mind automatically assigns it a future. Even people. Yours is the most fascinating case of head trauma I have ever seen."

"You've been listening to Dr. Ecarius. You think I have a brain injury ..."

"Almost reverse amnesia, really. You remember things that have yet to happen . . . and may never happen."

John Alden smoked from the pipe. "And you, Dr. Henry Wadsworth Hightower, are so much more than you appear to be."

"No," Hightower told him, "you are mistaken. I am just an old and fat, retired university president in a small town in

Upstate New York. Hardly the place to change the course of history."

"Yes, but the ideal place to prepare others to change the course of history." John Alden breathed deeply. "How do you think this ends?"

"I don't know. Tell me how you see it ending. Your worst case scenario."

The time-traveling professor of criminal justice thought it over. "If Franklin Roosevelt were to be killed . . . to never be elected president . . . then America may never recover from the oncoming depression, and the country goes into the second world war unprepared, or not at all. Fascism, or communism, or both, rule the day . . . and eventually the earth."

"Sounds like a pretty dramatic future, whether the governor lives or not."

"And so I ask again . . . how do you think this ends?"

Hightower shrugged his shoulders. "For you, I fear, not well."

A pall suddenly fell over the den. The old man sensed it, an unwelcome stretch of silence. "Then, Mr. Alden, let us again pretend you are from the twenty-first century. The riddle you brought with you . . ." Hightower asked in a detached tone of voice, ". . . two men must die . . .?"

"Yes."

"And you are sure your serial killer murders for sexual reasons?"

"What other reason could there be?"

"Political."

John Alden took another puff of the pipe. "Explain."

"As misguided as the killings were, the suffragists murdered here in New York were murdered to prevent women from obtaining the right to vote. The mistress you claimed in your time, the one your serial killer murdered, was a woman who had just been appointed to the United States Senate. Now we suspect your killer is going to try and kill Governor Roosevelt here in our time . . . ergo . . ."

"That doesn't explain my wife."

"Let us theorize some more. Perhaps he wasn't killing your wife. He was killing your unborn child . . . probably a girl."

John Alden was flabbergasted. "Why would anybody kill an unborn child?"

"You claim the both of you are traveling unstuck in time. I believe your man to be a political assassin. Put the two together and he was killing your child for what he believes that child grows up to be. A senator? The first woman president?"

The blood was rushing to his head, as was the opium. John Alden put his hands to his face, momentarily speechless.

Hightower went on. "That brings us back to why you are here. And we still don't know who his second target is."

"'*Two men must die*,'" Alden said, remembering that storm-laden night. "'*You can't stop it this time*.' That's what he said."

"Are you sure that's exactly what he said?"

John Alden felt wonderful, dream-like smoke filling his throat, his lungs, his brain. "Hell, I'm not sure of anything anymore."

"Again, assuming the governor is his main target . . . might his other potential victim be a student here?"

"Why travel through time to kill a student?"

"The same reasoning applies. He would not be killing the student for what he or she is . . . but rather for what he or she is to become."

The displaced college professor inhaled, a long, last puff. Then Lady May removed the pipe from his hands. He leaned his head back on the couch. "Think what you could do with Cornell University if I had brought you a newspaper from the future."

"Or better yet, a book on the twentieth century."

"I am that book," John Alden suggested.

The old man shrugged again. "And yet, Mr. Alden, we find ourselves with far more questions than answers."

The professor closed his eyes, losing himself in an opium mist.

The old man continued his analysis of the tortured soul. "Talk to me of the woman you say was your wife . . . your Katelyn."

John Alden kept his eyes closed. In this opiate state his beautiful Katelyn was like a figure from an uncertain dream. "I can't."

"When did you commit your adultery?"

He opened his eyes. "Right after Katelyn told me she was pregnant."

"Not uncommon."

"We were in shock," Alden said, recalling the day. "We thought we were too old to make a baby . . . that it wasn't in the cards. Hell, after that stunt I pulled in Oregon, we never even dreamed we'd end up married." Then he realized he was talking about his wife after all, and he suddenly stopped.

"Then tell me of the woman you say was your mistress."

THE ADULTERER

She was blonde and beautiful, John Alden explained to the old university president, in the candlelit radiance of an Ithaca opium den. He found it much easier to talk about his lover than it was to talk about his wife. Her hair, he said, had the glow of those spermaceti candles. And she had brains. The governor had appointed her to the coveted office of United States Senator from the State of New York after the elected senator accepted a cabinet position in the new administration. Before that she had represented the Finger Lakes region in the United States Congress, and before that she was a firebrand at the state legislature in Albany. Like John Alden and Katelyn Richter, she was born and raised in the hills of Ithaca, but unlike them, she chose to stay at home after high school, graduating summa cum laude from Cornell and then beginning a distinguished career in public service. This wonder woman never married. Had no children. Politics was her blood. But passionate people need multiple outlets for their unbridled passion.

They would meet at a downtown hotel in a room on the upper floors, with a splendid view of the lake. High enough so that they could see, but not be seen. One afternoon, in the dead of winter, they stayed so late it was dark by the time they said their goodbyes. They were dressed again and at the door to the room. It was his role to leave first. She would wait a half hour before departing. If anybody ever put them in the same room at the same time, then he was simply there to discuss funding for his criminal justice courses at the university. But they were never caught. Smart people are just better at concealing their illicit behavior.

"If we had met at another time . . . do you think . . .?"

"No," he told her, before she could even finish the question, "you're my lover. Katelyn is my wife. There's a difference, you know. Women just don't understand that."

"Explain it to me."

He threw on his sport coat and then reached for his winter coat. "Franklin Roosevelt didn't die with his wife; he died with his lover. And they had been lovers for thirty years. Did it diminish his love for Eleanor, or his place in history? At what point does it stop being an affair and become instead a poignant relationship?"

She turned down his coat collar, smoothed it out, then she wrapped her arms around him at the door and they took their goodbye kiss. And then they just kept on taking.

Minutes later, there she was, the new United States Senator from the State of New York, pressed up against the hotel window getting penetrated hard from behind by a married man, and an ex-cop no less. Had it not been for the darkness of the evening, they could have been seen by all. But wasn't that the idea? Sex thrives on risk.

He could see the twinkling lights of downtown Ithaca through the luminosity of a light snowfall. He could admire the snow-laden pines on the hills across the way. He could marvel at the giant black hole of unfrozen water that was Cayuga. And all the time he was pushing deep inside of her, his chin was up against her golden hair. He could hear the crazy, heavy beating of her heart. She was collapsing. He was the only thing holding her up. It was the kind of sex a man dreams about. That is what the newly appointed senator was to him. Dream sex. But unlike her, he could never escape the feeling they were being watched. The university was a society of glass walls. He exploded inside of her. Then she leaned her forehead into the freezing glass to cool her face. He wrapped his arms around her and held her there.

OF TEA AND OPIUM

"**A** sensuous story, to say the least," said H.W. Hightower. "But except for the political office involved, your tryst could easily have taken place in our time."

"But it did not," John Alden said, emerging from his opiate stupor. "It happened in my time."

Lady May was before them, bowing with her usual grace. "May I get tea for my honored guests?"

"Lady May, we would love a cup of your tea," the old man said to her. "It is the best tea in all of New York." When she had gone, the president emeritus turned back to his visiting professor. "I fear if everything you say is true, then your serial killer will not wait long to strike. After your lectures and your pronouncements, suspicion for any killings here in Ithaca would almost certainly fall upon your shoulders. If your time-traveling madman is among us . . . he knows this."

"I agree. Roosevelt won't be here until commencement. We need to find out who his other target is."

Evil That Walks Through Time

On the same night John Alden and H.W. Hightower were getting stoned in an Ithaca opium den, a colored man nicknamed Night Train was having the boot put to him in an Ithaca barn. It would take weeks for the old assistant football coach to recover from the beating he took that night. The welts and the bruises would eventually disappear, his ribs would mend, and he would return to his odd jobs, but he would never forget the beating.

The old man had spent decades in the hills of Ithaca. He could remember as a young man coaching with legends like Pop Warner and Gil Dobie. He had helped them win national championships, including the 1915 championship team with the great Bobby Bill. The Ghost Runner. He would have been a head coach himself had it not been for the color of his skin. Still, university president H.W. Hightower had been good to him. They shared a love of books. The library in President's House with its wealth of knowledge was always open to him.

He also knew of the legends of Ithaca Falls. All of the ghost stories. Hell, he even made up a few stories of his own to pass on to his grandchildren. But the most haunting story he ever told was the one he told police while in the county hospital.

The Ithaca Motion Picture Company was paying him to be a night watchman out at the barn that served as their studio—to keep an eye on their sets, their props and equipment. He had always scratched out a living doing these odd jobs. Besides being the assistant football coach, he was also paid as the athletic trainer and the groundskeeper.

In the barn was a bed that had literally been fitted out for a queen, so he could sleep most nights. Out back, they had built a French village complete with a cobblestone street in what was once a cornfield. He did not understand movie making, but they paid him well, and at his age work was anything an old man could physically accomplish.

It was raining the night he took the beating, and the west wind whistling up from Cayuga Lake carried with it the promise of even more rain to come. The old coach was lying half asleep across the bed, fully clothed in farmer's overalls, his boots dangling over the side so as not to get the silky sheets muddy. Suddenly there came a pounding clatter, as if someone was banging at the barn door. This was almost certainly the doings of the wind, for he had never before been disturbed. His nights in the barn were solitary, but for the costumes, the sets, and the tall, lethal prop with the angular blade that they had constructed at the back of the barn.

He wiped the sleep from his eyes and pushed open the big barn door. A cool, wet wind slapped his face. Slapped him awake. He peered into the rain, but it was too damn dark to see anything except for the faint outline of the clock tower up on East Hill. Then an outsized shadow draped the corner of his eye. Before he could turn into it and give it shape and form, a sturdy stick struck the back of his head and he fell forward into the mud. Now dazed, the old coach got to his knees and put his arthritic fingers to the back of his head. Felt a mix of rain and blood. He at first believed the wind had dropped him with a tree branch, but then the stick deliberately felled him again. Now lying in the mud, too weak to rise, he found himself being hit again, and yet again. He was being beaten by a shadowy force with a heavy stick. Beaten like a dog. When the shadow was done thrashing him with the stick, it put the boot to him. First in the gut, breaking his ribs. Then the shadow stomped on his back and on his head. Finally the old football coach lay perfectly still, face half in the mud, pretending he was dead. He was rooted to the ground in severe pain and bleeding in a dozen places, a broken old man who had one summer when he was young helped farm the very land he now guarded.

When at last the beating ceased, when he realized he might be allowed to live after all, he forced opened one swollen eye. Just a slit. But it was enough to see the malevolent shadow move into the barn.

He got a good look at the back of the monster. His assailant was standing tall in black boots, a cape, and a dark, slouchy hat, and this whole fascination moved with an otherworldly air about it. Seemed to know what it was looking for. It drifted toward the back of the barn, to the two wooden uprights that stood nearly fifteen feet in height. There it stopped, frozen, almost as if it were worshiping the damn thing. A crossbar and a blade was secured at the top of the two uprights. The monster in the boots stared up at the deadly apparatus.

The old coach observing all of this had little experience with ghosts and ghouls, only the local tales he had heard, but he knew on this night he was witnessing the embodiment of evil, that undying kind of evil that everybody knows is out there. The evil that walks through time.

Suddenly he felt icy cold. His bleeding head throbbed with pain, his vision was blurred, but he later told police he saw the entire head of the shadowy monster turning slowly around on a motionless torso, inexorably rotating, until a face void of features seemed to be staring at him backward. Like a scene out of some future horror movie.

STRAIGHT HALL

"Crime fascinates me," she said. "Cops fascinate me."

Hot and smart in anybody's time, John Alden had liked this woman from the start.

After a lecture on psychosis, Caitlin Dewey met him for coffee on the patio deck of Straight Hall. On this day everything was right with the spring weather. High pressure had settled in after the rain. The sun felt good. They had a view of the grassy slope that rolled down to the woods that hid the gorge and the Rickety Bridge.

"Did you hear about the old football coach?" she asked.

"I did. President Hightower is beside himself. He's an academic. I'm afraid he doesn't deal well with the violence of the real world."

"Who would do such a thing?"

"A killer of women. If the old coach had been a woman . . . do you think that monster would have left her alive?"

Caitlin Dewey pondered the question. "Where did you meet her . . . the senate beauty from the future, I mean . . . the one you say was murdered?"

"She was speaking here at Cornell," John Alden told her, satisfying her curiosity about the women in his life. "I remember she explained to the students that day that *alma mater* was Latin for *nourishing mother*."

"It is."

"Cornell University, she told the students that day, was her nourishing mother."

Caitlin Dewey leaned forward, sticking that beautiful face of hers into his weather-beaten face. "Talk to me about your future last case with the New York City police."

"There were three women murdered, butchered really, in three states," he told her, recalling the details. "New Jersey, Connecticut, and Pennsylvania. They all had three things in common . . . beauty, brains, and public service."

"Why hadn't somebody figured this out earlier?"

"The killer spread them out over five years, and in three different jurisdictions."

"He was a serial killer."

"Yes, a classic case."

"How did this involve your *future* New York?"

Her constant use of the word *future* had a mocking ring to it. "Because he lived here. Upstate New York was my guess . . . Ithaca, Syracuse, Binghamton . . . a college town."

"How did you become involved?"

"State police in Trenton contacted me after my book was published. They asked me to draw up a profile of the unidentified subject and to keep it under the radar."

"*Radar*?" she asked.

Sorry he had used the word, he told her, "It's a device invented in 1941 that sends out radio waves for finding out . . . forget it."

"Okay, forget *radar*. What did you determine?"

"That our unknown subject was a serial killer with a flair for the dramatic. That the killings in New Jersey, Connecticut, and Pennsylvania were all related. That the killing of a public servant guaranteed him the headlines he craved. That the un-sub lived in Upstate New York. And that his next target would be a high profile public servant from New York City . . . most likely the first woman elected to the United States Senate from the state of New York."

"And this is the older woman your blonde beauty replaced when she accepted a cabinet position in the administration of the colored president?"

He thought she was close to making fun of him. "Yes," he said emphatically.

"I see. So in the future a woman actually does get elected to the United States Senate?"

"She does."

"Did she know of the murders?"

"We told her office of a threat."

"And?"

"They said it was too vague . . . but they would increase her security."

"And then . . .?"

John Alden sipped his coffee, all the while admiring her beauty and her curiosity. "There are only two ways to catch a criminal, now or in the future. You hunt him down . . . or you set a trap and wait for him to walk into it. Not having nearly enough to hunt on, we set a trap for him."

"What happened?"

"My educated guess, based on the profile, was that he would attempt to assassinate her at Cooper Union, down in the village. He has a keen sense of history. It was to be a small evening event. Little publicity. Little security. He could have easily reached her . . . coming or going. But then somebody leaked the threat. I suspect her staff. The newspapers publicized the extraordinary security, and it turned into a three-ring circus. The next day, following an uneventful speech, the police looked stupid . . . especially me. We aren't credited for preventing crime. We are only credited for catching criminals. Not only did we not catch this guy . . . in law enforcement circles it was believed the man only existed in my mind. The case left my reputation in tatters and raised even more questions about the accuracy and effectiveness of criminal profiling."

"There are more than a few people," she reminded him, "even here at Cornell, who think psychology is junk science."

"That doesn't change in the future, even here at Cornell. But those three women in those three states did not kill themselves."

"The cases could have been unrelated."

"So they told me." Now he recalled for her the aftermath. "They said I was under extreme duress and I was ordered to undergo a psychiatric evaluation. That evaluation took place at Bellevue, and in the New York City Police Department, once you check into Bellevue, your reputation never checks out. So I quit the job and I came home to Ithaca."

"And you married your old high school sweetheart."

He repeated what she had said, almost to himself. "And I married my old high school sweetheart."

"I would think," Caitlin went on, carefully measuring her words, "that if a New York City police detective were to check into Bellevue, it would have to be a bit more serious than a botched investigation."

He did not answer her.

"But after your release, in your estimation, a serial killer was still out there."

"He was. He just didn't concern me anymore."

"Until your old high school sweetheart of a wife was killed." Again, he did not answer her. The sun moved behind the hall. Left them in the shadows. "What time is it?" she suddenly wanted to know.

"I don't know . . . I don't wear a watch. Never have."

Caitlin Dewey reached out and put a hand over his unadorned wrist. Her touch was magnetic. "If in your mind your story is true," she said, "did you ever stop to think that because of your books, and your reputation, and because of that trap you set for him, and the publicity that resulted from that trap, that this so-called serial killer knows a lot more about you than you do about him?"

"Serial killers don't come after cops," he told her. "Now or in the future. We are the one entity they fear."

The Murder of All Time

The first murder in Ithaca in the year 1929 took place amidst the heavy rains of April. At the beginning of the season there was no thunder to go along with these sheeting rains, no lightning, no howling winds, just relentless downpours that stretched on for days at a time. But that was about to change. On the last night of April it had already been raining for three days. H. W. Hightower was seated in his private library at President's House, among magical bookshelves lined with timeless history. Open on his lap was a leather-bound copy of Dante's *Inferno*, as translated by Henry Wadsworth Longfellow. Hightower despised the work of his namesake, believing it to be an inferior translation. The senior scholar was working on a paper recommending professors and students alike avoid this particular rendition, and further suggesting that the definitive translation of Dante Alighieri's masterpiece had yet to be written, a not-so-subtle suggestion that the consummate lucubration might be penned by a Cornell man.

On the table beside him was a glass of Scotch and a day-old copy of *The New York Times*. The venerated newspaper was reporting that reform-minded governor Franklin Roosevelt had initiated an investigation of Tammany Hall regarding the sale of judicial offices, and that the governor had also appointed a new warden to the infamous Sing Sing prison. The last paragraph of the story on appointments mentioned, almost in passing, that the governor had chosen a new captain to head the criminal investigations unit of the New York State Police—a one-armed detective and a veteran of the Great War. His name was Evan Murphy. This bit of police news made Hightower think again of the terrible beating taken by his colored football coach. He recalled the hours the two men had spent together among the books of this enchanting library in President's House.

The president emeritus had been sitting alone with Dante, the devil, and *The New York Times* for hours, hoping that John Alden might come down and join him for a nightcap. But it was getting late. He glanced up at the timepiece hanging on the wall and listened to the ticking of the clock's pendulum, a sound resembling the steady beat of the human heart. It was nearing midnight. The witching hour. He pulled his gold watch from his vest pocket to ensure the two timepieces were synchronized. Deadly accurate. Assured fates were aligned, he snapped the watch closed and returned it to his pocket. The sound of the rain on the window panes was making the old man sleepy. So was the Scotch. Yet he did not want to sleep. Few old men do. Something in the night air was forcing him to stay awake.

THE PROFESSOR

On the night of the murder, John Alden, his .38 Super automatic in hand, was upstairs in his third floor room, standing at the window, gazing out at the incessant rain. Ithaca was funny that way. He knew the region was infamous for its inclement weather, but when his mind wandered back to his childhood years in the small town on Cayuga's waters, the sun was always shining. It was as if nothing memorable had ever happened in the rain.

He glanced over his shoulder at the picture of the Cornell football player hanging on the wall. Bobby Bill. The Ghost Runner. As the weeks passed and John Alden became more comfortable living in this bygone era, he had learned to be more circumspect, to put more weight on his head injury and less emphasis on his mysterious origins and his knowledge of future events. He turned back to the rain, popped a wad of opium into his mouth and then chased it with a swig of Coke. The laudanum mix relieved his pain and elevated his state of mind, but the potion could not chase away the spirits that were haunting him. He recalled again his trip to rainy Oregon and seeing his beautiful Katelyn for the first time since his return from the war—in bed with her first husband.

Through the weather he could barely make out the silhouette of the magnificent clock tower where Caitlin Dewey played the chimes. On this night a concert was scheduled at midnight.

He gulped another swig from the bottle of Coca-Cola. And that is when he saw it, a bright yellow convertible, like a warning beacon moving through the night. It was the sports car of Royal S. Copeland III, tearing through campus in the rain, no top, torrents of water pouring over its driver. It was a strange hour and strange weather to be out for a drive, even for a young fool like Copeland. John Alden tried to swallow his hostility along with the Coke.

He also knew at this hour President Hightower would be downstairs, sitting alone in his library of mystifying books. He thought of joining him there. John Alden squeezed the grip of the gun and kept his eyes peeled for shadows moving through the rain.

THE MAD DOCTOR

At the same time John Alden was downing a wad of opium in his room at President's House, Dr. Victor Ecarius was wrapping up a night of research amidst his collection of body parts on the second floor of Hell Hall. Despite his dour disposition, and despite the fact that students and faculty thought of him as a morbid creature, he hated the rain. Foul weather brought out the worst in him. His student assistant, the ungainly Jim Dorn, had just left for home after compiling notes on intelligence and biology, and then rambling on for an hour with his own notions of the social pecking order of the human race. The doctor poured himself a stiff drink and wandered over to the window, near the operating table he kept wired for electroshock therapy. He winced at the outline of Sage Chapel, haunting in the storm, considering it his mission to drive religion from the field of science. Then he stared down the hill at President's House and thought of the man who called himself John Alden—the man of a thousand secrets, limping over the hills, growing stronger every day. What if, for the sake of academic argument, he really was from the twenty-first century? What if he really was what he said he was, a Harvard-educated, New York City detective from the year 2010? At the very least, John Alden was an unintended force of nature. The uninvited guest. A man who seemed for now to be as big a mystery to himself as he was to others.

The doctor watched with a measure of concern as the shadow of his assistant, Jim Dorn, dashed through pitchforks of rain and then disappeared over Libe Slope, as if washing into the abyss. The boy was blind as a bat. Dr. Ecarius shook his head.

And that is how the night left him—the mad doctor of Hell Hall standing before the laboratory window like Mary Shelley's Dr. Frankenstein, wondering if perhaps within every human brain there lived a monster.

THE BEAUTIFUL STUDENT

And there was yet another person out and about on that rainy night—Caitlin Dewey with the big brown eyes, the girl whose interest in John Alden seemed almost preternatural. It was a feeling she could not explain, a sentiment that had haunted her from the first time she saw those brooding Irish eyes of his, when he limped out of the shadows and into the candlelight on the night of the dinner party. She had been hoping the rain might let up before she had to walk up to the clock tower for the midnight concert. But there was no break in the storm, and Caitlin set off across the campus under a black umbrella. She entered the clock tower alone, shook the weather from her shoulders, and then climbed nearly two hundred stairs to the musty timbered loft, where she removed her raincoat and took her place before the controls. The lighting was poor. A chill filled the air. Killing time, she rubbed the goose bumps from her arms and thought about the ex-detective-college professor who claimed he was from the future. Was he? Or were his detailed lectures on crime just the ramblings of a deranged mind? As Caitlin Dewey waited patiently for the huge clock to strike midnight, the campus beauty let her highly-educated mind wander over the possibilities of helping treat a man who sincerely believed he had come to them from another century.

THE PRIEST

Looking back on that night of horrors, Father Wallace Dougal could not tell police what it was that drove him out into the stormy weather and over to Sage Chapel. He pushed through the carved oak doors and removed his soaking wet hat, and then his raincoat, and he stomped into the deserted church. He crossed himself before the altar, then lit a pair of candles before resting his tall frame in the front pew before the apse. The dark oak wainscoting appeared black in the candlelight, while above it an elaborately embellished scheme of branches and vines snaked through shadows and time. The Catholic priest listened to the rain dancing on the roof, as if the weather were mocking him. How does one know when evil creeps in under the cover of good?

The tirades against the university and its non-religious mandate were severe and endless. Infidel Cornell. New York City newspapers called the young school a sinkhole of corruption and a hotbed of sin from which few students came away uncontaminated. One detractor went as far as saying Cornell students were a "crowd of dissolute roughs and felonies were a frequent occurrence among them." At times the Scottish priest felt as if he had wandered into collegiate hell. The more his fundamentalist followers demanded an ounce of religion from the university, the more Cornell blandished its non-sectarian creed and its progressive ways. Even getting the administration to publicly admit that the school had at least been founded on Christian principles had proved impossible. Perhaps the silver-haired priest could pray away his frustrations. Then he heard the chimes in the clock tower. It was midnight.

THE TWINS

The chimes tolled twelve times. Then the concert began. On this night it was Beethoven's Fourth Concerto, an enchanting piece famous for its solos. The bells rang out through the rain. The very first rumbles of spring thunder broke over the hills and mixed eerily with the chimes emanating from the clock tower.

Identical twins Belle and Amanda Parrish took the witching hour literally. On the night of the murder, the beautiful blondes were dressed all in black as they set out from President's House to worship the earth and the rain. Their mother had been a witch, as had been their grandmother. It was a religion older than Christianity. Talk of mental illness in the family was nonsense to them. Just another witch hunt. In the circular drive that fronted the house they glanced back at the third floor window, where they saw the tall shadow of a man step back away from the light, the curtains before him billowed by the wind.

THE RICH KID

His expensive yellow roadster came to a dead stop on the edge of campus. The engine was flooded. Literally. The car did not run well in foul weather. Plus, it had no top. He sat in the rain behind the steering wheel and swore like a sailor. Royal S. Copeland III had that old blue sense of entitlement. The skies were not supposed to rain on him. He was too vain to wear a hat. He found them silly. His bare head was soaked. His long tweed coat clung to his slender frame like a soggy blanket. In the middle of the night he had gotten the call to report to the "barn," the name they had all given to the movie studio. The Ithaca Motion Picture Company wanted to shoot in the storm. Capture the realism. Now he was on his way there, to perform an insignificant part in a less-than-significant movie. In his heart he believed he should have leading roles in Hollywood feature films. The young man saw himself as Douglas Fairbanks, John Gilbert, and Rudolph Valentino all rolled into one. The consummate star. He could see the clock tower up on the hill, and he could hear the chimes trying mightily to break through the storm. He recognized the piece as Beethoven's, but he was unsure of which composition.

Suddenly, lightning livened the skies over Cayuga Lake and thunder rolled his way. The music abruptly stopped. The Copeland boy stepped from his roadster. Felt the pouring rain upon his shoulders. Take away his exaggerated sense of privilege and self-worth and he really was a handsome young man. Intelligent. Well built and well bred. He was supposed to have gone to the University of Michigan like his father, but by the time he had finished prep school, he had grown sick of hearing about the glory of Michigan. So he chose Cornell, in part to stay in New York, and in part to spite his old man.

He did not scare easily, but now he was consumed with fear of the rising storm. The brilliant future he envisioned for himself, and his country, seemed suddenly threatened. Almost all that he could hear was the falling rain and the approaching thunder. And yet there was another sound, constant and barely discernible in the night. It was the sound of raging water sluicing through the gorge before dropping over Ithaca Falls. Then came a flash of lightning, and he saw two feminine figures in hooded cloaks coming his way. He was pretty sure they were in the movie. He saw another figure with an umbrella emerging from the clock tower. The sodden Copeland shuddered. A gust of wind cut through the hills, and suddenly tree branches were dancing about like wailing banshees.

The young man did not really care for Ithaca. Or even Cornell. Everything was too small. Everybody too provincial. Most of all he did not like the Harvard-educated detective who was limping around campus in the guise of a college professor and claiming to be from the future. There was something about the man's act he found immoral. Disturbing. Intimidating.

He watched as the figure with the umbrella moved away from him. Meanwhile, the two figures in the hooded cloaks were coming right for him, their twin robes billowing in the wind. Royal S. Copeland III did not know it then, but he was about to land his leading role. In fact, he was about to star in one of the most memorable scenes in the history of American cinema.

THE ANACHRONISM

John Alden would later tell police he had just wanted to walk in the rain. He wanted to shower on the streets of Ithaca, to be washed clean of the bad dream he was living. With the first bells of the midnight chimes he tucked the gun beneath his belt and threw on his suit coat. Buttoned it tight and turned up the collar. Grabbed his cane. At the foot of the wide staircase that was the spine of President's House he noticed a light still burning in the library. The retired university president had come to mean the world to him. But the professor knew his Cornell history. The old man's days on this earth were numbered.

The glass of the green-shaded lamp was aglow on the reading table, but he found the library vacant. The only sound was the rain outside the window and the ticking of the clock on the wall. An empty glass of Scotch sat next to Dante's *Inferno*. In a notebook were handwritten annotations on the text, but they were hard to decipher. John Alden picked up the notes and admired the old school calligraphy, shaky as it was.

It was while studying these comments on Dante's version of hell that his eyes were once again drawn to the books that lined the shelves. Ever since the night of the dinner party he had intended to return to the library, alone, and study some of the unusual texts, but each time the thought arose he had been too tired, or too pained. Now with a slight limp he moved to the shelves. Standing there, he slowly and deliberately enunciated the titles lined up before him. "*Dr. Faustus*, by Christopher Marlowe. A classic," he said. "*Fables*, by Aesop. Child's play. *Reflections on the French Revolution*, by Edmund Burke," he went on. "Who but Burke could make getting your head chopped off boring?"

John Alden continued his running commentary to the next shelf, proud of all the books he had read in his lifetime. "*Confessions of an English Opium-Eater*, by Thomas De Quincy." He had only recently read that one. He grinned at the title, and then he moved on.

"*The Making of the President 1960*, by Theodore H. White . . ." Even before the complete title was out of his mouth, the time-traveling professor iced up. He dropped the notes on the floor along with his gold-headed walking cane, and he reached out for the book. It was encased in a blue cardboard sleeve, for its own safety and preservation. He slid it out of the protective sleeve and examined the copy, a special hardcover edition. He had read the book at Harvard. It was a model of political reporting, considered the best book ever written on the trials and tribulations of American presidential elections. But his Harvard edition had looked nothing like this. The book was missing its original dust jacket. Its dark blue cover was severely discolored and stained. The binding consisted of broken sewing. He opened it. The whole text block, the body of the book, was brittle and soiled, washed out, as if the book had been fished out of a creek. This made for each page being twice as thick as it should have been, and difficult to handle, as some of the more frail pages were detached. He randomly flipped the opening pages of the tainted work. It landed on page eleven and he read: *"Thus it had been an easy and leisurely afternoon in the grand hall of the Waldorf-Astoria, as it slowly filled with cigarette smoke while Royal S. Copeland III and Richard M. Nixon took their naps and the nation waited for the Waldorf in New York City and the Ambassador Hotel in Los Angeles to report what was happening."*

John Alden flipped more pages, not believing what he had just read. In a chapter on the Democratic primary in Wisconsin in 1960 it read: *"Where Hubert Humphrey could staff but two offices in Wisconsin, Copeland could staff eight of the ten congressional districts with superior personnel. It was the long-established connection of Copeland's family, friendships, and social background that provided him with the talent. Four of the ten districts were staffed by Ivy League Cornell classmates."*

John Alden tore through the fragile book, still incredulous. Yet another chapter told of Copeland's heroics in the Navy during World War II. In fact, on every page that he turned to, the name of John F. Kennedy had been substituted with the name of Royal S. Copeland III.

"Anachronism?" Ecarius asked, wanting the definition.

"Something out of its proper place and time," answered John Alden.

"Yes," Ecarius told him. "Anachronisms are everywhere in Ithaca. One has only to look."

"Hightower!" Alden screamed. He limped out of the library and ripped through the house. Halted at the foot of the staircase. "What is this?" he demanded to know at the top of his lungs while holding the broken book aloft. But there was nobody in sight to acknowledge him. There was only the echo of his voice, the sound of the rain outside the front door, and the resonance of Beethoven's chimes rolling over the hills of Ithaca. John Alden turned to the front door. He glanced again at the extraordinary book in the palms of his hands. Then his detective's mind, his twenty-first century mind, put it all together. He dropped the future manuscript on the floor and ran from the house, leaving the front door wide open, the wind and the rain washing over the scattering pages of *The Making of the President 1960.*

"Two men must die . . ."

Hightower had been right. The killings were political. Franklin Roosevelt and Royal S. Copeland III were the targets. Future presidents, their progressive programs would transform America for generations.

John Alden ran with a pronounced and painful limp through the Arts Quad in the pouring rain. In the opium den Hightower had asked him if he remembered hearing the killer correctly on the Rickety Bridge the night of the Halloween storm. He had not.

"Now two men must die and all will be changed. Go back. You can't stop it. Not in this time."

The madman had said, *"Not in this time."* So John Alden was sent chasing him through time.

Fighting his way through yet another storm, the ex-New York City police detective was mad at himself for having bungled the details, angry for letting his personal hostility toward the Copeland boy cloud his judgment. The rich in America had a long tradition of charity, philanthropy, and public service, especially in New York. Their fate could no more be determined by their school days than could that of the poor.

John Alden drew the gun from his belt. Soaking wet, he clutched his bum leg and ran up College Avenue, ran beneath the giant clock on the chiming tower, following the path of the yellow roadster he had seen disappear in the rain. While he ran, a thousand arguments raked his brain. A running debate. Was tonight the night Royal Copeland was to die? And if it was, for the sake of history, should the rich kid even be saved?

THE CORPSE

The handsome but arrogant young man was not found until morning. It was one of those grace-filled, sky-blue mornings that follows a midnight storm. He was sitting at the wheel of his yellow roadster, parked across the street from Eddy Gate on the edge of Collegetown. His right hand was at rest on the steering wheel. His left elbow was bent casually over the driver's side door, almost as if he was going for a spin in the country. Except for a crimson ring around the collar, his grey tweed suit was free of blood. Free of wrinkles, for that matter. But the suit was also free of the man's head. At first glance it appeared to be a prop, a headless dummy from some horror movie, like the bloody flicks they made at the Ithaca Motion Picture Company. Then the first blood-curdling scream of discovery split the morning sky, and everybody within earshot knew that fair and shining Ithaca had a murder on its hands.

END OF BOOK ONE

"The ticking of the clock on the mantelpiece seemed to him to be dividing Time into separate atoms of agony, each of which was too terrible to be borne."

—Oscar Wilde
The Picture of Dorian Gray

The Guillotine

The steel blade weighs 15 pounds. The weight attached to the blade weighs 66 pounds. The drop to the human neck is 88 inches. It takes 7/10 of a second for the blade to fall. Power at impact is 888 pounds per square inch. The blade cuts through the neck in 0.005 seconds. The professor of criminal justice knows all of this as soon as he sees the guillotine up on the silver screen. He is an expert in the art of death. This guillotine flickering before him in black and white is comprised of two 14 foot uprights joined by a crossbar. The internal edges have been greased with tallow. The famous angled blade is weighted to ensure a swift, clean cut. The system is operated via a rope and pulley, while the whole construction is mounted on a high platform. A stage for all the world to see.

A mob is gathered at the foot of the guillotine. Some people up front are dressed in black robes, including two young girls, and though it is a silent film, they appear to be chanting. The executioner takes the stage with the whirl of a dancer. He is recognizable in an instant. He is the villain from the storm on Halloween—the man the professor chased down Libe Slope and across the Rickety Bridge—a tall man in black, with a face cadaverous of complexion and partially hidden behind a mask. A floppy hat hides his forehead and shields his eyes.

A horse-pulled cart with the prisoner arrives over cobblestone streets. This appears to be a movie about the French Revolution. The elaborate set is the town square of a village, with the great steeples of the Paris churches visible in the background. No expense has been spared. The extras number in the hundreds. Some in the crowd are waving banners. A man hoists into the air a severed head on a stick. The sky is leaden. Threatening. Women in specially-built bleachers are holding umbrellas. There is a drum corps, uniformed soldiers with percussion instruments strapped from their shoulders. The crowd is crazed with anticipation, giddy with excitement, like in the moments before the opening kickoff of the Harvard–Yale football game.

More uniformed soldiers drag the prisoner from the cart and up steep wood stairs. Soldiers with muskets and bayonets block any retreat.

The prisoner is dressed in a ruffled white shirt. Black breeches. His feet and ankles are bare, having been robbed of his shoes and stockings. He is a tall, handsome man. A man of advantage, with the mien of a privileged education. He is being dragged to his death kicking and screaming. Literally. If this be acting, his is an unbelievable talent.

Then at the base of the guillotine, something odd happens. Instead of being placed face down in the guillotine as is the norm, the prisoner is being strapped onto the death table of the decapitation machine face up, Robespierre-like, so that he can see the blade crashing down. Witness to his own death. Furthermore, there is no basket to catch his decapitated head. Performers in silent movies act with gestures and eyes. It is obvious the prisoner is screaming "No! No!" over and over again as the last strap is tightened and his head is locked into place.

The movie is well directed, with fluid camera movements and innovative lighting. A cinematic exercise in psychological horror. The professor cannot help but admire the talent involved. It is what happens next that makes film history. There is only one long master shot, and it is from a high angle that includes both the head and the feet of the prisoner. One continuous shot. No cutaways, no close-ups, no camera trickery whatsoever.

Now the sky above the guillotine turns a more ghastly hue. Clouds of black and gray lurch forward as if in anger. The weather as a prop, as a malicious character. The masked executioner removes a tin of white powder from his vest pocket. He puts a tincture to his nose and sniffs. Then with sweeping and dramatic gestures the executioner throws the handle. Everything that follows is instantaneous. The rope and pulley swing into action. The blade falls. The prisoner's eyes burst wide open. Then his head topples to the stage and rolls, coming to rest at the feet of the executioner. Blood pours from the neck of the torso.

The executioner picks up the head immediately and displays it before the crowd. Before the camera. Is a severed head aware of its fate? For a good five seconds the prisoner's head retains ocular movement. Makes direct eye contact with the camera lens. His facial expression is one of terror as he glances about. His lips tremble as if he is murmuring inaudibly. Then the young, intense eyes on the severed head of the prisoner slowly close, the way a pair of eyes drifts off to sleep. The iris of the camera closes slowly on the cackling visage of the executioner, head in hand.

The professor of criminal justice sits alone and listens to the rhythmic flapping sound of a film that has run out of one reel and spun onto another. The film stock used in the silent era is cellulose nitrate, a close chemical of nitroglycerine. It is explosive and highly flammable. Cellulose nitrate is also chemically unstable. It begins to decay from the moment it is created. But this film is in remarkably good condition, as if being viewed in the year it was produced. And so the professor is left to wonder—is this really a silent movie, or is it the black-and-white after-dream of a madman on opium, watching another old movie on another dull, dark and soundless night?

BOOK TWO

ITHACA, NEW YORK

1929

The One-Armed Cop

He wore the scowl of a serious bulldog, had sandy hair devolving to gray, and he kept this hair cropped short and hidden beneath a black fedora. He always wore a suit. A dark suit. Tailored. Expensive. The man looked like a million bucks standing alongside other detectives, dressed in cheap suits they could barely afford. His suit coat was cut wider at the waist so that it flowed neatly down his compact body, leaving no bulge from the revolver he carried on his hip. But there was a glaring oddity to the pricey suits worn by the dapper detective. The sleeve of the left arm was empty, the flat cuff pressed neatly into the hip pocket. Because of this handicap, and because of the classy lifestyle he embraced, there were never-ending rumors about Evan Murphy. That he was on the take. He was in somebody's pocket. Had to be. How does a man with only one arm, many asked, not only retain his job with the New York State Police, but actually rise to the rank of captain? There was only one flaw in their crooked cop theory. Murphy solved cases. He made arrests. Put murderers away. And he had a reputation for never missing the execution of one of his collars. When they strapped these coldblooded killers into the electric chair at Sing Sing, the one witness they could count on to see them to their grave was Evan Murphy of the New York State Police.

That a senator's son had been decapitated at one of the first and largest coeducational universities in the country set off a newspaper war. A journalistic feeding frenzy. Infidel Cornell. The New York City tabloids picked up on the grisly murder as soon as the story hit the wires. By the end of the day the murder had been tabbed *sensational,* spawning national headlines, and political recriminations. Arriving trains were flooded with reporters. Radio news reports were updated on the hour. At the time of the 1929 murder, Cornell was still a young university, but with large aspirations. It was located in a small town in the heart of a big state, and the killing shook the tight-knit community to its core. Swallowing their pride, the authorities in Ithaca immediately called the state police in Albany and requested assistance. In the meantime, local cops and volunteers swarmed over the Homeric hills in search of a killer.

It was Franklin Roosevelt who had promoted Evan Murphy to the rank of captain, making him the Empire State's number one detective—and it was murder that brought the state's number one detective to the hills of Ithaca. Royal S. Copeland Jr. was the United States senator from New York, a doctor by trade, and a prominent Democrat. The murder of his son while attending Cornell, a second-rate institution still in its infancy, sent the powerful politician into a barely-controlled rage. He demanded justice from the state's new governor.

The case was a detective's nightmare. Small town cops and big time politicians. A dead, rich college kid and career academics. The tension on campus would be palpable.

Before the war, before he had lost his arm, there had been a series of murders in Upstate New York. All of the victims women. Suffragists. Despite Albany's offer of assistance, local cops had zealously guarded their turf. There was little collaboration between jurisdictions. The murders went unsolved. This lack of cooperation among law enforcement agencies was crippling. It had to change.

Still, as he made the long train ride upstate, it was another angle that intrigued the one-armed cop. Stories about the time-traveling professor from Cornell had already reached Albany. The state police captain carried the professor's suspiciously thin file on his lap. It was not only the idea that this John Alden was claiming to be from the future that fascinated Murphy; it was also the fact that the mystery man who had washed ashore at the foot of Ithaca Falls was claiming to be an ex-cop. A New York City homicide detective. Now, pulling off something like that would be no small ruse.

A PLEA FOR HELP

The forever-president of the university was especially shaken by the atrociousness of the crime. The old man had never married. Had no children of his own. The students were his offspring. Even in retirement, he felt responsible for every last one of them. H.W. Hightower wanted desperately to help. The president emeritus had noticed over the past weeks that John Alden had shifted most of his attention to the recovery of his injuries and to his lectures on the psychology of crime, with less emphasis on what would happen in the years ahead. It was almost as if the man was slowly forgetting what he had claimed to be, and where he had claimed to have come from. From a psychiatric point of view, this was a good thing. Hightower suspected it might have something to do with the girl that played the chimes. But now the university needed the cop that was clearly inside of him.

The president emeritus was making his way across the Arts Quad, having come from an emergency meeting with the Board of Trustees. He was dressed in his portly best and swinging his cane in an agitated manner when he saw his visiting professor sitting on the front stoop of President's House, waiting for him. He was angry. It was apparent the man had been up all night. His clothes had been drenched and dried while he wore them. His unkempt hair looked as if it hadn't seen a comb in a full moon. His eyes were red.

"You knew," said John Alden, struggling to his feet as Hightower approached. "You knew the kid was to die."

"I knew no such thing. How dare you?" Hightower raised his cane as if it were a pistol and pointed it at Alden's chest. "May I remind you that you are the wide-eyed sage limping around my campus claiming to know the future. The ghastly murder of one of our most prominent students would have been a particularly nice thing to know."

"I tried to warn you. What happened to the book?"

"What book?"

"*The Making of the President 1960*," Alden told him. "The book where Royal S. Copeland the third is elected President of the United States."

"There is no such book. In point of fact, there is no book in the house on American presidential elections, much less on an election that takes place thirty years hence. May I suggest you search the Cornell Library . . . under *fiction*."

The warm spring sun was shining down on them as they argued, the first sunshine in days. Students, still upset by news of the murder, were stopping to watch.

The two men lowered their voices, but hardly their intensity. The Harvard graduate pointed to the window at the far end of the house. "That library of yours is littered with books I've never heard of."

"And you, the learned John W. Alden, know of every book ever written? I was unaware my friends in Cambridge were graduating students of such a fantastic caliber. I inherited that library from my predecessors. I have tried to add to the esoteric collection, and I will leave the entire anthology to my successors . . . minus, of course, your imaginary book on the presidential aspirations of the Copeland boy." The old man rested his weight on his cane using both of his hands. "Perhaps young Copeland was not meant to be saved."

Now there was a break in their debate as John Alden fought to catch his own breath. He wiped his brow and then put his hands to his hips, spreading his suit coat and revealing the .38 Super automatic tucked beneath his belt. "What the hell do you want from me?"

Hightower took note of the weapon. "You have knowledge of police work. You have detective skills. How and when you acquired these skills and knowledge, I do not know. But the university's future is fragile. Something like this . . ."

"Murder."

"Yes. This must never happen here in Ithaca again. Please help."

THE SCENE OF THE CRIME

After discussing the situation with the shaken old man in more measured tones, John Alden left President's House and for the first time intentionally wandered away without his cane. And without his gun. He made his way to the county morgue in town to have a look at the headless body. Then he limped back to the scene of the crime by following the footpath through the gorge until he reached the edge of Collegetown.

The late afternoon was still sunny and warm, first day of May warm, but already the omnipresent clouds could be seen gathering over Cayuga Lake. The long walk back from town made him feel good and bad at the same time. He was beginning to think that perhaps he had ditched the cane a day too early. He was tired now and his leg was sore. John Alden limped up to the driver's side door of the yellow roadster that had been owned by Royal S. Copeland III. He peered inside. Two uniformed Ithaca police officers watched him, more curious than concerned. Hours had passed since the discovery of the body. The headless corpse had been removed, yet the car remained at the crime scene, exposed to the elements. And to onlookers.

The heavy rains had washed the sporty car clean. The interior was waterlogged, but spotless. There was no sign of a struggle. John Alden had arrived at this time and place in search of a killer of women. Now he was confronted with the murder of a young man. Still, the ex-cop believed his worst fears had been realized. The serial killer he had chased down the hills and into the gorge, the caped man he had struggled with on the Rickety Bridge, and with whom he had tumbled into the raging waters and then washed over Ithaca Falls, had made the same trip he had made. Back in time some eighty years or more. "And what are you two supposed to be doing?" Alden asked the Ithaca cops.

The two cops were dumbfounded. They did not appreciate being questioned.

"We're waiting for the state dick," a slovenly officer informed him.

"The state dick? And who the hell is the state dick?"

"That would be me."

John Alden turned when he said that. Saw him standing there as if he owned the space. He was what Alden called "a serious cop." Command at first sight. The man knew how to dress. He knew how to carry himself. He knew how to speak softly, yet with a measure of authority that was never to be questioned. "I didn't mean any disrespect. My name is John Alden. I'm a guest lecturer here at . . ."

"I know who you are, Professor," the man said, stopping him mid-sentence. "I'm Captain Evan Murphy of the New York State Police." He did not show a badge, or even offer to shake hands, yet the absence of these gestures did not seem rude. What he presented instead was an air of confidence.

"You fought in the war?" Alden asked, nodding at the empty sleeve.

"I did. The 69th."

"The Fighting 69th. A mostly Irish, New York regiment. I remember watching a movie about you guys when I was a kid."

"So in the future they make a movie about our war exploits?"

"They do. In fact, it's called *The Fighting 69th,* though I'm having a hard time recalling who was in it."

Murphy watched him closely as John Alden struggled with his memory. "I heard you saw some action yourself?"

"In my day, I was an MP."

"The MPs I knew were mean bastards. But, damn, they kept order." He had a gruff voice, a smoker's voice, and every once in a while he would raise his fist to his mouth and clear his throat. "That's quite a dodge you've got going there, Professor."

They both circled the car, a small crowd of the curious gathering to watch. "And just what is it, Captain, that you think I'm dodging?"

"It's really a play on the old amnesia dodge."

"How so?"

Murphy paused at the passenger side door. "You have no identification papers . . . because you're from the future. You have no criminal record . . . because you're from the future. You say you were with the military police . . . but yet you have no military records. You have no medical records, no school records, no paper trail whatsoever . . . because you're from the future. Feigning madness is one of the more dastardly ways to hide your true identity."

John Alden stood beside the driver's side door where the rich kid had been found without his head. They talked across the car. An odd couple. One in a sleek suit, a priceless tie, and a fedora perfectly angled above his face. The other in a disheveled suit coat, with no tie, and with no hat to cover his shaggy head of hair. "Do you really believe I'm feigning madness, Captain?"

The one-armed cop cleared his throat before answering, all the time examining the car. "When I was in the hospital in France, recovering from my wounds, there was an amnesia patient at the end of the ward. I never really met him. His head and face were all bandaged. Most of us in that ward were from New York... you know, fought together, bled together, hospitalized together. I don't recall if he was with the 69th, but somehow they determined that this particular soldier was from Ithaca. But that's about all they could get out of him. Doctors think he might have been referring to the ancient Ithaca. You know, the one in Homer's *Odyssey*. They pretty much figured he had a college education. A lot of Greek studies. The kind of stuff they teach at Harvard and Cornell."

"You never went to college, did you, Captain?"

"No, never had the opportunity."

"And you resent those of us who did."

"*Resent* is not the right word."

"Still," Alden told him, "you possess what I would call a blue-collar intellect. Not to mention street smarts coming out your ears."

"I'll take that as a compliment."

"It is."

"Anyway, this amnesia patient I'm telling you about . . . some of us thought it was just a dodge to get out of the service. You know, his ticket home. Sure enough, day after they took off his bandages . . . he was gone. We figure he got the hell out of there before anybody recognized him. Nobody ever knew who he was, and nobody I talked to ever knew where he disappeared to."

Unmoved by the story, John Alden shrugged his wide shoulders. "If he was hospitalized with head wounds, I don't see how he could be accused of shirking his duty. Maybe he went back to the front to be with his men."

"Yeah, maybe that was it. He went back to the front."

John Alden returned the discussion to the crime. "Why was this car left sitting here?"

Captain Murphy again looked the roadster up and down, his face registering a glimpse of disdain. "Oh, I expect they were waiting for me. What would you have done with it?"

"I would have had it in a garage by now, with a full forensic team swarming all over it."

"A full *forensic* team?"

"It's from the Latin word *forensis,*" Alden explained. "The application of scientific knowledge to legal or criminal matters."

"And how would you have handled the crime scene here, Professor . . . *forensically* speaking, I mean?"

John Alden scanned the hilly campus behind him. He read the concerned faces of the gathering crowd, now made up of students, faculty, town folks, out-of-town reporters straining to hear the conversation, and local cops. Some in the crowd were clearly angry. Crowds at murder scenes can grow hostile fast. "I would have set up a command post away from the crime scene," he said, pointing up the hill. "This murder was staged for shock value. The man was decapitated someplace else and then fitted back into the car with the precision of a hand into a glove."

"That would explain the absence of blood. What else, Professor?"

"I would have isolated this area and protected the scene. Determined all paths of entry and exit to this spot and then searched them for evidence. I would have kept all unauthorized persons from entering the crime scene. I would have identified and retained for questioning the person who notified police. I would have detained anybody who arrived at the scene before I did. I'd have separated the witnesses so that I could get independent statements. I would have kept a chronological log of each and every person who entered the crime scene, including badge numbers and titles . . . doctors, detectives, photographers, reporters, et cetera."

"Including you?" Murphy asked.

"Especially me. And I would have taken copious notes and photographs," John Alden told him. "Now all of that has been lost."

"You know a lot of cop talk. I'll give you that. Truth is, that's exactly what I would have done. But even after the governor handed me the case . . . it took me hours to get here by train. Now, we can't be faulting the Ithaca police. They haven't seen a lot of murders. Not like you and me, huh?"

"What now?"

Captain Murphy reached his one hand into the car and popped open the glove compartment. Fingered through the contents. "You tell me, Professor. What do we know so far?"

John Alden took a deep breath. He was being played, but felt he had no choice but to play along. "From the events on the night of April 30, 1929," he said, "we can surmise the following . . ." Then the alleged-ex-cop-turned-college professor-turned-time-traveler rattled off what he believed had happened. "The killer used the heavy rain to his advantage. It concealed his approach. It washed away clues and literally covered his tracks. The victim ..."

"Mr. Copeland."

"Yes, Royal S. Copeland the third was lured to his death. Literally walked to his execution. The car never moved. The victim was decapitated at an unknown site and then returned here to the car, where the scene was staged for presentation."

"And was young Mr. Copeland a random victim, or was he targeted?"

"He was targeted," Alden told him. "He was the son of a United States senator, and he had a very promising future."

"And in your estimation . . . would his death alter the future?"

"Every man's death alters the future."

"Why cut off his head?" Murphy asked.

"Besides the shock value . . . it was a statement about capital punishment."

"How so?"

"Capital punishment derives from the Latin word *caput*. It means *head*. The forfeiture of the head."

Murphy nodded his own head, not agreeing or disagreeing. "Senator Copeland is a doctor by trade. He doesn't believe in the death penalty . . . do no harm, and all that stuff. I wonder if his son's murder will change his mind. How about you . . . do you believe in capital punishment, Professor?"

"I do not."

"And come the year 2010 . . . have Americans evolved beyond capital punishment?"

"We have not."

"Funny, I'd have thought we would have. And what is it you call such killers?"

"I believe this one is a serial killer. A psychopath . . . but now with the addition of a political agenda."

Murphy lifted a piece of paper from the glove compartment and read it. "Yes, that's it, a *serial killer*, with a political agenda. And didn't you tell your students here that these serial killers like to inject themselves into the investigation?"

"Sometimes, yes."

The one-armed cop slipped the piece of paper beneath his suit coat. Pocketed it. "According to my files, Professor, you also told of your wife being murdered by this serial killer. Your beautiful Katelyn." He spelled it out. "K-a-t-e-l-y-n." Then he paused for effect before asking, "And what year was that?"

"You're very thorough, Captain Murphy."

"That I am." The state cop covered his mouth to squelch another cough. "It almost seems from your own testimony that this serial killer, as you call him, is not as much interested in killing others as he is in tormenting you." That drew no response, so the man from Albany refocused his attention on the driver's seat of the car. "And how, exactly, do you suppose young Mr. Copeland lost his head?"

John Alden hesitated before answering. He glanced over his shoulder at the growing crowd, angry in a frightened way. Then he lowered his voice as he turned back to the state police captain. "From the sharp angle, and from the clean cut to the neck, my guess would be a guillotine."

Murphy glanced up at the clouds building over the lake and laughed, an expressed amusement just short of a mocking cackle. "That's the thing, you know . . . we just don't see a lot of guillotines lying around this part of New York. Who do you think might have one of those?"

John Alden shot right back. "Traveling magicians might have one. Theaters might have one. It wouldn't take much effort to convert a prop into a working machine. You might even check with the Ithaca Motion Picture Company. They just might have a guillotine lying about."

Infidel Cornell

John Alden crossed over the East Avenue Bridge on foot. He paused mid-span to rest his leg, just long enough to look upstream at the suspended skeleton of the Rickety Bridge, where his odyssey had begun. An electric railcar crammed with students rolled down the curve and onto the bridge. Rang its bell. John Alden stepped from its path. The passing students eyed him with hostility and suspicion. Anybody watching the time-traveling professor from the campus above would have seen him continue his journey by crossing the road bridge and then disappearing into the woods on the far side.

The sun swam in and out of the clouds, in and out of the trees. He turned his coat collar to the spring breeze and thought about what Hightower had said to him in the depths of the opium den: *"Every place you go, everything you see . . . your mind automatically assigns it a future . . . Yours is the most fascinating case of head trauma I have ever seen."* In what was now woodland that rolled from the lake to the hills, John Alden envisioned parking lots, modern dormitories, and campus halls. But in this new reality of his, this 1929, there stood only acres of trees. He continued on, down a trodden path, following the directions he had been given.

The professor of criminal justice stopped before a meadow at the edge of the tree line. A barn lay across the way. Everywhere he looked, things were springing to life. He reached into his breast pocket and withdrew the letter that had traveled with him through time, the letter he wore over his heart, and the same letter that had survived the raging waters and the spill over Ithaca Falls. The one-armed cop from Albany asking him questions about the murder of his wife had unsettled him.

Katelyn had not dated the letter. Even if she had, what would it have proven? He wished now he had kept the envelope it arrived in, with the stamp and the dated postmark—October 23, 2009.

His beautiful Katelyn was still living in Oregon when she read a magazine article about a New York City police detective who was rewriting the book on American crime. Not only, the article reported, was he solving the most heinous of crimes, but he took the time to put his experiences and his expertise into words and then get the manuscript published. Katelyn, she later told him, had tried to get her hands on the groundbreaking work but was informed it was a police textbook and unavailable to the general public. Still, the story of the small town boy who grew up to be a big city detective released in her a hometown pride she had almost forgotten.

By the time she had entered high school, a cute but awkward girl, John Alden was already a local legend. She watched the golden boy from Ithaca play football with an unparalleled passion. Where other girls found the game too violent, or too complicated, she grew to admire the gridiron paradox of brute force versus elegance and poise. She could appreciate the thrilling beauty of a deep pass, or the grace and geometry of a long run. By the time she was a senior, and now a beautiful young woman, she had become attuned to the game's strategies, once likening it to a swift and violent chess match played by muscular men.

When she at last came across the magazine article, Katelyn was already separated from her alcoholic husband. Years of marriage washed up in gin and tonic. For the first time in her life, she was alone. The remembrance of days past, she told him, became overwhelming to her. She recalled the steep hills of her youth, with swift flowing waters rushing into lakes shaped like giant fingers that stretched across the landscape for miles. She recalled the first snowfalls of winter and the first rumbling thunderstorms in early spring. And then there were those wonderful, long walks with her grandmother. She remembered her first kiss, and losing her virginity to the football hero in the eternal mist beneath Ithaca Falls. And no matter where she walked in her old hometown, she always found herself staring up at the great university on East Hill.

What is it that makes a woman sit down and write a letter to her first beau after so many years have gone by? Maybe it took a bad marriage, but something stirred deep inside of her as she neared the fortieth year of her life. She wanted desperately to reach back through time and grab hold of some of the magic from her youth.

Katelyn penned the letter longhand, with slow, loving strokes, and with words that had been etched in her memory a lifetime ago. More and more as she wrote she longed for home in the hills above Cayuga's waters. This was a yearning she had never expected. When she was finished with the letter, when she was confident she had made a complete fool of herself, she addressed it to the bright and athletic detective at the New York City Police Department. She even went as far as putting a postage stamp on the envelope. She would, of course, never mail the thing. She told herself it was simply an exercise in recovery. Therapy. She placed the letter on a console table near her front door, where she eyed it each and every day.

Then one day the letter was gone. Katelyn had told how she panicked. She was even more horrified when she learned that her soon-to-be-ex-husband, who had noticed the letter sitting there on his way out the door, picked it up and handed it to the mailman.

Hello Darling,

I hope you don't mind my writing you after all these years. I read an article on you and all of the wonderful things you are doing with the New York City police department. What a terribly fascinating job you must have. My God, the things you must see. How do you keep from losing your mind? I remember my grandmother taking us on the train to the city. She loved it there. Said the city was timeless, and that in her youth she had once fallen in love with a New York City police detective. The canyons of Manhattan. I was in awe, but I couldn't imagine ever living there. In those days I could not imagine living anywhere other than our Ithaca. It really was a magical place to grow up, wasn't it? I have not been back in years. But my mother is old now and too often ill and she can no longer make the long trip out here to Oregon, so I may be back that way soon. Is there any chance you'll be in town?

You seem to have put your troubles from the war years behind you and built a career. And what a career you're having. I'm proud of you. I'm sure all of Ithaca is proud of you. Yes, as I said, I've read all about you, though nobody would lend me that book of yours. Not for us non-cops is what I was told. But I'm a pretty tough cookie. I'll bet I could handle it.

My marriage is over. Thank God. I stayed in it way too long. I ended up living with a ghost of the man I married. Like any colossal blunder, one wonders where it all went wrong. Isn't it funny how the mistakes we make when we are young follow us the rest of our lives?

Anyway, I hope this letter finds you well, and that I haven't made too big a fool of myself for writing to you after all these years. It would be nice to hear from you.

Love,
Katelyn

Nothing can be more flattering to a man than when an old love looks him up years later. The ultimate compliment. The ex-detective from New York City carefully folded the timeless letter and returned it to the breast pocket over his heart. Then he set off across the spring meadow for the barn. For the world of make believe.

NAMING A SUSPECT

The two men started down Campus Road, the American elms towering over them. Days had passed since the murder, with still no arrest.

"Tell me more about this Bobby Bill."

H.W. Hightower viewed the blue sky hanging overhead, and then the menacing clouds that were forever forming over the lake. He walked hurriedly, a load of books in his arms, term papers separating the pages. The old man had more energy than men half his age. Another rally had been scheduled on Libe Slope. Father Dougal and his Moral Way crowd. The president emeritus was not invited to speak. In fact, he was being fingered for the years of blasphemy and debauchery that had led up to the murder. Still, he felt obligated to attend, if only to observe and to listen.

"Bobby Bill," he answered, "was one of Cornell's first All-American boys. Captain of the football team, and national champions in the year 1915. He also had a sharp academic's mind." Here he hesitated, remembering back to that championship season. "Then in his last year here, he captained the eleven to a record of nine wins and one loss. We might have been headed to the Rose Bowl had it not been for that one loss."

"Who did they lose to?"

"*We* lost to Harvard. The Crimson eleven were all but unbeatable in those years. Still, if anybody could beat them . . . it was the Ghost Runner, Bobby Bill, and his Big Red teammates."

"And why do you think the Ghost Runner and his Big Red teammates lost?"

"The rain, mostly. The game was played here in Ithaca late in the season. It was cold and rainy. The field was a quagmire. By the end of the first half, from up in the stands, you couldn't tell one player from the next. Twenty-two indistinguishable men caked in mud."

"And Bobby Bill?"

"He played a great game, as I remember it. Played his heart out. Perhaps literally."

"How do you mean?"

"There were rumors about a romance gone awry. Perhaps a break-up the night before the game. Anyway, near the end of the fourth quarter he ran for a touchdown all the way into the Woods in the south end zone . . . and he disappeared."

Evan Murphy picked up his step, trying to keep pace with the old man. "Bobby Bill's famous disappearing act."

"You've heard of it?"

"I saw a similar act in the war."

They hurried by the massive Barton Hall, which had served as an airplane hangar during the Great War. The ROTC trained there. Cornell had provided over four thousand commissioned officers for the war effort, and 264 Cornell men had lost their lives in that first ever world war.

"Your cynicism is unwarranted, Captain Murphy. In his years at Cornell, Bobby Bill purported himself as a gentleman, a serious student, and a great athlete . . . and in that order."

"And if he were alive today, this Bobby Bill would be about the same age as this John W. Alden . . . isn't that correct?"

"May I remind you that due to his amnesia, we do not know Mr. Alden's exact age."

"And may I remind you that Mr. Alden is not claiming amnesia. On the contrary, he's been quite emphatic about who he is. And where he's from."

"That being the case . . . yes, Bobby Bill and Mr. Alden would today, I guess, be in the same age range."

"Don't you think it's time to confront Mr. Alden about his identity?"

"For what purpose?"

"Because he's a suspect in a student's murder."

Hightower stopped cold, taken aback. "You certainly don't believe Mr. Alden is capable of such a ghastly crime?"

"Mr. Alden all but predicted that ghastly crime."

"Mr. Alden," Hightower told him, "came to Ithaca in search of a killer."

"Yes, a killer who has no more records than Mr. Alden. A serial killer, no less, with a political agenda. Now if I'm putting this story together correctly, didn't those suffragist murders back before the war . . . didn't they begin about the time this Bobby Bill of yours disappeared?"

"Mere coincidence. Now how about one of our football coaches, a colored man who has devoted his life to the university, being beaten to within an inch of his life out at that movie studio barn?"

"He's on my list of people to be interviewed."

"I should hope so." Hightower hurried on, rushing past students on their way to the big rally. "I admit the past six months are a puzzle I have yet to solve, but I firmly reject your theories regarding Mr. Alden. He's here to help."

"You're an academic, Mr. Hightower. Are you familiar with *Occam's razor*?"

They came to a stone foot bridge that brooked a stream alongside Stately Hall. Tulips were in bloom on the banks. Hightower halted on the bridge and again checked the sky, calculating how far and how fast he had to walk before the sun disappeared and the rain began to fall. "Before I was a university president, I was a scientist. Yes, I know of *Occam's razor.* Though I am surprised a policeman would know of the principle, no offense intended."

"None taken."

"*Occam's razor* is often expressed in Latin as *lex parsimoniae* and is attributed to the fourteenth-century English theologian and Franciscan friar Father William of Ockham. His exact words were . . . *'entities must not be multiplied beyond necessitate.'*"

"Yeah well, in plain old cop talk it means the obvious answer is the answer."

"A simplistic interpretation of the principle, to be sure."

"The Irish have an even more simplistic interpretation of the principle. Don't introduce leprechauns into the equation, unless necessary."

"I can assure you Ithaca is leprechaun free. Ghosts, yes, but no leprechauns."

The state police captain pulled his fedora down a notch to keep the sun from his eyes. He fished a pack of Lucky Strikes out of his coat pocket. Stuck a smoke between his lips. Then he returned his right hand to the coat pocket and pulled out a small silver lighter. With a quick flick of his wrist a flame danced to life, and he used it to light the cigarette. Replaced the lighter in the pocket. All of this was done with a fluidity of motion. He sucked the smoke into his lungs and then blew it into the air.

"Take a look around, President Hightower, at your precious university. You have a charlatan in the guise of a visiting professor giving nonsensical lectures to students about time travel and future events, plus *modern* police work. You have a doctor in a laboratory up there on the hill collecting and preserving the brains of the condemned and the destitute. You have a motion picture company running around your campus making movies about murder and mayhem, starring your own two nieces, who, by the way, claim membership in a covenant of witches. For some bizarre reason you have organ music playing at midnight. And you have a Scottish priest of some sort up there in that haunted castle you call a chapel organizing rallies and preaching eternal damnation for the whole damn lot of you. And now you have the headless corpse of the son of a United States senator. One of your own students. Is it any wonder the politicians in Albany and the newspapers in Manhattan look at Cornell University and shake their heads in bafflement, if not outright contempt?"

"With all respect, Captain, I think what we have here is not only a difference of opinion . . . but a difference in class."

"Yes, all of you are oh-so-smart and I'm just a dumb, Irish, one-armed cop."

Hightower hurried along. "I do not buy your dumb Irish cop act any more than I bought Mr. Alden's dumb Irish cop act. Do they teach that routine at police school? Now if you'll pardon me, I'd like to arrive at that rally before the rain. Will you be attending?"

"I might stop by. Give a listen." He flicked some ash to the ground. "Where is this football stadium I keep hearing about . . . the one where Bobby Bill disappeared?"

"Just follow Campus Road down the hill. You'll see the Crescent." And the old man left the police detective standing near the Collegetown Bridge.

THE RALLY

By 1929 America's universities had been divided into three distinct types. The private, endowed universities. The great state universities. And Cornell. Not only was the university on East Hill separated from the rest of New York, it was physically separated from the very town it sat in, looking down on lowly Ithaca from a perch 447 feet above Cayuga's waters.

By the time H.W. Hightower arrived on the steps of the library, ahead of the rain, the big Moral Way rally was already underway. Libe Slope was packed from top to bottom with students, faculty, and townsfolk, all of them standing and straining their necks to hear the speakers. The size of the rally was monumental when compared to the modest rally of only a month earlier, when he and John Alden had limped across campus together for the first time.

Libe Slope was just that, a gently sloping hill before the Cornell Library. It was the beating heart of the campus. The place to meet. The place to rally. The place to party. In just four weeks' time would come "Slope Day," a tradition observed by students who wanted to blow off steam on the last day of spring semester, mostly by consuming alcohol and shouting obscenities. On Halloween night the slope was literally a grass bed of depravity. But the winds of change that were blowing across America were also blowing across the campus on East Hill. Many believed the Roaring '20s had gone way too far. Even some progressives at Cornell were fed up with liberal ways. There had to be a better way, they argued. A more moral way.

On the brow of Libe Slope, at a microphone, stood Father Wallace Dougal, erect as a statue. H.W. Hightower winced at the sound of his voice. The invention of the modern microphone with large speakers that amplified the human voice was something a polite society could have done without. He found the loud, electronic voice shrill. It lacked the intimacy of radio, or the sincerity of a well-spoken lecture. Used before the masses, the modern microphone seemed to Hightower a diabolical tool.

The clouds were inching their way up the hill, but for now the sun still shone on the priest's face, as if he had been approved by God, revealing a silver-haired man with a noble, but craggy face, who used his ancient Scottish brogue to berate those who did not believe as fervently as he believed—a Catholic priest who cherished what he called *historical confirmations* of biblical events. He spoke with a criminal passion on the murder of Royal S. Copeland III.

"Should we be surprised," the priest told the crowd, "when women are allowed to wear their skirts at knee length? What's next, above the knee?" There was none of the snickering or shouts of derision that might have followed that remark only a few months ago. Hightower could see women in the crowd were feeling uncomfortable.

"Should we be surprised," bellowed Father Dougal, "when the laws prohibiting alcohol are blatantly disregarded? Should we be surprised when an American university actually forbids religion in its charter?" The crowd was growing loud and restless. "Should we be surprised when, under the guise of science, men are allowed to desecrate the human body?"

Now the crowd turned their attention to the windows of White Hall. Hell Hall. The figures of two slender men could be seen watching the rally in a second story window. There were angry shouts from the crowd of, "No! No!"

"And should we be surprised, my children, when a movie company is allowed to freely roam our campus, filming ungodly scenes of rape and torture?"

"No!" The crowd had been whipped into a frenzy. The president emeritus thought the only thing missing was the pitchforks.

"Shame on you, Cornell," the priest shouted into the microphone. His voice with all its Catholic certitude roared down the hill and across the Ithaca plain. "Infidel Cornell!"

COMING HOME

Disappointed in his search, John Alden closed the door on the world of things that are not what they appear to be. He had found no instrument of death in the barn. There was no sign of a blade that could have cleanly separated a man's head from his shoulders in one fell swoop. He walked the grounds of the fake French village in search of clues. In his own day he would have had a forensic team comb the grounds with a magnifying glass. Now all that he could afford the investigation was a visual inspection, and it revealed no death scene. No traces of blood besides those visible in the doorway. But they were movie makers. It was their job to bring an entire time back to life, only to tear it down and move on, leaving behind a mere black-and-white remembrance set in cellulose nitrate. Disappointed as he was, he had gotten to the film set ahead of the Ithaca police, and ahead of the one-armed cop from Albany.

At the edge of the fake village the time-traveling professor stopped and stared up at the modest spires that decorated East Hill. He could hear the shrill anger of a man screaming into a microphone. The fury of his voice as it echoed through the woods was at odds with the peaceful nature of the land.

It had been strange to come home again. For so many years he had believed he never would. New York City was exciting. The heart of the universe. Why, John Alden asked himself, after four years at Harvard and twelve years as a cop on the streets of New York City, would he ever want to return to the provincialism of Ithaca? Yet when he was released from Bellevue Hospital following weeks of dark dreamlessness, it was not the sounds of the city that beckoned him. It was instead the mystic pull of Cayuga's waters and the haunting echoes of what might have been that called him gently back to the hills of his youth. So he boarded a train at Grand Central Station and, as if traveling through time, came home to Ithaca, eventually accepting a teaching position at the university.

For months after his return he walked the scenic campus with tunnel vision, his destination in sight but never really seeing the world around him. He felt the urge to write. He began looking into the history of Ithaca, not knowing whether he simply wanted to write a local history book, or whether he wanted to take a stab at writing the great American novel. He found the years leading up to the Great Depression particularly interesting. Every now and then he thought of writing up the case that had sent him over the edge. True crime, they called it. All the true crime writers he knew lived in New York City. But he did not want to go back there. Besides, how do you write a story whose ending is still unknown? On most days he just longed for simpler times. A more simple life. Then he got the letter from Katelyn, forwarded to him in Ithaca by the New York City Police Department.

Some women are unchanging. They never age. Never really die. They travel through space and time without a blemish to their bodies or their souls. In the minds of the men who loved them in their youth, they remain pure and faultless. Near angelic. Such was the case with Katelyn Richter. He had not seen her since that night in Oregon, when at the point of a gun he woke her and her husband from a rainy night's sleep. Had it been nearly twenty years? He remembered standing in the doorway of her Oregon home, squeezing her tight and telling her how much he loved her, before setting out into a thankless night of never-ending drizzle. Since that night the emotionally wounded soldier had been a Harvard student, a graduate student, a New York City police detective, an acclaimed author, and an honored professor of criminal justice at a prestigious university. But through it all the pall of loneliness and the loss of what might have been never left him.

At heart, Ithaca is a small town. Deaths do not go unnoticed. The announcement of the passing of Marlene Richter in the spring of the year 2010 appeared in the *Ithaca Journal*. It said she was survived by her daughter, Katelyn, of Portland, Oregon. John Alden and the romantic fool in him carefully read the obituary.

It was on an exceptionally warm night, only a month earlier in 2010, when John Alden was ambling down Old Elmira Road from the university. Out of instinct, out of memory, he had stopped on the sidewalk before the girlhood home of Katelyn Richter and stared up the hill at the house. Sometime in the years that he had been gone the screens had been removed from the front porch. Now it was wide open. Inside the house, only one light was burning. The dim light appeared to be coming from the back of the house, in the kitchen. He put a foot on the first step, as if he might just go up the hill and knock on the door. He had gotten the letter Katelyn had written to him from Oregon, but he had yet to answer it.

"You made my daughter happy," came the old woman's voice, fighting for every breath. "Any fool could see how much."

John Alden was startled. Caught off guard. He had been a cop. He did not like being caught off guard. He snapped to attention. Now he could see her up there, the shadow of an old woman sitting in a rocking chair on the front porch. A cigarette in her hand. "I'm sorry, Mrs. Richter. I didn't see you there."

"Her husband was well-to-do, you know." Her raspy, elderly voice drifted down the hill, barely making it to his ears. "He played golf and tennis with the best and the brightest of Portland . . . is what I was told. I thought she was lucky to be admitted into that circle. We were always considered plain. That's why she never came back here. That's why when you came looking for her after the war . . . I told you to get lost." She laughed, a mean laugh. "I heard you took me up on it." John Alden watched as the tip of her cigarette glowed bright red in the night before fading back to orange. "It was sometime in those high school years when I noticed her beauty, and the effect she had on men. She was like her grandmother that way. Her grandmother was always filling her head with nonsense. They were a pair . . . those two. Real beauty skips a generation, you know. Katelyn never dated in high school, until you came along."

"I know."

"Of course you know. In high school you were one of them. Until her senior year, you never gave her a second look. She wore big, ugly glasses and she sang in the choir."

And those were the last words he heard the old woman choke out. *"She wore big, ugly glasses and she sang in the choir."* The old woman coughed up a lung, and John Alden turned and moved on down the sidewalk.

Then he was reading her obituary in the *Ithaca Journal*.

A MOTHER'S FUNERAL

The Revolutionary War-era cemetery rested above Heights Road, on the slopes of a hill that rolled down to Cayuga Lake. The trees and the grass were springtime green, thick and moist with new life. It was raining, not hard, just a steady wisp, much like that night in Portland when he last saw her. A small crowd stood around the casket that sat before an open grave. A pastor was reading from the Bible. "Ashes to ashes," and that kind of stuff, a requiem for an old woman who was born and raised in Ithaca, married in Ithaca, gave birth and raised a child in Ithaca, and at long last died alone in Ithaca.

"Our father who art in heaven…" John Alden mumbled along with the crowd, but he found little comfort in words from the Bible.

He saw her dressed in a sleek black dress, appearing more stylish than mournful. Somebody held an umbrella over her head, but raindrops still glistened in her hair. She was staring at the casket, an absence of tears in her eyes, but a lifetime of grief written across her face. A face forever young.

When the service at the burial site had concluded, he kept his distance and watched as long lost relatives and old friends expressed their condolences, giving Katelyn hugs, wishing her well, and then starting for their cars. He did not know what to say to her. He thought of turning and walking away. But then she spotted him. A smile broke across her face, one of those perpetual natural smiles that John Alden so admired. Katelyn Richter started his way.

"Hello, John Alden." She embraced him as an old friend, her mother's casket resting on the hill behind them.

"Hello, Katelyn." He stepped back and opened his coat. "I'm unarmed."

"I'm glad," she said with a mild laugh. She did not seem to care that a skit of rain was still falling, even as the clouds were breaking up over Cayuga Lake.

They were seldom apart after the day of the funeral. A life lost. A new life begun. Their marriage was a simple civil ceremony in the quiet town hall up the lake in Seneca Falls. It was almost anticlimactic, for they had already settled into living together. They moved into the white clapboard house on Old Elmira Road, a five-minute walk to the university. Katelyn went back to school. The college professor and the adult student. And every night when they went to bed, John Alden wrapped his arms around his beautiful wife and cupped his hand beneath her breast and drifted off to a dreamland he had never before known.

Because they were approaching middle age, their plan for a family was simple. They would have sex until their eyes watered. If Katelyn got pregnant—wonderful. If she never got pregnant—then they would become self-indulgent, world-traveling academics. Perhaps for the first time in his life, John Alden found himself happy. And he would have stayed that way, and life in this new century would have been good, if only his life as a cop had not returned to haunt him.

THE CRESCENT

At last he got to see the famed crescent, the unique crescent-shaped football stands that seated twenty-one thousand fans for the games at Crescent Field. "Are you the man they call *Night Train*?" the Albany cop wanted to know.

He was a large, colored man and he was working a rake with a religious zeal at the fifty-yard line when Evan Murphy approached him at Crescent Field. Murphy had been told that besides being an assistant football coach, the man was also the athletic trainer and the groundskeeper—a quiet man, it was said, who never got the glory but was more a part of the Big Red football team than any white coach could ever be. His hair was flecked with gray now, and Murphy counted as many age lines on his face as there were yard lines on the gridiron. There were also on his face the remnants of welts and bruises. Still, the man maintained the mien of an athlete, with the broad shoulders of a linebacker. "Marvin would be my Christian name," he answered, "the name my mama gave me way back in another time. But the boys here have been calling me Night Train for so many years . . . that's the name I come to use. How'd you'd end up in Ithaca, they'd ask me. I told 'em . . . I took the night train from Brooklyn. The name just stuck."

"That was quite a beating you took out at that barn."

"I played me some real football back in the day, back before the reforms President Teddy Roosevelt ordered. In those days you could take a man's head off. That was some mean football. Monster gave me that beating out at the barn snuck up on a sleepy old fool . . . that's all."

Evan Murphy observed the rake and the turf. "Getting an early start on it, I see."

Coach Night Train did not look up. Concentrated on his work. His field. He was as comfortable and confident with a rake in his hands as was a quarterback with a football. "Those damn movie people were here the other day making their silly movie in the middle of my field. Actually painted the dirt green. Ain't that a laugh. Damn movies are black and white." He waved a hand across the dirt in front of him. "This here is where the game is played," he told his visitor, "between the forties. Hard to keep grass here during the season, so in the springtime it's like bakin' a cake. You want to run your rake over it ever so gentle like, more like a massage than a good raking. Work the dirt. Smooth it out. Then you lay down your seed. Let the rain fall. Let the sun bake it. And watch it grow. A blade of grass is a precious thing on a football field. We get us some onion rain and this place will green up real pretty."

"Onion rain?"

"That rain that falls unexpectedly in late spring, after the onions have been planted. Could be on its way today." He stopped his work and leaned on the rake, resignation playing out on his face. "Then it all be nothing but mud come November, about the time we play Princeton in the finale, with the season on the line."

"Coach Night Train, I'm with the state police in Albany."

"I know who you are. It's a big college in a small town. You're here about that rich boy's murder?"

"I am."

"Damn shame, that business." He sized up the cop standing before him. "Now you look like you could have been a nasty ole guard, or maybe a fullback."

"Actually, I'm more of a baseball fan, but I used to play some two-handed touch."

The groundskeeper glanced down at the empty sleeve pressed into the coat pocket. "Is that a joke?"

"Yes, it is," said Murphy, without cracking a smile.

But Coach Night Train laughed. It was a loud, honest laugh. "That's a good one. A one-armed man saying he played two-handed touch."

Murphy removed his felt hat to wipe the sweat from his brow. Then he kicked at the ground while making note of how dark and moist the dirt appeared. "You have to be the only Negro in Ithaca."

"Yes, sir. Sometimes seems that way. Every once in a while there'll be some colored students here at the college, but they'd be those uppity niggers from New York City, or maybe Philly, or Buffalo. They all see me out here with my black hands in this beautiful black dirt and then they don't want anything to do with me. Hell, I probably read me more books than all of them put together. Fact is, President Hightower let me the use of his own personal library up at the big house. Yes, sir, read me some good books up there. Books you ain't never going to find in no normal library."

"And they tell me you've been here a long time."

The old football coach searched the stadium around him. "Been more than thirty years now. I've seen me some of the best damn football in America."

The state police captain knelt down and grabbed a handful of the black dirt. Ran it between his fingers, as if he might have grown up on a farm. "I was just in the hall back there admiring the old photographs and all the trophies. Do you remember a student athlete named Bobby Bill . . . they tell me he was a favorite of yours?"

Coach Night Train smiled at the memories. "Ole Bobby Bill. That boy was a legend, a living legend. I wasn't there to see it myself, but tale has it he once dove seventy feet into a gorge pool to rescue a drowning dog."

"And then?"

The athletic trainer and groundskeeper brought his focus back to the cop. Back to the present. "I thought I heard tell Bobby Bill was killed in the war."

Murphy shook the dirt from his fingers and stood. "There's no record of that."

Coach Night Train turned and pointed into the south end zone, where the tall stately pines served as an evergreen backdrop known as the Woods. "When they built the stadium here," he explained, "they were careful not to touch that big ole grove of trees down there."

"It's beautiful. I've never seen a stadium quite like it."

"Ain't no place like it. Anyway, last time I seen Bobby Bill, he ran into those woods, a football under his arm. Kind of the way I like to remember him."

"Bobby Bill's famous disappearing act. Like his magic act?"

Coach Night Train laughed. "Yes, sir. The boy had him a magic act . . . some of the stupidest damn tricks you'd ever want to see. But he did have this one trick . . ."

"Where he would disappear after sitting in a chair with a blanket thrown over him?"

"Yes, sir, that's the one. I played his assistant. I'd be the man up on stage who would throw the blanket over him. Seemed that boy could disappear for real. Never explained the trick to me." Here the coach seemingly got lost in those days gone by. "Then one Saturday afternoon, don't remember what year that was, but it was the end of his time here . . . he breaks away on one of his long touchdown runs and then disappears into those woods. Guess he just kept on running."

"Do you know why?"

"I heard tell about a girl . . . Kate-something was her name. She dropped Bobby Bill like a muddy football and ran off to Oregon with some rich boy . . . is what I heard."

"Seem to be a hundred stories about how the man disappeared. Do you think you'd know Ole Bobby Bill if you saw him again?"

Coach Night Train laid the rake across his shoulders and hung his arms from it. Stood there at the fifty-yard line like a scarecrow. "Oh, I don't know about that. They come here just big ole boys, you know, and four years later they leave here strapping young men, educated and all. Then they all come back for a game some ten, twenty years down the road and they're grown men with boys all their own. I hardly recognize 'em. Time does funny things to a man. It changes him, you know?"

"Have you ever seen this professor who calls himself John Alden?"

"Oh yeah, that crazy man says he's from the future, been limping around campus with a gold-headed walking cane. I heard him speak one night at President's House. Says a colored man is one day gonna be the President of the United States." Coach Night Train shook his head. "Ain't that a laugh. Yeah, he came to question me about the beating I took out at the barn. Said he'd been out there."

"He said he'd been out at the barn . . . the movie studio?"

"Yes, sir."

"He say what he found?"

"He say what he didn't find. That guillotine."

Murphy stepped into him. "They had a guillotine out there?"

"Yes, sir. Never saw them use it . . . 'course I was only there after everybody went home . . . but it was standing all spooky-like in the back of the barn."

"And now it's gone?"

Coach Night Train pointed to the welt beneath his eye. "Don't know . . . ain't been back since."

Murphy was angry that the alleged professor of criminal justice had once again beaten him to a crime scene. Not only that, but now he knew there had indeed been a guillotine in Ithaca, just as Alden had suggested. "Might this John Alden character be the same Bobby Bill?"

Coach Night Train raised an eyebrow at the question. "I heard someone else suggesting something 'bout that. Can't say I'd recognize him, though. He sure didn't recognize me."

"So when he first saw you, there was no look of recognition?"

"No, sir, none at all. I thought he was kind of a glassy-eyed man, you know, always staring beyond you. A colored man gets used to that, but this was different. Makes you wonder what he sees."

"Did you have any other contact with him?"

"There was one afternoon early this spring during a toad-strangler when I had my truck parked back there at the north end of the field . . ."

"Excuse me," said Murphy, baffled by the language, "a toad-strangler?"

"Yeah, that's a heavy downpour in this part of the state. Rain off the lakes. Comes down in buckets. You don't want to get yourself caught standing in a toad-strangler. And if you're in the gorges . . . whoa!"

"I see. Go on."

"Yeah, so I'm sitting in my truck waiting for a break in the weather, 'cause I ain't going out there. But somebody was. I saw me a shadow of man standing right here at the fifty-yard line in the pouring rain all by himself, leaning on a walking cane, looking up and down the field like maybe he once owned it. You can always tell the old players. They kind of tiptoe onto the field, like they're in a church maybe, and they just stand here. I think that's what he might have been doing."

"How long did this man stand here?"

"Till the rain let up some. Then he limps away."

"Into those woods?"

"Maybe. Rain like that made it hard to see."

Two Cops on Death Row

There was no stopping the clock. The minute hand ticked past 9:00 p.m. The Nor'easter kept closing in. And so did the execution. Thunder over the Palisades grew ever louder and lightning flashed with increasing intensity, illuminating from shore to shore the dark waters of the Hudson River. The crowd that had gathered below the walls of the notorious prison kept one eye trained on the storm clouds and one eye fixed on the narrow window of the death house. Cell 17.

Inside Sing Sing Captain Evan Murphy took the long walk down the elongated hallway. The felt hat he wore like a helmet stayed on his head. The empty sleeve of his suit coat stayed pressed into his hip pocket. There was a bulge in his right coat pocket, but it was not his gun. He had been relieved of his revolver at the gate. A giant window in the gloomy hall just outside the cells allowed him to see the exercise yard, and beyond that the section of the death house that held the execution chamber, known among prisoners as the "Dance Hall." He was sandwiched between two prison guards. It was obvious from their heavy gait and their deliberate demeanor that, like the prisoners themselves, these men did not like cops. The large guard leading the way stopped before Cell 17. He tore open the leper-squint and peeked inside. Slammed it closed. Then he found a skeleton key on a large key ring and inserted it into the brass lock. The heavy door swung open with a loud creak. The creaking hinges were by design.

Murphy stepped before the cell. Thunder shook the walls. The prisoner was lying awake on his bunk, his head beneath the window, his white-socked feet to the door. What struck the state police captain first was the man's physical appearance. He was thin and pale, with a ghastly pallor of the skin. Almost ghostly. His hair had been cropped short, and there was a glassy gleam to his eyes. The muscles on his once-manly frame had all but withered away, so unlike the manifesta-

tion of the hale and hearty college professor he had met at the crime scene that day in Ithaca. As the years passed the police captain had observed that every inmate locked away in the death house eventually wilted away, as if stricken with a deadly cancer. And each and every one of them became mentally disturbed to some degree. If they weren't a bit off-kilter when they arrived, they were certainly off-kilter by the time they took the long walk. Some heard voices. Others saw visions. A few went stark raving mad. The condemned man in Cell 17 claimed he saw the future.

"Ten minutes," said the large, surly guard. "Door remains open. We remain here."

With that the guards stepped back to the tall window, each one of them flanking the door, allowing the cop and the prisoner a tincture of privacy.

Murphy stepped inside the cell. Gave it the once over. A flash of blue lightning lit up the window. Grimy green walls. Gray concrete floor. Black bars over a rusty screen. A dim light bulb. A bunk. A toilet. "You don't deserve this."

Thunder continued to rumble. "I do not."

"Yet here you are."

"Yes, and much to my chagrin, here you are. You're persistent. I'll give you that."

"I'm a cop," he said. "I brought you something." The police captain reached into his coat pocket and pulled out a bottle of Coca-Cola. "The warden OK'd it." After watching the slightest of smiles steal across the prisoner's face, Murphy held up the Coke bottle and signaled to the guards. The large, surly guard with the skeleton keys rummaged through his pants pockets for a utility knife with a bottle opener. He entered the cell. Popped open the Coke bottle and then returned to his place at the window outside the cell, fingering the bent pop bottle cap in his hand.

The prisoner sat up on the bunk. Murphy handed him the cold drink, still wet with condensation. The prisoner took a giant swig, choking on it. It was as if the Coke brought him back to life. He wiped his mouth and put his feet up on the bunk and leaned back against the wall, like a man in a bar enjoying his first beer in months. He used the bottle to point up at the window. "Hell of a storm coming."

"I was listening to the radio on the drive in. It's wreaking havoc up and down the Eastern seaboard."

"Any power failures?"

Murphy laughed. "None in New York . . . that I know of." The state cop glanced out the window at the approaching weather, then down at the crowd gathered below. In the stormlight he thought them pathetic. "The governor has ruled out a stay of sentence," he said, turning back to the prisoner. "Besides the shooting, you remain a suspect in the death of the senator's son."

"I'm not expecting any forbearance."

"What are you expecting?"

"Death."

The prisoner spoke with a melancholy consistency, and Murphy was exasperated by the answer. "Was this your plan all along?"

"My plan?"

"In your mind . . . was this your plan to get home . . . back to where you claim to have come from?"

The condemned man took another swig from the bottle. "Hightower once told me that it took an ungodly storm and a bolt of electricity to get me here . . . and it'll take another ungodly storm and a bolt of electricity to get me home."

"What got you here was a tumble over Ithaca Falls, and had it been up to me, I'd have thrown you back in the drink." Murphy unbuttoned his suit coat, probably as relaxed and informal as he ever got. "Speaking of Hightower, he says he has a word for you."

"Let's hear it."

"Petrichor?"

"The word can be found in the Oxford English Dictionary," the prisoner said, educating his visitor. "Petrichor is the smell accompanying the first rain after a long period of warm, dry weather."

"Why didn't I know that? And I'm guessing you have a made-up word from the future going back to him."

"Googol."

"Googol. And what in hell is a googol?"

"It's the numeral one, followed by one hundred zeros. First known use . . . 1938."

"Six years hence."

The prisoner stole another swig of Coke. "In my day," he said, recalling his future past, "with a different spelling, it becomes a verb. To Google."

"You're crazy, Professor."

"And you're a fraud, Murphy."

"How so?"

"You're still not convinced of my guilt."

"I'm not convinced you were competent to stand trial. You belong in Bellevue . . . not Sing Sing."

"Yet here I am."

"Tell me . . . in this futuristic fairy tale of yours . . . do you get back in time to save your wife?"

"Probably not . . . but I think I'll come to accept her death."

"Because you killed him?"

He chugged the Coke, then leaned forward. "Yes, because in the end, I killed that son of a bitch. He'll never again be a problem in your time . . . or mine."

"But if there was a second shooter in the clock tower . . . and by that I mean you being the first shooter . . . then your man, your serial killer, is still out there."

"No . . . the shooter in the clock tower was just a misguided youth. I got my man."

"You keep telling yourself that, Professor."

Then a voice bellowed behind them. "Time, gentlemen! Time!"

"Are you a witness?" the prisoner asked.

"I am," said the one-armed cop.

"Then I guess I'll see you out there."

Captain Evan Murphy of the New York State Police stepped out of the cell. But just before the surly guard closed the door on their visit, he turned back to the prisoner, who was still sitting on the bunk, savoring his Coke. The smaller guard stepped into the cell to collect the bottle. "Humor me," Murphy said to the prisoner. "If you should somehow get back to this future New York of yours . . . will you find out what became of me? What kind of life I lived?"

The condemned man raised his pop bottle in salute. "You're a fraud, Murphy." Then he stole the last swig of Coke, wiped his mouth, and handed over the empty bottle. "But, yes, I'll look into it."

The Head of the Water

Captain Evan Murphy stuck his finger beneath the chin of the decapitated head of Royal S. Copeland III and tilted it upward so that his detective's eyes could get a better look at the damn thing. The boy's head sat on a table next to the film editing machine. The head itself, bloodless in its current manifestation, appeared to have been separated from its torso at the neck with one swift cut, the efficient work of a guillotine. Just as John Alden had guessed. The edit room of the Ithaca Motion Picture Company was built into the loft of the barn that housed their makeshift studio. Captain Evan Murphy stood before the table and examined both the head and the machine. The world of make believe.

The head did not really look all that much like the Copeland boy, more of an approximation, but then the head was made of wax, and it probably appeared real enough on film. He let the wax head rest on its severed neck and turned his attention to the editing machine. It was an upright Moviola, with four different reels winding through two dozen rollers. The relevant footage had been loaded for him. All that was left for him to do, he was told, was stick his detective's eyes into the viewer and feed the machine the workprint, a positive copy of the film negative.

His moviemaking experience began.

The first scene he views is a master shot. The chalkboard held before the camera reads: **Execution. Scene 1. Take 1.** It is a beheading in a French village in another time. On a high platform before a crazed crowd stands a guillotine. An executioner appears in a mask, a floppy hat, and a black cape. The man playing the part is Dr. Victor Ecarius of the infamous body parts collection in Hell Hall. The casting is pitch-perfect.

Next, a horse-pulled cart arrives with the prisoner. Cornell student Royal S. Copeland III is indeed playing the part of the condemned man. He is dragged, kicking and screaming, up the high platform and over to the base of the guillotine, where he is strapped in. Face up.

The executioner snorts a white powder, undoubtedly meant to be cocaine. A nice touch, thinks Murphy. Most people think the cocaine problem arrived with the twentieth century. No, cocaine had been a drug problem for hundreds of years. Hell, Sherlock Holmes sniffed cocaine. The state cop continues to thread film through the Moviola. He watches intensely as Dr. Ecarius, in the dramatic guise of an executioner, throws the handle to the guillotine blade. The Copeland boy screams his head off. The crowd goes crazy.

And then the director yells, "Cut!"

There is a wild round of applause from the crowd. Everybody is clapping. Up on the platform the Copeland boy is unstrapped. He rises, smiling, head quite intact, and along with Dr. Ecarius, he takes a bow before the extras. On film, everybody is having fun.

"Where is this guillotine?" Murphy asked the director.

"It was dismantled after the scene and used to build something else. Hey, that's Hollywood."

But they were not in Hollywood. They were in Ithaca. Murphy stuck his face back into the edit machine.

The next shot is a close-up of Royal Copeland screaming his head off as the blade supposedly plunges downward toward his neck. He is an incredibly handsome young man, even getting his head chopped off. After the take he is unstrapped and somebody brings him a glass of water to ease his ailing throat. Again the crowd gives him a round of applause. He waves to them.

After that scene comes a close-up of the blade descending.

The last scene Murphy views is another master shot. Same crowd. Same scene. It is **Take 2**. This time it is obvious to Murphy that the body strapped beneath the guillotine is a mannequin. A dummy. Ecarius snorts his cocaine. He throws the handle. The blade falls. The dummy's wax head is separated from its torso. It rolls across the stage to the feet of the executioner. Ecarius picks up the head by the hair and displays it before the crowd. Again, the crowd is ecstatic.

Captain Evan Murphy of the New York State Police backed out of the viewer and rubbed his eyes. Amazing. In just a matter of seconds he was able to leave 1929 and step back in time, into another century. He suddenly had a new appreciation for the wonder of film. He stared hard at the wax head resting on the table.

THE ROWBOAT

According to Iroquois legend, New York's Finger Lakes were created when the Great Spirit reached out to bless the land and left behind an imprint of his hand. Cornell geologists, however, told a different story. They said the six long and deep parallel lakes were carved from the glaciers of the last ice age. But there were certain effects left in the wake of the glaciers that science could never explain, and so it was that during the American centuries the cavernous waters of Cayuga Lake became the most mysterious finger on the Great Spirit's giant hand.

John Alden and Caitlin Dewey set out onto the mystifying waters from the Cornell boathouse. It was warm. Roll up shirtsleeves warm. The idyllic weather had springtime love written all over it. They floated outward with still plenty of time to enjoy the sunset. Then John Alden began to row north, slowly up the lake.

Ithaca sat at the southern tip of Cayuga Lake, the longest of the famed lakes. Almost 40 miles in length. At its widest the water was 3.5 miles from shore to shore. Its deepest point was 435 feet. Because of its size and depth, the lake rarely froze over in the wintertime. And ever since the first Iroquois settled along its shores, people had reported strange, dull rumblings coming from the lake's depths. The sounds were usually heard at dusk in the spring and summer and were most distinct midway down the lake. The Iroquois believed the rumblings were the voice of an angry god. Early settlers considered them omens of disaster. Cornell scientists tried to attribute the booming noises to the belching of natural gas released from the rock rifts at the bottom of the lake. Historians had a more idealistic explanation. The Guns of Cayuga theory. The dull booms were the distant echoes of the guns that General George Washington had ordered used to lay waste to the British-loving Iroquois Nation and its settlements around the lakes.

Their outing in the rowboat seemed a fantasy, like a scene out of a Hollywood romance. Not a cloud graced the sky. He asked her about the afternoon matinee they had just seen.

"I thought it was a bit risqué," Caitlin told him.

He was surprised by her answer. "Why?"

She seemed surprised by his surprise. "Why? I mean, it was a movie about infidelity. Shameless adultery. Divorce. It was sad."

"It was about young couples making mistakes, marrying the wrong people, and then trying to correct their mistake years later."

"And that is what you saw?"

"I saw a movie about unrequited love, betrayed friendships, and the disease of alcoholism." John Alden looked up at her baffled face. "I've always liked that movie. I found it bold and insightful, especially considering the year in which it was made."

"John, that movie was made this year—1929."

"My point exactly."

Caitlin Dewey shook her head in mock disgust. "I'm afraid I don't share your enthusiasm for the movies. Like that movie they're shooting here. God only knows what kind of mayhem they're up to . . . including your two girlfriends?"

"You mean Hightower's twin nieces? Why would you suggest something like that?"

"I've seen the way they look at you."

"I'm old enough to be their father. For that matter, I'm old enough to be your father."

"Nonsense."

"And how old do you think I am?"

Caitlin Dewey had the latest edition of the *Ithaca Journal* on her lap. "Isn't that what we're all trying to figure out?"

"You couldn't leave the newspaper behind?" he asked her with a playful grin.

Her beauty was striking. She was dressed in white. White blouse. White skirt. The outfit set off her eyes and her hair, which reflected the colors of autumn. There was something inimitable about this Caitlin girl, a timelessness John Alden could not resist. He felt immeasurably drawn to her. She kicked a pair of white sandals from her feet. Now barefoot, there was excitement in her voice as she read the newspaper. "It's all about the riots and the big fire at Auburn prison," she said, staring at a front page photo of a prison building engulfed in flames. "But then, if you are who you say you are . . . you should have known about these riots."

John Alden was dressed in a white shirt with rolled-up sleeves and a pair of khakis. Tennis shoes with no socks. He kept on rowing. "I did know of them. Not the specific date, but the Auburn riots and fire of 1929 led to some badly needed prison reform."

"So you just let it happen?"

"When it comes to the future, I have to examine all of the angles."

Caitlin voiced her doubt with a sigh, then buried her face in the newspaper. "It says here one of the largest employers of the Finger Lakes district is the Auburn state prison, on the north end of Cayuga Lake. It was established in 1816. It is New York's oldest prison with a long, grim history, of which this fire is only the latest embarrassing chapter."

While he gently rowed the boat, John Alden recalled his college studies on the history of America's penal system. "Auburn prison was the first facility in America to confine its prisoners to cells. I believe the cells were three-and-a-half-feet wide, seven feet long, and seven feet high. The smallest possible space in which a human being could both stand up and lie down."

"Yes, and it says here the traditional American prison uniform, consisting of horizontal black-and-white stripes, originated at Auburn prison."

"That's true. And the prisoners were all shackled together, marched to a work site and not allowed to speak a single word. Their punishments amounted to torture."

Caitlin finished the article. "Here at the end it says . . . 'in 1890 at Auburn the first person in the world, a murderer from Buffalo, was put to death in an electric chair. Then in 1916, all executions were shifted to Sing Sing.'" When she looked up, John Alden had stopped rowing. His face was flushed. "What's wrong?" she asked.

"Nothing," he told her, shaking his head. "Just a moment of *déjà vu*. I'm guessing you know what that is?"

"It's French," she answered. "It means *already seen*. The term was coined by a French psychic researcher named Emile Boirac in his book *The Future of Psychic Sciences*. Sigmund Freud calls experiences of *déjà vu* the *uncanny*. But since you claim to be from the future, your premonitions can't really be *uncanny* . . . can they?"

"Are you making fun of me, Caitlin Dewey?"

"Not in the least."

John Alden stuck the oars back in the water. "The most likely explanation of *déjà vu* is not that it's an act of premonition or prophecy, but rather that it's an anomaly of memory. It only gives the impression that an experience is being recalled."

Caitlin Dewey tucked the newspaper beneath her seat. She motioned to the top of the hill. "Perhaps, but there are researchers right here at Cornell who are trying to establish a link between *déjà vu* and mental illness. Specifically . . . schizophrenia, anxiety, and multiple personality disorder."

"Multiple personality disorder. There's a mouthful."

"It describes persons who think they're two different people sharing the same body."

"I know what it is. But in the future it's called dissociative identity disorder. Is that what they're saying about me now?"

"Before the murder you were the subject of ridicule and derision. The Pilgrim."

"And since the murder?"

"Now you scare people. The Suspect."

"You sound like Captain Murphy."

Water from the oars splashed her, and Caitlin Dewey wiped the droplets from her arms. "I know this isn't nice to say . . . but I don't like men who are missing body parts."

"That's not politically correct."

"What does that mean?"

"Speech marked by a progressive attitude on issues of race, gender, and physical disabilities. May I remind you that your new governor leads from a wheelchair?"

"So you think those stories are true?"

"They're true. Polio. His legs are useless. Any photo you see of him standing . . . he's being supported by braces. Basically propped up."

"I believe then the newspapers are complicit in a cover-up. And to think he's going to be our commencement speaker."

"How did you end up here at Cornell?" he asked her.

"Oh, my mother was from Ithaca. I grew up hearing about the legends of Cornell, and of the gorges that lead down to the lake. Mother made the place seem almost mythical. She met my father while vacationing . . . and they lit out for Oregon. Father was from Portland."

He rowed further up the lake, the verdant green hills silently slipping by, while the spires of Cornell University grew smaller and smaller by the oar stroke. "Will you be going home for the summer . . . back to Oregon?"

"No," she told him. "Mother is coming here for commencement. I'd like you to meet her."

"Yes, I'd like to meet your mother."

"All right then, but no talk of the future," she warned him.

The visiting professor rowed hard, leaving the university on the hill behind them. "All right," he agreed, "no talking to your mother about the future. Besides, every time I open my mouth to talk about future events . . . there is trouble."

"Then stop talking about future events."

The setting sun on his face felt like a gift from the gods. The exercise of rowing was stimulating. "Here's what we will do, Miss Dewey . . . I will tell you things of tomorrow, and you will explain how it is I know of these things today."

"That sounds fair. Let's play."

With every stroke they rowed deeper onto the lake, and on this day they were the only two people out on the water. He paused atop this watery isolation to contemplate life in the time ahead. The life he swore he once knew. "This very year," he said to her, "two men, working separately and independently, will transmit and isolate light in a vacuum tube. The Radio Corporation of America, known to you and me as RCA, will take this discovery and produce an invention called *television* . . . and life in America will never again be the same."

Caitlin Dewey shrugged her shoulders, unimpressed. "It's essentially radio, except with moving pictures. It's already being speculated on. If this discovery took place this year, then you probably came across it in a scientific journal, but instead of phrasing its potential as speculation, you state it as fact. It's a word game you play. You're very good at word games. What else have you got?"

John Alden admired her thinking, and her beauty, and he resumed his rowing. "A generation later, television is followed by the invention of personal computers . . . radio-sized boxes connected to keyboards, with one in virtually every home. These computers can crunch and compute millions of bits of information in a matter of seconds. And all of these personal computers are interconnected. Think about that . . . you merely type a question into your very own computer and within seconds you have a plethora of answers to choose from. Literally a world of information at your fingertips."

"Glorified adding machines."

"Caitlin, sweetie, I'm talking about a bit more than that."

"And do these computers ..."

"Personal computers."

"Yes . . . do these personal computers wipe out famine, stop wars, alleviate poverty, or put an end to crime? Do they make everybody rich and happy, with full employment and a four-day work week?"

The sun was beginning to set behind the pines on the western shore. Again John Alden stopped rowing and let the small boat drift north on Cayuga's waters. "No," he confessed, "they do none of those things."

"These personal computers of yours sound to me like nothing more than information and entertainment . . . neither of which is knowledge or enlightenment."

Just as the sun began to disappear in the west, the moon was beginning to show itself in the east, hanging like gossamer above the distant spires of the university. Caitlin pointed to the lunar sky. "Do we make it to the moon?"

"We do," he told her, staring up at it. "In 1960, a very young and handsome American president declares without doubt or reservation that we will put a man on the moon before the decade is out. And we do. It becomes one of the proudest moments in American history."

"And in your mind, John Alden, what becomes of this young, handsome American president?"

John Alden dropped his eyes. "He's assassinated." He thought about that for a somber moment. "It was supposed to be the Copeland boy," he said, almost talking to himself. "But apparently, from what I've read, if you kill a future president, a different future president simply takes his place."

"Ahh," she gasped, in mock surprise. "A fairy tale prince for a president, and a man walking on the moon. It's nothing but a romantic's version of the future. The assassination lends the tale tragedy, earning it a dose of reality. You're quite the storyteller."

Alden picked up the oars. "And you, Caitlin Dewey, are quite the cynic."

It was then they heard the booming noise. More like cannon fire. It rumbled from beneath the lake then bounced off the hills, tantamount to rolling thunder on a sunny day. The mysterious gunfire sound unnerved him. John Alden stuck his oar deep in the water, as if with one bold stroke he could propel the boat back to shore.

Caitlin Dewey glanced around at the peace and serenity of the whole scene now being disturbed by the fading rumble. She looked into the anxious eyes of John Alden. "But you grew up here. You've certainly heard this before."

"I have. That doesn't mean I like it. Let's get off the water."

He pulled hard on the oars, but the right oar got caught in a bed of long weeds floating just beneath the surface. It almost felt as if the weeds were pulling back. Finally the weeds released the oar and John Alden watched the face of the paddle slowly rise to the surface. But it was bringing something along with it. Something round and hard. Then, just before it broke the surface, John Alden could see the round object had eye sockets. It also had an open mouth and holes for a nose. Then the oar popped free of the water and thrust the round object up and into the boat.

Caitlin Dewey screamed so loud the echo of it outdid the cannon fire, bouncing off the hills and rolling crazily across the surface of the lake. At their feet between them was the decomposing head of Royal S. Copeland III. The cut at the neck was perfect.

Caitlin was standing now, trying to get away from the dead boy's head. She grabbed the newspaper and threw it at the decayed face. The boat was rocking recklessly from side to side.

"Sit down, Caitlin, you'll swamp the boat. Sit down!" John Alden ripped apart the pages of the newspaper and laid the front page over the head at the bottom of the boat.

Caitlin Dewey dropped into her perch and shot her arms to the side in an attempt to keep the rowboat from capsizing.

And that is how their romantic rowboat trip ended, the two of them floating precariously on Cayuga's waters, scared out of their wits, with a decapitated head rolling back and forth on the planks beneath their feet, hidden under a newspaper picture of a prison building engulfed in flames.

The Clock Tower

Captain Evan Murphy stole one last drag from his cigarette and then tossed the smoke onto the sidewalk and crushed it with the ball of his shoe. He tipped his head skyward, holding onto his hat, and stared straight up at the clock tower. A classic phallic symbol for university pricks. The long black hands said it was nearing four o'clock. He took a deep breath and swore to himself, "Here we go . . . damn it."

The detective from Albany stifled a cough with his fist and then swung open the door and started up the stairs. He took it slow, pacing himself, one laborious step at a time. There was no rail to hold on to, and so the higher he climbed, the more his balance waned. The hardest part of losing his arm had been losing his balance. The connection between his brain and his body had to be recalibrated. At every other landing there was a vertical slit in the stone, a window where he could look down and see how far he had come, and then wonder about how much further he had to climb. This was his one great phobia. A fear of heights. The loss of his arm only exacerbated the problem. As a cop his handicap forced him to use his wits, because he would never win a foot race. Or a climb. When he guessed he was halfway up the tower, halfway to the clock, he stopped and leaned his back on the stone wall. Straightened his tie. Put his hand to his mouth to smother another cough. Then he pressed on, ever upward, one step at a time.

At last the stairs opened up to the clock room. It was like a fortress inside a tower. Heavy, rough-hewn timbers encompassed the room. The workings of the four-faced clock were clearly visible. The four clock faces presented a classic visage to the campus. No matter where you were on campus, he was told, you could always lift your eyes and see the time. Captain Evan Murphy of the New York State Police had never visited a place so obsessed with time. The faces of the clock were made of white opal-flashed glass, and the hands were made of carved teakwood painted black. Each face was ten feet in diameter. The hands were five feet long. There was a giant keyboard at the center of the room that looked as if it might have been stolen from the movie set of *Phantom of the Opera.* But he was disappointed to find nobody at the controls. He looked up. More steps.

The next landing brought him into the bell tower, and that's where he found her, her arms clasped behind her back, gazing out over Ithaca, with all of its natural and supernatural wonders. The figure she presented from behind was one of a slender form. The dark blue dress she wore showed off her shape without advertising it. Her shoes were the stylish but practical shoes a woman would need to roam the hilly campus, and to climb the stairs of the clock tower. "There you are," he said to her, out of breath and clearly relieved.

Caitlin Dewey turned fast and spread her arms wide, as if to stop herself from falling through the open arch. "My God . . ." she exclaimed.

Even in fear she was a classic beauty. Chestnut eyes, with a face of ageless perfection. "I'm sorry," he said to her, holding out his hand. "I didn't mean to startle you. I didn't see anybody at the organ."

"Chimesmaster," she said, putting a hand to her chest and calming herself.

"Excuse me?"

"I'm not an organist. I'm a chimesmaster. I play the chimes."

"Chimesmaster, organ grinder . . . it's all the same to me."

"Were you expecting a little monkey?"

"No," he said. "A monkey probably couldn't get up here." Evan Murphy worked his way over to the arch beside her. "Wow," he exclaimed as he gazed out at the view.

"It's quite spectacular, isn't it?" She was more relaxed now, having recaptured her breath.

"Reminds me of that old joke," said Murphy. "It's not the end of the world, but you can see the end from here." Then he looked down at the sidewalk. Lost his balance. Staggered backwards a step or two. He put his hand to his mouth and coughed up a storm.

"Are you okay?" she asked.

"Yes," he said, somewhat embarrassed. "Just a bit dizzy . . . not unexpectedly."

"Vertigo," she informed him.

He pulled a handkerchief from his coat pocket and wiped his mouth. "Is that what they call it?"

"It's a dizzy sensation that causes a loss of balance. It's usually associated with heights . . . though, technically, a fear of heights is called *acrophobia*."

"I like *vertigo*. I'll have to remember that word." She seemed older than she looked, and it wasn't just the college education. There was a wizened beauty to her. Murphy inched back to the ledge between the stone columns. Attacking his fear. Again he took in the incredible view—all of Cornell, the whole of Ithaca, and out beyond, the hills of the Finger Lakes region. This time, being more careful, he inched his neck through the arch and checked out the sidewalk below. "This would be a great sniper's nest. Did anybody ever fall out of here, or maybe jump?"

"No," she told him, "they jump into the gorges. It's just as lethal, and infinitely more dramatic."

Evan Murphy stared out at the great body of water called Cayuga, incomparable in the distance. "Isn't that the lake down there where you were rowing with John Alden when you discovered Mr. Copeland's head?"

"Yes."

"That must have been quite a shock."

Caitlin Dewey folded her arms. "It was horrid. I've never experienced anything like it."

"By the way, my name is Murphy," he said by way of introduction. "I'm with the state police."

"Yes, I know who you are. They say you work for Governor Roosevelt?"

"I do."

"Is it true what I heard about him?"

"Do you mean about his legs? Yes, he's confined to a wheelchair."

There ensued an awkward silence, and Murphy used it to get to the reason he had climbed the stairs. "I heard you were friends with the Copeland boy."

"I was."

"And now you're friends with John Alden."

"I am."

"Do you think our Mr. Alden hails from the twenty-first century?"

"I do not. But I think he believes he does, and belief can be a powerful force."

"And all of these prognostications of his?"

"Educated guesses. Extrapolation."

"Yes, that's what your President Hightower thinks, too. This John Alden sure does go into the specifics though, doesn't he?"

"His certitude is amazing."

"Yes, he appears to be an amazing man. Says he's chasing a killer." He got no response from her. Murphy grabbed onto his dark fedora to stop it from leaving his head and sailing out over the campus. That's when he noticed how uncomfortable she was with his missing arm. "It's windy up here. How high up are we?"

"One hundred seventy-three feet." The answer sounded know-it-all, and she shrugged her shoulders. "We have to know the details because of so many visitors . . . one hundred sixty-one steps to the top, twenty-one bells . . . that sort of thing."

Murphy pointed down at the old science hall. "And is that the building they call Hell Hall?"

"Yes it is. And I don't want to know what goes on in there."

"That's where they took his head. Mr. Copeland's, that is. Dr. Ecarius is going to have a look at it."

"Is he a suspect?"

"Dr. Ecarius? I have no reason to suspect him. Do you?"

"Do you mean other than the fact that he collects human brains?"

"The infamous brain collection." He turned to her, trying to put her more at ease. "Where are you from?"

"Oregon."

"Long way away. How did you end up here?"

"My mother was from Ithaca."

"That's interesting. Would your mother have known Bobby Bill . . . also known as the Ghost Runner?"

Again Caitlin Dewey placed her hands behind her back and moved toward the arch, admiring the view. "I never heard that name until I arrived at Cornell."

"And what did you hear?"

"That he was some kind of football god way back when. I think I also heard he went missing in action during the war."

"So the story goes."

"They're really a dime a dozen, you know."

"Who's that?"

"Football players," she answered. "They live for the moment. One glorious Saturday afternoon. I almost feel sorry for them." Then again she shrugged. "But it's tradition."

"I like tradition," Murphy said, moving beside her. "It's what bonds us." They both spotted Father Dougal standing before Sage Chapel. He glanced up at them without acknowledgment before moving into the church. "Did you ever kiss him?"

"I beg your pardon?" exclaimed Caitlin.

"John Alden, I mean. I'm just trying to establish your relationship with the man who calls himself John W. Alden. Do you know what the 'W' stands for?"

"I do not."

"It's William . . . John William Alden. Funny, because do you know what the great Bobby Bill's middle name was? It was Alden. Robert Alden Bill . . . Cornell University, Class of '17 . . . if he hadn't disappeared."

"Ithaca is a small town. Family names merge all the time. It's called marriage."

Then, without warning, the bells went off. Westminster chimes. *"I summon the living, I mourn the dead."* Evan Murphy was stunned. It was like being caught in a musical earthquake. He reached out his one hand and braced himself against the stone wall. His head was ringing. In closing, the bells struck four times. Four thunderous times.

Caitlin Dewey seemed bemused by the one-armed man trapped in the bell tower, cowering against the wall. "I have a concert at four," she said to him. And then the eternal beauty from Oregon slipped down the stairs and out of sight.

Head of the Table

Night had fallen. Windows stood open all over campus. The spring air hung hot and heavy. Sticky. An unexpected heat wave had bubbled up from the southeast and lingered like an early and uninvited guest.

The severed head up from the depths of Cayuga Lake lay on the examination table at Hell Hall. A single light bulb dangled above the cranium, throwing a harsh light on the subject. Dr. Victor Ecarius turned the decomposing head of Royal S. Copeland III over in his hands. He ran his spidery fingers across the dead-white face. Then he used a magnifying glass to examine the sockets of the missing eyes. "The fish ate them," he announced.

"You're sure?"

"There is no evidence of slicing and removing."

"And your conclusion?"

Ecarius turned the head upside down and again examined the detached neck. "It appears to me as if our Mr. Copeland have lost his head to a guillotine. A real guillotine."

The one-armed cop drew a deep breath. An angry breath. "Just as Mr. Alden speculated."

"We may not know who Mr. Alden really is," Ecarius told him, "but the man sure knows death."

Captain Evan Murphy of the New York State Police inched his fedora back from his forehead. "He knows death far too well, as far as I'm concerned. But he has no working knowledge of a guillotine. Not like you, Doctor."

Ecarius laughed, that mocking laugh he used in the movies. "If, Captain, you're alluding to my minor movie role . . . I was witness to a shiny piece of tin slicing through a carved ball of wax. I believe it was all captured on film. And, yes, I do like a good movie."

President Emeritus H.W. Hightower stood back away from the table, where he could watch the examination without getting too close to the putrid skull. "Let's not jump to conclusions," he warned.

Father Dougal stood silent beside him.

"What's the preacher doing here?" Murphy wanted to know.

Father Dougal spoke up, his Scottish accent always more pronounced when he was angry. "The *priest* is here to insure Mr. Copeland is given a Christian burial. With his brain intact."

Dr. Ecarius rolled his eyes. "The good father," he told the state police captain, "thinks I'm going to harvest the boy's brain."

"Are you?"

"His brain is of no use to me . . . even though I suspect it's perfectly preserved, owing to the icy lake water. Cayuga is reluctant to give up her dead."

Murphy turned to Hightower. "Do you know the size of that lake?"

"I do," answered the old university president.

"Forty miles or more?"

"Over a hundred square miles, to be more precise."

"And what are the odds," Murphy wanted to know, "that this once-missing head appears at the end of Mr. Alden's oar, and then jumps into his boat with a flick of his wrist?"

Hightower nodded his head in agreement. "The odds are astronomical, Captain Murphy, but there are other forces at work here."

"Or more likely, the sleight of hand of an amateur magician. Alden brought the head with him to the boat."

"Why would he do such a foolish thing," Hightower countered, "and implicate himself in the murder? I think we can all agree that the man who calls himself John Alden is, in his own mad way . . . brilliant."

"Aren't you the one who told me," Murphy argued, "that after waiting years to marry the love of his life . . . the first thing he did with his new wife was cheat on her with another woman? This deceiving son of a bitch is toying with us. He is, in fact, everything he lectures about. A psychopath with a political agenda. He's not from the future . . . but he certainly wants to alter the future."

"For what purpose?" Hightower wanted to know.

Father Dougal spoke again, with less anger in his voice. "Perhaps there's a higher purpose to all of this."

"Oh yes," said Dr. Ecarius. "God forbid we should let science get in the way."

"And what did your science do for that boy whose head you're rolling around the table?"

"Is the question rhetorical, Father Dougal, or would you like an answer?"

"Gentlemen, please," scolded Hightower. He was old and overweight. The humidity that had sneaked up from the south was killing him. He wiped his brow with a soiled handkerchief. "Can we discuss our next move?"

Evan Murphy was emphatic. "I say we bring him in."

But Hightower objected. "There has to be a better way other than to just arrest the man and accuse him of the most ghastly crime in this town's history."

Murphy threw up his one hand in frustration. "May I remind you the governor is coming to your campus? Should we just wait until this lunatic commits a worse crime?"

TROUBLED MAN ON A BRIDGE

It was getting late now. Nearing midnight. While the lights, and the arguments, were still burning in Hell Hall, student lamps were being extinguished up and down the hills of the university.

John Alden stood center span on the Rickety Bridge, alone, suspended above the water that rushed to Ithaca Falls. It was cooler in the gorge by several degrees. A breeze was palpable. The stars were out. A crescent moon hung like a movie prop above the tree line. The Iroquois called it the moon of the new canoe. The earth, the sky, the moon, and the water—the professor of criminal justice found it all very humbling.

There could be no doubt about it now. He was a suspect in the murder of young Royal Copeland. The circumstantial evidence against him was overwhelming. The only question seemed to be when they were going to come for him. If he were the detective in charge, John Alden would already be in handcuffs and on his way to Albany. The former cop understood now, perhaps for the first time, a suspect's will to flee. He himself was feeling the need to disappear. But disappearing had never solved his problems. Besides, he was being watched. There were shadows among the trees. No doubt, Murphy's men.

The bells in the clock tower struck twelve times. Reverberated through the gorge. A midnight concert was scheduled. The chimes rang out. To visitors, this music at midnight was either charming or downright annoying. But to natives of Ithaca, and to the students of Cornell who came to the fabled hills from all corners of America, the chimes in the midnight hour felt as pleasant and reassuring as home and apple pie. After four years at the university, many could not sleep until they heard the echo of the music.

John Alden listened to the chimes, a melancholy tune he could not readily identify. On this night he did not know who was at the keyboard, but he wondered if it was the girl he so admired. If Caitlin Dewey had questions about his mental stability before their outing on Cayuga Lake, she surely had to believe him a cursed man now. Death followed him like the plague. His relationship with her seemed all but doomed. And she was his only connection to his future life. His future wife. His own beautiful Katelyn.

Time travel was draining. Exhausting. Only the outlines of things to come were visible. Everything else was yet to be. It was depressing beyond all of the words in the dictionary. The man with the twenty-first century mind stared downstream, and as the falls thundered, he recalled a few lines from a novel by his future favorite author, a Cornell alumnus: *"Aren't the gorges beautiful? This year, two girls jumped into one holding hands. They didn't get into the sorority they wanted."*

It was tempting to take the big leap. To disappear into the rushing water. To wash over Ithaca Falls and then down and into the lake. To sink to the depths of Cayuga and float ghost-like for generations in a watery grave while waiting to be born again. No opium could assuage his feelings on this night. No bottle of Coca-Cola could quench his thirst to be done with it all. The chimes played out. The sliver of a moon slipped behind a gossamer of a cloud. His had not been a normal life. John Alden had somehow come unstuck in time. And his unraveling had begun a long time ago.

THE CASE AGAINST HIM

"With all respect, Captain Murphy, I have to agree with President Hightower." It was Dr. Ecarius speaking now, the tall, skeletal man in the lab coat, with the warlock features and the mismatched eyes. He placed the severed head on the table so that it was facing the room. The four men stood surrounded by brains resting in jars of formaldehyde, a grand jury of the dead gathered for a hearing in Hell Hall. "If we move too fast, and without a solid case, I'm afraid Mr. Alden will, as they say in police circles . . . bolt."

Now Evan Murphy took the floor. Not even the arresting heat could loosen the tie around his neck or remove the hat from his head. He made his case. "John Alden washes up in the gorge with a head injury after going over Ithaca Falls in a storm. Was he really wrestled from the bridge, or did he jump? He concocts a story about being from the future, 2010, making some outrageous predictions . . . yet some of his predictions are already being speculated upon." He held up his hand and counted off Alden's predictions with his fingers. "A second world war. A stock market crash. A New York governor in the White House." He pointed to the severed head on the table. "He predicts a grisly murder. Ithaca gets a grisly murder. He takes one look at the headless corpse in the morgue and states that it was done with a guillotine. There just happens to be a mock guillotine in Ithaca . . . or there was. He goes for a row at sunset and the victim's head magically leaps into his boat. But this is the kicker . . ." Murphy paused here for dramatic effect, raising his one arm in the air and pointing a finger at the ceiling. ". . . It's not that the son of a bitch knows police work . . . it's the fact that he knows so damn much about cold-blooded killers. No cop knows that much. He's in their heads. Why? Because he is one."

"Ridiculous," declared Hightower. "He claims to have been a *profiler*. His job, as he described it, was to get inside their heads."

But the one-armed cop plowed on. "He's not here chasing a *serial* killer. He is the *serial* killer."

"I reject this without reservation," Hightower answered.

Murphy continued. "Mr. Alden feared this killer of his would strike again in Ithaca. But there had been no murders in Ithaca until his arrival."

"You're talking about the ramblings of a mad man," Ecarius interjected.

Murphy now opened the palm of his hand and spoke for the room. "Yes, yes, at last something we can all agree on.

Everybody here thinks John Alden is mad, to some degree. He's admitted to President Hightower and to the Dewey girl that he was once locked up in the psych ward at Bellevue Hospital. Under what name, we do not know."

The night air was stifling. Insects flew in through the open windows, seeking the lights. Hightower wiped his brow and swiped at a moth. He shifted his substantial weight, uncomfortable with both the weather and the discussion. "My family is no stranger to mental disease. But there are degrees of madness. Mr. Alden would have to be so delusional he does not realize that he is the man he is chasing."

There was a sudden suspension of talk as everybody caught his breath—Captain Evan Murphy, Dr. Victor Ecarius, Father Wallace Dougal, and H.W. Hightower, PhD. A breeze would have been welcome, but only flying insects made their way through the open windows. There was no relief from the sultry air.

"Off the record . . . what drugs do you have him on?" Murphy wanted to know.

"Laudanum," said Hightower, "for his leg."

"And Coca-Cola," added Dr. Ecarius. "Off the record, of course."

There was nervous laughter.

"And what of the girl?" Murphy asked, pointing out the window to where the clock tower stood, and where the chimes had ceased.

"Caitlin Dewey," said Father Dougal. "To hear President Hightower tell it, Mr. Alden has been fixated on her since the night of the candlelight dinner."

"He believes she might be his late wife's grandmother," Hightower informed them.

"There has to be some connection between the two," agreed Ecarius. "I have a theory. Perhaps if I could question him?"

Father Dougal was curious. "And when you say 'question him,' do you mean question him with your needles and your drugs? Or are you going to hook him up to your electrical device?" he asked, pointing to the operating table by the window. "That's not questioning. That's torture."

"Do we want niceties," Ecarius asked, "or do we want answers?"

"I'll be doing the questioning," Murphy assured the priest. "Now what of this guillotine?"

"Ask the good doctor," said Father Dougal. "He's been helping them make that damned movie."

Ecarius shot right back. "Oh yes, Father, if the church can't blame it on science . . . then for God's sake, blame it on Hollywood."

"Was the guillotine built for the movie used in any other scenes?" Murphy wanted to know.

"Not that I know of," Ecarius answered, "but we're only given the pages for the scene we're shooting that day. Besides, the guillotine was a cheap prop. And as I stated previously, my involvement with this latest movie is minimal. I run through campus at nighttime in a cape, scaring the hell out of people. It's fun."

"By the way," asked Murphy, looking around, "where's that scrawny assistant of yours?"

"Do you mean Jim Dorn?" asked Ecarius. "Jim took a well-deserved night off to study for his finals."

"Any chance he was in this movie with you?"

"Gentlemen, please," said Hightower, exasperated by talk of movies and guillotines. "Final exams begin at the university in less than four weeks' time, followed by commencement, and all with lingering uncertainty. A resolution to Mr. Copeland's demise would be most desirable."

"Your esteemed president is right," said Captain Murphy. "I've been here weeks, with little to show for it. Governor

Roosevelt will be here for commencement. He's not going to arrive in town with this unsolved murder hanging over our heads. No pun intended."

"We could steal a page from one of Dr. Ecarius' movies," suggested Father Dougal, "and run Mr. Alden out of town before the school year is out."

"He's not going anywhere," Murphy pronounced. "Not this time. I've got two men sitting on him now. He'll not be pulling his disappearing act on me."

"My guess is, Captain, that you're assuming he's the long lost Bobby Bill," Hightower said. "Yet nobody in Ithaca has recognized him as Bobby Bill."

Evan Murphy waved off the old man's argument. "His face got shot up in the war. He's aged. He claims he's somebody else. He still has a bag of tricks from his magician days. It's not surprising people wouldn't recognize him years later."

"And what of his police training?" Ecarius asked. "His knowledge of crime is astounding. Are you suggesting that after going missing in the war, he suddenly turned up as a homicide detective in the New York City police department?"

"Look . . . I don't know." The police captain was exasperated. "I haven't figured it all out yet. So don't the bunch of you go figuring you're smarter than me." He looked at the severed head on the table, the head where the fish had eaten the eyes and the waters of Cayuga Lake had bleached the skin the color of skimmed milk. "My mind is made up," Evan Murphy declared. "I'm bringing that crazy son of a bitch in."

The Interrogation

It was a basement room in the Ithaca police station. Because the station house sat in the flats downtown, on Clinton Street between the two gorges, its basement was literally surrounded by water. The interrogation room was stark, dark, and dank. Smelled of mold and mildew. Buckets of water could have been wrung out of the air. The cinder block walls that lined the subterranean room had originally been primed white and then painted hemp green, but they had never been repainted. Years of moisture had flaked the paint and softened the cinder. The bare concrete floor was ground in grime and paint chips. A door with a rusty latch was kept closed. There was a metal table in the center of the room and two metal chairs, all trimmed with rust. A lone yellow light bulb hung down from the ceiling on a long, frayed cord that looked downright dangerous. It was an interrogation room right out of an old gangster movie.

John Alden sat alone in this shadowy lit room. He wore an unbuttoned vest over a wrinkled white shirt, but with the neckline wide open, giving him the appearance of an aging athlete. In the humidity his uncombed mop of hair stuck to his neck. Stuck to his forehead. His sleeves were rolled up to his elbows. He had been left waiting. A common police tactic. His leg was bothering him. He longed for the opium, but the ex-cop was all too familiar with its addictive nature.

It was well past midnight now. Another police tactic. Interrogate them at the end of the day, when they are dead tired. Mentally exhausted. He remembered the music from the clock tower as he stood on the Rickety Bridge, and he could not help but wonder if perhaps it had been Caitlin Dewey at the keyboards after all. The human head up from the bottom of the lake had rocked their boat, and their world. They had not talked since.

The door to the dank room finally creaked open, and in walked Captain Evan Murphy of the New York State Police. He was dressed in another new suit, with the necktie pulled tight, the dark fedora in perfect balance with his head, and the armless sleeve pressed neatly into the coat pocket. The bulge of his revolver was barely visible through the expensive material. He was of that special breed of cop that never sweats. John Alden had always admired their sort, as opposed to the third degree kind, those dumb cops who beat suspects senseless. Even in his time Roosevelt's man from Albany knew psychology would catch more crooks than a beating with a rubber hose. Still, the one-armed Mick had a hard-boiled way about him. He kicked the door closed with the heel of his shoe.

This was strange. Never before had John Alden sat on this side of the table. The piss-colored glare of the light bulb was annoying, as it was meant to be. It was beginning to affect him in the way the hellish candles had affected him on the night of the candlelight dinner. He rubbed his sore leg.

The one-armed cop dropped a file folder onto the table. He flung it open with his one hand and silently fingered through the papers inside. Alden had used the tactic often. It did not matter what was in the papers. In fact, they were usually old crime reports unrelated to the offense. Just make it look like you've gathered a ton of information on your suspect. "John W. Alden, PhD," Murphy finally said, "esteemed professor of criminal justice at Cornell University. My, my, my, such a lot of brains around town and so few guns."

John Alden had to laugh. "This is classic film noir."

"What's *film noir*?"

"It's a movie . . . a long, dark chase with death at the end."

"Yeah, I heard you like the movies." Murphy remained standing so that he could look down on the suspect. "I heard you like word games, too."

Alden shrugged. "What have you got?"

"Torture?"

"It comes from the Latin verb *torquere*. 'To twist.' Torture being the classic shortcut for the incompetent detective."

"The tombs?"

"The criminal courts building in Manhattan."

"The Island?"

"Blackwell's Island. It's the New York City jail . . . soon to be relocated to Rikers Island."

"Up the river?"

"The Hudson River up to Sing Sing."

"Dead man walking?"

"Death Row . . . the walk to the electric chair."

Murphy shook his head in mock amazement. "Very good, Professor. You certainly have a cop's vocabulary. Now, do you know why you're here tonight?"

"So that you can try to intimidate me . . . browbeat me into confessing to the murder of young Royal Copeland."

"Are you confessing to his murder?"

"You know, in my day we have the right to remain silent. We have the right to an attorney, and to have that attorney present during any questioning."

"Well, today is not your day. Have you ever been a murder suspect before?"

John Alden searched the room of discolored walls before answering. "In my time, I *may* have been a suspect in the murder of my wife, and in the murder of a United States senator . . . also a woman."

Murphy raised an eyebrow. "I can understand you being a suspect in the murder of your wife, but why would they suspect you in the murder of a senator?"

"We'd had a relationship."

"You cheated on your wife?"

"I did."

"Did the police arrest you?"

"There is no law against cheating on your wife."

"I meant for the murder, wise guy."

"They did not."

"Lack of evidence?"

"No, they had an even bigger problem. I didn't kill either one of them."

Murphy returned to the papers in the file folder. "John . . . that's kind of an all-purpose name, isn't it? John Doe, Dear John, when Johnny comes marching home . . ."

"What's your point?'"

The state police captain turned over another sheet of paper. Perused it. "Point is . . . we're here tonight to find out once and for all who you are." Now he looked directly at his suspect. "And by that I mean, who you really are. Because you're not John W. Alden from the twenty-first century. You've never been married. You never went to Harvard. No woman has ever been a senator from New York, much less murdered. And you've never been a New York City police detective."

"Are those the facts?"

"Those are the facts. I do believe, however, that you served in the military. I'll give you credit for that one. You've got that war-haunted face, which is why, I suspect, nobody recognizes you. And you did play football."

"I played some high school ball. What of it?"

"I think it was a lot more than that."

"Is this the Bobby Bill theory?"

"You know of him?"

"I grew up in Ithaca. I'd heard of Bobby Bill the same way I'd heard of Babe Ruth, and Jim Thorpe, and Hobey Baker."

"Curious, though, that you claim William as your middle name, because his middle name was Alden. Robert Alden Bill."

"We were both from Ithaca. Our families might have been related by marriage."

"Yeah, that's what the girl said."

"What girl?"

"Caitlin Dewey."

John Alden swallowed hard. "Point is," he said, "all those people lived years before my time."

"Before the time when you disappeared?"

"Before the time when I was born."

"And what year was that, Professor?"

"That year was 1968."

"Let's get back to reality . . . 1929. Where were you on the night of the murder of Royal Copeland?"

John Alden leaned back, comfortable that he had won an early round. "I was in my room at President's House."

"Doing what?"

"To the best of my recollection, I was eating opium and drinking Coca-Cola with a gun to my mouth."

"And when you'd finished your meal?"

"I went downstairs to President Hightower's private library. I remember it was raining. I don't sleep well in the rain."

"And maybe you got restless . . . got up and went out."

John Alden thought it best not to mention the book he had found in the library. It was still missing. "The last thing I would do is go out in the rain. Thunderstorms . . . I'm scared to death of them. Always have been."

Murphy nodded his head, an understanding nod. "Heights are my bugaboo. Cops . . . we all have one, don't we?"

"We do."

"Tell me about the girl."

"What girl?"

"The girl you took rowing. Caitlin Dewey."

"She interests me."

"Why?"

"Because I'm a man, and she's a beautiful young woman. As the kids in my time would say . . . duh!"

The slight had no effect on Murphy. "I think it goes deeper than that," he said. "Hightower tells me that you believe Caitlin Dewey is your late wife's grandmother."

"She may well be . . . I don't know."

"Did you know Catlin Dewey's mother back in your college days?"

"No . . . because I didn't go to college back in her mother's days. And neither did most women."

"Except at Cornell." Murphy let his point sink in. "The way I hear it, her mother and Bobby Bill were once an item, away back in those more innocent times."

"No. Your time line is off. Caitlin is over twenty years old."

Now the police captain shoved his hand into his other coat pocket. Ignored the file folder before him. "A broken heart can make a man do a lot of strange things. Send him in wayward directions."

"I wasn't around back in those more innocent times, so I couldn't tell you."

"You know, Mr. Alden, or whatever the hell your real name is . . . maybe you've convinced this wide-eyed coed that you're from the future . . ."

John Alden cut him off. "Caitlin Dewey doesn't believe I'm from the future any more than you do. Nor does President Hightower, Dr. Ecarius, or Father Dougal. If you want to accuse me of being a fraud, Captain, that queue runs all the way down Libe Slope. Get in line."

Interrogating a murder suspect was serious business, but John Alden had to admit he was somewhat enjoying himself, going toe to toe with the best cop New York state could throw at him.

Captain Murphy fished a pack of Lucky Strikes out of his coat pocket. "Smoke?"

"I don't smoke. Neither should you."

Murphy lit up a cigarette and re-pocketed the pack and the lighter, all with a steady one-handed motion. "How does one alter the future?" Murphy asked him.

The cigarette smoke sucked the oxygen out of the room. Made the air in the room almost unbearable. But John Alden tried not to show it. He considered the question. "A second-rate actor assassinates an American president in a theater. A Southerner ascends to the White House. History is forever changed."

"What's done is done . . . why does it matter?"

"Because the consequences go on," Alden told him.

"What do you think of Governor Roosevelt?"

"I think he's going to be one of the greatest leaders in American history. In fact, Blackwell's Island is to be renamed Roosevelt Island."

"Is that right?" Murphy let loose another stream of smoke. "So if someone were to, let's say, shoot and kill the governor . . . that would certainly alter your future, would it not?"

"It would significantly alter both of our futures, Captain Murphy."

The one-armed cop pulled out the chair across the table and took a seat. He blew smoke into the yellow light. "Look, Professor," he said, "I'm just a cop. I ain't got none of your fancy education …"

"Boy, that education of mine really bothers you, doesn't it? Especially considering your claim that I never went to Harvard."

"No, you went to Cornell."

"What is it with you, a class warfare thing?"

"Why did you kill Copeland?"

"Why do you beat your wife?"

Murphy let loose with a good chuckle. "That's good. I'll remember that one."

John Alden leaned forward on the table and stared Murphy square in the eye. "We could do this all night, Captain. I have a distinct advantage over you."

"And what is that?"

"All I have to do is tell the truth. You, on the other hand, in order to keep your story going . . . that I am not who I say I am, that I am, instead, the great Bobby Bill, and I magically returned to Ithaca and killed Royal Copeland . . . must continually lie."

"Interesting you would use the word *magically*." Captain Murphy exhaled again. Smoke swirled in the harsh light like a ghost. "Do you think you're the first soldier disillusioned with war?" He flicked ash off the end of the cigarette and onto the floor. "Do you think you're the first veteran who comes home from some war-torn country and stages violent attacks on the people who sent him there? We got the goods on you, Professor. You're going up the river. In fact, give me one good reason why I shouldn't lock up your sorry ass right now."

"Because you have no evidence against me . . . only unanswered questions and a string of bizarre circumstances. Trust me, you've never before seen a case like this."

Evan Murphy snuffed out his cigarette on the metal table. "It's true. I might not have enough evidence to make a murder charge stick . . . but I have more than enough evidence for a state judge to declare you insane."

John Alden felt a sudden chill in the hot, humid night. "You can't do that."

The one-armed cop leaned into the lingering smoke beneath the bare bulb. "No, but I know somebody who will do it for me."

Electroshock Therapy

For centuries physicians had been fascinated with the idea of using electricity to treat certain mental diseases and long-term head injuries. As far back as biblical times, men of medicine noticed that people suffering delusions or depression showed remarkable recoveries after suffering a seizure, or after receiving the proverbial blow to the head. Not only did their moods change dramatically, and usually for the better, but they often recovered lost memories and had restored to them their powers of cognitive thinking. Even Benjamin Franklin reported nearly going into convulsions after putting his finger to the key attached to his kite. The jolt of electricity left him feeling giddy for days. So why not use electricity to induce seizures, a sort of electrical blow to the head? At least that was the thinking of Dr. Victor Ecarius.

When John Alden came to, when he had regained consciousness and shaken the cobwebs from his forced sleep, he found himself shackled to the ghastly-looking operating table that stood before the tall windows in the brain collection laboratory of Hell Hall. It was late. Outside the windows overlooking Libe Slope, in the faded glow of a street lamp, he could see light rain falling, bringing with it a measure of relief from the heat. Within the shadows of the laboratory itself he saw row after row of jars filled with formaldehyde, the human brains inside of them facing him, judging him, like a jury made up of the convicts he had put away. A fire hose was mounted on the wall. A crimson blanket hung next to it. The lab reeked of ammonia wash.

Leather straps circled his ankles and his thighs. Leather handcuffs secured his wrists to the table. Another leather strap stretched across his chest, squeezing him as tightly as any python would, while a shorter strap across his neck, in the manner of a dog collar, would choke him should he attempt to sit up. He had been stripped bare and fitted with a burlap diaper. The sight of the diaper sent his large body convulsing with rage. John Alden tore at the leather shackles as if he were already in seizure. His face was red. Saliva spewed from his mouth.

Dr. Ecarius placed a calming hand across his forehead. "Relax, Mr. Alden. You will eventually lose control of all of your muscles," the doctor told him. "As a result, you'll experience a bowel movement. Don't be embarrassed. We'll clean you up."

There had been a sanity hearing before a state judge. A local yokel. The hearing was a sham, with none of the protections afforded future defendants. Then he was taken to a jail cell to await a ruling. While in jail he ate a God-awful meal served with a disagreeable tea. He fell fast asleep on a rancid cot. And then—

Jim Dorn, the skinny, ungainly grad student who had asked the first derisive question in the parlor of President's House on the night of the candlelight dinner, was standing on the other side of the table. Dorn was dressed in a soiled and wrinkled lab coat. He hugged a clipboard to his chest and constantly adjusted his glasses, every inch of him a portrayal of the mad assistant to the mad doctor. "I cut short my studies for finals to be here tonight," he said. "This is medical history."

John Alden had grown up here. He knew the Dorns of Ithaca. In school they studied hard, made the grades, but they were dirt poor and were never accepted by their classmates. He rolled his eyes to the top of his brows in a vain attempt to see what was attached to his head. But it was better he could not see it, for it appeared as an electric football helmet, with snakes protruding from the top. "Why are you doing this to me?" he managed to choke out.

"We're trying to help you," Dr. Ecarius assured him in a sincere voice. Then he passed his fingers over the luminous dials of the control panel. "Have you ever before had this type of treatment?"

"No," Alden said. But the fright showed in his eyes as he scoped out the power box.

"Then how is it," Ecarius asked, "that you know so much about electroshock therapy?"

John Alden found himself staring into the abnormally-colored eyes of Dr. Ecarius, one black and rat-like, the other injurious red. He spit out the word, "Pigs."

"Pigs?" Ecarius was baffled.

But his assistant was insulted. Jim Dorn removed his glasses and took a threatening step toward the table. But Ecarius put out his hand, stopping him dead in his tracks. "Explain," he ordered.

"Slaughterhouse pigs," Alden told them. "It was difficult to get the pigs to hold still so that their throats could be slit. So someone had the bright idea of using electricity to shock them into unconsciousness . . . then they slit their throats."

"And did this method work?"

"Yes."

Jim Dorn piped up. "But didn't the electricity kill the pigs?"

Alden hated answering to this sycophant of a student, but he could see that Ecarius was waiting for a reply. "No," John Alden explained to them as best he could. "In fact, some of the pigs woke up more lively than ever, and they had to be zapped again."

"How do you know all of this?" Ecarius asked.

"It's the history of electroshock therapy. It's taught in the psychology departments in all of the universities, including Harvard."

"How can they teach the history of a therapy that does not yet exist?"

He felt they were trying to verbally trap him. "I don't know . . . I just learned it. Before I went over the falls, I had an eidetic memory."

"Eidetic?"

"It's from the Greek word *eidos*," Alden told the doctor, breathing hard. "It means *form*."

"I know what it means."

Again Jim Dorn spoke up. "Are you claiming to have a photographic memory?"

"There's no such thing," Alden said, correcting the student. "It's a myth." He struggled to free himself, but it was like being hog-tied. "Now I remember things, everything, but it's all mixed up."

"What kind of things?"

"My life . . . episodes . . . things . . ."

Here Ecarius began his planned interrogation. "Are you from the twenty-first century?"

John Alden was near tears. "I don't know anymore."

"Are you mad?"

"No, I don't believe that I am."

"Well, let's find out." Dr. Ecarius lifted a large rubber plug from the table. The plug was of a blood-red palette. "I'm going to introduce fifty-five volts of electricity into your brain for one second. Bite down on this. It'll ease the shock and keep you from swallowing your tongue."

Alden clenched his teeth and shook his head *no*, as if he were a petulant child.

"Very well," Ecarius told him, retaining the rubber plug in his fist. "Now, what is your full name?"

"John William Alden."

"Where were you born, Mr. Alden?"

"Ithaca, New York."

"And in what year were you born?"

"1968."

With that answer Dr. Victor Ecarius reached over and twisted the numbered dial on the power box. The electricity shot through John Alden like a bolt of lightning. It was a burning, rattling, excruciating pain that pulsed through his entire body and got him shaking and screaming at the same time. Ecarius jammed the rubber plug into his mouth, and now the alleged time traveler welcomed it. He bit down hard and finally felt the convulsing pain leaving his body, as if someone had pulled the plug to a tub of acid.

Ecarius yanked the rubber plug from his mouth. "What is your name?"

"John Alden," he choked out.

"Where were you born?"

"Ithaca."

"And in what year were you born?"

"I don't know."

"Good," Ecarius told him. "That's good. What is your occupation?"

"I was a detective. New York City. I teach at the university now."

"Why did you come here now?"

"I'm after a serial killer."

"There is no such term," Ecarius reminded him.

"He's killed multiple times, but I screwed up."

Ecarius winced. "Screwed up?"

"His killings are political. He's here to kill again . . . two men."

"And in your mind . . . who was his first victim in Ithaca?"

"My wife."

"No, it was Royal Copeland. There is no record of you having a wife."

"I had a wife. He butchered her."

"What was her name?"

"Katelyn. My beautiful Katelyn."

"Spell it."

"K-a-t-e-l-y-n."

"There were no murders here in Ithaca before your arrival. Is it possible this beautiful Katelyn of yours was killed in another place?"

"No, it was another time, but she dies here in Ithaca."

"Did you kill her?"

"No. I loved her."

"Most people murdered are murdered by a loved one. Are you this so-called serial killer? Are you in pursuit of yourself, Mr. Alden?"

THE MURDER OF HIS WIFE

It was late. Past 11:00 p.m. A quarter moon was buried beneath Ithaca's ever-present clouds. The specter appeared in the night as a human bat, a kind of Dracula fleeing the scene of a crime. Only instead of flying, this bat was running, his cape flapping in the wind. Yet even walking home in the dark, John Alden could make out a bloody little thing being carried like a treasure in the palm of his hands.

"What kind of bloody little thing?" the Ithaca police would later ask him.

"Like about the size of a mouse."

"And you believe this was the fetus?"

This caped man ran up the steep residential street toward the university, past the old homes that had been built for the first generation of college professors. At first John Alden was not even sure if the man was fleeing the big white clapboard house they had inherited on Old Elmira Road, but his police instincts kicked in and he hurried up the sidewalk. He bounded up the concrete steps to the front yard and then up the flight of wooden stairs to the porch. The front door was wide open. There had been a struggle. He rushed inside and called her name. "Katelyn!"

She was naked on the hallway floor that led to the bathroom. The murderer had surprised her as she came out of the bathroom at the end of her shower. The bathroom door was open. The light was on. Moisture still hung in the air.

Detective First Grade John Alden had been to a hundred crime scenes, but this was his wife's crime scene. His very own Katelyn. His mind was suddenly torn between emotional horror and the calm, detached professionalism of a homicide investigator:

Note the exact time. *Twelve minutes past eleven.*

What is the apparent cause of death? *Her throat has been slashed to the bone.*

Is the murder weapon present? *No.*

Note the position of the body. *On her back, splayed across the floor.*

Are the bloodstains wet or dry? *Wet.*

Is the blood bright red or brown? *Bright red.*

What is the condition of the body? *Stabbed. Torn. Mutilated.*

Examine the hands. *Her defensive wounds are obvious.*

Is there any jewelry? *Her wedding ring is missing.*

Anything else missing? *Her stomach has been cut open.*

"Katelyn," he cried out. "Oh, Katelyn, what have I done to you?"

"Were those your exact words?" the Ithaca cop wanted to know.

What he had done was convince Katelyn to marry him, leave Oregon, and return to their hometown of Ithaca, where they were to live out some midlife fantasy about an academic's life in a small upstate town.

But now on a hallway floor, his life was a nightmare without end. He dropped to his knees at her feet, his mouth locked open in shock, tears streaming down his face. He wanted to hold her, cradle her, but the horror of her remains was overwhelming, and his cop's brain was telling him not to touch anything. Against his police instincts, he used the telephone in the house to call for help.

He was outside now in the cool night air, sitting on the top step of the porch, his face buried in his hands. When he finally looked up there were a thousand red lights flashing beneath him. The neighbors had gathered at the foot of the hill, beyond the yellow police tape. An aging, bald-headed detective in a cheap Sears suit was seated next to him.

Another detective, a tall and much younger man, was standing on the steps, looking down on him, notebook in hand. "Well, Professor," he said, with a hint of sarcasm in his voice, "it shouldn't be too hard to spot a caped man running through campus. It's not like it's Halloween or anything."

"Why were you away from the house?" the older cop asked him.

"Pizza."

"Excuse me?"

"We had a fight. I went out for pizza."

"What was the fight about?"

Despite his Ithaca roots and his return to his old home town, he was an outsider to these cops. He was the New York City big shot, the so-called murder expert teaching at the university. Since arriving at the scene, these local cops had done everything by the book—the very book John Alden had written:

Immediately remove the suspect from the crime scene.

Note and preserve any evidence found on the suspect.

Do not permit the suspect to wash his hands or use the toilet.

Do not permit any conversation between the suspect and any other parties.

Record all spontaneous statements.

Observe behavior of the suspect. Drunk? Drugged?

Is he emotional or unemotional?

Yes, in their eyes, in their provincial Ithaca eyes, he was the number one suspect in the murder of his wife.

MORE ELECTRICITY

"What time is it?"

Dr. Ecarius glanced up at the clock on the wall. In bold italics beneath the hands it read, *Ithaca Calendar Clock Company*. He leaned over his patient, his human guinea pig. "I find you strangely obsessed with time, Mr. Alden." They were nearly nose to nose, only now John Alden's nose was fire-engine red. Near-bursting with blue veins. "But your insights on future events don't interest me. I see them for what they are. Parlor tricks. Now, murder didn't visit Ithaca until you arrived . . . and you arrived here in Ithaca on Halloween night, 1928."

"There were other murders," Alden told him.

"That night you washed over the falls . . . who were you chasing?"

"I thought he was a serial killer. I now believe him to be an assassin."

"How do you know? Perhaps he was just a man in a cape. It was Halloween. They were making a movie."

"I recognized him as the man fleeing my house after the murder of my wife. He also fit the profile. And he ran."

"It was raining. He was running to get out of the rain."

"He attacked a woman."

"Again, how do you know?"

"I heard her scream."

"Again, I say, it was Halloween. This is Cornell . . . there was a lot of drinking and a lot of screaming."

"No. He tried to kill again."

"And what year was that?"

"It was 2010."

Ecarius jammed the blood-red plug back into John Alden's mouth. Alden bit down hard while at the same time trying his best to scream in protest. The electricity again coursed through his veins, head to toe, splintered his bones, ripped into his muscles like a bear's claw, throwing him into convulsions of ungodly pain. He messed himself. When Ecarius finally pulled the plug from his mouth, there were tears pouring from his eyes. He fought to breathe, like a man whose head had been forced under water. Now he could smell his own feces. He could feel his urine pooling beneath his legs.

Dr. Ecarius used his thumb to gently wipe the tears from Alden's face. "Mr. Alden," he said in a most paternal voice, "the year was 1928, wasn't it?"

"I don't know anymore," Alden sobbed.

"It was Halloween night, 1928. The whole campus was drunk. We had a storm. For some inexplicable reason, you chased a man in a costume. During the pursuit of this man, you fell from the Rickety Bridge."

"We both fell."

"Let us deal with you now. We're making progress. Real progress. Next time you slip into the future, I'm going to turn up the dial and administer one hundred and ten volts for a full one second."

"No, please don't . . . please . . ." He was reduced to begging.

"Mr. Alden," Ecarius asked, "have you ever served in the military?"

"Yes."

"With whom?"

"Military police. US Army."

"Did you see combat?"

"Yes, it was terrible."

"And what year was that?"

John Alden tried to shake his head, but his head was strapped in place. "I don't know."

"Good," Dr. Ecarius told him. "That's really good, Mr. Alden. We're here to wash away all of your false memories and then retrieve your real memories. You say your name is John Alden?"

"Yes."

"Is it possible that's not your real name?"

"I don't know."

"Might your last name be Bill? Robert Alden Bill? Everybody called you Bobby Bill. You were the Ghost Runner."

"I don't think that I am."

"For now we'll continue to call you Mr. Alden. Is that okay?"

"Yes."

"Mr. Alden, you were born here in Ithaca in the year 1896."

He pulled hard against the straps until the leather was cutting into his skin. "No, I'm older than that . . . look at me."

"I am looking at you . . . and I see a man who served in the Army, but it was during the world war."

"World War Two?"

"No, Mr. Alden, there has been no second world war. You served in the first ever worldwide war. The Great War. Do you remember?"

He continued his struggle with the constraints. "I'm trying. Please, I'm trying . . ."

"You never went to Harvard, Mr. Alden. You went to Cornell. You were in the Class of 1917, but you left Ithaca without graduating."

"No. Harvard, '95." John Alden knew as soon as the words had left his mouth he had made a big mistake. The plug was forced back into his mouth, but he spit it out in a fit of anger. Then one hundred and ten volts of electricity were shot into his brain. The screaming was so loud it seemed to be coming from outside his body. He messed his diaper a second time. Mostly fluids. He blacked out from the pain. He may have been out a minute, or it may have been an hour. The pain made it difficult to keep track of time.

When he came to, Ecarius was standing over him. More impatient now. Ironically, the only sympathy in the room was now in the eyes of the young man hiding behind the thick glasses. The mad doctor's assistant—Jim Dorn.

"While a student at Cornell," Dr. Ecarius explained, in a matter-of-fact way, "you got a girl pregnant. She ran off to Oregon without telling you of the pregnancy. The baby was a girl."

"You're crazy," he spit out, foaming at the mouth.

"And is President Hightower crazy? Because he told me the story. Bobby Bill got a girl at Cornell pregnant. But she never told him. She didn't go the Caribbean to sail. She went to the Caribbean to have the baby. Then she took the baby, found a husband, and she began a new life in Oregon. And after the war . . . you went out there to confront her."

"No. That's another man's life."

"And through it all she sang the glories of Cornell."

"No!" cried John Alden. But before he could protest any further, another one hundred and ten volts of electricity was shot into his brain.

THE OLD MAN IN THE RAIN

The old man viewed this trial by fire from the safety that distance affords. He stood outside Hell Hall in the rain, bathed in the soggy yellow glow of a street lamp, where he watched through the tall windows as this experiment called electroshock therapy was carried out. The entire procedure would last a mere ten minutes. There would be ten treatments, one every other day. During that time the patient would be locked up in the basement of Hell Hall, like a prisoner during the Inquisition. It was for his own good. Still, the old man's heart felt leaden. His stomach weakened. The foul weather played havoc with his bones, especially his knees. He leaned on a cane, the same gold-handled walking stick John Alden had once used to navigate the sidewalks of the hilly campus. An Ithaca judge had ruled that the man's brain was temporarily insane, and he had released the mystery man and his troubled mind into the care of H.W. Hightower, PhD, president emeritus of Cornell University. This legal maneuvering sounded cruel, almost a betrayal, but it was really an act of subterfuge, a last-ditch ploy Hightower had used to keep John Alden out of jail. The man was, after all, a murder suspect, and the old president was using every trick in the Cornell law books to help him remain free of charges—liberated so that he could pursue the real killer, a madman who was sure to strike again. And then again. *Ad infinitum*. But was that kind of killing even possible?

The young writer F. Scott Fitzgerald, the obnoxious little Princeton drunk of a novelist John Alden was so high on, was once quoted as saying something smart—that the test of a first-rate intelligence is the ability to hold two opposed ideas in the mind at the same time, and still retain the ability to function. H.W. Hightower was a master of *horology*, the study of time. He believed, at least in theory, that time travel was possible, but he still could not bring himself to believe John Alden had traveled back through time, some eighty years.

Dr. Ecarius, on the other hand, believed John Alden suffered from a rare form of amnesia. That he was, instead, the Ghost Runner. The great Bobby Bill. An All-American football player drowned in heartbreak and wounded in war—and lost forever to all those who once knew him. His talk of future events was nothing but educated guess work. Mere predictions.

The old man wiped the rain from his eyes. It was an incongruous sight, raining outside while the lightning strikes were coming from the inside—inside the laboratory windows of Hell

Hall. He watched with trepidation as once again faux lightning lit up the tall windows and another one hundred and ten volts of electricity were shot into the tortured brain of the man who called himself John Alden. As the rainwater streamed down his aged face, the once all-powerful university president, his *eminence grise,* listened to the anguished screams of the former New York City police detective. Screams that floated out over the mystic hills and the haunting gorges of this strange and fascinating land they called Ithaca.

END OF BOOK TWO

"He knew the things that were and the things that would be and the things that had been before."

—Homer's *The Iliad*

The Dance Hall

Prisons echo. The footsteps in the hallways echo. Voices echo. Even the whispers echo. Sing Sing had an echo all its own. At 10:00 p.m. they came for him. He heard the echo of their footsteps marching down the row. Then four uniformed guards and the warden escorted the most infamous prisoner in America from his cell on Death Row to the pre-execution chamber, the prison cells nearest the chair. He made the walk down the lonely corridor in his stocking feet. In the pre-execution chamber at Sing Sing it had become a tradition for the guards to play any phonograph music requested by the prisoner—that is how the pre-execution chamber became known as the "Dance Hall." This prisoner requested Al Jolson, the only singer of the day he was familiar with. And so as he left his small cell on Death Row, his home for the past three years, and he made his way past the block of cells where other men were waiting to be executed, he was able to listen to and appreciate the sweet melancholy voice of the Jazz Singer.

After you've gone and left me crying
After you've gone, there's no denying
You'll feel blue, you'll feel sad
You'll miss the dearest pal you've ever had

It was the first real music he had heard in years, and each plaintive note was a symphony to his ears.

The CBS radio network had won a court fight to carry the execution live. This would be a first in American broadcasting. Some thought it a victory for First Amendment rights, while others thought it was a perversion of both the medium and of justice. With that legal victory the Ithaca Motion Picture Company won permission from the courts to film the prisoner's electric demise. A cameraman with a camera mounted on a tripod filmed the prisoner moving slowly down the corridor before turning into his new cell. The black-and-white footage that survived the fire was grainy and filled with shadows, as the movie industry had yet to learn how to film using only natural light. Still, the surviving film reel shows a lofty, but skeletal-looking man shuffling behind a courtly dressed warden and a Catholic priest—a tall, hooded friar. Three uniformed guards brought up the rear, while the prisoner himself seemed a scarecrow draped in baggy clothes. His lack of shoes and the white stocking feet made him appear saintly and poor. His face was bony, his eyes hollow. His hair, cropped short in prison, was now peppered more gray than brown. There was no conversation during this long, short walk, no audio at all, as if everybody involved in this black-and-white reel were merely going about their business in as professional a way as was humanly possible.

Further down the corridor a radio announcer stood leaning in from the doorway of the execution chamber itself. His coat was off and his cuffs were unbuttoned, but his tie was still pulled tight around the neckline of his white shirt. He wore a large headset over his ears, and he was trying to stretch the cord of the large microphone he gripped in his hands. With the radio equipment restraining him, he was barely able to lean into the doorway far enough to see the prisoner, where he put on his best Walter Winchell voice. "From my vantage point here in the doorway of the execution chamber, I can now see the prisoner . . . the very assassin who tried to shoot Governor Roosevelt before he was elected president. This is the madman who has claimed all along he has come to us from the future. Well, this so-called man from the twenty-first century has now left his twentieth-century cell on Death Row, and he is being marched down the hall to the cell nearest me. Yes, here he comes. There is music playing in the background. Perhaps you can hear it. I believe it's an Al Jolson tune . . ."

Everything seems lovely
When you start to roam
The birds are singin', the day that you stray

But later, when you are further away
Things won't seem so lovely
When you're all alone

"Folks, these are truly amazing sights and sounds. The prisoner appears very composed for a man who, in an hour, is scheduled to die a horrible, electrifying death. And, God willing, you will hear it all here on the CBS radio network."

But God was less than willing. The storm that was ravaging the East Coast was closing in on Sing Sing. Already the radio signal meant to carry the execution was weakened and crackling with static.

The three cells nearest the chair were different from the cells strung out on Death Row. More cage-like. There was no solid iron door. Only steel bars. The condemned man would be under full observation until his death.

When the bars to his new cage slammed closed and the bolt shot home, the prisoner strolled to the narrow window and gripped the steel bars. Al Jolson continued his concert out in the hallway. The movie camera was relocated to the front of the cell door, but the prisoner kept his back to it. He could see the dreaded Nor'easter now crossing the Hudson. The Palisades on the far shore had been swallowed whole in a sea of swirling black clouds, and the dark river water appeared to be rising up to meet those clouds until one could not tell where the earth ended and where the hellish weather began. The flashes of lightning in the storm were so intense they stung his eyes, and the thunder that followed had evolved from that distant-rumbling kind of thunder to the shattering-crack-of-an-explosion kind, as if trees in the neighborhood were being felled and homes were being leveled. The crowd below the prison was fast dissipating as hundreds scrambled for the shelter of their cars. Even the burly guards standing vigil outside the cell flinched at the sounds of the storm. They knew this Thursday night execution was anything but routine. This was to be a night out of the ordinary, and in that frightening sort of way. Thunder literally shook the walls.

It is best, he was advised, not to stare too deeply into the abyss. Cornell's president emeritus had translated Nietzsche's quote to the prisoner. "Battle not with monsters, lest ye become a monster, and if you gaze into the abyss, the abyss gazes also into you." Now as the prisoner stared into the teeth of the approaching Nor'easter, he remembered watching the storm clouds that were forever building over Cayuga Lake, never knowing whether they would gather force and race up the hill to the university, or just slowly dissipate over the enchanting water. He recalled the never-ending rains of Ithaca that brought with them so much depression, and yet so much green luster. In fact, it was raining that hot spring night they strapped him to that table in Hell Hall and fitted him with that ungodly helmet. The condemned man remembered the searing pain from the electroshock therapy. Now he found himself dwelling on the long two minutes it would take to end his life.

But in the weeks that followed that electrifying experimental therapy, he was never sharper. Never more in control of his wits. It was a natural high no drug could replicate. His police instincts, along with his college education, were dragged to the forefront, as was his military bearing, while the demons of his past took a seat in the back of his mind. If that time-traveling killer had hoped to shock the time-traveling cop from his tail, he had only succeeded in doing the opposite.

Mammy . . . Mammy, I'm comin'
Oh, Lord, I hope I'm not late
Look at me, Mammy. Don't you know me?
I'm your little baby!

BOOK THREE

ITHACA, NEW YORK

1929

The Heat

The heat wave that arrived in late spring not only lingered on, but it increased in intensity. Pretty much put a stranglehold on the entire East Coast. It remained blistering hot as Cornell students began preparing for their final exams. The temperature topped 90 degrees every day. The cool winds off the lake all but ceased, and the humidity was hell. But in the spring of 1929, there was something else in the New York air besides moisture.

Confidence in the stock market remained strong, although the trend of the market was generally down. On the New York Stock Exchange sales were still above four million, and frequently rose above five. Those in charge of finances at Cornell University continued to borrow and trade with the same speculative zeal as did the rest of the world. People in Ithaca who had invested their life savings in the stock market believed in their hearts they were getting rich. But the unusual heat and the sudden eerie stillness of Cayuga Lake carried with it the portent of change. And things *were* changing.

Ezra Cornell had established a university open to all, regardless of race, sex, religion, or lack of religion, or even pecuniary condition. In the nineteenth century this was revolutionary, and in her first sixty years of existence, Cornell pretty much stayed true to her lofty principles. But suddenly secret amendments were being added. Near the end of the semester vandals broke into Hell Hall and caused extensive damage to the equipment and specimens of Dr. Victor Ecarius. The Moral Way was suspected of being behind the attack, as the words GOD, NOT SCIENCE had been painted on the wall in pig's blood.

Meanwhile, two colored girls, both of them returning Cornell students, were escorted out of their rooms at the Dormitory for Women and assigned rooms on Cascadilla Street, seven blocks from the university. There was also a movement to restrict an unsatisfactory Jewish element at Cornell, and a New York state senator identified several student clubs at the school that appeared to him to be subversive. In a widely-reported speech in Albany the senator charged that Cornell University was a center of revolutionary communistic activity. The board of trustees and the current president of Cornell remained shamefully mute on the issue, but President Emeritus H.W. Hightower would not stay quiet. He told the *Ithaca Journal*, "If we had no communists at Cornell, I would feel it my duty to import a few."

The old president's quote only stoked the flames of prejudice. The Moral Way called for another awakening rally on Libe Slope. In Albany, advisors were urging Governor Roosevelt to cancel his commencement speech at the controversial university. Besides the tension and the unrest, there was still the unsolved murder of Royal S. Copeland III. Roosevelt's one-armed police captain was ordered to remain on campus.

And once again, to the chagrin of many, roaming free in the heat and the hills was the visiting professor of criminal justice. A man who had mysteriously washed ashore at the foot of Ithaca Falls during a thunderstorm. A lonely savant with head injuries who claimed to know of the things to come.

A LIST OF HIS OWN

They did not speak of his treatment, even though he was in effect a ward of President's House, still under a court order that said he was temporarily insane. As painful as the electroshock therapy was, John Alden had to admit the results were positive. Hell, they were electrifying. Where he once felt lost in a time that was not his own, he now felt in full command. Not only a man of his time, but a man of both times.

The professor of criminal justice believed the next big event would be the stock market crash in the fall. If his memory served him correctly, there would be a financial scare in the spring. A six-month warning. Yet there was little he could do about it. Nor should he. The coming crash would result in years of misery, but from that tribulation would emerge a lifetime of good.

On this sweltering day he sat at a small desk before an elm-shaded window on the third floor of President's House, the High Victorian Gothic mansion with the dark wood and leaded glass windows. From his perch he could look out across the Arts Quad and keep tabs on the campus. He could see the clock tower, and behind it the Libe Slope drop off. On a quiet night he could hear the water tumbling over Ithaca Falls. The window was wide open now, but it did no good. The midday heat was omnipresent. A lot of the students were crowding under shade trees, while others moved toward their classes at a tortoise pace. John Alden rolled his sleeves up past his elbows and undid another button to the front of his white shirt. The back of the shirt was sticking to his skin. He peeled it away, wiped the sweat from his brow, and picked up a fountain pen. He removed the blue steel cap and began scribbling notes on the murder of young Royal Copeland. His personal list of suspects. It was his first work on the case since his release from the dungeons of Hell Hall.

For starters, there was Dr. Victor Ecarius, the mad scientist of Hell Hall. His name went at the top of the list. Seemed the man with the odd-colored eyes could not wait to hook up John Alden to his electrodes. Question him. Shock him. The doctor was an official collector of body parts, and all in the name of science. He had begun his morbid collection back before the war, around the same time as the unsolved suffragists' murders in Upstate New York. His biographical and physical characteristics matched the profile. On the other hand, the professor of criminal justice had been aware of the doctor's controversial research long before he washed over Ithaca Falls. Ecarius would in the future debunk his own theories, that intellect was based on the size and shape of the human brain. The doctor would then go on to more credible research and take a respectable place in Cornell history. Hardly the biography of a serial killer —or a political assassin.

There was, however, his equally mad assistant, Jim Dorn. Dorn's name went on the list, too. The awkward grad student lacked the intellect of his mentor, but he was young and passionate about his work. He was a native of Ithaca, and he had the personality of a sociopath. He also possessed the youthful strength and willpower it would take to kill through time. Was it possible he had taken the research of Dr. Ecarius and perverted it, used it to further his own misguided beliefs?

On the subject of misguided beliefs, he next penned the name of Father Wallace Dougal, the Catholic sage of Sage Chapel and the spiritual leader of the Moral Way. John Alden, himself a onetime patient at Bellevue, and a Catholic in poor standing, recalled a Friedrich Nietzsche quote as he wrote the priest's name. *"A casual stroll through the lunatic asylum shows that faith does not prove anything."*

The priest fit the profile. The man was not a Catholic, he was a *papist*. His perversion of Catholic ideology was filled with ignorance and hate. In John Alden's own time the priests of the Catholic Church would be accused of every sordid crime imaginable, from the sexual molestation of children to conspiracy to commit murder. This priest seemed determined to bring religion to Cornell University—and only his brand of religion—even if it killed him.

He heard them giggling at the door below. The Bobbsey Twins. Amanda and Belle Parrish. But while the Bobbsey twins had been fraternal twins, the Parrish girls were identical twins, or as their uncle called them—identical trouble. John Alden watched as they skipped out across the quad, oblivious of the heat. Seemingly oblivious of reality. Were they just a pair of bimbos dabbling in witchcraft, or were they something more malevolent? They had been out and about on the night of the murder. In fact, they were bound for the same destination as the victim Copeland, to shoot a scene in the pouring rain for the Ithaca Motion Picture Company. The ex-detective jotted down their names on his list of suspects, though more as witnesses than killers.

Then there was the specter of Bobby Bill, the All-American football player and soldier gone missing. An Ithaca man. John Alden slowly printed his name, one capital letter at a time. Then he turned his head and took a long, hard look at the picture of the football player hanging on the wall across the room. If the man still lived, he also would be the right age with the right physical traits. Unlike the other suspects, Bobby Bill had been famous for his vanishing acts. An amateur magician disappearing on stage from a chair beneath a blanket. A football player disappearing into the end zone during football games. A heartbroken young man disappearing from Ithaca, about the time the suffragists' murders began. And finally, a soldier disappearing from war. Was it possible he, too, had come unstuck in time? John Alden turned away from the haunting picture and turned back to his list. Next to the name Bobby Bill he wrote in cursive, *The Ghost of Cornell.*

All four of the men on his list fit the detailed profile of the unidentified subject he had drawn up, a serial killer and political assassin bent on altering the future. Meanwhile, Captain Evan Murphy of the New York State Police had on his list only one name. John W. Alden. The one-armed cop had made plenty of noise with his unhappiness that the so-called time-traveling professor was once again roaming free. He was boldly predicting

Alden's flight, and not into the future. Somewhere out there on the crowded, steamy quad was a cop in the guise of a student with his eyes trained on the third floor windows of President's House.

He again heard the heavy front door to the mansion open and close. John Alden put down his pen and peeked out at the drive below. H.W. Hightower had just stepped out of the house. He wore a dark suit with a natty bow tie. A bowler topped his head, even in the damned heat. No doubt the old man was off to some formal meeting, still a living, breathing creature of that gilded age. Alden leaned his head far out the window in hopes of catching a breath of fresh air. But the only air available was stale, sizzling, and miserable. "Do you know in the future what it is men do on such a hot day?" He answered his own question. "They remove their coats and ties."

Hightower turned and smiled up at him, a beaming smile that spoke to how relieved he was that there were no bitter feelings. "Brilliant. The wisdom of our future generations astounds me."

"Don't be modest. You must surely remember Willis Carrier."

"I do. A prominent alumni of Cornell . . . a turn-of-the-century man, if my memory serves me correctly."

"He graduated from here in 1901, with a masters in engineering," Alden reminded him. "One year later he devised a machine to moderate the temperature and humidity of a Brooklyn printing plant. He founded the Carrier Engineering Corporation back in 1915. This invention of his, air conditioning, is slowly spreading to other factories as we speak. Unfortunately for you, because of the coming economic depression and another world war, air conditioning doesn't become popular in commercial buildings and homes until the 1950s."

Suddenly the chimes sounded in the clock tower. The noon concert. The president emeritus glanced up at the four-sided clock. The hands sat together at the top of the hour as if in prayer. He turned and looked back up at John Alden and spoke while dabbing his forehead with a white handkerchief. "I fear I cannot wait that long. If I should succumb to a heat stroke on this afternoon in Dante's Hell, please have yourself a wonderful life, Mr. Alden . . . in whatever time you choose to live it." Then the rotund old man, still light on his feet, ambled off and into the hottest part of the day, swinging his gold-headed walking cane.

A glass of water sat on the desk, dripping with condensation. There seemed more water on the outside of the glass than on the inside. John Alden stole a sip. It dripped all over his shirt and onto the floor. A few droplets spilled onto his notebook, running the ink on his list of suspects. He dabbed at the paper with a napkin while swearing at the delay of air conditioning.

Through the window he caught a last glimpse of the old man disappearing in the heat, but before he waddled completely out of sight, he was seen stooping down to pick up a piece of wastepaper off of the sidewalk, not allowing anybody to trash his campus.

What of H.W. Hightower? He was the seemingly forever president of the university, still residing in President's House, the unorthodox sage with the private library of beautifully crafted, yet unrecorded books. As an expert on horology, the study of time, it was almost a certainty the old man knew of the strange powers of the vortex sometimes created at the foot of Ithaca Falls. It was Hightower who had once told John Alden of an old Indian legend of an Iroquois brave who fell into the deep gorge during a raging battle and disappeared over Ithaca Falls. It was believed the young brave was drowned, though his body was never found. A generation later the brave miraculously returned to the shores of Cayuga Lake seemingly having not aged a single day. He told the elderly chieftains of the coming of the white man and of the eventual demise of the Iroquois

Nation. They did not believe him, but his everlasting youth scared them to death, so they banished him to the deep woods west of the Great Spirit's fingers of lakes. But instead of leaving, the still mighty warrior collected in his arms a tribal mystic, an older woman who had never wed. It was said together they leaped into the deep gorge, and clinging to one another in the rushing water, they disappeared over Ithaca Falls.

"And you think this young warrior had seen the future?" Alden asked the old man.

"Don't you?"

"Perhaps. But more likely he had seen Boston."

"And his still youthful appearance all those years later?"

"Elementary," the ex-detective said, putting reason to legend. "It wasn't really the lost warrior. It was his son. And the old woman he grabbed . . . was his mother."

Hightower himself was too old and misshapen to be the actual killer. But could he be the killer behind the killer?

"Eminence grise. *It's French. It means the power behind the throne. An advisor or decision-maker who operates secretly or unofficially."*

John Alden at first hesitated— he thought so much of the old university president—but reluctantly he put his fountain pen to the ink-stained paper and added the name of H.W Hightower to his growing list of suspects.

The chimes from the noon concert were at their end. The last bells echoed through the heat and the hills. John Alden could not help but wonder again if Caitlin Dewey was the chimesmaster at the controls. He still believed her to be his late wife's grandmother.

"Cheer up, Pilgrim. If you're telling the truth . . . your mother-in-law is not even born yet."

The point had been made in a fit of sarcasm by the Copeland boy on the night of the candlelight dinner. If those in the future had yet to be born, could they still be saved? Or would they, like President of the United States Royal S. Copeland III, be erased from history—as if they had never existed?

The Lab Assistant

The heat of the night made everybody miserable. Nobody knew this Ithaca. The entire student body found themselves longing for the cool, rainy, snowy Ithaca they had come to know and love—the wood-strewn hills where one could experience three of the four seasons in only an hour's time. No, this stretch of heat was from some parallel universe. Some other time. This heat was murder.

Lab assistant Jim Dorn found himself sweating profusely while sweeping up shards of glass in the shadowy bowels of Hell Hall. The lanky grad student had been sweeping up bits of glass for days, a result of the vandalism. The cleanup and repairs would take a month. The stench of ammonia wash was overwhelming.

Left undamaged in the attack was the operating table with the leather straps and the power cords, along with the electric football helmet and its generator, probably because the morons who broke in under the banner of God could not figure out what purpose the contraption served. But Jim Dorn knew of its significance. It was an electric revolution in the science of the human brain. The experiment conducted on John Alden, or whoever he was, was already being trumpeted as a success. And Jim Dorn was helping to write the scientific paper about the research, a paper sure to be published in the most prestigious journals of academia. His name would be on that paper for posterity. This was an unimagined honor for an Ithaca boy of once lowly status. As a child he had hunted in the nearby woods—and not for sport, but for that night's supper.

It was the witching hour, and his bubble of pride was suddenly burst by a shuffling sound and a passing shadow at the far end of the lab. Dorn at first feared the vandals were back, that they could not accept their victory was temporary, and that the mess they made would eventually be cleaned up and the experiments would go on.

"Who's there?" he called, adjusting the black frames of his glasses.

But there was only darkness, nothing more, just the silent burden of the heat playing games with his brain. He returned his broom to the task at hand.

Dr. Ecarius was a genius, Dorn believed, and he was honored to be working for the man. But Ecarius never went far enough fast enough. Instead of plunging forward into the great unknown, he would let the smallest facts hold him back. To Jim Dorn this seemed an incredible waste of time, and the importance of time had been drilled into him.

Suddenly there was that sound again, almost ghost-like. Somebody was in the lab. This time Jim Dorn was sure of it. He carefully set his broom aside and grabbed a scalpel off a table, but just as he stepped forward to investigate, he was seized from behind. Found himself in the grip of a serious strength. His precious glasses were ripped from his face. Then a wet rag, soaked and fresh, was over his mouth. He was a science major. He recognized the sweet smell instantly. In fact, so saccharine was the odor that it was choking him into a state of unconsciousness. There was a gurgling noise that might have been coming from his own mouth. He struggled mightily against the fumes. But his great effort was for naught. The lab assistant went limp.

A LESSON IN CHLOROFORM

When Jim Dorn came to, the first thing he did was spew vomit onto his lab coat. He kicked about some but found he was strapped in. The electric football helmet was tied to his head. He was nearly blind, but he could make out the blinking lights on the control panel. With enlarged and frightened eyes he focused on the tall man standing before him.

"Hello, Jim. Did you enjoy your little nap? Trust me, I know the feeling." John Alden towered over the lab assistant. He was examining Dorn's glasses while at the same time shielding his nose with the back of his hand from the smell of vomit, and from the smell of the chemically soaked rag. "Chloroform . . . I'm guessing you know what that is?"

Dorn swallowed the taste of his vomit. "It's an organic compound with the molecular formula CHCI3," he choked out. "Can I have my glasses, please?"

John Alden turned the black frames over in his hands. "Christ, I've drunk from the bottom of Coke bottles that aren't this thick." He carefully placed the glasses back on the lab assistant's face. "There you go . . . now you'll be able to see what lies ahead." The ex-detective leaned over his suspect. "Chloroform, as you no doubt recall from your studies, comes from a multitude of natural sources, most of them seaweeds. They make a dense, colorless, and oh-so-sweet-smelling liquid, whose vapor just happens to depress the central nervous system. It's a common solvent in laboratories, so I figured there would be some on hand." John Alden wiped away a trickle of sweat from his brow. He unbuttoned his vest and rolled up his sleeves, as if it were time to get to work. "Chloroform was once a popular anesthetic," he went on, "but it had a tendency to induce heart attacks. Even still, in your day, here, it can be found in toothpaste, cough syrup, and a lot of ointments. It's phased out in the future . . . that heart attack thing. However, even in my day, chloroform is used to extract morphine from poppies." Alden tapped his leg. "Lucky for me, huh?" Now he adjusted the electric helmet on the grad student's head, making sure the fit was good and tight. "You see, chloroform, I know. Criminals have used it for years to knock out their victims." He passed his fingers over the luminous dials of the control panel. "But this electricity stuff . . . I just don't know much about this." He put his fingers to his lips, like he had just been struck with a thought. "Oh, wait. I guess I know more than most people." Then he turned and walked to a nearby table and picked up a glass jar with what looked to be a piece of charcoal preserved in formaldehyde. He displayed the jar before grad student Jim Dorn, strapped tight to the operating table. "Now if I remember correctly, and my memory has become a volatile issue on campus . . . Dr. Ecarius told me this specimen here is the brain of a man who died in the electric chair at Sing Sing. Would that be right?"

"How did you get in here?" Dorn wanted to know.

"Old habit of mine . . . sneaking up on people. I was very good at it in the future."

"What do you want?"

"I want you to answer my questions . . . most truthfully and honestly. And should you choose not to . . . well, then I'll just have to start playing with these dials here." John Alden held the fried brain in the jar under his arm while he again let his fingers run over the numbered dials. "The thing of it is, Jim . . . what makes it so risky . . . is that when I was hooked up to this contraption, I could never really see the exact dosage the good doctor was administering. I mean, yes, he told me . . . but I never really saw what knobs he controlled here, or for how long." He put a finger to his forehead. "Again, it's a memory thing."

The pupil of the human eye can grow three times in size. The wide eyes of Jim Dorn grew that much and more. "What do you want to know?"

John Alden held the jar with the shriveled brain up to the lone light bulb burning in the lab. "They have a saying in basketball, or they will have a saying . . . teams that like to press don't like to be pressed. I found in my line of work that's pretty much human nature. Bullies don't like to be bullied. People who inflict pain on others have an overwhelming fear of having pain inflicted on them. And serial killers, those morbid little creatures who live off of fear and control, live in fear themselves of the cops coming to kill them." He lowered the jar. "Tell me about Ithaca Falls."

"It's a big waterfall . . . that's all."

"We both know it's much more than that."

"Those are ancient Indian legends."

"Are you referring to the vortex stories . . . time travel?"

"There's no such thing. It's the stuff of fiction."

"No, Jim, time travel is science. Albert Einstein even has a theory."

"His special theory of relativity suggests we can move forward through time . . . not backward."

John Alden held the charcoal of brain before his eyes. "Well, for now let's forget about what year it happened . . . but somebody in Ithaca murdered my wife. That same person also murdered a United States senator. Said person went on to murder the son of a United States senator. And all of my instincts and all of my training tell me this same person is going to try and murder Governor Roosevelt when he arrives here for commencement."

"Do you think it's Dr. Ecarius?"

"You tell me, Jim. Have you ever seen the good doctor at the foot of Ithaca Falls?"

Dorn swallowed hard, again choking on his vomit. "I have."

"When?"

"Last autumn. I kind of followed him."

"Tell me about it."

"It was late. Midnight. I was walking home. He was way ahead of me. Then he cut through the woods and I followed him because I was curious. I knew that wasn't his way home."

"And what did you see?"

"It was dark, but I could see him at the foot of the falls arguing with somebody."

"And who would that somebody be?"

"My eyesight is not so good from a distance, even with my glasses on, but from his size and shape I'm guessing it was the old school president . . . Dr. Hightower."

"Could you hear what they were arguing about?"

"No, it was the night after that big storm. The falls were way too noisy."

"Wrong answer." John Alden replaced the brain on the table. "Unfortunately for you, Jim, I grew up here. I know what the human voice sounds like at nighttime in the gorge at the foot of the falls." He picked up a rubber plug. "Here," he said, shoving it roughly into Jim Dorn's mouth, "bite down on this."

COOLER DAYS

After eight days of hot, unbearable classrooms, the heat wave finally broke. A Canadian high pressure system slipped slowly across the Great Lakes and then over the Finger Lakes, and it ushered in cool, breezy air, along with steel-blue skies. Now the weeks leading up to finals seemed to fly by like minutes. Time at warp speed. Green leaves emerged on all of the trees, and chilly rains would fall at night and then the sun would shine all day long.

On a bright day in May a popular honor student from an affluent Philadelphia family threw himself headfirst into the gorge, his broken body washing ashore before it neared the falls. Everybody was shocked. For a day or two. Then life at Cornell returned to normal. The baseball team was losing as many games as they won. Preparations were underway for Governor Roosevelt's visit. And posters by the Moral Way were plastered across campus announcing their big year's end rally.

John Alden noisily kicked a chair aside and spread the bound newspapers across the reading table in the Cornell Library. Students nearby shot him a harsh, apprehensive glance, but he no longer cared for their approval. He was increasingly comfortable in his own skin, living in their own time. He flipped through the faded, yellowing pages until he found the edition he was looking for:

THE SENECA FALLS
Tuesday, June 5, 1917
SUFFRAGIST LEADER FOUND DEAD
Foul Play Suspected

His eyes were not as good as they once were. Still standing, he placed both of his hands on the table, leaned in close, and bore holes through the front page.

> Eliza Rhea, 39, a local leader in New York's burgeoning suffragist movement, was found dead in her home this morning. Police Chief Robert Oaks believes foul play was to blame but assures Seneca Falls there is no threat to public safety. His statement suggests the unmarried Rhea knew her killer. Hers is the second death of a suffragist in the Seneca Falls area in the past six months . . .

"Who would a suffragist leader let into her home?" He wondered this aloud, and now students studying in the library shushed him, as if they wanted to strangle him.

So John Alden left the reading room and stood by himself atop a spiral staircase in the tall bay windows of the library that overlooked Libe Slope. He loved libraries, or at least he used to. The preservation of knowledge. The preservation of time. This library echoed the cathedral plans of medieval builders, with a nave and transept, only the high altar in this place of worship was the circulation desk. Cornell had been one of the first universities in America to encourage students to check books out of the library for study. This particular spot, atop the winding staircase, was also one of the most beautiful and most private places on campus.

The professor of criminal justice watched as the noontime crowd gathered on the pastoral tableau that was Libe Slope. Echoing their last rally, this gathering of the sanctimonious right promised to be even larger. American flags, dozens of them, were being lined up behind the podium. The holy rollers were wrapping themselves in the pageantry of the stars and stripes. Liberal thought would be under attack.

Then John Alden heard below him the cautious limp of someone working his way up the wobbly staircase. Someone with the same idea as his, to watch the rally from the perch of the library. He hated the intrusion, but the visitor did not surprise him. "From listening to you climb the stairs," Alden commented, "I would have thought you had only one leg, as opposed to one arm."

Captain Evan Murphy clung to the railing, the white knuckles glowing on his only hand. "My heights bugaboo," he said, finally resting at the top. "I think I told you about it." As always, the state cop was dressed to the nines, from the shine on his black shoes to the folds in the black fedora atop his head. He was forever the dapper detective. "I hear you've been asserting yourself, Professor."

John Alden himself had come to loathe the dress of the day. Where he had at first felt uncomfortable on the buttoned-up campus in the buttoned-up times, he was now the campus contrarian, usually sporting a white shirt proudly open at the collar, sometimes a vest, but never a hat. "Imagine an ex-cop asserting himself."

"Gain anything useful?" Murphy wanted to know, catching his breath.

Along with his investigation into the still unsolved murder of Royal S. Copeland III, John Alden had learned that Captain Evan Murphy of the New York State Police had been put in charge of security for the visit of Governor Franklin Roosevelt to Cornell University. "It seems," he said, "that certain men on campus like to meet and conspire at the foot of Ithaca Falls in the midnight hour."

"Not the most bizarre thing I've heard of on this campus," Murphy told him, observing the rising crowd on Libe Slope, "but not a crime either."

"You're going about this all wrong, Murphy. You started with a conclusion . . . that yours truly, John W. Alden, is a con man, and that he likely killed Royal S. Copeland III because he saw him as some kind of threat to his future plans. And then you set out to prove your conclusion. That, my dear captain, is a detective's recipe for failure. You should have gathered the facts and then followed them wherever they led. It's Detective Work 101. In the future, I write a book about it."

"Every fact I've gathered since arriving in this bedeviled town has led me right back to you."

"C'mon, Captain . . . in your heart, do you really believe I killed the Copeland boy?"

"In my heart I believe you're a fraud."

John Alden shrugged his wide shoulders, a gesture of hopelessness. "Fraud is not murder," he said. "And fraud is not going to do harm to Franklin Roosevelt."

Murphy was angry. "Now why do you say that?"

"Say what?"

"That thing about harming the governor."

"Because," John Alden explained, "it is the surest way to alter America's future." He nodded at the collection of American flags lining the slope. "You have no idea of the country Roosevelt is to inherit, and of the legacy he's to leave behind."

"And you think this serial killer of yours is aware of these changes to come and is out to harm the governor . . . before he becomes president."

"I'm almost sure of it."

"And what if say, strictly for security reasons, I were to lock up your crazy ass until after the governor's visit?"

John Alden looked him square in the eye, one cop to another, veteran to veteran. "That would almost certainly prove my innocence . . . but it could also result in the governor's demise."

"I don't want to hear that kind of talk."

"And what of that kind of talk?" he asked, pointing to the podium.

Father Wallace Dougal was at the microphone. The sun was shining down upon him. The crowd was going wild with applause. With a weird forest of American flags fluttering behind him, the Catholic priest held an oversized Bible high in the sky and began calling God's wrath down upon the university on the hill. The crowd was loving it. And America's religious right, under the leadership of men like Father Wallace Dougal, were loving it.

"I have a lot less on him than I do on you," Murphy told him above the roar of the rally.

"I'm not surprised," John Alden said to him, "but I have an idea. Are you doing anything tonight?"

THE GIRL AT THE RALLY

John Alden had spotted her from his perch in the library. She stood like a saint at the foot of the slope, a part of the crowd yet separate from the raucous rally before her. He left the library and skirted the idiotic-patriotic rabble, making his way down the hill until at last he sauntered up beside her. She ignored him at first, a worried look on her face, undoubtedly wondering about the place of women in this new America she was all of a sudden hearing about. He stood silent beside her, admiring her beauty and her youth. Through the loudspeakers came the tinny voice of Father Dougal warning against the threat of a socialist flood. The priest was surrounded by young people who hung on his every word. The Ithaca Motion Picture Company was filming the event from the bed of a hay wagon. The footage was bound to appear in a newsreel or a movie.

The religious fervor of the Libe Slope rally seemed strange for an American campus, and doubly strange for a university like Cornell. It was as if the entire student body saw a big change coming, and it scared them. So they sought refuge in religion draped in the American flag, where lies were accepted as truth, where they were promised new textbooks that falsified history, and where men like Franklin Roosevelt were suddenly considered socialist sinners. "Godless!" bellowed the Catholic priest, for what seemed the hundredth time.

"They told me you were in the hospital," Caitlin said between applause.

"I was having my batteries recharged."

"So tell me, what year were you born?"

"I don't play that game anymore."

She was angry with him. "You dangle the promise of closeness and then you just disappear. I'm beginning to suspect, as others have, that you've got disappearing down to a science."

They listened to more of the priest at the microphone, bringing God Almighty to Ithaca. He was the carnival barker on a stage writ large. The thousands gathered on the slope of the hill were being driven crazy by his holy pronouncements.

"Do you have money in the bank?" Alden finally asked her. "Does your mother have money in the bank?"

"Well, of course we have money in the bank." She stepped away from him, as if she were actually more interested in what the priest had to say.

"Caitlin, listen to me," he said, stepping closer. "For the time being, take all of your money out of the bank. I know it sounds counter-intuitive, but in the days ahead, money outside of the bank will become more valuable than money inside the bank. If I'm wrong, you can always put the money back. But if I'm right and the banks collapse . . . you and your mother stand to lose everything."

She motioned to the crowd. "None of this makes any sense. This is the dawn of a new age. Times have never been better."

"You're right, a new age is coming . . . but, Caitlin, it isn't pretty."

Caitlin Dewey turned and stared at him now, as puzzled by the man as she was by the rally.

John Alden did not know what to say to her anymore. So he leaned in and kissed her, just lightly on the lips. It was their first kiss, undying in its poignancy, and she seemed surprised by it. Then he stood back and thought of how he must be confusing the hell out of this young woman.

MIDNIGHT AT THE FALLS

The Catholic priest who had so stirred the young masses was the first to arrive at the foot of the falls. It was a Thursday night, the twenty-third day of May, 1929, a rare, clear night in Ithaca—the kind of night where the Iroquois would have gathered beneath the stars on the shores of Cayuga Lake and traded stories of the constellations. A full moon with the brightness of a headlamp sent deep shadows cascading up and down the gorge. And though it was getting late in May, water still flowed heavy and fast over the falls, creating a white noise almost musical to the ears. Father Wallace Dougal stood before the eternal falls as if in a trance, as if he were about to drop to his knees and pray to its mythical powers.

"Are you expecting somebody, Father Dougal?"

The priest turned when he heard that. He was disgusted. "I should have known you'd be here. What do you want, Ecarius?"

"It's Dr. Ecarius, and I was about to ask you the same thing."

The two antagonists were face to face when they heard a loud, rustling sound, like a bear making its way through the woods to the water. They both turned to watch. They saw the rotund shadow of the quintessential academic emerge from the path between the trees. This big old bear of a man was draped in a spring coat and was calmly swinging a cane.

Father Dougal stepped toward him. "What is the meaning of this, President Hightower? More of your hijinks?"

The old man seemed surprised by the accusation, as well as the company. "Father Dougal, might I guess that you, too, received an invitation?"

"I got a note."

"As did I," said Ecarius.

"May I see them?" asked the old man, holding out his hand. He adjusted the spectacles perched on his nose and strained to read the writing in the moonlight.

Meet me at midnight at the foot of Ithaca Falls
The future depends on it

Hightower examined the scrawl. "It would seem the three of us have gotten identical invitations. For what purpose, I do not know."

"Look there!" Ecarius pointed to the infamous Rickety Bridge up the falls and down the gorge. Beneath the luminous moon two identical female shadows draped in hooded dresses skirted the planks north to south. "It seems," Ecarius said, "the Hightower family is out in full force tonight."

"I can assure you, gentlemen, I am not behind this ruse."

"Then who are we waiting for?" Father Dougal demanded to know.

"Alden," declared Ecarius, turning back to the men. "John I-know-the-future Alden . . . that's who we're waiting for."

"True," said Hightower, staring up at the falls. "I did not see our mystery man this evening. But then after what you did to him, I'm surprised he knows his name."

"He does not know his name . . . that was the whole point of the experiment."

"Then allow me to introduce myself," came a cry from deep in the woods. "John W. Alden, Detective: First Grade. New York City Police Department. Retired." All three men were startled by the force of the voice. They turned to look, but they all turned in different directions. It was as if the disembodied voice was coming from multiple places, as if the falls itself had captured a vocal influence and was now hurling it down the gorge.

Ecarius, angry, shouted into the night, "Another one of your magic tricks, Mr. Alden? I'll have you up on charges for what you did to my student."

"You can't, Doctor. For the time being, I'm legally insane, remember? It's like blanket immunity."

Now President Hightower addressed the dark of the woods. "What is the meaning of this, Mr. Alden? I know deep down you are bitter about the therapy, but yours is a most unusual case."

"I'm not bitter. Turns out electricity can be an eye-opening experience."

"Where are you?" Hightower asked, confused by a voice whose source he could not see. "This is most irregular."

"It's an anomaly of sound," came the voice through the trees. "Ithaca is famous for them. This stretch of the gorge is particularly interesting. I'm sure someday there'll be a scientific explanation for it . . . but basically the human voice is amplified over the falls. It's almost like those ancient Greek theaters, where an actor's voice could be heard loud and clear even in the furthest seats. We first learned of the spot when we were kids. We shouted up a storm down here. As curious teens we would come down here at night and listen to young couples making love."

Dr. Ecarius called back. "We can now add voyeurism to your long list of symptoms."

"I got suspicious when your man Dorn told me he followed you down here one night . . . but that he couldn't hear a thing that was said because of the falls. I knew that to be a lie. This is better than an amphitheater. Isn't that right, Captain Murphy?"

Now the three visible men beneath the falls grew more nervous. They visually searched the deep-wooded gorge during the spooky silence that followed, the concern on their faces clearly registering in the white moonlight.

"I guess the cat has his tongue tonight," John Alden's voice told them, "but I believe two out of three of you would like to see the good captain lock me up."

"You belong locked up," Ecarius shot back.

"What do you want?" Father Dougal demanded to know.

"I want the man who killed the Copeland boy . . . and then I want to go home."

"You are home, Mr. Alden," Ecarius told the night. "You're just too ill to realize it."

"Tell me about Ithaca Falls, gentlemen."

"It's a goddamn waterfall," Ecarius said, swearing for the priest's sake. "Name me a college town and I'll name for you all of the silly legends that come along with it."

"Do you mean like Bobby Bill, the Great Ghost of a Cornell football player, disappearing into the trees following touchdowns?" came Alden's rejoinder. "Or Bobby Bill diving into the gorge to save a puppy? Or the Bobby Bill who went missing in action?"

"Bobby Bill was all too real," Ecarius assured him. "The only mystery is whatever became of him . . . or should I say *you*."

President Hightower again addressed the night. "Dr. Ecarius and I and Father Dougal are all in agreement on that particular subject, Mr. Alden. I think even Captain Murphy would agree. Robert Alden Bill was a Cornell man . . . and his whereabouts have not been known in years."

Father Dougal, unable to see the man who had lured him to the falls, waved the piece of paper in his hand to the moon. "What does all of this prove? A cryptic note like this could have gotten a hundred students here tonight."

"Sometimes as cops we just like to stir things up."

Dr. Victor Ecarius stepped toward the creek and peered across the water, suggesting he had discovered Alden's hiding place. His shrill and unpleasant voice changed now from anger to sarcasm. "Since we're all gathered here tonight beneath your mystical falls, perhaps you could endeavor to entertain us with more of your tricks, Mr. Alden. Tell us something of the future." Now the scientist was at the edge of the rushing water, waving his hands in a mocking gesture, a crazed expression on his face. "Father Dougal and I will be mere footnotes in Cornell history, if we're remembered at all. But President Hightower is a living legend." Here he challenged the disembodied voice, his stick-like figure in the moonlight being the most menacing of the three. "If you grew up in Ithaca, if you taught criminal justice at Cornell University, as you claim, then you certainly knew of H.W. Hightower . . . even in the year 2010. So, Mr. Alden, tell President Hightower when it is he is to die . . . and how he is to die. Because if you're from Cornell's future, you surely have to know."

"This is a fool's game, gentlemen," Hightower said, more to himself. "And a very dangerous one."

"Yes, I know of President Hightower's death," responded the mellifluous voice in the trees, "but I'm not cruel enough to say . . . even though I suspect President Hightower is more aware of the future than he's willing to admit."

Hightower spoke to the shadows of the deep gorge. "I know only of the past, Mr. Alden, because I lived so much of it. I know nothing of things to come. One must live a very long time to realize how little they know of the world . . . and even less of the future."

"Then let me tell all of you of the days to come," boomed the voice that seemed to have traversed time. "One of us here tonight has committed multiple murders . . . and is planning to kill again. In the not-so-distant future that man will meet a fiery form of justice." There was a long silence. Then came the bells from the clock tower. The midnight concert. "This has been fun," said the voice of things to come. "Goodnight, gentlemen."

Slope Day

Slope Day began bright and sunny in Upstate New York, a beautiful morning in late May. This unofficial student celebration was not nearly as decadent as Halloween night, but it was just as infused with alcohol. Slope Day was the last day of spring semester classes. The day would be followed by the stress of finals week, followed shortly thereafter by commencement. So on this brilliant morning thousands of Cornell students, thinking *themselves* to be brilliant, gathered on Libe Slope, as they had been doing for years—basking in the sunshine, drinking from flasks, flirting shamelessly, trashing the lawn, and swearing up a storm. Meanwhile, their freshmen brethren were busy erecting the skeleton of a gigantic bonfire at the foot of the slope.

But within an hour of the revelry's launch, clouds began building over Cayuga Lake. And then the dark clouds rolled slowly up the hill to the university. Skies were completely overcast by noon when the rumors reached Ithaca. Something was happening on Wall Street. Something horrific. It was said entire fortunes were being wiped out in a matter of hours. A frightful collapse. There was word of panic in the streets.

At Cornell an emergency meeting was called by the Board of Trustees, and throughout the afternoon administration bigwigs could be seen migrating towards President's House. Ghostly white faces were slipping in and out of the Gothic mansion on East Hill, and the most ashen face of all belonged to the financial administrator, Livingston Hughes, who had berated John Alden on the night of the candlelight dinner.

In truth, a wave of fear had swept the market. People began to sell. The *Times* industrial average was off 10 points for the day. Banks began curtailing their loans in the call market, and the rate on broker's loans shot up to 14 percent. Each new share price that marched across the ticker was far below the previous price. It seemed to many on this day that the boom market was over. The Roaring '20s had reached their end.

Rumors at Cornell continued to grow like the poisonous weeds in the gorges. Soon a large crowd of mostly drunken students had gathered on the great lawn before President's House. The very next week their parents would begin arriving in Ithaca for commencement festivities. The governor of New York was coming to town.

Inside President's House, H.W. Hightower dispatched a messenger to the third floor to retrieve John Alden, but he was told the mystery man was nowhere to be found. Hightower was not surprised. John Alden was not an I-told-you-so kind of man.

So in the small town of Ithaca, New York, in the midst of a financial crisis, a crowd gathered on the lawn beneath a canopy of elms to hear from an old man who had supposedly surrendered his authority long ago. The board urged him to make a statement. Stop the rumors. Ease the fears.

It was late afternoon and daytime dark by the time the president emeritus stepped onto the second floor balcony overlooking the quad. There was no applause, only a drunken silence. The gray clouds overhead had rolled to a stop. Even the wind and the birds seemed suddenly still. The old man stared down into the youthful faces crowding before him and remembered a time in New Haven when he himself was young. The dream and the desire to return to that age overwhelmed him, and he choked up before speaking. Then he cleared his throat. Strength and confidence were imperative. These students had to believe the bright future they dreamed of, the future they were working toward, was still within their grasp. John Alden had warned that what mostly lay ahead for them was depression and war—that more than any generation since the War Between the States, they would be asked to sacrifice.

H.W. Hightower, PhD, president emeritus of Cornell University, straightened his top coat and puffed out his chest. "If you people are here today to sing me *Happy Birthday*, you have been terribly misinformed." Laughter filtered up from below. There was no hostility in this crowd, only concern. "I wish to speak to you about the events on Wall Street today. It seems there was some wild speculation this morning, followed by some panic selling, but the crisis was pretty much quelled by noon. We have been communicating by telephone all day with our financial representatives in New York City, and I can assure you the stock market is fundamentally sound. In point of fact, it is technically in better condition today than it has been in months. In the morning, trading on the market should start laying a foundation for a constructive recovery. As for the university . . . I am confident the diversity of our investments will insulate us from any financial catastrophe." Then he waved his big fat hand in mocking annoyance. "So go, future generations. Enjoy the fiery night. Next week, finals begin."

There was a great round of applause for the aging and retired university president.

But back inside President's House, nobody was smiling. While all of the bankers and most politicians were speaking of how sound the market was, and that this single black day was only a correction, one prescient politician recognized the near sudden crash as a portent of things to come. Governor Franklin D. Roosevelt, speaking in Poughkeepsie, harshly criticized what he called the "fever of speculation" that had gotten the country headed in the direction of a giant collapse.

THE BIG RED BONFIRE

By the time the market closed on Slope Day there had been a slight rally, somewhat easing fears across the country and throughout the hills of Ithaca. People left President's House thinking the worst was behind them. Even the weather got better. When the warm sun finally set on Slope Day, everybody on campus donned letter sweaters and sweatshirts and drifted toward the giant pile of wood erected at the foot of Libe Slope.

The word *bonfire* comes from the words *bone* and *fire*. *Fire of bones*. The Celtic people believed the time between the beginning and end of the harvest was when spirits could travel freely between this world and the spirit world. The bones of animals were culled and burned as offerings. Cornell's Big Red bonfire on the green at the foot of Libe Slope was almost thirty feet tall and had taken a week to construct. Seemed each freshman class was after a record. How high could they build the beast? Thirty feet was a new record, built from railroad ties, scrap from local farms, and fallen timber from the nearby woods. The Ithaca Motion Picture Company contributed two 14-foot uprights and a crossbar. When the skeleton of wood was completed, it had the appearance of a monster of a man set to devour the entire campus.

As had been done for years, a senior student was awarded the privilege of igniting the fire of bones. He was costumed as Vulcan, the Roman god of fire. Ablaze in a red cape and black face paint, he represented the triumph of spring over winter. "I do tonight what the gods have been doing since man's time on this earth began," the devilish figure shouted to the crowd. "I set fire to wood and light up the night." Then he took the flaming torch and jammed it into the foot of the beast. The flames began unhurried and then they slowly grew while they climbed, until it seemed all of Ithaca was ablaze.

CAITLIN

On the night of the Big Red bonfire Caitlin Dewey stood at the foot of the slope, mesmerized by the flames, only a few feet from the spot where she had stood and watched the Moral Way rally. Before her was a fire to behold. Flames climbed to the heavens and then shot to the stars in perfect teepee formation. The bonfire burned brilliant shades of red and orange, the colors of autumn. The crowd around her stood in silent awe. Through the fire she could see the dancing outlines of the clock tower, the chapel, and atop the hill the gables of President's House, where what seemed like the speck of a candlelight was flickering in the third floor window.

As suggested, she had taken her money out of the bank and had convinced her mother to withdraw her own savings. Already there were stories about runs on banks, and of other banks abruptly closing. John Alden's first big prediction was bearing fruit. Her mother, money in hand, had boarded a train in Portland. She would be arriving in Ithaca soon. They were planning on together attending the commencement festivities, including the speech by Governor Roosevelt.

"What the hell was that?"

Caitlin Dewey saw nothing, but she turned to hear the conversation.

"Looked like another costume."

She saw a creepy shadow float by the corner of her eye. It was near the woods that led to the Rickety Bridge over the gorge. Caitlin turned back to the fire and saw the devilish Vulcan with the blackened face, torch in hand, standing statue still at the foot of the flames. He seemed for the moment to be staring right at her. Then she caught a bit of another conversation coming from behind.

"Did you see that?"

"See what?"

"A man with a hat and a cape . . . and I think he was wearing a mask."

"Really? The god of fire must have his men out in force tonight."

Caitlin thought little of it. It was Slope Day. Bonfire night. The weather had cleared. The stock market had rallied. The student body was drunk and giddy. The night breeze still had a bite to it, so the heat from the bonfire felt good to her. She checked the watch on her wrist. It was her night to play the chimes. The last midnight concert of the school year.

Suddenly there was a symphony of screams. Caitlin was startled. She jumped back as the top of the bonfire toppled over and sent sparks shooting into the night. The screams were followed by laughter as the thrill of it all settled in. The fire was burning down. Caitlin wished the sights and sounds, the pure joy of life in college, could last forever. But the bonfire was crumbling. She checked her watch again and then set off for the clock tower.

She made her way up the hill, the flames dancing beneath her. By the time she reached the sidewalk to the clock tower, she was alone. She turned to see the crowd, still entranced by the bonfire. Vulcan had his back to her. When she turned again, she saw an ominous shadow disappear between the trees and the library wall. A chill ran down her spine, and she picked up the pace. Then came the overwhelming feeling she was being followed. She was too scared to stop, so she pivoted as if she were a ballerina and walked backwards. And then out of the elms he came.

He was a big man in a mask beneath a floppy black hat. He spread his arms and his black cape extended like the wings of a bat. Then he reached for her neck. But Caitlin Dewey stopped on a dime and let loose with a scream that broke through the night. It was a loud, frightening scream that disrupted the drunken crowd at the bonfire below and sent hordes of them racing up the hill.

She did not faint, but her cry for help was so loud and exhausting it drained her of strength, and she dropped to her knees. The man in the mask stumbled backward with the sound of the scream; then he recovered and vanished as fast as he had appeared. Her fellow students were gathering around her.

"It was that creep in the black cape. I saw him limping away."

"He tried to attack her."

"Let's spread out . . . and keep your eyes open."

It was Vulcan himself who at last helped her to her feet. "Summon the police," he told the students. The Roman god of fire held Caitlin Dewey in one hand and his torch in the other. "Come on, we'll get her over to President's House."

"No," Caitlin told him. "I have to play the chimes."

"My dear," said the god of fire, "there'll be no chimes tonight."

"Oh, but I must," she insisted. "It's tradition."

The Grandfather Paradox

It was another bright morning in Upstate New York. A spring day to be worshipped. Captain Evan Murphy of the New York State Police picked up the Sunday paper on the steps of President's House.

The Ithaca Journal
May 26, 1929
ITHACA PREPARES FOR GOVERNOR'S ARRIVAL
Events on Wall Street Heighten Roosevelt's Visit

Murphy put the headline up to his face and hit the doorbell with his elbow. He had been listening all weekend to the reports about the short-lived panic on Wall Street. Most thought it a one-day event. Few thought it was the beginning of the end. However, any way they spun it, the day had almost played out as John Alden had predicted it would. The mystery professor had also been right about the strange gathering of men in the midnight hour at the foot of Ithaca Falls.

Governor Roosevelt would be in town in just five days. There was still an unsolved murder, and now the attempted assault of the Dewey girl. The chimesmaster. Under normal circumstances he would have advised the governor to cancel his visit, but the calamity on Wall Street had suddenly given the New York governor a national stage. Murphy elbowed the doorbell again.

A graduate student answered the door. Then the young man led the police captain upstairs, where he pointed to yet another, more narrow flight of stairs that led up to the third floor. Murphy made his way up the dusty steps. The door at the top of the stairs was open, allowing a breeze to cut through the room. John Alden was seated at his desk before the window overlooking the quad. He was writing.

"Top of the morning to you, Captain," said Alden with a touch of sarcasm in his voice.

"Morning." Captain Murphy conducted a police search with his eyes.

It was a small but cozy room. The ceiling jutted up and down at sharp angles, giving the room an asymmetrical configuration. There was a bed. A four-poster. The bed had been made that morning with military precision. There was a small chest of drawers sitting against a wall, a mirror hanging above it. And there was a closet with no door or curtain, where very few clothes were hanging. A thin-legged nightstand stood beside the bed. On the nightstand beside some books was a wind-up alarm clock with two large oxidized bells at the top and a copper hammer between them, waiting to strike. As opposed to being futuristic, the clock had the dull sheen of an antique. Old world. Murphy walked into the room, tossed the newspaper onto the bed, and picked up the alarm clock. Examined it.

"What did you expect to find," John Alden asked his guest, "computers?"

"I don't know what a *computer* is . . . and I really don't know what to expect from you anymore."

John Alden rose from the desk and moved uneasily beside Murphy. He grabbed a fat dictionary from the nightstand and returned to the desk.

Murphy watched him walk. "You're limping again."

"I twisted my ankle," Alden said, taking his seat. "Not hard to do in Ithaca."

"You heard about the attack on the Dewey girl?"

"I did. I was hoping to see her later."

"Sounds like it was your man."

"It does."

Murphy raised the alarm clock to the tip of his nose, as if he were trying to figure out what made the damn thing tick.

"The green alarm bells are made of copper," Alden told him. "From the Latin word *cuprum.* Over a long period of time oxygen corrodes copper, giving it that patina."

"Time eroding a clock. Oh, the irony." Murphy placed the clock back on the nightstand. "Why would this serial killer of yours stage an attack five days before the governor's visit? I mean, another murder would almost certainly lead the governor to cancel his visit."

"A killer can't control his impulses. You know that. He may also have been getting back at me for our little stunt at Ithaca Falls."

"Or last night's attack was a copycat. Somebody who knew the killer's every move. Somebody who very much wants the governor to cancel his trip to Ithaca."

Alden paged through the dictionary. "If that was the case . . . then Caitlin Dewey was never in any danger. No harm, no foul."

"If I were to toss your room right now . . . what are the odds I would find a mask and a cape?"

"If you were going to toss my room you would have done it a month ago."

Murphy pulled open the top drawer on the chest of drawers. He lifted by his fingertips the black handgun, as if it were an oddity he had never seen before. Then he raised his eyes to the mirror and saw John Alden watching him. The police captain addressed the man in the mirror. "What the hell kind of gun is this?"

"It's a Smith & Wesson .38 Super automatic. It's built on the frame of the regular Army .45. It has an incredibly flat trajectory and makes a hole the size of my fist. They just went into production this year. I bought it off an ROTC colonel."

Murphy, not happy, dropped the latest in American weaponry back into the drawer and closed it. "I prefer a good revolver . . . thirty-three ounces of weight in your hand, with a six-inch barrel. By the time a man pulls the trigger on a revolver, he's well aware of what he's doing." He turned away from the reflection in the mirror and addressed the man. "So tell me . . . what kind of weaponry are we cops carrying in the future?"

John Alden continued paging through the dictionary. "Most police have switched to the automatics, but with larger clips. Other than that, things haven't changed much."

"Do we still shoot the bad guys?"

"Oh hell, yes. There're more bullets flying through the air than ever before."

The one-armed cop moved slowly across the room, his eyes drawn to a picture on the wall. It was a framed photograph of a Cornell football player. Murphy inspected the sepia image. "Robert Alden Bill," he stated, as if for the record. "Also known as Bobby Bill, a.k.a. The Ghost Runner."

"Yes, they tell me that's who that is."

Murphy nodded. "I recognize him from the photos down at the field house." He gestured toward the mirror. "A striking resemblance, don't you think?"

John Alden looked up from the dictionary and glanced at his own reflection in the mirror. He shrugged his football wide shoulders. "I don't see it. The picture was hanging in the room when I arrived . . . or at least it was here by the time I regained consciousness."

"I'm sure it was," Murphy said. He lifted the frame with his pinky finger. Peeked behind the photo. There was no discoloration of the wallpaper. "I'm willing to bet Hightower himself pounded in the nail the frame hangs from."

"*Schadenfreude,*" Alden said, his fingers settling on a word on the page.

"Excuse me?"

"*Schadenfreude*. What does it mean?"

"I don't know . . . it sounds German. I might have heard it used during the war."

"It is German," Alden told him. "It means enjoyment obtained from the trouble of others. First known use . . . 1895."

Murphy nodded. "Seems to be a lot of *Schadenfreude* on this campus."

John Alden finished reading to himself the full definition of the word. Then he asked, "Why are you up here?"

"Governor Roosevelt is arriving Friday . . . come hell or high water. How much danger is he in?"

"I really don't know."

"I think that you might."

John Alden scribbled his own more simple definition of *Schadenfreude* into his notebook and then closed the dictionary. "Have you ever heard of the Grandfather Paradox?"

Murphy stepped away from the photograph of Bobby Bill. "Sounds like some college boy theory to me."

"That's exactly what it is. Science fiction elevated to scientific theory . . . an inconsistency at the very heart of time travel. If you travel into the past and murder your own grandfather before he meets your grandmother, where does that leave you? Do you cease to exist, or do you continue living on, but in that time period? Your grandmother meets someone else, and your brothers and sisters may or may not be born . . . they just have different parentage."

"Either way . . . your grandfather has been murdered."

"Not necessarily," Alden told him. "Another theory posits that you cannot murder your grandfather, because *you* are the paradox. Say you go to shoot him . . . the gun jams. Or another person steps in the way. Or police shoot you first. What seems like luck in your grandfather's time was really the universe contriving to prevent the act. Your grandfather cannot be killed by *you*. You, however, are expendable . . . because *you* are not supposed to be there."

"So under your college boy theory, it's possible Roosevelt can't be killed here?"

"Well, not by his grandchildren. He's destined to become president."

Captain Evan Murphy picked up the newspaper off of the bed and again read the headline. "And the stock market . . . remind me again . . . what's that destined for?"

"Trust me. By the time Roosevelt is president . . . your stocks will be burnt toast."

THE FLYING LEAP

In the week that followed that day of panic, the stock market rallied. It soared so high that in the end that one drama-filled day was all but forgotten. It was said of the spring of 1929 that never in world history had so many people become so rich so fast.

The little man stood at the highest peak of the highest bluff on the Fall Creek gorge. No path led up to this crest. The only access was to skirt the trees through the woods and then climb the rocks. In the boulder-strewn gorge below, the ever-rushing water rounded a bend and formed a pool. It was a swirling but strangely inviting pool. Cornell legend had it that it was from this point the great Bobby Bill perfected a swan dive into the pool to rescue a drowning dog. A myth for sure. Livingston Hughes stood statue-like at the same exact point, his small black eyes gazing down at the water, just beyond the tips of his toes. Dressed in black tails and tie, he looked like the little man atop a towering wedding cake, sans a bride.

Livingston Hughes was a banker by trade. He knew numbers. Stocks. Securities. Margins. Collateral loans. Interest rates. If that one day of trading, that black day on the market, had proven one thing, it proved to him the stock market was far from being "fundamentally sound." It was as broken as was a shattered vase, and it had been replaced by a funhouse mirror. In just one single, eye-opening day, Livingston Hughes had been given the ability to do what John Alden claimed only he could do. He could see the future. He knew the worst was to come. And then the worst would worsen. As opposed to a minor correction, the whole economy was tumbling face forward into the abyss. The mystery man who had washed up at the foot of Ithaca Falls with the temerity to predict economic ruin had been right all along. When in the coming months the Board of Trustees got a look at the numbers, the real numbers, the finance administrator would be out of a job, if not in jail. In truth, it was doubtful Livingston Hughes would ever work again. At least not in finance. And what else does a numbers man do?

He had never been drawn to nature—books and equations were his love—but somehow Livingston Hughes had found himself drawn to Ithaca. The landscape was unearthly. And then there was the university. President Hightower, an enigma himself, had convinced the banker to stay. But he had needed little convincing. Now, glancing downstream, he could see the Rickety Bridge outlined against the setting sun, and beyond that the gold-glittering water rushing over the edge of Ithaca Falls. It was the roaring sound of the cascading spray that now graced his ears. Even before John Alden's arrival, the university's finance administrator had heard the stories about the falls. Maybe he, too, would be given a second chance.

In the end, he heard voices. They were far away, but strangely distinct. They were talking about the stock market crash, shocking rumors about brokers throwing themselves from towering windows into the streets of Manhattan. A myth for sure.

And then the unremarkable Livingston Hughes gorged out. With his arms held tightly at his sides, he fell face forward. Literally toppled head over heels in the direction of the mystic water that raced through the gorge on its way to Ithaca Falls.

The Ghost of Cornell

It was pouring rain the day the Harvard eleven came to Ithaca. They had traveled all the way from Cambridge to play the reigning national champions, the Big Red of Cornell University. Only this year a bid to the Rose Bowl was on the line. The most prestigious athletic event in college sports. The long train ride west. New Year's Day. Pasadena. Sunshine. Oranges and roses. Parades and beauty queens. This would be the capstone of any player's career, but in this game all eyes would be on one player in particular. Cornell's All-American quarterback. Bobby Bill.

There seemed no pass the Ghost Runner could not complete, no tackle he could not escape. His uniform slipped from defenders as if it were greased. When playing on defense, his own tackles were inescapable. His nose for interceptions and fumbles allowed him to lead the nation in those two categories for the second straight year. On the day of the big game, Ithaca's very own Bobby Bill had it all.

All, except the woman he loved.

It was the night before the Harvard game, and the two lovers found themselves at the foot of Ithaca Falls. The sky on this night was luminous, as opposed to the mountains of clouds that would descend on them the next morning. Stars shone like diamonds. There was a full moon. The Hunter's Moon. Season's end. The spires of the university could be seen protruding from the trees atop the gorge. The evening air was late autumn cool. The waterfall was as magical and musical as ever.

"I have this idea for a new trick," he told her, trying desperately to change the subject. He spoke with the enthusiasm of an eager child. "Coach Night Train loves it. On stage I have two glass vats filled with liquid, you know, like those jars of formaldehyde in the labs. In one vat

the liquid is crystal clear. But in the other vat, the liquid is ink black. Then I take a book . . . some rare history book from President Hightower's personal library . . . something like that. I show the printed pages to the crowd. Then I dip the book into the vat of clear liquid. The water turns black. People gasp at the heresy . . . at the damage being done. When I pull the book from the magic vat . . . the pages are blank. Every last one of them. Old man Hightower has a heart attack. A hundred years of history have just been erased."

"That sounds fun, Bobby."

"Wait, that's not the best part. Then I dip the blank book into the other inky liquid. And when I retrieve it . . . all of the pages are freshly printed. Then I make a joke about rewriting history. Obviously, I need two different books, but identical in appearance. The trick is making the switch."

She seemed to be paying him and his silly magic act little mind, her own thoughts lost somewhere in the water tumbling over the rocks. "They say those who wash over the falls vanish. They disappear for eternity."

"Yes. It's called drowning. Cayuga swallows them whole."

She was a brown-haired, brown-eyed beauty, her splendor even more radiant in the moonlight. "Bobby, don't be so unromantic."

"Then don't leave me."

She turned to him and raised her eyes up to his eyes. "I have a chance to go sailing in the Caribbean with friends . . . for once in my life, to leave the snow and the cold behind me. I've never been out of Ithaca, Bobby. Please, let me go."

"What . . . with those snobs from the Upper East Side of Manhattan? Is that what you want?"

"Yes, maybe it is."

"Oh yes, they all want to be our friends . . . until the end of football season. Then they'll drop you and me both, like a couple of freshman flunkies."

"You're a god here in Ithaca, Bobby Bill. But to me, this is just a suffocating little town in a great big world. I'm moving on. And you

should move on, too." She put her hand to his heart. "Bobby, you are so smart. I overheard President Hightower talking about you. You could be so much more than just a football player."

"I don't understand any of this."

"Please, stop saying that."

"Then explain it to me."

"There are things, Bobby Bill, that are simply beyond you. You are blind to them."

Now anger was seeping into his voice. "You couldn't wait until after the game?"

"This isn't about football."

"You've had sex with me. You can't just . . ."

She dropped her hand. "I can't just what?"

"There are rules."

"No, Bobby . . . those rules only exist in your mind."

The All-American boy was standing at the foot of the falls, near tears now, trying desperately to think of something to say to her, something to change her mind. As it turned out, this was the last thing he said to her at Cornell, his plaintive voice carrying out over the gorge. "Will you be at the game?"

The whole football game had a dreamlike feel to it. Actually, it was more like a nightmare. The rain and the mud had put an end to the passing game. Even the running game was a slow motion trod. The first half of the contest was sluggish and painful. Scoreless. In the third quarter Harvard managed a touchdown on an end run, but they failed to convert the extra point. Then came the fourth quarter, and the rain began to fall even harder. The fans in the stands were emptying out. Up the hill the students ran. Into the parking lot.

Standing mid-field, hands on his hips, he saw her up there. She was left sitting alone in the bleachers that lined the hill, her arms crossed over her knees, her head bare, her wet hair framing a beautiful face exposed to the weather. The rain was washing over her. He himself was caked in mud. She could have no way of knowing which player he was. Then she got up, turned her back on the sodden field, and walked slowly up the stairs between the bleachers.

On the top step she was met by a priest. That new priest. He took off his coat and draped it over her head. Then the priest turned, his collar to the field. Made the sign of the cross. Blessed the players. Forgave them their sins. Then he escorted her out of the stadium.

He watched her go. Between plays, Bobby Bill stood in the mud and watched the love of his life walk up the hill and out of the stadium. There was something deep in his heart that told him he would never see her again. Not in this lifetime.

The ego of the All-American boy does not allow for failure, much less rejection. One by one players were being carted off of the field, felled from exhaustion. But even on the field it was hard to tell which players were out. Mud had obscured their faces. Erased their numerals. Robbed them of their identity.

It was nearing the end of the game and Harvard controlled the ball, and the clock. A simple pitch to the left was called. The Harvard quarterback pivoted in the mud and pitched the ball to his halfback, moving in a straight line behind his blockers. The halfback was hoping to get around the corner and slog down the sideline, as he had done for Harvard's only score. But this time there was a Cornell player waiting for him, a big man who had fallen for none of the shifts and fakes. He had shed his blocker as if he were just another layer of sludge. And though his face was plastered in mud, rendering him unrecognizable, the Harvard running back knew from the killer look in his eyes that the Big Red football player was the lethal Bobby Bill. He braced himself for the hit. Tried to protect the ball. But the Ghost Runner was just too damn fast, and too damn mean.

Bobby Bill planted his shoulder into the runner's midsection. The ball went flying from his arms. He buried the Harvard back deep in the earth of Ithaca. Then he spun around to see the football plop into the mud beside him. Bobby Bill climbed to his feet, scooped the ball out of the muck, and he took off running—towards the Woods.

It was like running through wet cement. Like running in chains. But as slow as Bobby Bill felt on this day, the Harvard eleven who were chasing him were even more deliberate. The diehards who remained in the stands rose to their feet, their screams but faint echoes when heard through the rain.

No yard lines were visible. The goal line had vanished in the first quarter. So Bobby Bill fixed his eyes on the goalposts, ten yards deep in the end zone. And that is where he ran. His sidelined teammates were like a squad of spirits cheering him on, and as always, the loudest of the loud was Coach Night Train. "Run, Bobby, run!"

He ran right between the goalposts, beneath the crossbar. Six points. Tie game. But that was all of the football the All-American boy had left in him. The Big Red were on their own now—because the Ghost Runner just kept on running. Through the pines.

He sprinted through the deserted campus, across wet grass and dead autumn leaves, the cold rain pouring over him, washing him clean. Somewhere on Libe Slope he dropped the football.

Bobby Bill ran down the hill to the woods above the Fall Creek gorge. He fought his way through the trees and onto the cliffs. And then he climbed. He climbed to a spot he knew well. To the top of the cliff. The highest spot above the gorge. The rain had turned the water below into a raging river that gathered in a pool at the foot of the cliff. But because of the sheer volume of water cascading above Ithaca Falls, that pool was now swirling, spinning with the force of a liquid tornado.

He stood there as noble as any warrior before him. Then, dressed in the full regalia of the Big Red football team, and with the leather helmet still atop his head, Bobby Bill, Cornell's Ghost Runner, executed a perfect swan dive from the edge of the cliff. With the grace of a hawk he plummeted, straight as a blade, seventy feet through the rain.

And then he hit the water. And then blackness. Like what happens come the end of a dream.

The Roosevelt Visit

When John Alden awoke from the dream, he was drowning in sweat. The sheets were soaked. He kicked them off. Sat up on the bed. Wiped his face with the palms of his hands. He checked the time: 7:15 a.m. The day after Memorial Day, 1929. The day Franklin Roosevelt was coming to Ithaca.

The 31st day of May in that most memorable year fell on a Friday, seven months to the day since John Alden had chased a serial killer through the university campus before tumbling from the Rickety Bridge into the raging water and then somersaulting over Ithaca Falls, where he was swallowed alive in an extraordinarily rare but powerful vortex. And though only 211 days had come and gone since H.W. Hightower had dragged him comatose from the shoreline, it seemed to him a lifetime. As if some eighty years had passed. He thought of the dream he had just been witness to, the unhinging of Bobby Bill. It had been a dream of remarkable clarity. The girl in the dream was a girl of haunting beauty, and her name *may* have been Katelyn, but she was not *his* Katelyn.

Showered and shaved, the time-traveling professor buttoned his clean white shirt and checked the oxidized alarm clock atop the dresser. It was 8:00 a.m. now. The governor's motorcade from the train station to the campus up East Hill was scheduled for ten. He had two hours to stop a killer. Outside he heard sirens. Fire engines in the distance. He tucked his shirt into his pants and then pulled open the top drawer. He lifted out the .38 Super automatic and checked the magazine. Seven bullets. He placed another bullet in the chamber. Eight shots in all. Eight chances. He slapped the magazine into place, checked the safety, and stuffed the gun beneath his belt in the back. Then he threw on a suit coat and took a good, hard look at himself in the mirror.

More strands of gray hair were showing in his disheveled hair. Added wrinkles had lined up to the sides of his eyes. He was aging fast. The ex-cop could see forty, and more. Also showing in the mirror that morning, just over his right shoulder, was the sepia photograph of Cornell football player Bobby Bill. Ithaca's great ghost. John Alden shook his head in amazement at both visages.

From the dresser drawer he lifted the letter from his beautiful Katelyn, the tattered letter that had traveled with him through the years. He slid it into his breast pocket. Pressed it against his heart. Then he left the small room where he had convalesced and limped down two flights of stairs, ready to tackle the day.

On his way out of the house he stopped in the kitchen and grabbed a bottle of Coca-Cola from the icebox. He pried off the cap with a bottle opener, popped a laudanum into his mouth, and washed down his medicine.

Outside, on the front steps of President's House, the Cornell professor swigged his Coke. Then he closed his eyes and lifted his face to the morning sun. In Ithaca, sunshine was a light to be worshipped. John Alden had awoken expecting storm clouds. Lightning and thunder. Wind and rain. But the day was picture perfect, marred only by a stream of black smoke to the north, beyond the Fall Creek gorge. When he again opened his eyes, the only clouds that could be seen were the puffy little white ones a child might draw. He followed the blue sky down to the tree line and then down to the rolling green lawns of the fabled university.

On the gravel drive that fronted the house stood a chauffeur before a waiting car. The black-uniformed man tipped his hat to John Alden, both of them acknowledging the special day that it was.

"Where's that smoke coming from?"

"It's from that big barn they use as a movie studio," the chauffeur told him, staring out at the smoke over the trees in the distance. "Looks like somebody put a match to the whole kit and caboodle. Probably that Moral Way crowd."

Then the door to the house was opened wide and President Emeritus H.W. Hightower, PhD, emerged. He was dressed to the hilt, almost comically. Yet somehow the round old man made it all work. A tuxedo showed beneath a black overcoat with black velvet lapels. A top hat graced his head. He came out swinging that gold-headed cane of his with an extra bounce in his step. At the foot of the stairs this legend of a university man paused and basked in the sunshine. "*Effulgence,* Mr. Alden?"

"Brilliance," John Alden answered, defining the word. "Radiant splendor."

"Yes, from late Latin . . . *to shine forth.*"

Alden took another swig of Coke. "*Plutonium*?" he asked, wanting the definition.

"*Plutonium,*" the old man repeated, letting the word roll off his tongue. "Sounds chemical. Perhaps one of those hazardous wastes of which you've warned us."

"*Plutonium* is a radioactive chemical . . . to be discovered by your friends at Berkeley in 1940."

"Those devils."

They had not really talked since the near catastrophe on Wall Street, or since the untimely death of their finance administrator, whose badly broken body did not surface until it had reached the shores of Cayuga Lake. "Cornell is headed for trouble, isn't she?" Alden softly asked.

H.W. Hightower surveyed the leafy campus. His campus. "This university, Mr. Alden, was built on hills," he answered, "and I mean that both literally and figuratively. Cornell has had her ups and downs in the past; she will have them in the future. Even I can see that." The old man stepped toward the car. The chauffeur opened the back door. "Now, I am off to the train station. I've been asked to ride with the governor in the motorcade."

"You moved the money, you sly bastard."

Hightower stopped. "Pardon?"

"The university's money," John Alden said, pointing the Coke bottle at him. "You moved it out of the stock market before the coming crash."

Hightower climbed into the back seat. The chauffeur closed the door. The window was down. The president emeritus flashed his house guest a diminutive smile, reflecting the cautiously good mood he found himself in. "Cooler heads may have shifted enough of the university's endowment to ensure Cornell's survival. Still, I suspect things will not be easy in the years ahead. I, too, saw the future last week." Then H.W. Hightower, PhD, waved his fat, stubby hand. "I've assured Captain Murphy that you are not a threat. So behave yourself, Mr. Alden. Today history is being made."

THE MOTORCADE

News reports of the governor's speech in Poughkeepsie had spread across the nation. The speech was an indictment of the banks, Wall Street, and Herbert Hoover and his free market policies. Some were coming to believe that Franklin Roosevelt alone saw the true nature of the problem. But others now saw the young governor of New York as the prince of socialism, and a threat to capitalism. Newspaper reporters flocked to Ithaca. The Ithaca Motion Picture Company had been hired to shoot newsreel footage of the governor's visit. The motorcade would wind up the hill on East State Street and then turn left onto

College Avenue. Then Roosevelt's car would angle through Eddy Gate and onto the Cornell campus.

It was before Eddy Gate that the crowd was the largest, where students, protesters, faculty, and the university bigwigs lined both sides of the street to both cheer and jeer the governor. It had been beneath the Latin words etched into the wrought iron arch of Eddy Gate that John Alden had begun the hunt for the killer of his wife.

"So enter that thou may become more learned and thoughtful. So depart that thou may become more useful to mankind."

Now the professor of criminal justice found a spot on the east side of the street, just outside the gate. With the sun over his shoulder, he had good sight lines. He would be able to see the governor's car coming up the street, along with the crowd across the street, plus the crowd to his left and to his right.

The Cornell marching band had assembled on a hill just inside the gate. They were tuning up, blowing their horns in a cacophony of combinations. Also inside the gate, John Alden spotted Belle and Amanda Parrish dressed in their ghostly garb —dark, hooded dresses that hung down to the ground. They had been staged for the cameras. The twins held baskets of flower petals. The Ithaca Motion Picture Company would shoot the motorcade coming through the gate and then passing by the twins.

Directly across from John Alden stood the Catholic priest, Father Wallace Dougal, chatting amiably with those around him. His hands were clasped behind his back. His Moral Way crowd was there to protest the governor's visit, but with the near-collapse on Wall Street they had suddenly lost their sheen. The mood on campus was changing by the day, and not in the direction of the Moral Way. In just one week's time Roosevelt's stock had risen dramatically, while the stock of the Moral Way, along with that of the Republican Party, had fallen with the near collapse of the stock market.

Chimes came bursting out of the clock tower. Their echoes graced the blue skies. It was ten o'clock. The priest turned to the tower and stared up at the hour hand.

Dr. Victor Ecarius was also standing across the street, awaiting the governor's arrival. The collector of brains and other body parts noticed John Alden staring at him. With his odd-colored eyes he tossed Alden a look of contempt. Then he turned away. Ignored his former test subject. The former New York City detective searched for the doctor's assistant, Jim Dorn. But the ungainly grad student was nowhere to be seen. John Alden swore beneath his breath. On this day he wanted all of his suspects accounted for.

And there was yet another man standing at Eddy Gate. He was actually leaning up against the gate's ivy at the back of the crowd. Because he was taller than most, his black face clearly stuck out in the sea of white faces that surrounded him. It was Coach Night Train, the keeper of legends of Big Red football—the old man who had been beaten at the studio barn and left for dead. Something inexplicable about the coach made the Cornell professor uncomfortable, and he turned away.

Now the minutes were ticking by, so slowly they could have been measured in years. It was 10:05. Anticipation was high. Then it was ten minutes past the hour. The crowd was growing restless, but in an eager way. There was an energized feeling among the people who lined the streets—that on this day in Ithaca something special was about to happen.

It was already fifteen minutes past the hour when John Alden heard a ghostly voice calling his name through the crowd. The voice sent shivers up his spine. He looked about. It was strange in that it sounded just like the voice of his beautiful Katelyn calling his name through the years. But it was not his murdered wife. It was Caitlin Dewey. She was across the street, but a half-block down. Her hand was in the air. She was trying to get his attention through the crowd and the noise. John

Alden put his hands to his ears to tune out the band. He smiled her way. Then he saw the woman standing beside her. His hands dropped to his side in disbelief. The woman was obviously Caitlin Dewey's mother, for she bore a striking resemblance to her daughter—older, yet somehow even prettier. He found it near impossible to keep his eyes off of her.

She was a bold brunette. A mother who still turned heads. Her beauty was undying. Her age, irrelevant. Her face was unforgettable. At least, it was unforgettable to John Alden. Because he had seen her only the night before in his dream, walking out of the stadium in the rain, leaving Ithaca, and Bobby Bill, behind her.

It was then the woman's eyes met his, a shocking look of familiarity—as if the two of them were staring down ghosts. Caitlin Dewey was still trying to signal him. She kept her hand in the air, waving. He knew what she wanted. She wanted him to walk down there and meet her mother. But now seeing her mother in person, he could not let that happen. Memories came flooding back to him, and these memories were phantasmagorical. He saw himself running through a grove of trees with a football tucked beneath his arm. In the next stride he was dodging bullets in a field of wheat with a rifle in his hand. Then came a series of explosions right before his face, and in the last blinding burst all he could think about was his undying love for a cheeky girl from Ithaca. It was not as if time were standing still; it was almost as if time were running backwards. A man's lifetime was flashing before his eyes, like a movie being shown in reverse. But whose life was it?

Caitlin Dewey stepped into the street, hoping to cross, but just then two state patrol motorcycles turned the corner and started toward Eddy Gate. The governor's car was right behind them. The crowd went crazy. The Cornell marching band struck up a Sousa march. Caitlin Dewey jumped back to the curb.

John Alden turned away from the two women. He blocked the confusing memories from his head. He was sweating, feared trouble was brewing. He wiped his forehead and concentrated on the task at hand.

Due to the protesters, and to the unsolved murder, security was tight. Behind the police motorcycles was the big black convertible. A touring car. Franklin Roosevelt sat in the back seat behind the driver. H.W. Hightower sat beside him. The driver appeared to be a plainclothes police detective, and in the passenger seat beside him sat the mayor of Ithaca. Captain Evan Murphy of the New York State Police was walking behind the slow-moving car, as was another detective. Two Ithaca squad cars followed the convertible, patrolmen hanging on the running boards.

The cheering grew loud as Roosevelt approached the gate to the university. The protesters, waving placards, feared they were being drowned out by the governor's supporters. They began forcing their way to the front.

The governor wore a gray fedora on his head. The sun was in his face. And what an illuminating face it was. John Alden was so taken by the sight of the smiling, waving governor that he almost forgot why he was there. The big convertible kept inching up the street, pulling directly between John Alden on one side of the street and Dr. Ecarius and the Catholic priest on the other side of the street. The university crowd was now stepping off of the curb, approaching the car. The protesters were being pushed back. Hands were reaching out to touch Franklin Roosevelt. He was grasping at them with pure joy. To date, it might have been the sunniest, happiest moment of his political career.

H.W. Hightower was all smiles himself. In the back seat beside the governor, he pulled the gold watch from the vest pocket of his tuxedo and he checked the time.

That was when the first shot rang out.

John Alden reached for his weapon at the sound of the gunshot. It sounded as if it might have come from the clock tower. He watched in horror as the mayor of Ithaca in the front seat of the car reached for his bloody throat. Across the street the priest was suddenly crossing himself. Then the crazed eyes of the priest, sadism written in his face, met the eyes of the time-traveling former New York City homicide detective, standing with his gun drawn.

John Alden saw Father Wallace Dougal pull a long shining object from inside his coat, and even though this priest was as smooth as a magician, he made one glaring mistake. For a second, and it was only a second, he allowed the blade to glimmer in the sun. The dagger was in his left hand. People were crowding the street, bringing the big convertible to a near halt. The priest stepped off of the curb. John Alden raised his automatic. It had been years since he had fired a gun. Hell, in his mind it had been over 80 years. *"Don't wait for the dagger; it'll be too late."*

The priest raised his right hand as if he were blessing the young governor of New York. His left hand floated out to his side. Then it happened. The priest moved his left hand, his dagger hand, toward Roosevelt. The sun shined off the metal. John Alden opened fire. He fired straight across the back seat. Roosevelt must have felt the heat of the passing bullets. He fired again. Then a third time. And a fourth time. The bullets were exploding automatically from his gun. But the priest was still moving toward the governor, the dagger reflecting the sun. The crowd was screaming in shock. People were diving to the ground. Others were pointing at the clock tower. Gunfire seemed to be coming from multiple directions. Then the mayor's head exploded. Blood and brain matter splayed the crowd. Even John Alden was surprised at the sound of the shots. He fired again, and again, only now he was finding his mark. The priest was jerking backward by the time John Alden got off his sixth and seventh shots. The bullets found their way into the priest's chest.

Bloodied his collar. The man of the cloth flew backwards, tripping over the curb and landing on the lawn beneath Eddy Gate. He was lying flat on his back now, staring into the heavens, the deathly metal still in the palm of his hand.

Captain Evan Murphy jumped onto the back of the vehicle and threw himself over Governor Roosevelt. "Go!" he screamed at the driver. "Go!" Even while Murphy was covering Roosevelt, the one-armed cop managed to draw his revolver. He leveled it at John Alden. But then he hesitated. Never pulled the trigger.

H.W. Hightower was leaning forward, trying to give comfort to the mortally wounded mayor. Hightower, too, was staring daggers through John Alden. The hate and the betrayal in both of these men's eyes was overwhelming. Then the car was speeding through Eddy Gate, where the band, seemingly oblivious to the gunshots, was still playing Sousa—and Belle and Amanda Parrish were tossing flower petals at Roosevelt's car as the governor was sped through the leafy campus to a place of safety.

THE RUN FOR THE BRIDGE

The shooting scene was pandemonium writ extra large. John Alden stood before Eddy Gate, smoking gun in hand. The Catholic priest was dead on the ground across the street, his body riddled with .38 caliber bullets. Hundreds of people were still running for cover. Others were pointing toward the clock tower. But many of the people who had come to see Franklin Roosevelt were now focused on the self-proclaimed time traveler with the gun in his hand. Uniformed police officers, guns drawn, were fighting their way through the crowd toward John Alden.

He could hear students yelling at him. "It's that crazy professor. He tried to kill the governor."

"He's killed the priest!"

"He had a knife," John Alden proclaimed, loud enough to be heard.

"Assassin! Assassin!"

"There's another shooter," said a girl, rising to her feet. "The shots came from the clock tower."

John Alden turned and glanced up at the clock tower. But the sun in his eyes was blinding. He turned back to the shooting scene. Down the street he spotted Caitlin Dewey down on the ground, in the arms of her mother. They were both crying. Now the Ithaca cops were only a few yards away. In fact, the only thing stopping them from gunning him down was the frightened crowd. In the melee he saw a uniformed arm reach down for the knife in the hand of the dead priest.

"Shoot the bastard! Somebody shoot the bastard!"

The time had come. He had a decision to make.

Then Coach Night Train was at his side. Shouting in his ear. In his face. "Run, Bobby, run!"

John Alden dropped his gun on the ground. He pivoted with the grace of the agile quarterback he once had been, and he sprinted through Eddy Gate. The Parrish twins tossed flower petals over him as he sprinted by them. The camera from the Ithaca Motion Picture Company recorded his flight. Even before he cleared the crowd, he heard the first warning. "Police! Stop!" Then a pistol shot sailed over his head. He cleared the crowd and ran between the towering elms toward the clock tower and the library.

In those first hundred yards of flight he forgot all about his age, about his aches and pains. He just ran. As soon as he reached the top of Libe Slope he knew his destination. He had only to reach the Rickety Bridge. The priest was dead. It had been him all along. He had surfaced beneath the falls some twelve years ahead of John Alden. Spent his time trying to murder the suffragist movement, one leader of women at a time. Then he had lain in wait. A serial killer. A political assassin. The evil that walks through time. But this time evil had failed. Franklin Roosevelt was alive. John Alden's job in this bygone era was done. Once on the bridge, he would willingly throw himself into the waters below and call upon Ithaca Falls to do the rest.

John Alden hurtled down Libe Slope like a wounded track star, his suit coat flapping behind him like a cape. The police lined the crest. Several dropped to their knees and took aim. Gunfire exploded behind him. Bullets whizzed by. He took a quick glance over his shoulder. The cops were now descending the hill in hot pursuit. In his day they would never catch him. But those days had long passed. He was running downhill fast on a bum leg, so fast that by the time he reached the foot of Libe Slope his feet were out of control. His balance was topsy-turvy. He stumbled and fell face first into the lawn. When he looked up again, blades of grass were stuck to his cheeks. The cops were still coming, making their way down the hill, closing rapidly. He brushed the grass from his face. John Alden got up and ran.

At last he reached the woods across the road. He felt as if his chest were on fire. He tried to calm the flames with the palm of his hand. His leg felt broken again. Now the best he could muster was a speedy limp. More shots rang out. He could hear the cops shouting. "He's going for the bridge."

John Alden made for the trees. Bullets ricocheted off the branches as he fought his way down the foot path. This was the very spot where he had once dangled over a cliff in his pursuit of a serial killer. Then, finally, it burst into sight. The rickety old suspension bridge where it had all begun. It had looked ominous then. Now it was a most welcome sight. All that was left to do was to take flight from the center of the span. And then pray.

John Alden grabbed hold of the rail and stepped onto the bridge. But he made only that one step. The next bullet caught him in the shoulder blade and sent him sprawling forward. Even before he hit the boards, a second bullet nearly tore off his left ear, grazing the corner of his eye. His bloody face hit the bridge.

"We got him! He's down!"

John Alden lay face down on the boards of the Rickety Bridge, blood running into the corners of his eyes. He played the shooting scene over again in his mind. The governor's smiling face. The shot from the clock tower. The priest drawing his dagger. He himself emptying his automatic. But in the end he could not get out of his head the way everybody had stared at him after he shot the priest. Christ, he had stopped a serial killer. He had saved the life of a future president. Yet all those provincial fools saw before them was a sad and delusional anachronism. A pilgrim they had doubted and mocked from the beginning.

Now the cops were on top of him. They swarmed over the bridge, making it sway.

"He had a knife," John Alden murmured.

"He was holding a crucifix, you murdering bastard."

"No, he had a knife," Alden repeated.

The cops wrestled his hands behind his bloody back. "I hope you live, you son of a bitch," said the cop, slapping on the cuffs, "so we can watch you fry."

"Up the river," another cop yelled, grabbing his head of unruly hair. "You're goin' up the river."

END OF BOOK THREE

"For everything to be consummated, for me to feel less alone, I had only to wish that there be a large crowd of spectators the day of my execution and that they greet me with cries of hate."

—Albert Camus
The Stranger

BOOK FOUR

SING SING PRISON

THURSDAY, NOVEMBER 10, 1932

Braving Time and Storm

Three years on Death Row. Time as torture.

It was 10:15 p.m. The Nor'easter was on top of them now. The lightning was continuous. The thunder was deafening. Winds were crazy, approaching hurricane force. The lights of Sing Sing began to flicker. As for the prisoner, he was now forty-five minutes and a mere forty feet from the death chamber. Out in the hallways that echoed, he overheard rumors of a postponement. The weather was that bad.

After his release from the hospital, after the bullet had been removed from his shoulder and his head had been bandaged, John Alden was arraigned at the county courthouse in Ithaca. That summer he stood trial for murder. He did not take the stand in his own defense. That would have played into the hands of the prosecution—forced him under oath before a jury and the national press corps to state for the record that he was a visitor from the twenty-first century. A sworn lunatic. Instead, his lawyer simply argued that he was an ex-cop who had shot the priest in defense of Franklin Roosevelt. At worst it was manslaughter, that even if the priest was not armed, the defendant believed the man was armed and threatening the governor when he pulled the trigger. Besides, the defense remarked, it was determined the mayor of Ithaca was killed that day by a different caliber of bullets, the shots presumably having come from the clock tower. It was also noted by the defense that Ithaca native Jim Dorn, the assistant collector of body parts in Hell Hall—and a kid so morally and physically blind that he probably could not tell Franklin Roosevelt from the mayor of Ithaca—had vanished following the shooting.

The prosecution reminded jurors that the defendant was not on trial for the murder of the mayor, and that the law had no reason to be looking for this boy called Jim Dorn. John Alden was also not on trial for the murder of Royal S. Copeland III, even though the newspapers made it seem that way. Nor did the state have to prove the visiting professor was a part of a conspiracy to assassinate the governor. No, the defendant was on trial for gunning down a Catholic priest. An unarmed priest. Police said no knife was found. The prosecution went on to argue that the man who called himself John W. Alden was also a dope fiend, and that even his identity was in question. Was he really an ex-cop? He could have been an ex-con for all anybody knew. He had appeared in Ithaca out of nowhere hell bent on talking murder, and murder is what they got. Case closed.

The trial lasted three weeks. Then the jury was sequestered. As had been done in ancient Greece, twelve reasonable men in the heart of Ithaca argued back and forth for three long days. A hopeful sign for the defense. But in the end, they returned a verdict of guilty. And then the judge sentenced John Alden to die in the electric chair at Sing Sing.

THE LAST VISITOR

Storm or stars, it was time to barber the prisoner for the chair. The last haircut. The prisoner hated haircuts. He was like Sampson that way. Always felt better and stronger with his shaggy hair. But on Death Row they kept his hair cropped short. Now, to his surprise, a new barber appeared at the cell gate, a large, rough-hewn man who carried only an electric shear and a small stool. In fact, he looked as if he might have been a trustee who worked in the stables. "Here, sit on this," the barber demanded, plopping the stool down in the middle of the cell.

The prisoner did as he was ordered. No less than three uniformed guards surrounded him. The barber plugged the shears into a long cord that snaked out into the hallway. Then he fired up the blades. The harsh shearing noise sounded more threatening than the weather. The barber put blades to scalp and simply shaved raw the prisoner's temples with the electric shears. Then he rubbed into the prisoner's scalp a cold and greasy, piss-yellow conducting gel. That was all. The worst haircut imaginable. The barber stooped down and with his bare hands ripped open the inside seam of the prisoner's right trouser leg. Ripped it up to his knee. The barber then shaved the hair from the right leg with the shears. He rubbed the prisoner's bare leg with the same conducting gel, as if he were rubbing down a horse. When he had finished humiliating the prisoner, the barber stood and took his leave.

Now it was 10:21. Thirty-nine minutes till his date with death. The prisoner sat on the bunk with his ridiculous haircut and stewed. His Bible lay unopened beside him. He quietly sang to himself, a refrain from Cornell's *alma mater*.

Sentry like o'er lake and valley
Towers her regal form,
Watch and ward forever keeping,
Braving time and storm.

The guards kept their eyes on him, but their ears were straining to hear the static-filled radio. Newscasters were trying to warn of the deadly Nor'easter now over New York while at the same time covering a live execution. And all the while their signal kept cutting in and out.

A curious thing had happened after the prisoner's conviction. During the trial the time-traveling professor was portrayed by the newspapers as a madman. He was mocked and scorned. The Pilgrim. The dope fiend. A conspirator and an assassin. He was pilloried, convicted, and hung out to dry. But after his imprisonment, ever so slowly, the winds that carry public opinion began to change in his direction. With every passing month, and then every passing year, more and more of what John Alden had predicted had come to be—including the Great Crash of 1929, the onset of the Great Depression, and just two days before his scheduled execution, the election of Franklin Delano Roosevelt as President of the United States. Those who were at the candlelight dinner party at President's House on the campus of Cornell University on that enchanting spring night in 1929 were especially moved by the turn of events.

The Sing Sing warden entered the cell. He was known as a reformer, and he had been appointed to his position by Governor Roosevelt. From his blue pinstripe suit and the no-nonsense demeanor of his bespectacled face, he could easily have been mistaken for a banker, but in this era of economic depression, prison wardens were being held in much higher regard than were America's bankers. It would have been easy for the prison population to demonize the warden, but they never did. The crooks in Sing Sing knew an honest man when they saw one.

"What's the box office take look like?" the prisoner asked him.

The warden smiled. "Not bad for a Thursday."

"I miss the movies."

"I wish I could have helped you there. Do you have any favorites?"

"Keep an eye on that Clark Gable. And James Cagney, and Spencer Tracy. You're going to like them . . . and there's a young actress named Bette Davis."

"I'll watch for them." The warden sat on the bunk beside him and put a hand on his shoulder. "I've been talking with our prison chaplain, and with that one-armed cop friend of yours . . ."

"He's not a friend of mine."

"Be that as it may . . . we all agreed that no man should die alone. There are thousands of people across this country who believe in you . . . and none more than those who knew you in Ithaca. Now what I'm about to do is highly unorthodox, but I've allowed for you to have one last visitor." The warden signaled the guards. Then he patted the prisoner on the back and got up to leave.

Her innocence and her beauty filled the open doorway, almost angelic in appearance. Her sweet face at first expressed shock at his ghostly visage, but then she smiled, a bold smile, and she stepped into the cell and sat beside him on the bunk. "Hello, John," she said in an intimate whisper.

"Hello, Caitlin," he said, a bit embarrassed. "You look wonderful, but you shouldn't haven't come."

"I couldn't stay away."

She was a few years older now, a bit more mature, her education complete, but the years had only added to her splendor. She was dressed in gray, with a pair of sensible black shoes. The rain and the wind had mussed her hair, yet to him she looked like a million bucks. He lifted her left hand and admired the engagement ring on her finger. "Is he a good man?"

"Yes, he really is. Do you see a future for us?"

He stared into the timeless diamond. "You'll have beautiful children," he assured her, "and they'll have beautiful children."

The cell gate was left wide open. It would remain that way until the last walk. The hallway outside the cell was filling with people—more guards, a reporter or two who had won favor with the warden, and some rat-faced stranger whispering asides into the ear of the cameraman from the Ithaca Motion Picture Company.

Caitlin watched them gathering, like crows on road kill. She lowered her voice. "You think you're going back there, don't you . . . to Ithaca in the twenty-first century?"

"I hope so," he told her. "I really do."

"How? Even if you lived the life you claimed to have lived . . . wouldn't the only way back to your mythical Ithaca be over Ithaca Falls?"

"I tried, Caitlin. After the priest was dead, I tried with everything I had to reach the falls. I saw you crying in your mother's arms . . . I knew you were safe . . . and I turned and I ran for the bridge. I would have flown over the railings . . . but they got me."

Caitlin turned her back to the crowd in the hallway. Put her hand to his face. "We're petitioning the governor for a stay of execution. We've been writing President-elect Roosevelt thousands of letters, asking him for mercy."

"I shot and killed a Catholic priest. My appeals are exhausted. There'll be no mercy for me." He took her hand in his. "Are you to be a witness?"

"God, no," she said. "Do you want me there?"

"No, please. That would be horrible."

There was another crack of thunder as flash lightning lit up the Death Row cells. Caitlin jumped at the sight and sound. She pulled her hand away from his face and put it to her heart, watching as the crowd in the hallway had the same reaction. "I don't know how I'll ever get back to the city tonight."

"How is your mother?" he asked, trying to pull her mind from the storm.

Caitlin Dewey relaxed a bit. "Three years on . . . and she's still upset."

"Does she say anything about me?"

"She says you reminded her of someone."

"I used to get that a lot."

"When I ask who you reminded her of . . . she dismisses the question. Says it's not important."

He leaned into her, so close as to share every sincere breath. "In the property room the Ithaca police have a letter. It was in my breast pocket when I was arrested. After I'm gone, I've instructed that the letter be turned over to you."

"Who is it from?"

"I believe it to be a letter from your future granddaughter. She's named after you . . . but with a different spelling. She wrote me the letter while she was living in Oregon. I carried it with me for years. It was in my pocket when I went over Ithaca Falls. Show it to your mother . . . I have a feeling she'll understand."

"I know about that football player," Caitlin said, tears now streaming down her face. "For years I thought it was just a rumor. Tell me it's you . . ."

"I saw your football player in a dream. It was the night before the shooting. But I wasn't him. Even in the dream, I was only a bystander. A fan. A witness to the unwinding of an All-American life."

"You mean, the way your life unwound?"

"Yes, I suppose."

"Is my mother in your dreams?"

"Yes, I dream of her. And you."

"How can that be?"

"The dreams here on Death Row are intense and otherworldly. I always think I will wake up and everything will be okay . . . that I will be back where I belong. But whenever I wake up, I'm still in Sing Sing. Still on Death Row." He touched her forehead with his. "I'm not insane, Caitlin. I'm not in a coma. I do not have amnesia. I'm not having some prolonged nightmare, like in some badly written movie. Maybe I did live another life in another time . . . I don't know. All I do know is that this day and age is not where I belong. I am who I say I am." He put his hand to her cheek. "You go see Captain Murphy. He'll get you the letter."

Caitlin Dewey wiped her eyes. Her nose was beginning to run, and she pulled a handkerchief from her pocket. "You're like fog in a mirror," she said, wiping her nose. "I see something in you . . . some part of me. I saw it the night of the candlelight dinner and I've never overcome it ..."

The Soldier

She had once called him provincial. A god in Ithaca but a mere mortal outside of it. Now as he ran through the wheat, the mortar fire exploding all around him, the provincial All-American boy had grown into a man of the world. A global traveler. A soldier. His wanderlust had led him to this place, to the bloody fields of France, where his line was now being overrun. He had taken command and signaled the retreat. The New York captain remained behind as long as he could in an attempt to cover their escape. But the shells were upon him. Sunlight filtered through the black smoke. The heat was murder. His wool uniform was suffocating.

The Great War they called it, but there was nothing great about it. Like a million men on both sides of the Hindenburg Line, he just wanted to go home. And so he sprinted through the wheat field, spent rifle in hand, as if his native soil were the goal line. It was the oldest tale of all. The homecoming. The return to the motherland. To his beloved Ithaca—to streams and waterfalls, and to giant, rocky hills, where moss-colored promontories jutted into elongated seas shaped like the fingers of a god.

The next shell landed in front of him. He saw an immense white flash, like the bright light that was said to await the dead, and then an upward blast with searing heat. The explosion was so loud it deafened him. No sound now. Like watching a silent movie. Then he was somersaulting backwards, through space and time. He landed on his back in a bed of wheat.

His face was broken and burned. Unrecognizable. His uniform was reduced to smoldering shreds. He was blinded. Still, he had visions. He saw things. Spiritual things and things not of his world. An instant later, he saw himself being born again. Living another life in another time.

"Captain! Captain Bill!"

They were looking for him. Through the shelling and the bursts of machine gun fire they were combing the wheat in search of their captain. But he was too weak to acknowledge their cries. Then he heard the frightened voices of his men begin to fade away, as did the explosions and the gunfire. The battle was going elsewhere. The armies were moving on. He flashed back to his Greek studies at Cornell. Actually garbled a few lines. "And so we sailed on, aching in our hearts for the comrades that we lost, but glad to be alive."

He made an effort to move, but it was as if he had been planted there, his legs one with the earth. The abortive effort made him laugh, more a pitiful chuckle. "What a waste," he muttered, tears forming in his eyes. "What a fantastic life I have wasted."

And then he was all alone, lying Christ-like on his back with only the wheat and the acrid wind to assuage his wounds. The black smoke was clearing now and he could see an indigo sky, a sky as blue as the waters of Cayuga. It should have been raining. Clouds should have obscured the heavens. But they did not. His view was endless. The sunshine off the wheat was golden. One should not have to surrender his time in this world on such a pretty day.

"I'll be back, my fair and shining Ithaca," he cried to the cavernous sky. "Only next time . . ."

The Execution

It was the big, surly guard who shook him awake. "You nodded off," he said to the prisoner, half sympathetic. "You're the first one I've seen who fell asleep while waiting to be executed."

The prisoner sat up on his bunk and wiped the soldier dream from his eyes. He looked around, momentarily confused. The brilliant bursts before him were lightning strikes. The explosions were thunder. But the smell of smoke lingered.

Caitlin Dewey was gone. She would marry soon and then even her surname would disappear. Still, she was a woman ahead of her time, and she had been remarkably brave about the whole sordid affair. In the end she had held back the tears in her eyes and left him with a long, loving embrace. The last thing she did was place the palm of her hand over his heart, as if counting the beats.

Despite the crowd congregating outside his cell, he was alone now, left by himself to contemplate the last minutes of his life as they slowly ticked away. So what does a man think about in those final minutes? What goes through the head of a condemned man when the only thing awaiting him is death? For this prisoner it was the women in his life who came to mind. In the end, they are what mattered the most—his mother, his wife, his lover, and young Caitlin Dewey. He wished he had had the opportunity to thank them while they lived. He wished he could apologize for the hurt he had caused them. It was almost as if he had lived two lives. One life had ended on the Rickety Bridge over the rushing water on Halloween night in the year 2010. His other life was coming to a close in another time in the notorious prison that sat on the banks of the Hudson River. Had this other life of his really been only those seven months in Ithaca, and three years on Death Row? Or had it been, as some suggested, closer to forty years—highlighted by football and war, by unrequited love and endless wandering?

The Nor'easter, it seemed, was saving its worst for Sing Sing. The prison was under an all-out assault from the weather. Besides the deluge of rain, the wind whipped up gales of river water and threw it full force against the prison walls. The crowd in the hallway outside the prisoner's cell closed ranks in fear.

At 10:45 the warden stepped into the cell. It had been determined the show would go on, the ritual of men killing other men on Thursday nights. "It's time," he announced.

"Yes," the prisoner said, admiring each electric burst outside his cell window. "It is time."

Two guards entered the cell next. The prisoner stood. Soldier straight. Chin up. Eyes forward. He held out his hands to be cuffed.

"There's no need for that," the warden said. "Just follow me and do what you're asked."

They stepped into the hallway. The unwanted crowd parted. The warden paused for a disapproving second before turning toward the death chamber. "Walk this way."

The priest was there—that kind and faceless voice that slipped through the leper-squint. But he would remain faceless. Turns out he was a friar. And a tall one. The hood of his modest brown robe was up over his head, and that head was kept bowed. With bowed head and folded hands he turned and led the warden and the prisoner down the hall.

There was a virtual parade behind them. One guard held a shotgun. The movie camera had been placed ahead of them in the death chamber. The long walk, the walk portrayed so melodramatically in so many movies, was in reality a very short walk, and it was relatively dignified. Then they entered the death chamber.

The prisoner was stunned by the brightness of the room, so much hellish light it hurt his eyes. He put a hand to his brow. There was a telephone on the wall beside him, and above the phone was a big round clock with a bloody red second hand. It ticked loudly. On his left side, nearer the chair, a fire hose was mounted on the wall. A crimson blanket hung next to it. In 1932, it was what passed for fire safety.

The polished oak chair reserved for him was situated at the front of the chamber, placed on a rubber mat before a wall of electronics. Leather straps dangled from it. A black curtain was draped to the exit side of the electric wall. This was where the executioner would hide, where only the warden could see him.

Two guards gently took one arm each and guided the prisoner to the chair. He was seated. Got his first look at the witnesses. He had to squint, but he could see that every chair was occupied and every inch of space was filled with people standing. If it were any other event, no fire marshal would allow so many people to be crammed into such a small space. Most of those present were men, but there were a couple of women scribbling notes while consciously avoiding his eyes.

The lanky newscaster he had seen in the doorway hours earlier as he was walked to the dance hall cells was now standing at the back of the chamber, almost hiding behind a big chrome microphone that had attached to its face the call letters CBS. The man held a headset to his ear, and his face looked even more anguished than the prisoner's. He was whispering into the mike, in the style of a golf tournament. "I say again . . . the prisoner has just entered the death chamber. They are moving him toward the . . . okay, are we on? Because I'm not hearing anything . . ."

The witnesses to his death were for the most part unfamiliar faces. Near anonymous. Was that his fate, to die in a room filled with strangers? He could feel the cold eye of the camera lens as it recorded his torment. Then he spotted him standing off to the right. A familiar face. A black face. An Ithaca man. It was Coach Night Train from Big Red football at Cornell, the man who had yelled at him to run following the shooting. They shared a secret smile. And they were being watched.

The dapper detective was leaning his good shoulder into the wall, the dark fedora still atop his head. The empty sleeve of his suit coat was pinned neatly into the hip pocket. Captain Evan Murphy of the New York State Police. Their eyes all met, each of them seeking an answer for why the others were there. All three of their faces remained stone cold. Each a mask of indifference.

There were no windows in the death chamber. The Nor'easter was locked out, but the growing tempest still made its presence felt. Thunder caused a rumbling of the walls. The lights continued to flicker. At times it seemed like a race to the death. Would the power hold until the prisoner was electrocuted?

Now the guards worked quickly and methodically, strapping the prisoner into the chair. There were a minimum of four straps for every appendage. Another strap went around his waist like a giant belt and squeezed his stomach until it hurt. Yet another strap was strung across his chest, pulling him back into the chair, forcing him to sit up straight. The ankle straps went on last, spreading his legs apart in an undignified manner. His face was flushed not with fear, but with embarrassment. Humiliation.

An electrician knelt before him as if in prayer and strapped a copper anklet to the calf of his right leg. Then he attached electrodes to the anklet. The black cord snaked away from him toward the electronics on the wall.

Now it was 10:55.

They had executed so many men and were so proficient at what they did that they were apparently ahead of schedule, and so the prisoner was left to sit there, strapped to the chair facing the witnesses. Nobody spoke. Hell, nobody breathed. Near two minutes of dead silence was unheard of in a room filled with so many people. It seemed even the Nor'easter felt silence was imperative. The prisoner waited in perfect stillness as the quiet faces in the room melted into the bright light. Then the light was diffused through his tears.

Finally the warden stepped forward. "Do you have anything to say before we execute the order of the court?"

He felt a choking sensation in his throat. He wanted to wipe the tears from his face. It all seemed so unmanly. He glanced about. "Thanks for the haircut," the prisoner finally stated. Then he softly added, "Time . . . it's time." He kept repeating that one single phrase underneath his breath until they lowered the headset on to the top of his head.

The electric crown was cold and steely. And it was tight. By the time they were done fastening the screws, he felt as if his brain were in the grip of a vise. Finally they plugged him in. He thought of how utterly ridiculous he must look. Almost comical. But nobody in the room was laughing. Then they dropped the black hood over his face.

The ritual had all been explained to him in excruciating detail, but still the hood surprised him. The darkness that enveloped him now was maddening. He could easily understand how men facing a firing squad refused the hood. But those men were being given an honorable execution. A soldier's death. He was to die a convicted murderer.

And there was a distinct odor to the hood. No sooner had it covered his face than he smelled it. It was faint at first, but he recognized it from the dream. It was smoke. The hood smelled of smoke, as if there were an unwanted fire burning in the distance.

Now shrouded in this smoky darkness, he could hear his own breathing. He could hear his heartbeat. He could hear the magnified ticking of the clock as the bloody second hand worked its way to the top of the hour. Still, the wait was hell.

Suddenly there was a screaming sound that may or may not have emanated from his own mouth. He bolted upright in the chair. The smell of smoke was now overwhelming. He pulled at the straps with the strength of a madman and with the skills of a magician. Then it was as if somebody were helping him. Now everything was happening fast, and he found himself breaking free of every restraint that had ever imprisoned him. There was a distant explosion, and before he knew it he was running. Then he was falling. Not burning, but falling. Then he hit the water.

John Alden was back in the water now and somersaulting head over heels through a raging torrent. He struggled to breathe as the cold water swallowed him. Yes, he was in total darkness, but it was a watery darkness. Not fiery. There was no burning sensation. If anything, there was an absence of pain as he tumbled through the black torrent. He knew in his heart he was back in Ithaca. His Ithaca. Then he began the final freefall and he knew he was plummeting over Ithaca Falls, that sudden exhilaration of life before death. He had made this incalculable fall once before. It was not death, but a mere suspension of life. A dream from which he could not wake. Again he was consumed with the feeling he was being dragged through time. Without notice he stopped tumbling. His head stopped spinning. And then John Alden floated ghostlike in the icy lake, suspended ageless in his watery grave. Waiting only to be born again.

THE FIRE

Even before the switch was thrown, there was the smell of smoke. Copse smoke, not flesh. Fire is funny that way. It has its own manner of announcing through scent whether it be friend or foe, even warning of its line of attack.

"Do you smell smoke?"

Captain Evan Murphy of the New York State Police did not know the man standing next to him, most likely a reporter, but he acknowledged the question with a nod of his head. Then the prisoner entered the death chamber and they forgot all about the smoky odor. The man who had just stepped through the door was a mere specter of his past. A shadow impersonating a mortal being. In just a matter of a few short hours the prisoner had further deteriorated. His face was vaporous white. The ugly haircut and the bright, eerie lights made his once handsome face more sallow still. His lofty body was skeletal. The blue prison garb hung on him as if two sizes too big. Murphy had seen it all before. Death Row was unsparing. In the end, the chair only finished the job.

Outside, the Nor'easter could still be heard zeroing in on its target. Sing Sing prison. The thickness of the walls was no deterrent. Inside, grown men had the look on their faces of children acting brave. The witnesses maintained dual focus, their eyes on the man to be seated in the chair before them, and their ears on the furious pounding of the weather on the outside walls.

The prisoner was guided to the electric chair. He glanced about, obviously bothered by the lights, and seemingly more curious than concerned. Then his face fell, as if he were disappointed by the turnout. That was when the prisoner spotted the old football coach. Murphy, too, had spotted the large black man, squeezing in alongside the fire hose and the blanket. The aging Big Red football coach had entered the chamber late. One of the last. What was he doing there? The warden controlled the list. Only a request from the prisoner could have gained him entrance.

Then the man condemned to death clearly fixed his eyes on the one-armed cop. Murphy met his gaze with a stare of his own. Two soldiers, two detectives, wholly caught up in the irony of the situation.

Evan Murphy continued his frozen gaze as they strapped the prisoner into the chair. This, too, he had seen before. But if his face was frozen, his heart was softening. In his thirty years as a cop visiting Sing Sing, he had never once felt an innocent man was being put to death. But in this case, he had his doubts. Might not it have been better to admit the delusional time-traveling professor to an institution of psychiatric care and study? Then those oh-so-smart men from the Harvards and the Cornells could trek to the nut house every week and bask in his futuristic wisdom. Rejoice in his vocabulary. Maybe someday make crime a science and teach it in the universities.

An electrician knelt before the prisoner and strapped an anklet to his right leg. Then he attached the electrodes. It was at this point that all sound ceased. Even the storm took a breather. The prisoner was forced to sit stone still and stare at the witnesses. Uncomfortable cannot even begin to describe the feeling in the room. The broadcaster at the back of the room had quietly laid down his headphones in disgust. Film could be heard spinning through the movie camera. A minute ticked by. Murphy longed to breathe, but even that seemed inappropriate. There was that telephone on the wall, and those who could not stand the sight of the man seated in the chair before them focused their attention on the line to the governor's office, as if they might be able to make it ring.

At long last the warden stepped forward. "Do you have anything to say before we execute the order of the court?"

The New York police captain leaned forward to hear the answer. In his experience never had a condemned man had anything of importance to utter in the end. Some said they were sorry. Others said, screw you all. Still others, try as they might, could not force a word through their trembling lips. "Thanks for the haircut," Murphy heard the prisoner say. He was barely audible. "Time . . . it's time."

It was as simple and as eloquent as anything he had ever heard from the chair. But even after the prisoner had finished speaking, his lips kept moving, in the way a head severed by a guillotine tries to talk without its heart. It reminded Murphy of a silent movie he had seen.

He knew what came next. They lowered the electric headset onto the prisoner's head and fastened the screws. This had always been the most ridiculous-looking part of the ritual. Once the headset was on, there was no room for the prisoner's dignity. Murphy watched the prisoner's face grimace with discomfort as the last of the screws were adjusted. This would also be the last time he saw the face of the man who claimed to have traveled through time. They draped the big black hood over his head.

The guards stepped away from the chair. Nothing was left to do now but wait for the second hand to round the top of the clock and then begin the sixty second countdown to 11:00 p.m.

It was during this last minute of the ritual that the smell of smoke returned. Stronger now. It was not cigarette smoke. Smoking was not allowed. It was not electrical smoke, which carried with it a hot, wiry odor. This was the smell of a burning house. Perhaps lightning had set a building aflame. Now everybody in the room noticed it. Concerned looks were exchanged. The warden had noticed it too, and Murphy watched as the head of the most notorious prison in America struggled to keep a businesslike face. The second hand on the clock completed its circle, and the warden hurriedly nodded his head in the direction of the black curtain.

That is when the screaming began.

The prisoner bolted upright in the chair as a confetti of sparks exploded out from the wall behind him. In a matter of mere seconds the death chamber was on fire. There was only one exit in the room, and the stampede toward it was instantaneous. The guards made no attempt to extinguish the flames, as to try would have been foolish. It was that kind of fire. But Coach Night Train reacted. The old man grabbed the crimson blanket beside the fire hose and he hurled it over the chair. Batted at the flames. But then the smoke and the rush of the terrified crowd forced him from the chamber.

Evan Murphy found himself pinned on the wrong side of the room, against the wall opposite the door. The smoke stung his eyes. He could hear the screams and the breaking of the overturned chairs. He put his only hand on the man in front of him and followed him toward the exit, like a halfback following his blockers. Through the smoke the only thing visible was the flames and the electric chair.

What happened next would incite furious arguments among those who were in the death chamber that night. And among those who were charged to investigate it.

"I saw the electric chair, and it was on fire," Murphy wrote in his official report. "Flames were climbing to the ceiling. Houdini could not have escaped it."

"It was on fire, all right," wrote the newspaper reporter Murphy had followed from the chamber. "But it was empty! There was nobody in that burning chair."

Different versions of the fire were endless, and each version was hotly disputed. Reporters and cops, prison guards, and Sing Sing administrators began a newspaper war over what had happened after the switch was thrown.

"The switch was never thrown," testified an electrician. "The fire burst through the walls and we were out of there. If the prisoner died, he was consumed by the flames."

"There was already smoke in my eyes," testified the executioner, whose name was withheld from the public. "I barely saw the warden nod his head. Then the flames exploded and I grabbed at something. I think it was the switch. Then we were all fighting for the exit."

Evan Murphy pushed past the burning electric chair. He had fought his way through the smoke and fire of the Great War, his arm hanging by threads—literally—but this was different. The flames were grabbing at his ears. He removed his hand from the back of the man in front of him and used it to shield his face from the heat. He kept his feet moving in the direction of the exit. Wooden chairs blocked his way. He kicked at them. He was coughing. Choking. Then he stumbled through the exit into the hallway and dropped to his knees. His hat was knocked from his head. Somebody grabbed hold of him and pulled him up and forward.

"The building's on fire!"

They were staggering down the hallway now, down Death Row.

Inmates were screaming to be released from their cells, trying to part the bars with their bare hands. "Help us!" the condemned men screamed. "Don't leave us here!"

Murphy looked over his shoulder and through the window to the exercise yard and saw the death chamber engulfed in flames. A guard raced past him in the opposite direction, toward the cells, keys in hand. He was going to release the Death Row prisoners.

Murphy followed the running, screaming crowd toward an exit, coughing and wheezing as he moved. He wanted to stop and vomit, but there was no time. At long last he pushed through a doorway and into the prison yard. The first burst of fresh November air felt like a gift from heaven, and he sucked it deep into his lungs. But the night itself was hell. The wind and the rain had reached Biblical proportions. He dropped to the mud and again breathed deep, using his one arm to keep his face out of the muck. Frightened people were hurrying by him, splashing him with prison mud. Once outside, nobody stopped to help. But it did not matter. He was safe now. He turned and sat in the mud, spit the death chamber smoke from his lungs. The rain poured over his face. Then he watched as the building before him went up in flames. Tears were washing the smoke from his eyes, the wail of sirens barely audible to him above the roar of the storm.

Fire, smoke, wind, and rain. Endless thunder and blinding lightning. No mortal man could swear on a Bible to what exactly he had witnessed on that God awful night—so Captain Evan Murphy of the New York State Police did not include everything he saw in his final report. But as he sat there in the mud fighting for every breath, the deadly Nor'easter washing over his suit, there was one last unearthly flare of lightning. And in that split-second of spectral blue light the one-armed cop swore on his mother's grave that he saw the silhouette of a lofty man in prison garb scaling the walls of Sing Sing and heading for the river.

"So we beat on, boats against the current, borne back ceaselessly into the past."

—F. Scott Fitzgerald
The Great Gatsby

The Homecoming

All this happened, more or less.

And here might well end the story of the time-traveling professor of criminal justice but for a pop bottle found floating in a pool of swirling water below Ithaca Falls. It was one of those classic Coca-Cola bottles, with the thick green glass and the embossed lettering. The bottle had been corked after a handwritten note was placed inside of it. In what year this discarded Coke bottle was found and who found it was never recorded. The only reason the note was saved at all, and then catalogued in the Collections Department of the Cornell Library, was because of the person to whom it was addressed:

To the Most Honorable H.W. Hightower, PhD
President Emeritus, Cornell University,
Ithaca, New York

Dear Sir,

I shall not date this note except to say it is five years on and I am where I belong and all is well. I will tell you this much —memories live forever. I have spent a career chasing the evil that travels through time, and my time in your time left me with memories enough for two lives.

On some moonlit midnight I will place this undated note into this bottle, seal it with a cork, and I will drop the bottle into the water that runs to Cayuga Lake. Then I will watch intently as this Coke bottle rushes along the surface until it reaches the lip of Ithaca Falls. Then over the falls it will go, much as I did, disappearing from sight in a torrent of tumbling water. What happens next we will have to guess at, but I see myself standing in the shadows above the shoreline waiting for the bottle to resurface beneath the falls. It never does. This brings a smile to my face, and a great deal of satisfaction to my life. Sure, the bottle may get smashed to bits on the rocks beneath the falls, its ink-stained message washed away in an instant—but maybe not. Maybe one fine morning—

So we beat on—

Forever yours
J. W. Alden

THE ASHES

It is springtime in Ithaca. More like a prologue than an epilogue. The copious snows of winter are gone. Nothing now but water. This water is flowing through the gorges in magnificent torrents, threatening to overrun their banks on the way to Cayuga Lake, that fantastic oddity of all of New York's waters.

On this spring night another full moon is floating high in a star-filled sky, the Passover moon, and its shining focus appears to be on two elderly men who long ago had dedicated their lives to the higher education of the young—two especially wizened men who marvel at the plumes of mist rolling like ancient spirits before Ithaca Falls. For a moment they simply stand at the edge of the woods in warm silence, enjoying the moonlight and listening to the roar of the water tumbling over the rocks. This experience has not changed since the first Iroquois took root in the same exact spot. The mighty sound of the erasure of time.

The two men are here on this night to spread the prisoner's ashes at the foot of the falls. The state of New York has finally released what they claim to be his remains. But the fire in the death chamber at Sing Sing had burned so hot and so fierce that there was nothing left behind but ash. No bone fragments. No hair. No hard-boiled blood, just charred pieces of metal, melted wires, and ash. Everybody knew the electric chair was among the ashes, but science was not yet able to single out human ash.

"Do you think he's really in there?" the old football coach asks, holding a battered book in his hands.

"The state wants to pretend," the president emeritus tells him, leaning on his cane and holding up the copper urn, "so we, too, can pretend."

Coach Night Train grabs hold of the fragile book with both his hands and then fixes his eyes upstream, at the skeletal silhouette of the Rickety Bridge that spans the chasm. "That one-armed cop is back in town. Had the nerve to ask me if maybe I started that prison fire . . . same way Ithaca cops asked me if I might have lit up that studio barn."

"Do you mean Captain Murphy? I'm surprised. The last I heard of him, he was in Oregon. What did you tell him?"

"I told him, 'No, sir . . . that fire was started by God.'"

"Good answer . . . and legally correct."

"Do you think he's still searching for him?"

H.W. Hightower nods his red, cheeky head. "I imagine the good captain will spend his well-deserved retirement searching for him. But he will not find him. He was not a man of our time."

"You knew all along who he was, didn't you?"

"As did you, Coach."

"Not all along. Do you think he got away?"

The old university president smiles. "I choose to believe so."

"Believe that somehow we get to live our lives over again . . . try to correct the wrongs?"

"At one time or another, we all believe we've lived a previous life. But what if we woke one day believing we had lived a future life?" The president emeritus stares down at the urn in his hand. "Two men sharing the same soul, but in different times. It's just a theory." He looks up again at the water spilling over the falls. The old man's eyesight is a fraction of what it once was, but it is still good enough to notice something unwanted floating by in the moonlight. "What is that there . . .?"

Coach Night Train spots a small green vessel speeding their way. "It's a bottle of Coca-Cola," he says.

"Please retrieve it, Coach. I will not have my campus trashed."

The old football coach hands off the book and then stoops at the edge of the rushing water and reaches for the corked bottle, but the water is running too fast, and the bottle slips past him and continues its journey. The man who spent a lifetime on the sidelines of the university stands and shakes the water from his hands. "Almost looked like maybe there was a note inside of it."

The president emeritus hands back the timeworn book. *The Making of the President 1960,* by Theodore H. White. "Thank you for its safekeeping, Coach. I do wish they wouldn't bring their books with them when they come through . . . it so complicates things."

"I'll return it to your library now," the coach tells him. Then he stares up at the falls. "Are you expecting others?"

"Who knows what the future will bring?"

Then the bells ring out from the clock tower. The chimes echo through the hills and drift down into the gorge. It is midnight. The bells strike twelve times. And then the concert begins.

Hightower holds out the urn. "Shall we . . .?"

Coach Night Train removes the top of the urn for the retired university president. Then H.W. Hightower, PhD, steps to the water's edge, the raging falls spitting at his shoes. With a tremor born deep in his heart, he spills the ashes into the water and then watches in the moonlight as the alleged ghostly remains of a local hero race swiftly downstream—spreading through shining Ithaca on the way to the shores of the lake created by the hand of the Great Spirit, where his legend will live for a long, long time.

THE END

Acknowledgments

The books most helpful in the writing of *Ithaca Falls* were *CORNELL: Glorious to View,* by Carol Kammen; and *CORNELL: Then & Now,* by Ronald E. Ostman, photos by Harry Littell; *Practical Homicide Investigation,* by Vernon J. Geberth; *Twenty Thousand Years in Sing Sing,* by Lewis E. Lawes; and *The Great Crash 1929,* by John Kenneth Galbraith.

I began writing *Ithaca Falls* in February of 2009. It sat on a shelf unfinished and untouched for almost two years. Special thanks are owed to New York literary agent Henry Morrison, who read a hundred pages and urged me to get back to work. I completed the book in November of 2011.

Thank you to Kate Ternus for her critiques along the way. To my sister Mary Putney for her unwavering support through both good times and bad. And to Christopher Valen and Jenifer LeClair of Conquill Press, who made publication possible.

S.T.

Also by Steve Thayer

Saint Mudd

The Weatherman

Silent Snow

The Wheat Field

Wolf Pass

The Leper

Not Sure What to Read Next?
Try these authors from Conquill Press

Jenifer LeClair
The Windjammer Mystery Series
Rigged for Murder
Danger Sector
Cold Coast
www.windjammermysteries.com

Brian Lutterman
The Pen Wilkinson Mystery Series
Downfall
www.brianlutterman.com

Christopher Valen
The John Santana Mystery Series
White Tombs
The Black Minute
Bad Weeds Never Die
Bone Shadows
Death's Way
www.christophervalen.com

* * *

Coming Soon

Apparition Island by Jenifer LeClair
Broker by Chuck Logan
The Search for Nguyen Phem by Chuck Logan
Windfall by Brian Lutterman
The Darkness Hunter by Christopher Valen
For more information on these titles go to:
www.conquillpress.com